CﬦNTINUUM . . .

I0691572

Ardyce West's Continuum Series weaves numerous interlinking stories through each book, blending a bit of self-help with metaphysical historical fiction about unsung heroes and sensitive souls from the present day and the past. The task of her dynamic and engaging characters is simple - to shift the consciousness of the world - one thought, one word, one act of love at a time. Their seemingly ordinary lives are, at times, quite astonishing through the mystery and intrigue of their mystical experiences, with interwoven stories and tales told with humor, romance, suspense, intrigue, and timeless universal wisdom.

APEIROS - book one

When Sophia Delaney returns to her earthly life following a near-death experience in a car accident, her awareness instantly expands far beyond the three-dimensional world. She soon discovers innate intuitive abilities, enabling her to tap into countless historic events through dreams of past lives, which over time expands her soul's journey.

As Sophia weighs her new awareness against the life she once knew, a mystical Lakota shaman introduces her to a conclave of people from around the world, called the Order of Apeiros, a culturally diverse collection of intuitive sages, seers, and shamans, whose spiritually gifted sensitivities, sacred talismans, and enlightened wisdom raise their vibrational energies in service of the earth and all her inhabitants. They invite Sophia to join them, for they are aware that she has returned to this lifetime as the most powerful oracle the world has ever known. Overnight, Sophia shifts from her everyday mundane existence to many lives of mystic wonder.

AETERNALIS - book two

Sophia's metaphysical journey through her many past lives leads to the startling revelation of a family she never knew existed. Empowered by her newfound ability to pull back the veils of time and space, Sophia learns the truth about the mother she never knew, and the dark secret her enigmatic father took to his grave. Sophia embarks on a quest for understanding and forgiveness as the Order of Apeiros unites in Colorado, introducing her to widely diverse and delightful people who share a common purpose. As Sophia learns more about her mysterious past, a persistent vision transports her to the fateful maiden voyage of the RMS *Titanic*, where she found true love and spiritual calling on a passage into destiny.

SIORAI - book three

The revelation of Sophia's long lost family brought deep joy, but profound sorrow as well, and now she must confront a demon from the past before she may fully embrace the future.

Her journeys take her and Michael to Ireland, where they discover ancestral roots that impel Sophia to continue her recall of a past life aboard the RMS *Titanic*, where over 1,500 souls were lost in the most infamous sea disaster in history. Lost and adrift among the many nameless souls in lifeboats on the frigid North Atlantic, Sophia vividly recalls the grief and despair suffered by the survivors, whose lives were forever changed by forces beyond their control.

In the meantime, members of Apeiros reunite to embrace beloved White Buffalo, who shares his noble legacy that foretells an eternal life

What Amazon.com reviewers are saying:

"After reading this book, I became more thoughtful that there is more to this world than our senses can perceive." - Jay

"Rich, dense, expressive, captivating... you really have to take your time to read her story in order to grasp all that she is saying, because it is so much more than a story..." - Jasper

"There were two journeys that took place. Sophia's amazing trek that came from the powerful descriptive words read within this book and my own expedition that I took with her." – Jewels

"I found myself really identifying with the main character and wanting to be in on her journey." - S. Cobb

"This author has a way of writing that is spellbinding and poetic, full of spiritual wisdom and insight....Ardyce West is a master storyteller." - S. Walsh

"I found myself being Sophia her story is mine. It's like the author Ardyce West channeled me and my journey!" - Carol

"...it was so engaging, it allowed me to reflect on my own life too, which was unexpected." – Mtina

"...takes you to places in history with her characters, and describes scenes with such clarity." – Judy

Ardyce West's Continuum Series novels are available at Amazon.com, BarnesAndNoble.com and other online stores

OUROBOROS

Also by Ardyce West

APEIROS
Continuum Book One

AETERNALIS
Continuum Book Two

SÍORAÍ
Continuum Book Three

I Never Heard You Cry
A Compassionate Journey Through Abortion

From her Travels With Digit children's series:
There Once Was a Kitty Named Digit
There Once Was a Kitty Who Traveled

On the Horizon:
RÉALTA
Continuum Book Five

OUROBOROS

COONTINUUM BOOK FOUR

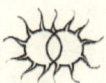

ARDYCE WEST

LoneWolf

Published in the United States of America
First edition published 09.01.2019 by KC LoneWolf
admin@kclonewolf.com
Colorado Springs, CO

ISBN-13: 978-0-9969544-6-4
ISBN-10: 0996954465

EBook edition also available on Kindle and other devices

Excerpt from
I Never Heard You Cry - A Compassionate Journey Through Abortion
Copyright ©2011 by Ardyce West
Used by permission

Author contact information: ardyce@ardyce.org

*To the memory of my parents, Elaine and Robert West,
both of whom were my greatest teachers
and now my spiritual guides.*

Prologue

Ouroboros (ôr-rob'-ôr-rus) - (Ancient Greek)
Infinity, eternality, and the totality of existence.

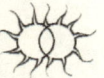

SÍORAÍ

Many came, but the one whose presence honored White Buffalo most was Crazy Horse, whose humble fortitude of the great warrior remained. Evangeline stepped forward and spoke for all.

"You have lived well, my love. The Grandfathers and all the Ancestors are pleased, for your walk has been one of the heart's yearnings. You have lived in a good way with your soul's work in this life, and you will accomplish even more as you move on. Come. We invite you to join us now, but it is up to you. Do you want to come with us to join with the Ancestors, or remain on Grandmother Earth?"

"I am ready," he said as he reached out for their extended hands that took him into their loving embrace - to travel the Great Ribbon of Stars to the Spirit World... into Síoraí... as White Buffalo breathed his last breath...

CHAPTER One

Sensing familiar feelings of more than a dream, and something other than a past life recall, Sophia slowly opened her eyes, taking notice of the full moon beaming its brilliance into the room. She was careful to slip quietly from under the covers, because even though Michael never woke himself up from his own raucous snore, the slightest disturbance could easily wake him from a sound sleep.

Not yet completely awake, she put on her robe and slippers and peeked out the window to take in the pristine beauty of the snow-covered moonlit valley in its crystalline perfection. More than surprised, she could not help but notice a mature white-tailed buck standing still in the snow, looking up at White Buffalo's window. The magnificent being turned his gaze toward Sophia and tipped down his massive antlers, as if bowing in reverence and respect.

Then she knew.

Now fully aware, Sophia felt a familiar presence in the room, which was a blending of the sacred earthly energies with heaven's eternality. Quietly, she walked downstairs to the kitchen, where she made herself a cup of calming peppermint tea. In the great room, she added a handful of kindling to the glowing embers in the fireplace, waiting for the fire to catch hold before adding several smaller split logs.

In the glow of the fiery blaze casting golden firelight and dancing shadows around her, she settled back onto the sofa that cushioned her in its soft embrace. She pulled up the woolen throw to shield her, not only from the chill in the room, but from her sense of great loss. The same afghan comforted White Buffalo many an evening as he sat in contemplation, watching the burning embers in the stone fireplace. No longer would she tenderly care for her dearly loved wise sage.

He was gone.

Wrapping her arms around her knees, she gathered the afghan under her chin. Sorrowful tears naturally flowed as the emptiness of grief's heartache took hold and assembled all the losses of those she loved so dearly who would no longer share this life with her as she knew it.

White Buffalo was more than an elder to Sophia. Even though he traveled all over the world most of his adult life, he was a selfless and humble man who respected the wisdom of the Ancestors, and lived from their guidance. To her, he was more of a loving grandfather. He unhesitatingly shared with her the entirety of his wisdom and knowledge, assisting her to grow into the wise woman she now was. As she knew about all those she had loved who moved on to their next greater becoming, she was certain she would know him again in another life - in another dimension. Beyond the grief, she already knew that his soul's presence, now free of the limitations of his humanity, would remain with her in ways she was yet to discover.

She laid down on the sofa, facing the blazing fire, and closed her eyes, but she was awakened by a slight vibration. Someone was on the sofa with her. She felt tiny paws walk up her leg, over her hip, and soon her petite four-pound Digit crouched on her upper arm, her front paws holding onto Sophia's shoulder. The welcoming sound of her tiny cat's purr brought Sophia peace as Digit laid her head down to sleep. As Sophia's tears easily flowed, Digit reached out and placed her paw on Sophia's cheek, enabling her to rest her mind and heart for a short while.

At least an hour passed, and after using a half box of tissues, Sophia finished her tea and quietly ascended the stairs. She walked to the bedroom on the cabin's northwest corner. As she opened the door, she noticed tiny golden lights floating throughout the room. She smiled as her heart welcomed thousands of angel spirits there in celebration of the life of White Buffalo.

She walked over to the edge of the bed, where White Buffalo peacefully laid under the covers. The only light in the room was the blue cast of moonlight reflecting off the snow through the window above his head. On the pillow, his long hair surrounded his face like a white halo. A slight smile remained on his face - forever serene - filled with eternal tranquility. She sat next to him on the edge of the bed and gently placed her right hand over his heart on the star quilt. Diverting her gaze to the window, Sophia half-expected to see the buck still standing in the snow, but he was no longer there. She looked for the deer's tracks, but there were none. The snow was no longer falling. Unlike the hours before, winter's night was completely still. No wind - no sound - only a tranquil peace filled the valley. There was no indication that the buck was ever there. All she saw was the yard covered in an immaculate, flawless shroud of snowy white, shadowed in soft layers of blue.

Until the sun began to rise, she sat next to her beloved White Buffalo and talked to him as if he could still hear her, believing that he was listening.

"My wise and wonderful sage, there are no words to tell you how much I love you, but already I miss you so. I know you are in a state of grace, far beyond my understanding, but I would feel at peace if you could let me know you are well, in a way that I will have no doubt it is you reaching out to me."

She then heard the comforting voice of White Buffalo:

My dear Sophia, together you and I are in the midst of this journey we call life eternal. I am still here with you. You will always know it is me, but you will now see and hear me in many more ways than when my feet walked on Grandmother Earth. You might feel me touch you as a whisper on the wind, or see me dancing in the gurgling stream. Many times when you peer into the night's darkness, you will see me blaze through the heavens of Grandfather Sky as I radiate my light over you before you go to sleep. Know that as you lay your head down on your pillow, my spirit will gently kiss your forehead, crowning you with the light of the heavens.

I am always with you, sweet Sophia. I always have been with you in many dimensions - in numerous lifetimes. I am now truly free of all human ways, with only Love to express. Remember when you were in Heaven, how you knew everything there was to know? Now, I too am aware of the Infinite - the Creator - Wakan Tanka, in unlimited ways far beyond that which I knew as a man. I now completely understand why you chose to return to your life on Grandmother Earth, so you could share with the world the eternality of Love and Awareness - that of God, the Absolute.

Since I am no longer with you in physical form, I will be with you in countless ways to help you do what you love. When in doubt, Sophia, remember that we leave the world of the physical plane to join with our spiritual eternality, which is the essence of our soul's journey in the constant upward spiral of our greater evolutionary becoming - to worlds without end.

And so, my dear Sophia, I am ever here to support you. Remember to call on me, but no longer remember me as an old infirmed man. Do not think of me as gone, because as you know for yourself, I have always been, and forever shall be eternal. I am right here... and everywhere.

CHAPTER TWO

*T*wo days later, White Buffalo's lawyer, Sebastien Rousseau, arrived at the cabin. He was the grandson of André Rousseau, the lawyer hired by White Buffalo's Grandmother Mika, who in 1960 arranged for White Buffalo to attend Tulane University as Scott Anka. He stepped in the door and carefully brushed the snow from his shoes.

"Welcome to Colorado, Mr. Rousseau. I trust your flight went well?" Sophia said.

"Please, call me Sebastien. Yes, my flight was uneventful, which is always good news." He was an elegant young man of sophisticated southern charm. "Thank you for arranging for a driver to pick me up, and for the delectable lunch you left for me. You don't get much to eat on the airlines anymore."

"It's a long drive up here, so we wanted to make it comfortable."

"Oh, it was beautiful, especially with all the snow, which I seldom see – or feel."

Sophia took his light coat and hung it in the closet. "Well, if you plan to spend any time here, we'll put you in a down parka and a nice pair of gloves."

Sebastien laughed as he set down his briefcase and overnight bag. "I thought I was prepared for cold weather, but I miscalculated the difference between New Orleans cold and Colorado cold."

"Only about fifty degrees difference," Michael said, walking in and extending his hand. "Mr. Rousseau, I'm Michael O'Hara."

"How do you do, Michael. White Buffalo told me so much about you."

"I can't tell you how much we appreciate your coming so quickly," Sophia said. "With all the arrangements we're making, I didn't expect we'd get to the legal matters this soon. I'm not certain why White Buffalo thought it was so important, but he must have told me a dozen times to contact you immediately after he passed. I hope this short notice wasn't an inconvenience."

"Most assuredly not," Sebastien said. "We of course were heartbroken when he advised us of his illness last spring, but since then the matters of his estate have been of the utmost importance to our firm."

"His estate?" Michael said, glancing at Sophia.

"Please," Sophia said, "come and meet the others." They led him into the dining room, where Darius, Gaston, and the other members of Apeiros greeted him.

After the introductions, everyone enjoyed Ellos' cinnamon rolls and fresh coffee.

"This is such a pleasure to finally meet everyone. White Buffalo told me that you are a group of people who hold the high watch for the world?"

"Yes, it's something very few know about," Darius said.

"I must say you are certainly my most fascinating clients, but I'm sorry we finally meet under these circumstances. Please accept my sincere condolences. I heard so many wonderful stories about White Buffalo when I was growing up, and I spent some lovely time with him on the phone these last few months."

"You're very kind," Gaston said. "He loved your grandfather dearly, and always felt forever in his debt."

"Your father and grandfather have been of great help over the years," Darius said. "They've been our family's legal counsel since World War II. I suppose you know your firm also represents my corporation, Delaney Hotels?"

"Of course!" Sebastien said with a laugh. "Before the digital age, my father dedicated a warehouse just for your company's files alone. As he will be retiring soon, I want to assure you that you're still in capable hands."

Mary entered and offered coffee refills.

"Mrs. Ello," Sebastien said, "these cinnamon rolls are-"

"Christello."

"I beg your pardon?"

"Mrs. Christello."

"Here we go," Michael said.

"I'm sorry, I thought Sophia said your name is Ello."

"She did, but what does she know?"

"Uh, Sebastien," Sophia said, "there's something you should-"

"Is he talking to you?" Mary asked.

"No." Sophia bit her lip to stop a laugh.

Mary continued pouring refills as she explained. "Christello's my name, but Ello can also be me, my sister, or a pastry. My friends call me Mary, but I prefer Ello."

Sebastien began to catch on. "I see, so let me begin again, Mrs. Ello, these cinnamon rolls-"

"S'matter? Don't you want to be friends?"

Sebastien laughed with everyone. "I would be delighted – Mary – and may I say these cinnamon rolls are exquisite."

Mary nudged Michael. "Hear that, sport? Exquisite. You need to work on your vocabulary."

"You have to give me the recipe to take home to my wife," Sebastien said.

"I don't care if you are a lawyer - I don't *have* to do anything." Mary walked back to the kitchen.

Sebastien looked around the room. "Did I miss something?"

"Wait for it," Gaston said.

Mary shuffled back in and handed Sebastien her coveted recipe. "Tell your wife the secret's in the yeast. Keep it warm." She straightened his tie and patted him on the shoulder.

Sebastien smiled. "Thank you."

Mary turned and looked at everyone. "So what are you waiting for? Carry on." She sauntered out of the dining room.

Michael sighed. "Now that we have the Ello blessing, I suppose this would be as good a time as any to get down to business." He brought a large box to the dining room and set it between his and Sebastien's seats.

"His personal effects, I presume?" Sebastien said.

"Indeed," Michael said.

"Very good." Sebastien pulled his briefcase and removed a dictionary-size pile of legal documents, stacking them neatly on the table. "I have here the trust and last will and testament of White Buffalo."

"Excuse me? Trust?" Michael said. He glanced at the box and back at Sebastien's paperwork. "All of that – for these gifts?"

Sebastien's eyes darted around the room. "Perhaps first I should read you his bequest that he revised six months ago, written in his own words. I would appreciate it if you save your questions and comments until I have concluded."

Gaston looked at Darius. "I have the distinct suspicion that good old Ska-T has been holding out on us..."

Sebastien cleared his throat to regain the room. "If I may? To wit:

"My dearest friends - my family, you are the ones of my intimate circle who remain here on Grandmother Earth. You helped me fulfill my purpose for this particular lifetime, supporting me along each step of my path. You touched me deeply in the way you each live your lives, through your awareness of Great Spirit - of love and the awareness of Its eternal qualities and Its simplicity of heart.

"This is my favorite quote of Jesus, 'Truly, truly, I say to you, whoever believes in me will also do the works that I do; and greater works than these will he do...' Jesus was talking about being an anointed one, which is everyone's true calling - to ascend in our consciousness above the conditions of the world - to live and breathe as the Infinite Intelligence, which I know as the Creator - Great Spirit. In this we serve the world through the wisdom of Love and Absolute Awareness in our day-to-day existence, as you all do so well.

"To complete my journey on Grandmother Earth, I request of you to place my cremains as follows:

- A third of my cremains are to rest with those of my beloved Evangeline in Golden Gate Park, Colorado.

- One third at the woods on Darius' property, scattered where the sweat lodge once stood. It was there that my father, Howahkan, interpreted my vision quest, helping me gain the continual wisdom of Wakan Tanka that became my life's work.

- Long before I was born, my mother, Wichahpi, saw through her vision quest that the soul of the great warrior chief, Crazy Horse, would live again in me. It is my desire to have the last

third of my ashes scattered at the Black Hills of South Dakota, where I was born, in honor of him, my parents, my great-grandfather Tahatan, and all of the Ancestors.

"I know this is asking a lot of you, but I trust you will find the time to make it your own sacred journey as you lay my ashes to rest on Grandmother Earth. Wait and see, for she will be happy when you do.

"My wife, Evangeline, and I did our best to live in a good way. We lived simply, and throughout our lives how greatly blessed we were. Evangeline inherited her family's wealth - both that of her parents and her grandparents - which included both businesses and landholdings in Louisiana and in Colorado. After our mother passed on, my sister and I inherited the substantial wealth of our grandparents, Mika and Jelani. Evangeline and I added our earnings from decades of our world lectures, wisely investing in vast tracts of land along Colorado's Front Range. For several decades we owned a large American bison ranch to help replenish the bison population, in support of removing them off the endangered species list. At the same time, Evangeline worked alongside me, traveling the world as I dedicated my entire professional life to the remembrance of the Lakota culture. Since we were unable to have children, our mutual desire was to provide higher education for indigenous peoples of all ages throughout the world. I can happily say that in the same way the family did for me, Evangeline and I returned the favor and provided college educations for many, some of whom you may meet over time.

"A year after Evangeline's passing, a reputable bison rancher made me a substantial offer to purchase the ranch. The timing was right. I sold it because we had accomplished our goal. He had a good reputation, and I knew the growth of the American Bison population would continue. I still lived simply, but I added the proceeds of the sale to my investment portfolio that incrementally grew into what I now leave to you all, with that of my stock port-

folio and mutual funds, valued at roughly 924 million dollars, and growing daily."

Everyone at the table gasped.

"Oh my Go- gosh," Sophia said.

Michael's jaw flopped open, and be blinked five times without a word - until he cried out when Sophia's fingernails clawed into his forearm.

"Did you know?" Darius asked Gaston.

"No! This is as much a surprise to me as it is to you!" Gaston said. "Why that old son of a-"

"Uncle!"

Sophia suddenly felt tapping on her shoulder. She turned to see who it was, realizing she felt White Buffalo's presence at her side. She smiled and sat back in her chair, completely still, just watching everyone else respond in shock and awe.

Sebastien raised his hand, indicating the need for silence before he continued. "With interest, projected assessments and the like, White Buffalo's financial holdings are valued well over one billion dollars."

"Good heavens!" Darius said. "This is a man who, since Evangeline passed, lived like a pauper in a one-bedroom flat."

"He drank ginger ale, for God's sake!" Gaston said.

Chayton smiled. "From the spirit world, Grandfather still teaches us."

"Definitely!" Sophia said.

"I realize this news comes as a shock," Sebastien said. "But if you'll indulge me, I must continue with the reading of his will, for it has important ramifications for all of you. Once we conclude, I'll be here for as long as it takes to answer your questions."

"I hope you packed for a few days," Michael said. He called to the kitchen, "Mary! More coffee! Please!"

Sebastien continued:

"To the thirteen of you, I bequeath 20 million dollars each, to supplement the good work you do in your part of the world." He kept his hand raised to quell the gasps as he continued to read, *"The remainder, I leave to the Order of Apeiros, in the form of a foundation to be utilized as follows:*

- One-eighth, I leave in increments over the next two decades to worthy foundations in support of sobriety of the Native American.

- One-eighth, I leave in support of foundations for the enhancement of the written word - for libraries and organizations that support writers who dedicate their lives to write and promote life-giving literature for the greater good of the world.

- One-quarter, I leave in support of worthy foundations for the arts - painting, sculpture, music, dance, and theatre.

- One-quarter, I leave to create a foundation for the college education of indigenous peoples of all ages.

- The remaining one quarter, I leave for the furtherance of the Order of Apeiros, itself."

Everyone was astonished. White Buffalo and Evangeline lived in such simplicity that no one would have guessed that they amassed such a fortune.

Sebastien continued, *"It is my desire that Chayton and Irina head up the foundation, under the legal counsel of the Rousseau Law Firm, and with the remaining members of the Order serving its board of trustees. Chayton's educational background, and Irina's multi-lingual abilities and years of experience working with people from all over the world, make them ideal partners to oversee the foundation's administration. You see, I was not just matchmaking for the fun of it. Of course, both Chayton and Irina must be in agreement to take on this noble cause.*

"As for my personal effects, I have very few items to give away, but I have left at least one for each of you..."

"I will read each bequest," Sebastien continued, "as Michael distributes the gifts White Buffalo left for you. There are a few items for the grandchildren of his sister, Little Deer, but I will only share with those of you in Apeiros what he left for you:

"Chayton, Grandfather is pleased that you have taken my place in the Order of Apeiros. You represent the Indian nations, and so I leave you my fan made of eagle feathers.

"I also leave you the chanupa, my sacred pipe, given to me by my mother. The pipe once belonged to my great-grandfather, Tahatan, a great warrior chief who bravely fought at Little Big Horn and at Wounded Knee. Tahatan gave my mother the pipe during the Inipi ceremony that preceded her four-day vision quest. It was there where she saw me, long before I became her son. She knew who I would be before I placed my feet onto Grandmother Earth. My sister, Little Deer, made the deerskin pouch with its intricate beading. Use both the pipe and the eagle fan in sacred ceremony to bless all those you serve."

Michael handed Chayton the items and touched his shoulder. Chayton wiped a tear and clutched the chanupa. "Aho mitakuye oyasin," he said as he reverently bowed his head.

"To Yesinia, I leave my Tibetan brass singing bowl, because your voice is like the sound of the angels. I received this from one of the Sherpas who assisted Evangeline and me on our month long pilgrimage to Mount Kailash in the Tibetan Himalayas. He was a most humble man who assisted us in every way possible. He carried our belongings, set up our tent to make us comfortable when we rested, and cooked us delicious meals. I will never forget his quiet strength of character, of which you possess the same qualities.

"Because you are a guide for people in their travels, I also leave you a rosary that once belonged to my beloved Evangeline. It is made of the finest beads of Brazilian amethyst. Amethyst strengthens and protects travelers. It connects with the angels, joining the earth plane with other worlds, while aiding one in their meditation and lucid dreaming."

Yesinia bowed her head as she gratefully accepted the gifts.

"To Irina, I leave a gold cross, which is embedded with rubies and pearls. A Catholic cardinal, who was the archbishop of Paris at the time, attended an Inipi ceremony that I held in the French countryside. As a gift, he gave me this exquisite cross and chain. Wear it well, knowing that you are the pearl who came out of the Black Sea.

"To Christofer, the painter of ancient storytelling, I leave to you a small, simple, framed painting from the Impressionist Era, of an outdoor café in Paris at night with the stars overhead. My Evangeline bought it for me at a Paris art fair, not realizing at the time it was of great value. I later had it appraised. As it turns out, the painting was an artist's study for his later painting, 'Café Terrace at Night,' by Vincent Van Gogh. Enjoy! I have cherished it."

"Oh my," Christofer whispered. He simply gazed at the painting, speechless.

"I also leave you my silver Zuni cuff bracelet. I have worn this since I was in college. It has great meaning, not only for its artistry of spiritual symbolism, but because it was a gift from my grandmother, Mika."

Christofer carefully placed the bracelet on his left wrist, and cupped his right hand over the intricate silver in gratitude.

"To Anja, I leave you a rare copy of the Koran, written in Arabic, translated into English. Its illustrated pages are beauti-

fully hand-written in calligraphy. I received it as a gift from a dear friend and colleague who is an American Islamic sheikh. He was born a New York Jew, raised in the Hebrew tradition. As a young man, he lived in India, where he became a Buddhist for the next 20 years. When he returned to the States, he became a professor of Religious Studies at the University of California, Berkeley. He once invited a Sufi sheikh to lecture his students, and fell in love with this man's passion for his faith. He soon became a Sufi and later a sheikh, himself. I respected him greatly, because of his tremendous love for Allah, which enhanced the love I have for the Creator, Wakan Tanka - Great Spirit.

"I also leave you my abalone shell in which I burn my sacred white sage from the Black Hills in South Dakota. Use it in all your world travels to cleanse yourself and all around you, so you will continue to serve others from the purity of your heart.

"To Ananta, I leave two precious items of great meaning. A Tibetan Buddhist Abbott from an ancient monastery in Kathmandu presented my beloved Evangeline this handmade silver filigree Tibetan prayer box, set with a blue topaz on its top. Some believe that topaz transcends time and space, with a lasting energy of joy and abundance of which you possess both qualities. This is a rare and priceless handcrafted piece made by Tibetans long before China occupied Tibet. No longer are they made in Tibet. Care for it well, and I invite you to use it to discover Divine wisdom and connection to the heavenly realm, even more than you already do, my dear.

"Before we left Kathmandu for the 32-mile, three-day clockwise pilgrimage around Mount Kailash, the Abbott also gave me these prayer flags. As we shared the journey with some of our dearest Buddhist and Hindu friends, we felt honored to carry these items during the ritual of holy pilgrimage, believed to bring good fortune in walking and living the prayer during the trek. The monastery in Kathmandu no longer stands because of the

2015 Gorkha Earthquake, but happily, the Abbott is safe and well, doing his good work in the world. His prayer, written in Tibetan calligraphy, remains in the prayer box along with a prayer I wrote especially for you.

"Lestari, I leave you a piece of meteorite that fell from the heavens. One dark night, Evangeline and I were camping in the Arizona desert. After I played my flute, I sat in prayer and meditation with my eyes closed, when Evangeline cried out, 'Scott, look up there!' I opened my eyes to see an unusual number of meteorites radiating streaks of fire across the night skies, but some appeared as if they were heading directly for us. There was no time to take cover, so with a heart of surrender, I stood up when I heard something hit hard against the earth just a few feet away. I shined my flashlight in the direction of the sound, and we soon found a piece of black rock the size of my fist, its surface melted as it traveled through space. I slowly reached for it, but I quickly stopped because it was too hot to touch. When it finally cooled down, I picked it up, immediately noticing how heavy it was, while marveling at the wonder of the Universe. Yes, the heavens are alive, and they are eternal and abiding - as you were named Lestari.

"I also leave you my native flute, along with the story of the first flute:

"Long ago, there was a young man whose heart was captured by a beautiful young girl. He constantly tried to get her attention, but she paid him no mind. Whenever he saw her, he rode his horse proudly, but no matter how hard he tried, nothing he did caught her gaze. One day, she and her friends were down by the river to gather water in their gourds, so the young man followed them. He began diving off rocks and swimming across the river to impress her with his skills, but again she seemed to take no notice. Feeling dejected, the young man walked into the nearby forest and sat down at the base of a cedar tree that no longer had life in it. As he sat there, thinking about the girl, he could not help but notice a red-headed woodpecker that landed on a hollowed limb above his head. Over time, the limb had hollowed out from the wind and weather, for it was a mere framework of grey. Then the woodpecker did what woodpeckers do, and began to peck holes along the length of the hollowed limb. He heard the consistent tap, tap, tap, as the woodpecker pecked, and eventually the limb broke off and fell to the ground right next to the young man. The limb landed in a way that the gentle wind blew through the holes, causing beautiful notes like angelic voices flowing through it. Mimicking the wind, the young man picked it up and blew into the limb's end. He found that when he covered the holes with his fingers, he could make beautiful, haunting music to match the feelings he felt in his heart for the girl. Until the sun set in the western sky, he sat underneath the old cedar tree, playing somber melodies. The young girl found herself drawn to the soulful sound coming from the ancient forest, and soon discovered that her heart was enraptured. Enchanted, she followed the music into the woods, where she found the young man sitting at the base of the cedar tree, playing the first flute given to him by the woodpecker. As she continued to listen, she fell in love with his music and could not help herself but to fall in love with the young man. The two walked off into the sunset, hand in hand, to live happily ever after.

"Tradition says, one of the uses for the flute is for courting, to attract a mate, but once you have your mate, you are to put the flute away and never play it in public again, because if you do, you might attract someone else.

"So, Lestari, play this flute in the privacy of your heart."

"Oh, I love this," Lestari said. "I shall cherish it forever."

"To Markos, I leave you a Coptic cross that came from St. Mark's Coptic Orthodox Cathedral in Alexandria, Egypt, which is the site where the remains of St. Mark are left. You are named after him. Evangeline and I were visiting Alexandria, and I felt guided to go into the church to sit in contemplation. After several *minutes, a monk approached me, saying he had attended my lecture the night before, for he was quite interested in the American Indians. From over his head, he removed this cross and gave it to my Evangeline as a gift.*

"I also leave you my first edition of Mark Twain's, 'The Adventures of Huckleberry Finn,' because not only do you possess a similar sense of humor as Mark Twain, you go about life in the way of his character - that adventurous, lovable scalawag."

Markos laughed as he accepted his gifts. "That I am, my sage, that I am."

"Shoshana, I leave you a tiny hand-blown glass bottle, made by an Israeli glass artist. Sealed within it is water from the River Jordan, which as you know, flows through the Sea of Galilee down into the Dead Sea. It is written that the Israelites crossed the Jordan at the last of their journey, before they entered the Promised Land. The story is told that John the Baptist baptized his cousin, Jesus, at the Jordan River. The events were significant in meaning, in both the Old and New Testament. Over the years, I have held this bottle during meditation and prayer, knowing that my prayers are of peace for the people who live on both sides of the River Jordan, as its waters flow to millions who have been in conflict for millennia. I see them finally living together in flourishing peace and tranquility. I was so greatly touched by the story of your father's work of peace as the Ambassador to Syria, I believe that your work as an archeologist gives voice to those who once lived on Grandmother Earth, and so they continue. As an archeologist, you are a bringer of truth and peace to the world.

"I also leave to you a pair of gold earrings, with each delicate dangle set with one of the Jewel Stones of the Twelve Tribes of the Israel. In Greek, the stone is called Topázion. In Hebrew - Pitdàh, otherwise known as peridot. It is one of the three stones of the south, attributed to Zebulon, the sixth son of Jacob and Leah. I bought them for my lovely Evangeline when we traveled to the

Holy Land, because her hazel eyes turned to the loveliest shade of green when her gaze turned to the golden light of the late afternoon sun."

"How beautiful! I shall cherish them," Shoshana said. She quickly put the earrings on for all to admire.

"Michael, I leave you my bear claw necklace. Many have wanted it for their museum, because it is quite rare, but I want you to have it. The bear symbolizes courage, physical strength, and leadership, but mostly it represents the protector, as you are for Sophia. You have been the protector throughout the ages, for this is the main purpose of your soul's journey. I also leave you my deerskin-beaded slippers that once belonged to my father, Howahkan, because you walk the Red Road. Like him, you are grounded to the core of Grandmother Earth with your gaze toward the eternal Great Spirit.

"Sophia, I have only one piece of technology that is worth passing along. I obtained this telescope when I was in college from one of my astronomy professors. He recognized that I had great gifts of seeing, and he gave me this so I could see far into the heavens.

"I leave you my star blanket that was handmade by many Lakota women. Each handmade stitch is a prayer. When you are using all your talismans together, and you travel to distances beyond Grandmother Earth, keep this star blanket around your shoulders, for the thousands of prayers will keep you safe and blessed by Wakan Tanka, Great Spirit.

"Sophia, I also leave you this small bottle of consecrated oil, once used by a very humble man. In his ministry, he administered healing through what they called, 'laying on of hands.' He placed a drop of oil on his finger and rubbed it onto his fingertips on his other hand before placing his hands on top of the head of the one in need of healing. He did this in union with another minister, while one spoke a prayer and the other served as witness. Through

the strength of 'when two or more are gathered' they became powerful conduits for healing. On several occasions, I witnessed miraculous healings take place through the faith of this humble man, who also did remote healing. From his home, he spoke a prayer for another, hundreds of miles away, in which healing would occur. So strong was his faith, that when someone picked up their phone to call him, they experienced a healing before they even spoke to him directly. I invite you to incorporate this consecrated oil into the work you do, with the same degree of faith.

"Lastly, Sophia, I leave you Evangeline's gold wedding band, and to Michael, I leave you mine. I have been witness to many devoted couples, but none is more loving than your blessed union. Thank you for welcoming me into your home and into your hearts."

"I believe this calls for a quick, second wedding," Gaston said.

"I'm good with that," Michael said. "What do you say, hon? Marry me – again?"

"Yes – again," Sophia said. They placed the rings on each other's right hand fingers. "These are so lovely. I adore them."

"To Darius, my cousin, my brother - I leave you my Buddhist Mala Prayer Beads, made of stunning blue lapis lazuli. The stone is a symbol of royalty and honor, gods and power, spirit and vision, as a universal symbol of wisdom and truth. They were a gift from a Buddhist nun, who assisted me for two weeks while I lectured in Thailand. She was a most petite woman, who at the same time possessed fearsome strength. She was my firekeeper during two Inipi ceremonies, which is not a job for the weak. Never did she waiver, as I know the same for you.

"I also leave you the most precious books of my collection, most of them first editions, many I read several times. Thoreau's Walden transported me to a world of nature that I sorely missed

when I spent my years in the mission school on the reservation. Emerson guided me with his transcendental wisdom, as Whitman's Leaves of Grass lit up my humanity. Edith Wharton, Rumi, Tagore, Krishnamurti, Yogananda, and Black Elk, among others, steered me through their insightful, spiritual writings. Lastly, I leave you the works of Yeats, for you share his Irish roots. His simple poem was a guide for my life. I know it also inspires our dear Sophia:

We can make our minds so like still water that beings gather about us that they may see, it may be, their own strength, and so live for a moment with a clearer, perhaps even with a fiercer life because of our quiet."

Darius dabbed his eyes with a handkerchief. "Dear me. Well, I know what I'll be doing the next few months."

"Gaston, my dearest friend, cousin, and soul-brother, I leave you the last of my bequests. Firstly, I leave you my Greek worry beads, made of the best green jade. During my travels, I kept them in my pocket so I could transfer my fear of speaking into the beads before I stepped on stage. In my later years, I kept them on top of the book I was reading, so that before I went to sleep I placed my worries and concerns in these beads. The stone brings good luck and friendship. Jade is the perfect stone for you, for it blesses who it touches with powers of healing and protection, but most of all, it is a dream stone, which accesses the spiritual world.

"Secondly, I leave you my buffalo robe, which first belonged to my great-great grandfather, the father of Tahatan. This buffalo robe came from a great being that lived two hundred years ago during the days when the bison ran free and flourished on the plains. Tahatan wore this robe in sacred ceremony during the Indian Wars at the Battle at the Little Bighorn and at Wounded Knee. He passed it on to my mother for her vision quest, and she, in turn, gave it to me when I was a young man for my vision quest."

"Look at that!" Gaston said. He pulled the robe close. "He knew how much I loved this. I always said, if you go first, I get the buffalo robe."

"What did he get if you were first?" Darius asked. "Oh, wait, I know..."

"The Cadillac," they both said.

Everyone laughed, but Gaston suddenly fell silent as Michael pulled out one final gift from the box. Gaston instantly recognized it, and tears welled in his eyes as Sebastien continued to read:

"Lastly, I leave to you my most sacred possession of all - one that only you know its significance - the pilsner glass."

"And so, we have concluded the bequest of Tatanka Ska, White Buffalo, otherwise known as, Scott T. Anka," Sebastien said as he gathered his papers and placed them into his leather valise.

Gaston could not help but break the silence as he softly wept.

Chapter
Three

While the rest of the group sat in silent shock at White Buffalo's big reveal, Sophia's attention diverted to the determined look in Michael's eyes as he stood. Clearly, he had a scheme in mind as he unbuttoned the cuffs of his sleeves and began to roll them up to his elbows.

"Ladies and gentlemen," Michael said, "I don't know about you, but I believe this very special moment calls for an equally special feast. It is Bohannan Time."

"Splendid!" Darius said. "Sebastien, you are in for a treat!"

Sebastien quizzically looked at Michael. "What time?"

"Please," Michael said. "I would appreciate it if you save your questions and comments until I have concluded." This brought great laughter. Michael turned to Sophia. "My love, if you will?..."

Unwaveringly, he walked to the kitchen area, clasping his hands together and turning his joined hands outward to stretch his arms and shoulders while cracking his knuckles. The unsettling sound jolted those left at the table from their stupor.

Michael was famished. The emotion of White Buffalo's bequest burned up all of his resources. Oftentimes, his answer to the strain on his spirit was to create something new out of seemingly nothing. On this day, it would be in the form of a sandwich, but not just your basic sliced-ham-

and-cheese-wedged-between-any-two-ordinary-pieces-of-store-bought-bread kind of sandwich. This sandwich would be a masterpiece.

Michael expressed his artistry in the kitchen with great passion, so much so that on his last birthday Sophia bought him a culinary attaché case, including every chef's knife he could possibly need, and an impressive collection of stainless steel bartending paraphernalia. Even for his special technique of making a sandwich, Michael took on the task with the same precision as when he wrote a book, or planned one of his architectural designs, with the final production reverse engineered in his mind before he began.

"Sophia, my *toque blanche*, please?"

Sophia walked to the pantry and retrieved a tall, white chef's hat and brought it to the master. Michael had to bow deeply so she could place it on his head. "I got him this for Christmas," Sophia said.

"My jacket..."

Sophia bowed slightly, backing away to the pantry and pulling out his fine, white double-breasted chef's jacket. She helped him into it. "He's very easy to shop for."

First, Michael cleared everything from the granite island and placed two large cutting boards at ground central. To the right, he meticulously laid out all the knives next to his sharpening rod, along with a two-foot wooden pepper grinder and a small crystal toothpick holder that held long bamboo knot skewers that looked like tiny swords chipmunks might use for swashbuckling. On the counter behind him sat a stack of plates, napkins, and a pile of forks, for one could not eat a Bohannan without a fork at the ready.

From the refrigerator and pantry, Michael gathered deli meats and cheeses, along with a wide variety of vegetables and condiments arranged above the cutting board in the order of intended use. The final addition - a hand-blown glass vinegar cruet containing his special recipe of gorgonzola salad dressing. At the ready in the drawer directly beneath the island were his cherished assortment of herbs and spices.

"The spices are arranged in alphabetical order, by the way," Sophia said.

Darius shook his head, "I dare say I *never* tire of watching this."

"It's the sheer precision in his handling of the condiments," Gaston agreed. "Not a drop spilled, nor a crumb toppled."

"Stunning," Markos chimed in, "simply stunning."

Michael raised his brow as he continued. "And from now on, you are being served by a *millionaire* Bohannan chef."

"Indeed!" Gaston said, rubbing his hands together. "I'm beginning to salivate."

Sebastien whispered to Darius, "What in the world is a Bohannan?"

From out of a long paper bag, Michael took a fresh baked French baguette, nearly a meter in length, and placed it on the cutting board to his left. With his serrated bread knife, he sliced it horizontally, leaving the slices face up. He then sliced a long loaf of pumpernickel in half. He was ready to begin. He looked at Sophia. "My dear? Aren't you forgetting something?"

"Oh! Right!" Sophia popped up and scurried to the stereo. "I got lost in that millionaire comment. Forgive me."

"Of course," Michael said.

Sophia clicked through a selection of background music for the occasion, carefully selecting the perfect piece to accompany her husband's culinary orchestration. Johann Sebastian Bach's *Brandenburg Concerto #3 in G Major* would be a perfect accompaniment. As the music began, Michael nodded at Sophia, quite satisfied.

Tying a long-wide chef's apron around his waist, Michael rubbed his hands together and used a sharpening rod to hone his knives to near razor blade perfection. Hearing the rhythm of the blades coursing across the rod, everyone now gathered to watch Michael perform his *Opus Gastronomicus*.

"How many for a Bohannan?" Michael asked. Thirteen hands instantly went up.

"And I don't even know what it is!" Irina laughed.

"Please, what is a Bohannan?" Sebastien begged.

Michael continued sharpening. "A Bohannan is a sandwich named for my maternal grandfather, David Bohannan O'Brien, who was a New York City policeman, and also the owner of a deli in Queens. One of my names is Bohannan, by the way. So, I carry on the tradition of his famous sandwich."

"Michael Bohannan O'Hara?" Shoshana asked.

"Oh, that's just the beginning," Sophia said.

"My paternal grandfather, also a cop, was Michael, so my full name is Michael Aengus Conlan Bohannan Liam Seamus Riordan O'Hara."

"It must take you ten minutes to sign a check," Markos said.

"My checks are a foot long. It took me years to remember every name, and the specific order, not to mention all the teasing I used to get from my friends. Some of them just called me Mac."

"Better than Mo, I suppose," Markos said.

"When I was born, my parents didn't want to insult any family members by not naming me after anyone of importance. You know – it's an Irish thing to be insulted - so, they named me after all of them, at least those who were still among the living. Most are dead now, so I suppose I could shorten my name to make it easier, but I've gotten used to them all. Actually, together they have quite a ring, don't you think?"

"Oh, no," Sebastien said. "Do you have any idea how many trust and inheritance documents I have for you to sign?"

"Perhaps he could just sign Mac, et al.," Gaston said.

Sebastien gave Gaston a look. "White Buffalo warned me about you. And so did my father."

"I'll have you know, Michael, I'm taking notes for when I return to Dharamsala," Ananta said.

Michael nodded. "Notes of all my names?"

"No - your artistry of sandwich-making."

"You'll have to let me know if it meets the approval of His Holiness the Dalai Lama. Now, the genius is at work. You may talk amongst yourselves…"

"One thing, Michael," Gaston said.

Michael awaited the silence for a moment. "Yes?"

Gaston searched the air. "Never mind, I forgot what I was going to say…"

"You've been into the scotch, haven't you?" Darius said.

"Just one." Gaston gave him an innocent shrug. "Dear brother, it's been an emotional day."

Michael pointed his sharpening rod at Darius. "You. Keep an eye on him, please?"

"Yes, Genius."

Michael began the Bohannan with a slathering of mayonnaise, ground mustard, and horseradish on one side of the bread - on the opposite slice, hummus and a pinch of garlic. He sliced a ripe avocado in half, whacked the pit with his knife, and with a slight twist, he easily removed it. After scooping out the avocado into a small bowl, he added a generous squeeze of fresh lemon juice, a smidgeon of Tabasco and Worchester sauce, and smashed it all together with a fork before spreading it evenly onto one side of the baguette. He topped off the first stage of the sandwich with fresh ground pepper.

Michael cooked with every color on the palette, believing that the more colorful the vegetables and fruits, the healthier his creation. He carefully prepared all of the needed ingredients, reverse engineering the finished product in his architect's mind before he began the layers, so the sandwich would not end up a big smutch on the plate.

Beginning with a mound of prosciutto on one side, layer by layer, he mindfully stacked each element of the sandwich like a well-constructed building, each in support of the next layer, carefully thought out, and finally finished with thinly sliced extra sharp cheddar cheese. With the wooden pepper grinder, he topped everything off with coarsely ground pepper.

"Can I get you a step stool to make it easier to distribute the pepper?" Sophia asked.

Michael smirked in her direction with the attitude of *don't interrupt the maestro*. He pointed the pepper grinder at her. "You keep your distance, my love. You're not allowed behind the island."

"Why the defensive posture, oh great chef, sir?" Markos asked.

"Whenever I cook, whatever is temporarily lying around on the counter, even for a brief moment - into the dishwasher it goes. I can be drinking a glass of water, and if I set it down for even a moment - into the dishwasher it goes."

"You'd put it in the dishwasher too, because the glass looks like he's eaten an entire greasy pizza," Sophia said.

"I'll turn my back to get a plate for whatever I'm fixing, and Sophia takes the cutting board - into the dishwasher it goes."

"I'm *really* not that bad," Sophia said. "But you will soon see why I clean up after him."

"I'll be using a paring knife, and I'll put it down to get something out of the fridge, only to find-" Michael stopped his diatribe, curiously noticing Sophia at work.

She tapped the sharpening rod three times on the counter, raised it along with her left hand, and like a conductor she waved as everyone said together, "Into the dishwasher it goes!"

Michael ignored her - ignored them. "I found my cell phone in there one time."

"Oh, you did *not!*"

He piled on the paper-thin roast beef next, Muenster cheese, and a layer of cucumber slices and sliced tomato, sprinkled with capers. Then, he added sliced red onion, a pelt of alfalfa sprouts, and fresh spinach leaves. Before he topped the sandwich off with the perfectly prepared slice of bread, he sprinkled the spinach with homemade Gorgonzola salad dressing.

"This is almost hypnotic," Chayton said. "I'm getting a little dizzy."

Using a bread knife, because by now the paring knife was too small to cut through the Princess and the Pea-type sandwich, he sliced his creation into three-inch, individual sandwiches, not perpendicular to the length of the bread, but artfully at an angle. He also reserved a similar layered vegetarian sandwich on the pumpernickel for those who didn't eat meat, carefully anchoring each individual sandwich with a bamboo swashbuckling skewer. He stepped back and raised his hands, admiring his work.

"Voilà! Ladies and gentlemen, submitted for your culinary enjoyment, I give you my Bohannan Salad in a Sandwich!"

Applause.

Sophia looked at the countertop and called it a mess.

Michael took a well-deserved, theatrical bow, his *toque blanche* clipping the range hood and toppling to the floor.

"Bravo!" Gaston cried.

Just as Michael placed his masterpieces on a large serving tray, the Ello Sisters walked in to begin dinner preparations.

"Whoa!" Lou said. "Jesus, Mary and Jerry Lewis! He made a Bohannan!"

"I'm hungry," Michael said.

"Hungry! Do you have a few fishes nearby to feed the masses with that thing?"

"I'm sharing it with everyone."

"I should hope so," Lou Ella said.

"I for one am famished! May I?" Gaston said, reaching for a sandwich.

"Please, everyone help yourselves," Michael said.

The gang eagerly lined up, taking plates and happily digging in.

"I hope you left enough food for the *rest* of the meals we have to fix," Mary said. "It looks like a tornado ran through the garden patch here!"

"You know how it is," Michael said. "A master chef cannot create neatly."

"It's gonna take you twice as long to clean this mess up than it took to eat that monstrosity," Lou said, "and that's saying a lot!"

"When I'm finished, I'll be hungry for dinner," Michael said. "It's all in the timing, you know. I'll clean up. Don't you worry."

"I'm not worried. I'm astounded," Mary said. "Be quick about it, the Ello Sisters are about to create an evening feast for you all."

"Hey, why don't you and Lou join us?"

"A Bohannan?" Mary said. "That'll ruin my girlish figure."

"Don't forget, we have some of that homemade vegetable soup simmering on the stove," Michael said, always trying to get in the last word. "There's plenty for all."

With a smile and a twinkle in her eye, Mary whacked him on the arm with a kitchen towel and placed the plates, soup bowls, napkins, and utensils on a tray. She took them to the dining room.

For once, Michael did get the last word...

Chapter Four

To begin their Bohannan experience, Michael created a non-alcoholic layered beverage for their enjoyment, made with grenadine at the bottom, and orange juice, lime juice, ginger ale, and a slice of lime.

"Let us all raise our glasses to our brother, White Buffalo!"

"Hear, hear!" They toasted their beloved friend.

"I call this the Tatanka Ska. Like White Buffalo, the drink is multi-hued, with a light bit of fizz. Underneath, we have a colorful surprise, which is deep in value, and rich in tone. May we all live so well," Michael said.

"To living so well!"

Afterwards, Michael served dishes of seasonal berries, topped with real whipped cream, not the kind spritzed from a can. The conversation throughout lunch was mostly pleasant small talk, but everyone was aware of Gaston's uncharacteristically melancholy demeanor. Normally, he would be cutting up with a quip or a humorous story.

"The sandwiches are a hit," Lou said as she and Mary cleared the dishes. "You're gonna put us out of business if you're not careful."

"I blame my appetite on mountain air," Michael said. "Food always tastes better in higher altitudes."

"Uh huh! Whatever you say," Lou said. "After all, you're the boss."

"Did you hear that, honey? Lou Ella says I'm the boss."

"Uh huh! Yes, deeear!" Sophia said with a pasty smile.

"Remember, I'll clean the kitchen, as promised. Come and join us," Michael said.

Mary and Lou joined the group again, bringing three plates of Ellos, and two pots of hot coffee.

Darius leaned over to Gaston and quietly said, "Are you alright? You're so quiet."

"All those years," Gaston said with a tear in his eye. "He always knew how to get to me... constantly subtle, but always with a zing. I believe it's a Lakota thing."

"Do you want to talk about it?" Darius asked, for everyone at the table became aware of their conversation.

"I suppose I owe it to him," Gaston said to the group.

"It was that final gift, wasn't it?" Sophia said. "The pilsner glass? You've been pretty quiet since you got it."

Gaston nodded and dabbed a tear. "I've rarely talked about this since that day so long ago. Darius knows most of the story, but he doesn't know some of the details." He took a deep breath, poured himself a cup of coffee, and added some cream before he began his tale.

"It was 1964. As I once mentioned to you all, White Buffalo and I were roommates at Tulane. I would soon graduate with my bachelor's degree in Business, and he, as Scott T. Anka, would graduate with a degree in Psychology, which took him only three years to complete. He continued on to get his masters and then his doctorate.

"White Buffalo and Evangeline dated since their freshman year, and I dated Evangeline's best friend, Dominique, during my junior and senior year. We were quite the foursome – inseparable, really. Rarely was there an occasion when we were not together. We always joked that it would take an act of God to separate us."

"Hold on," Sophia said. "Dominique? Why, Uncle, you've never mentioned her."

Gaston smiled and lightly patted her hand. "It all began with Mardi Gras that year. As you all know, Mardi Gras lasts for two weeks. At that time, spring break took place during the second week of Mardi Gras - the most celebratory time of the entire event. I suppose the school administration figured we would not miss too many weeks of school if they paired it with New Orleans' biggest event of the year. So, like everyone else, we students celebrated, ate, sang, danced, and celebrated some more. We got very little sleep, but goodness, did we have fun. I confess I did not remember much of what happened, but I'm fairly certain it was a good time."

"I can attest to that," Darius said, "for I distinctly recall the four of you parked your Cadillac on our front lawn one of those nights, and you took a three a.m. dip in the swimming pool – fully clothed."

Everyone laughed. "Yes, well it was very warm that night, unseasonably so for February, and it also saved us many quarters at the Laundromat."

"This is confusing me," Michael said. "We all knew White Buffalo in his later years, and he never drank alcohol. But I remember you told us about your early days together, which included many stories of him drinking."

"When White Buffalo first came to New Orleans, he didn't drink. As a youngster, he witnessed the ravages of alcoholism on the reservation. It ruined so many lives of family and friends, and he was determined to escape a similar fate. He was a few years older than the rest of us, and because of his upbringing on the reservation, he was a bit more mature than those of us who'd led easier childhoods. He also felt an obligation to Sebastien's grandfather and his mystery patron, who he later learned was his Grandmother Mika. Sebastien's grandfather risked his professional reputation to help both White Buffalo and his sister, Little Deer, get into college, so our straight-laced cousin toed a rather strict line early on.

"But, although I didn't notice it at the time, nor was I particularly concerned at that age, a subtle change in White Buffalo took place during our final year of school. He was so successful in his studies as he accelerated through the curriculum, that by his own admission later, he became rather smug and overconfident."

"Hardly a punishable offense for any bright, handsome young man just reaching his prime," Darius said.

Gaston smiled. "He *was* the all-American boy everyone emulated. So, despite the pressure of finishing his undergraduate studies with a bang, White Buffalo loosened up a bit that year, and he quite often burned the candle at both ends when it came to the social climate on campus. Like most of us, he wanted to fit in, so he joined us on the weekend debauchery much more often that year, and partied until night turned to day, especially during Mardi Gras.

"One night, he bought a souvenir pilsner glass with 'Mardi Gras 1964' printed on the side - this very glass." Gaston raised it for all to see. "For the next several weeks, he drank from this glass, making it a ritual, I suppose. We really lived it up like foolish young boys often do, believing nothing could get in our way. Life was good, and we were there to celebrate every moment of it. We were invincible.

"So, we made it through Mardi Gras, and we were back at school, hitting the books for final exams and looking forward to graduation. White Buffalo kept that pilsner glass on his desk, anxiously waiting the next weekend when he would put it to good use. Graduation came and went, and then came the wedding."

"White Buffalo and Evangeline?" Sophia asked.

"No, no, dear. Dominique and me."

"Uncle!" Sophia said. "You never told us you were married! I've always wondered!"

"You're getting a bit ahead of my story, dear," Gaston said.

"Oh – I'm sorry."

"Not at all. Anyway, when June came, Dominique and I planned to get married in the typical falderal of a traditional southern wedding. Nothing was left undone. We selected eight attendants each. Those girls' dresses were in every shade of pink satin and tulle. Darius and White Buffalo would stand up with me, accompanied by six of our university friends. We intended this to be the most elaborate wedding New Orleans ever saw."

"Tell us more about Dominique."

"Oh, she was a dark beauty of Jamaican descent, with Cherokee and African blood. Her ancestral grandfather was a full-blooded Cherokee, originally from Virginia. Forcibly taken from his family and shipped to Jamaica, he worked out his indenture for eight years on a sugar plantation. After liberated from his indenture, he soon married a beautiful African girl. They began their lives together, raising a family on their own small Jamaican sugar plantation, which grew with each generation.

"Dominique had the longest, thick black hair, with a mesmerizing shiny sheen nearly down to her waistline, not to mention those big black eyes of hers, like polished onyx. Already, I was in partnership with my father in his antique business, while Dominique did the books. We had a promising future all planned."

Everyone listened intently as Gaston continued, but there was an air of uncertainty where this seemingly enchanting tale was going.

"The night before the wedding, we had a typical bachelor's party. We went down to Bourbon Street and lived it up, as usual, but we did cut it short around 3 a.m. Everyone made it home safely, and we all got some sleep into mid-afternoon. At 6:30, the guests began gathering at St. Louis Cathedral, the oldest Catholic cathedral in the United States, located just two blocks from the Mississippi River. Oh, it was quite a sight. The sanctuary was decked out in every pink flower possible. The bridesmaids - all eight of them - in their pink satin high-heeled shoes, pink hats, like English fascinators, and gowns of every shade of pink meringue waited in the vestibule to precede Dominique down the aisle. It was as if pink champagne exploded all over the foyer - all of them a twitter, giggles, and flowers.

"I saw White Buffalo just before I left for the church. He was wearing his black tuxedo. You should have seen him dressed up with his black pompadour styled just so, on that full head of hair. At the time we called him 'Red Elvis' not meaning any disrespect to his Native heritage, because Elvis was part Cherokee. All through college, no matter where we went, women could not take their gaze from him, but he never took notice, because he only had eyes for Evangeline.

"Dominique dressed at home for the wedding, and White Buffalo volunteered to be her chauffeur. He arrived at her parent's home, and he said she came down the stairs, dressed in a floor-length gown, with layers of white satin, tulle, and lace. On her head was a silver tiara of white pearls with a long veil that trailed behind her. She carried an arm bouquet of white calla lilies and light pink long-stemmed roses that draped over her left arm, with long vines of ivy that gently fell to the floor. What a sight. He told me he could hardly take his eyes from her radiant beauty. Before they left the house, he took a few photos of her, posed on the stairway.

"My father loaned White Buffalo his beloved white 1959 Cadillac Eldorado Biarritz Convertible, complete with a red dash and distinctive tail fins, so he could deliver the bride in regal style. She was truly a modern day American princess, all in white, seated on those white leather seats. He gently helped her into the car, knowing he was transporting precious cargo for safe delivery to his best friend for the beginning of their life together.

"The wedding was to begin at 7 p.m., but by 7:45, there was no bride walking down the aisle. The guests were restless, the others in the wedding party confused, and there I stood with Darius and my other groomsmen, wondering if my Dominique had gotten cold feet and perhaps White Buffalo was trying to talk her out of leaving me at the altar."

"Oh, Uncle," Sophia said, taking his hand as he began to lightly weep. "She left you?"

"No," Gaston said, dabbing the tears. "Around eight, a policeman arrived and told us there was a car accident."

"Oh no!" Sophia gasped.

"White Buffalo had pulled out into an intersection after the light turned green, and a drunk driver ran the red light and struck the passenger side of the Cadillac, instantly killing my Dominique."

The room fell silent, save many tears and sad whispers. Now Darius openly wept.

"Oh, my sweet Uncle," Sophia cried, taking Gaston in her arms.

"White Buffalo was terribly injured, and taken to the hospital, suffering from a severe concussion, a broken arm and ribs, but he managed to ask the policeman to go to the church and tell me what happened."

"Oh my God," Michael whispered. "Gaston, was he drunk?"

Gaston smiled and composed himself. "That's the irony of it. He was stone sober, the blood tests said it was so. Imagine that? How reckless we were with the drink in those days, but he never would have put Dominique in danger like that. He hadn't taken a drink since the night before, he was sober as a judge, and a drunken driver killed my Dominique and nearly took the life of my best friend.

"Needless to say, our lives instantly changed. We weren't children anymore, and the world was no longer our playground to do as we pleased without consequence. My heart was in tatters, and unfortunately, White Buffalo blamed himself."

"But it was not his fault," Chayton said.

"Of course it wasn't," Gaston said, "and I never for one moment blamed him. But he second-guessed himself for a long time, saying, perhaps he was hung over and not clearly alert enough to see the car coming. He wondered if he had only left a little bit later - or earlier - or if he had taken a different route to the church... the list continued to play out in his mind. It was a very difficult time for all of us. Darius, White Buffalo, and I shed many tears of grief together that summer, and I dare say if not for them and my entry into Apeiros, I might not be here today."

Darius reached over and rubbed Gaston's shoulder. "Or, if not for your forgiveness and support, White Buffalo might have never become the man we all knew and loved."

Gaston smiled and held up the beer glass, his eyes wet. "He later told me, before he picked up my sweet girl, he put this in his valise and placed it on the floor behind the driver's seat, intending to put it to good use at the wedding reception. This pilsner glass was the only thing that remained undamaged. For over fifty years, he kept it in a prominent place, as a reminder of his humanity, he said. He even took it with him wherever he traveled across the globe.

"From that day forward, White Buffalo vowed he would never take another drink, saying he would not become just another sad statistic. In his mind, someone like him killed his best friend's bride. I never blamed him. Who could have avoided the situation, given the same circumstances? It just happened."

"Now you can understand why White Buffalo left his bequest of twelve million dollars to assist Native Americans with their sobriety," Darius said.

"Whatever happened to the drunk driver?" Markos asked.

"He spent some time in jail, but in those days drunk driving wasn't punished very severely. He eventually got out, and we never heard anything from him. No apologies."

"I can assure you, from my experience," Sophia said, "what goes around comes around, as they say."

Gaston touched her hand. "Indeed, it does. That is the deeper meaning of this gift that White Buffalo left. I confess we both had hatred in our hearts for a time, but White Buffalo's spirituality buoyed us and helped me turn that dark energy to the light. We traveled to the reservation and attended several sweat lodges that summer. There, a most marvelous medicine man helped heal our hearts. It took years to completely surrender, but we both came from the experience determined to preserve Dominique's memory by dedicating ourselves to strive for excellence in our lives."

"Uncle," Sophia said, "has there ever been anyone else?"

"No, I never married. Over the years, I've spent quality time with several wonderful women, but none compared with my Dominique. I always called her my dark angel, because she was so petite and sweetly angelic. Now she permanently remains so in my mind. But she never walked down the aisle with me. We never were married, never had children, nor did we have the life of our dreams. It did take an act of God to separate us after all."

Everyone, including Sebastien, Lou, and Mary were in tears. Again, silence reigned.

CHAPTER Five

Michael was already asleep. While lying next to him, Sophia could not help but review all the happenings of the past several days. Most people didn't experience so many events in a year, much less in a week.

In the wake of this past emotion–packed week, all Sophia could do was cry silent tears.

Michael awoke, feeling her tremble. He wrapped his body around hers and held her close as she broke down, sobbing. Her pillow soaked up all the tears that for days she had kept at bay. Feeling the security and warmth of Michael's body next to hers, Sophia finally fell into a deep sleep, soon returning to the adventures of her dreams, as she recalled her former life as Luciana, her ancestral grandmother.

Prior to the most recent events, Sophia dug deep into the history of one of her most famous ancestors. Sophia's great-great grandparents, the *RMS Titanic* survivors, Jocelyn and François Delacroix, were both descendants of the renowned French clairvoyant, Michel de Nostredame – more popularly known as Nostradamus. Like her ancestral grandfather, Sophia was also an oracle and a visionary. Naturally, she wanted to learn more about the famed seer. She found it quite interesting that with each recall of her many past lives, or with the visions into her ancestors' lives, she discovered each one to be a healer, oracle, or one with prophetic powers - able to tap into the Infinite Intelligence - the wisdom and eternality of God. Each one lived a life filled with love - love for their families, love for the work they did in the world, love for their communities, and respectful love for themselves.

Sophia could not help but wonder about her many lifetimes. They were a compilation of the consciousness and collective wisdom from whence she came. She wondered if she questioned her origins because she still doubted her spiritual gifts, not yet able to accept that she, like her ancestors, had the power to affect change for the betterment of the world around her. In the recollections of each of her past lives, she learned more about the powers by which she, too, was greatly gifted, for they were an integral part of who she was in the world. But, she could feel that something still seemed to be missing.

Although she continued to search deeper into her past, she was certain what she sought was not "out there." Instead, it was most likely an absent piece hidden within her that needed to rise to the surface. Nevertheless, she realized it was up to her to unveil it for the benefit of her present lifetime, and for the eternality of her soul's journey, and ultimately for the evolutionary upward spiral of the Universe. The answers would come. Of that, she had no doubt.

Sophia began her inquiry into the life of her ancestral grandfather by researching his known history, most of which referred to his famous quatrains. What she found most interesting was his history long before his renown, discovering who and what influenced the famed seer and healer to write such prophecies. However, that night she was not surprised when, in greater detail than before, Sophia returned to the past life of what she thought of as her ancestral grandmother's renaissance resort and health spa, in the year 1539.

Luciana was the sole proprietor of a small, but very successful inn along a well-traveled seaside road on the outskirts of Genova, Italia. Oftentimes, unbeknownst to the weary traveler, one would leave the inn revitalized in greater ways than their original intention, for not only was the inn a place for travelers to have a meal and bed down for the night, it was also where some gathered to restore their health and well-being.

A widow for several years, Luciana was an extremely independent woman in her early thirties, with long dark chestnut hair tied away from her face in a stylish chignon at the back of her neck. Her golden brown eyes emitted great wisdom that came from journeying through life with years of challenge. Yet there was a mystic edge about her, with an awareness far beyond the sun and moon's passing. Those who possessed the same numinous charm could easily recognize in others similar qualities of the mystical beyond that of the world.

Extraordinarily skilled in the healing arts, Luciana created custom concoctions of herbal remedies and tonics to bring one to physical healing. She also had a gift for scrying and forecasting while reading a person's future life events with the use of her water filled golden bowl. Other seers and soothsayers less insightful than she were envious of her ability to heal, which came naturally without effort. Those who had no concept of her spiritual gifts considered her a sorcerer, or worse, a witch. Yet, Luciana felt no such challenge with any of them, for she possessed a seemingly odd combination of humility paired with tremendous confidence in her spiritual gifts in the understanding that her powers and abilities were sourced by something greater than she ever could be on her own.

It was, however, the time of the Medieval Inquisition, an institution of the Catholic Church from which no one was exempt, which brought fear to most people in Europe. Empirics, apothecaries, midwives, and those like Luciana with the gifts of healing and prophecy were in danger. Women, in particular, were targets at that time, whether they were in the healing trade or not. Denied a higher education, women were not allowed into university. Becoming a physician, in particular, was a profession for men alone, who were deemed the new authority in the healing trade. As a result, people like Luciana had to do their healing work behind closed doors, away from the eyes of the Church lest they be found guilty of heresy, condemned for witchcraft, and almost certainly sentenced to death.

In addition to heretical accusations, the Church sought out offenders to blame for issues of concern, such as bad weather, poor crops, and disease. Deeply rooted in the story that Eve was the original source of evil, it was an underlying belief that she was responsible for the fall of Adam. Therefore, women not only became targets for the Inquisition, they were also controlled and denied any sense of authority.

Among other endemic diseases at that time in history, the plague consumed the lives of millions, reducing the population of Europe by a third. The Church was hard pressed for answers. So that the Church would not lose faithful followers and financial patrons, it was, therefore, important for a scapegoat to take the fall for all the difficulties.

By trade, Luciana was an innkeeper, but privately, she was a seer and healer in the shadows, possessing extraordinary abilities. She consulted her angels when working with an ill patron by peering into the golden vessel of sacred waters, foretelling what she needed, so she could bring them to healing. Beyond time and space, she communed with the spirits, and ultimately her God on High, knowing just what to do, which herbs to administer, what tonic to create, and what words to offer in the form of a blessing. She knew her power did not lie within her own abilities, but instead her authority came *through* her because she opened up, as a conduit, to the wisdom of the Eternal. If her patron was able to unite with her in her belief, healing became their reality.

Energetically, Luciana's vibration was so high that it shifted most anyone from the lower frequency of illness to one that was much higher, enabling them to receive the radiance of health through her belief. She easily healed livestock, for animals did not possess the filters that kept them from healing energy, thus increasing the farmer's prosperity. Her reputation for healing spread along the coastline in northern Italy. Like her ancestor, the Oracle of Delphi, she performed miracles beyond any other healing modality of the time. In truth, she knew the wisdom that came through her was sacred, holy, and divine - directed from God. In that awareness, she felt protected from lesser energies, carefully keeping aligned in the presence of the eternal now, free of fear and the entitlement of the lesser ego's stronghold.

In the early summer of 1539, a stately and elegant Frenchman came to the inn. Something intriguing about him drew Luciana's interest, yet in his quiet reserve, it was obvious that he was tremendously disheartened. Not wanting to call attention to himself, he sat in the darkest corner of the room with his head in his hands, facing the rough surface of the wooden tabletop. Typically, Luciana left her patrons to themselves until they made a request for food or drink, but it was not difficult to sense that this man was in need.

"Monsieur, I thought you might enjoy a plate of hot stew with fresh bread and a flagon of honey wine."

Surprised by her attentions, he looked at her and nodded, his face revealing the obvious pain he could not hide. He briefly rose from the table and bowed to her. "Merci, Madame. It has been some time since someone exhibited such kindness to me, nor have I enjoyed a warm meal for at least a fortnight."

"May I?" She smiled, motioning to the chair across the table from him. "My duties are done for a while, if you would care to share with me what is heavy on your heart." She laid down the weighty hand-hewn oak tray on the table, placing the pewter plate of food and mead in front of him, and then slowly took her seat.

He was in desperate need to release the burden he carried. After eating a few bites, sensing that she was a trustworthy soul, he began to reveal his story.

"Merci, Madame. If I may introduce myself, my name is Michel de Nostredame. Just weeks ago, I fled my homeland of France to avoid the inquisition by the Catholic Church. However, that is the least of my troubles."

"Yes, I must say, there is hardly one of us who is not in fear of the inquisition, but please tell me more."

"I am afraid that my memory clings to the pain as if it were yesterday. It has been four years since my cherished wife, and my young daughter and son all died of the Black Death. As it was, I was away from home, attempting to alleviate the suffering of those with this horrific disease, for I am a physician and an apothecary. I wish it were not so, but I was not there to save my *own* family."

"I extend my condolences for your tremendous loss." Long before Luciana approached him, she recognized his grief cloaked in melancholy, clearly resulting from a traumatic defeat. She knew all too well the mindset where nothing of value seemed to exist within the distressing anguish of grief's despair. She listened with compassion as he told his tale.

"Thank you," Nostredame said. "You are so kind to offer me your attention, but please forgive me for going on without first asking your name."

"I am remiss in not introducing myself before I sat at your table. My name is Luciana Nervetti de Genova. I am the proprietor of this inn."

"It truly is a pleasure, Madame."

"The pleasure is mine, Monsieur. Please continue."

"As an unfortunate consequence of the deaths of my family, the financial support of my community ceased, as well as my patron's benefaction, with their attitude being, if the doctor could not heal his own family, he must be in league with the devil. I have lost everything - my family, my home, my community, my profession, and my credibility that took years for me to gain."

Being a gifted healer of not only concerns of the physical body, but also that of the mind and soul, Luciana believed she could be of help, simply because it was not long ago that she stepped out of grief's shadowy abyss following the death of her husband. If her new patron would allow it, she could assist him out of the dark of night, into the light of day. It would take time, and it appeared he was rich in time, with nowhere to go and nothing to do.

"I have no way of knowing what you have endured, but from my experience, I *do* know grief. As the memories of loss soften, they become enriched into textures and colors - becoming a remembrance of those you have held most dear. Grief is not a place to reside, for it is a passageway into something far beyond what is now in your purview. Mourning certainly is not an indication of weakness, nor is it a lack of conviction. It is the price of love. We strongly grieve, because we love so deeply."

He looked at her with tears welling in his soulful eyes. "I appreciate your words of compassion, Madame."

When he reached for the flagon of mead, she noticed a long jagged gash on his forearm, giving her an opportunity to offer some needed care.

"Ah, my arm... shortly before I arrived here, my horse took an unfortunate scare along the path, causing me lose my balance. In the fall, I injured my arm on a protruding tree branch. I haven't taken the time to dress the wound myself."

"Monsieur, as it is for all healers, who is it that will heal the healer? If you follow me upstairs, I will dress your wound. Bring your drink with you."

Luciana gently washed the injury with fresh water and dried it with a clean cloth before she applied a poultice made of honey, calendula, myrrh, lavender, and comfrey. She wrapped a clean white rag around his arm and tied it at his wrist.

"If you plan to remain for awhile, I will address your injury until you are healed, but you are the one who will heal yourself by returning to the center of your being. In you, life is being recreated, and if you allow me, I will help you remember who you are at the core. This is where healing lies. It is not in the salve I treat your arm with, but more so within your belief."

An apothecary himself, he was enchanted by her. Furthermore, she had in her possession some captivating pieces that caught his attention, the first being the amethyst crystal that hung from a long gold chain around her neck. Never had he seen a piece of jewelry so simple, yet exquisite. Captivated by its elegance, he sensed it emitted great power. He continued to look around the small room filled with bottles of concoctions on tables and shelves. Clusters of varied dried herbs hung from the rafters, but what caught his greatest interest was a flawless golden bowl sitting on the table next to a flaming chalice, both made of the same lustrous metal.

Intrigued by this woman, her healing arts, and the inn itself, he responded, "I will stay for a time, for there is nothing immediately calling me. I believe this will be a welcome resort for my healing."

"You are most welcome to stay as long as you like to restore yourself for your upcoming travels. As you can tell, I too must resist the questioning eyes of the Church. I keep my deeper healing arts in the shadows, typically offering them in the night's darkest hours.

"Come with me. I have the perfect room for you, overlooking the sea. It is the quietest corner room, away from the noise of the inn. There, you will find a comfortable, clean feather bed, where you are welcome to rest your weary body and heal your wounded heart for as long as you desire. After you are rested, if you are willing, may I offer you a reading? It may be of some assistance to help you move toward your future..."

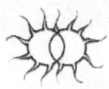

Chapter Six

The next morning, everyone gathered at the cabin for breakfast. After the long evening of legal paperwork the night before, and Michael taking hours to sign his full name on dozens of documents, the mood among the members of Apeiros was decidedly weary.

Darius addressed the group. "Since we've had such a deeply emotional and meaningful time together, might I make a suggestion? Our dear White Buffalo would not have wanted us to go our separate ways so weary with grief and sadness over his passing. Perhaps we should use our final two days together and take advantage of Colorado's winter beauty. The weather has cleared so beautifully. Sophia, do you think the roads are clear for a mountain drive?"

"Of course! Colorado weather is a blizzard one day, and fifty degrees and sunshine the next. A drive along one of the nearby mountain roads will certainly be plowed by now, and I have a great idea for a destination. Bring your wallets for a pleasant diversion and a little taste of the old wild west – saloons, gambling, dancing girls..."

"You know our group needs to keep it clean, don't you, Sophia?" Markos said with a mischievous grin.

"Pray tell, oh great Casanova, do you think I'm suggesting some kind of nefarious escapade?"

"But of course! However, I must say I do not need my wallet for such things."

"Bring it anyway. I'll surprise you, and certainly, I'm sure there will be many women where we're headed, if you desire."

"My, that sounds intriguing," Markos said.

"Many of them have blue hair, but you'll have your pick."

"Excuse, please," Markos said. "Did you say *blue* hair?..."

A change of scenery was more than welcome. Michael borrowed Jameson's van to drive half of the group, while Sophia took the rest in their SUV. The Ello Sisters joined them for the fun of it, and Sebastien came along, for Sophia told him he could have lunch, and then catch an airport shuttle at their intended destination.

They caravanned along the Peak-to-Peak Highway, enjoying some of the most beautiful scenery in Colorado. Thick layers of snow covered everything, from the highest mountain peaks, down the steep valleys, to the road in front of them. Pine, fir, and blue spruce held coated branches of icy white for hundreds of square miles far into the distance, with massive clusters of sleeping black and white aspens in their thin vertical salute to Colorado's blue skies overhead.

"We're coming into Central City and Black Hawk," Sophia said. "They're historic mining towns of the 1800s, but today they're known for legalized gambling. Back in the day, Central City was known as 'the Richest Square Mile on Earth.'"

They ate lunch at the Fireside Kitchen in Black Hawk, as Sophia and Michael shared some of Central City's interesting history. "This narrow valley we're in is called

'Gregory Gulch,' named after John Gregory who, in 1859, discovered gold in what was named 'the Gregory Lode.' In two months time, the population grew to 10,000 gold seekers who came to find their fortune in gold, silver, and copper. Thus, Central City was born, soon to be the leading mining center in all of Colorado. At one time, over 60,000 people lived in this narrow valley. Now the population of both towns is not much more than 800."

"When did they legalize gambling here?" Chayton asked.

"It was in the early 1990s," Michael said. "Both towns were virtually ghost towns before then. The idea was to revitalize the merchants, who thought they'd make a killing with mom and pop casinos, but eventually the big corporations came in and swallowed everything up. Now you see nothing but big name casinos here."

"I'd rather imagine these two towns were rambunctious in their day," Darius said.

"This truly was the Old West," Sophia said. "I read, in 1861 alone, they recorded over 200 fistfights, about 100 revolver fights, a dozen knife fights, and one dogfight. Amazingly, no one was killed. In 1871, the Republican Convention was held on the second floor of Washington House. Things got a little crazy, and the entire second floor collapsed down to the Recorder's office on the first floor below. With it went 200 men in attendance. Interestingly enough, no one was injured. The building is now a museum, and it still stands as the oldest public building in the state."

"A lot of famous people made their mark in Central City," Michael said. "Marie Curie, known as Madame Curie, mined some property for radium, south of the Glory Hole Mine, which she used in her studies in Paris. The first

Stetson Hat, manufactured here, became the prototype for all cowboy hats."

"I have always heard the name Baby Doe Tabor," Irina said. "Was she here?"

"Yes," Sophia said. "She was the wife of Horace Tabor, a famous silver magnate. Baby Doe was his second wife, but she once lived in Central City and Black Hawk with her *first* husband, who was a very poor miner. I'm not sure when she earned her reputation, before or after she married Horace, but she was considered the most beautiful, flamboyant, and alluring woman of the mining West."

"Hers was a sad story, though," Michael said. "She caused quite the scandal when she married old Tabor, who was about 25 years older than her. He dumped his first wife for an upgrade to Baby Doe."

"Ah, a trophy wife," Gaston said.

"She was the talk of Denver society for awhile," Michael continued, "but old man Tabor lost his fortune a decade later when the bottom fell out of the silver market in the late 1890s. He died without a penny, and Baby Doe deteriorated for many years until she froze to death in a ragtag cabin up in Leadville. She was 81."

"How very sad," Irina said.

"Colorado was quite the rags-to-riches-to-rags mining state, from what I've read," Darius said.

"Oh, yes," Sophia said. "Over 17,000 mining claims are in the southern end, here in Gilpin County. Many of the shafts go horizontally into the mountainside, but others go straight down, with the deepest over 2,000 feet. In 1874, most of the buildings in Central City burned to the ground in a wildfire, but the city was rebuilt of brick and stone. Twenty-eight of the buildings built before 1900 still stand today."

"After lunch, let's walk up to the Teller House," Michael said. "In the 1870s, it was reputedly the finest hotel west of the Mississippi River, and some say from Chicago to San Francisco. So, Darius, I guess your ancestors had a little competition, here in the Old West."

"I do say," Darius agreed. "Wouldn't you love to know what went on here?"

"Legend has it that miners laid a pavement of 26 ingots of solid silver, so President Ulysses Grant wouldn't dirty his boots when he stepped off the carriage during his visit with his friend, Henry Teller. Congress, at that time, was debating whether to back the U.S. dollar with silver or with gold. In order to show no favoritism, President Grant didn't use the silver walkway, but stepped up on the wooden boardwalk instead."

"Who was Henry Teller?" Lestari asked.

"He was the first elected senator when Colorado came into statehood in 1876. Three months later, he served as the Secretary of the Interior under President Chester Arthur. Years later, he was again elected as a Republican to the Senate, representing Colorado for 25 years, however ending his career as a Democrat."

"I've always heard about the opera house here," Gaston said.

"Yes," Sophia replied. "In fact, Horace Tabor built the Central City Opera House in 1878 - a community theatre, where they performed everything from opera to vaudeville. Even though it took horse and cart to bring all the building materials uphill, surprisingly the building was finished 100 days from the time of its groundbreaking. It was one of the most costly, but significantly well-built structures in Colorado history, made of iron, brick, and stone, with walls 16 inches thick. Some of the most famous performers were Buffalo Bill, P.T. Barnum's Circus, Houdini, and Oscar Wilde. Today, there are still theatrical and musical performances during a good portion of the year, with a packed house during their summer opera season."

"Tell them about Madam Lou Bunch Day," Michael said.

"Oh, that's funny. Every year, on the third Saturday of June, Central City celebrates Madam Lou Bunch Day, which began with the filming of an unused scene in the movie, 'The Duchess and the Dirtwater Fox.' Louisa Bunch was the last operating madam of Central City's red light district. In the early 1900s, when an epidemic of tuberculosis affected the miners, she turned her brothel into a makeshift hospital, and she and her 'sporting girls' nursed the sick and dying. So now, each year, the day begins with the Madam Bunch Bed Races. The 'sporting girls' and miners race down the street in old iron beds. The miners dress as such, while many of the women wear bustiers, fishnet stockings, laced up boots, and feathered hats. The day ends with the Madame and Miners Ball. I guess you could take that a number of ways. Anyone want to return in June for the festivities?" Sophia turned her focus particularly toward Markos.

"Sophia, are you implying that I'm a bit of a letch?" Markos said.

"Huh? I didn't hear you." Sophia smiled.

"Nothing... just an observation."

"I don't know if some of you remember the late 70s TV series, 'Centennial,'" Michael said, "but it was filmed in the Denver area, including here in Central City. Other movies were filmed here, as well."

"When we go to the Teller House, I'll show you 'The Face on the Barroom Floor,'" Sophia said. "I particularly like this story, myself. In 1936, The Central City Opera Association commissioned a local artist named Herndon Davis to do some paintings and sketches of the famous mining town. At the time, he was staying at the Teller House, where he did some work there as well. He had an idea to paint a picture on the barroom floor, but the hotel manager and the bartender would not allow it. About the same time, an argument ensued with the project director, who fired Herndon and subsequently told him to leave Central City. Since it was the last night of his stay, he decided to leave them with something to remember him by. He convinced the bellhop to lend him a hand.

"So, at midnight, they went down to the bar, and Herndon went to work while the bellhop held a candle so he could see what he was painting. He finished around 3 a.m. What he left was a portrait of his wife Nita, and today it remains. It's truly beautiful. People have written songs and performed a chamber opera about the painting of the Face on the Barroom Floor..."

After lunch, the gang took a little walking tour, which ended up at one of the large Black Hawk casinos, surrounded by dozens of tour buses. Sophia had a good laugh at Markos' expense as he perused a virtual sea of slot machines, attended by hundreds of elderly ladies on day trips from dozens of Denver area retirement communities.

"I've never seen so much blue hair in my life," Markos said.

"Go get 'em, tiger," Sophia said. "You have a pretty good chance, right up until four o'clock or so...."

They all decided to have some fun and gamble a bit, agreeing to meet back near the Fireside Kitchen at 5 p.m. for dinner before driving back to the cabin. When they gathered again, they shared tales about their day.

"I found myself drawn to the dollar slot machines, mesmerized by all those bright lights, bells, and whistles," Gaston said.

"What is it with you and bells?" Darius asked. "You're always ringing that blasted elevator bell at the cabin."

"It reminds me of home, at the store," Gaston said. "A customer walks in, the bell rings over the door, next thing you know, I ring up a sale." He winked at Sophia. "It's the same thing in the casino – it's the sound of money. I saw one elderly lady win two hundred dollars, and I was entranced."

"And it no doubt only cost her four hundred to do it," Chayton said.

"Ding, ding, ding," Darius said. "Money alright. Right out of my pocket. It took me only twenty minutes to lose fifty dollars. That silly machine just swallowed up what took me an entire month to earn, fifty years ago. So, I decided to go to the hotel spa and get a massage."

"I thought you were kind of shiny with a spicy scent," Gaston said.

"There's nothing like having a beautiful woman rub oil all over your body. It transcends all things of this earth," Darius said with a big smile on his face.

"Well, I met a woman," Markos said.

"When *don't* you meet a woman?" Christofer said. "You and women - no matter where we go, there's *always* a woman."

"I am Greek. I can't help it. She was a charming little old lady-"

"Blue hair!" Sophia said as everyone laughed and chided Markos.

"It was silver-blue," Markos said, "and she was absolutely lovely. She comes up here once a week on the bus from Denver."

"So, how did you manage that encounter?" Ananta asked.

"I sat down at a slot machine near her, and she began talking to me. What can I say? It's my Greek charm," Markos said, exhaling on his knuckles and rubbing them on his lapel.

"I think it's sweet," Sophia said.

"Thank you," Markos said, a bit defensive. "Her son takes her to the bus down in Denver at 9:30 a.m. every Tuesday. He gives her $100 to spend on her meals and gambling. She spends the entire day, and eats her lunch and dinner here, because the food is very inexpensive. She gambles all day, and at seven o'clock she catches the bus back to Denver, where her son waits to drive her back home. I tell you, she has it down to a science. She knows which machines are loose, and most of the time she takes home more than her son gives her to spend."

"Did she tell you which machines to use?" Lestari asked.

"She was very generous and informative. She even took me to the machine that usually pays off for her, offering it to me."

"You charmer you," Shoshana said.

"I'll have you know I won three-hundred dollars, and she was very excited for me. Afterward, I took her for coffee and a piece of pie. Her husband died ten years ago – he was a retired Air Force officer. We had a lovely time. What can I say? She was a nice little old lady. And get this – she's 90!"

"Wow," Michael said. "If I make it that far, I hope I have enough in the tank to go gambling every week."

Markos shrugged. "She seemed lonely. She just wanted someone to talk to – to be acknowledged. I hope she enjoyed our visit as much as I did."

Sophia smiled at Markos. "You made her day, Markos. I'm proud of you."

"How about you, Anja?" Markos asked, pushing the attention away from himself.

"I've never gambled before," Anja said. "I didn't know what to do, so I played the quarter slot machines. Easy enough. I won $120.00, but I spent $50.00 doing it. So, I'm ahead by $70."

"Not bad for a first try," Christofer said.

"Mary played the nickel slots the entire time," Lou said. "$50 goes a long way with nickels."

"Did you win, Mary?" Anja asked.

"I came ahead about $20, but Lou did better."

"Did you play the nickel slots, too?" Christofer asked.

"Oh, hell no," Lou said. "If I put money in a machine, I at least want a soda out of the deal."

"So, what did you play?"

"I'm not as cautious as my sister here. I played a little Texas Holdem and plucked a few pigeons for a hundred bucks," Lou said, quite proud of herself. "Then I went and rolled the bones. 26 straight rolls with 15 passes. I cleaned house for four hundred. Had everybody hollering. They gave me free champagne, and I don't mind sayin' I'm a little dipsy doodle right now."

Anja whispered to Christofer, "Did you understand what she said?"

"Yes. She first played a few hands of poker, and outsmarted her opponents, and won one hundred dollars. Then she played craps, and she successfully rolled the dice 26 times without losing, and made her point 15 times and won four hundred dollars. Finally, the management gave her apparently an abundance of champagne, and she is now hammered."

"Damn straight," Lou Ella said. "I thought I said all that."

"Mary," Michael said, "you're in charge of your sister."

"Got her."

"So, Lestari," Sophia said, "did you try your luck?"

"I tried my hand at roulette. I remember seeing an old American western movie with cowboys at the roulette table," Lestari said. "At first I doubled my money, but shortly after I lost it all - but it was fun."

"I played craps with Lou," Ananta said. "I like rolling the dice. It makes me feel as if I am in control, rather than letting a machine do all the work. When Lou got on a roll, a big crowd surrounded the table, and we cheered her on. It must be my inner extrovert at work."

"Did you win?" Mary asked.

"I did! Thanks to Lou, I won $170, plus what I came with."

"Did anyone else win?" Michael asked.

"I did!" Yesinia said. "I played Blackjack."

"*You* played Blackjack? Amazing!" Gaston said.

"I love that game. I always sit at the left side of the table so I can see everyone's cards before I have to make a decision," Yesinia said.

"Do you count cards?" Christofer asked.

"No, I just sit very still and ask my intuitive guidance whether to draw, hit, or when to double-down. It almost always pays off."

"So, you won. How much?" Gaston asked.

"$250, including my original fifty!"

"Whoo Hoo! Way to go," Michael said. "Guess who's buying dinner?"

"Crab's legs, steaks, and baked potatoes on me!" Yesinia said.

"And I'll buy the drinks!" Lou Ella said. "Bartender!"

"Mary," Michael said. "Your sister…"

"I got her."

"All right, then!" Michael said. "Let's get dinner. I'm hungry."

"Who'd have guessed," Lou said.

They walked through the casino together, headed for the Fireside Kitchen.

"I did pretty well," Shoshana said. "I played a machine that was all things Egyptian. It made me feel at home."

"Did you feel like you were at a dig?" Chayton asked.

"In an entirely different way - I doubled my money, which was more than I was expecting," Shoshana said.

"I played Blackjack, too," Christofer said. "I did pretty well for about an hour, but then I got cold and lost most of my winnings, just like water flowing through my fingers. But I still have my $50, so I won't go hungry."

"I won a little, then I won a lot," Irina said. "I played a little bit of most everything, trying to get a feel for what would work for me, when I noticed a woman who was playing a quarter slot machine for quite a long time. She left her seat without winning a thing. That was definitely the place to go next. Within ten minutes, all the bells were going off and the lights were flashing. Before I even took in how much I won, the officials were right there, getting me to sign papers for taxes."

"Yep, they appear out of nowhere!" Michael said. "How much did you win?"

"So, tell us. We're itching to know!" Yesinia said.

"$1200!"

"Whoa! Are you serious? I'm coming with you next time we do this," Lestari said.

"Dessert is on her!" Michael said.

"Chayton, how did you do?" Gaston asked.

"I won some, but not like my wife here. I won an extra $30 over and above the original fifty. I played craps, too. I spent the rest of my time basking in the glow of Irina and her winnings."

"My enchantress of a wife did quite well playing Blackjack," Michael said. "There she was with seventeen on the table, and she took a hit."

"No one hits a seventeen," Markos said.

"No one but Sophia," Michael said, "and I didn't hesitate to point that out. Even the dealer gave her a chance to change her mind, but not my little flower. She said hit it. I said don't. She said shut up and hit it. So, I shut up and the dealer hit it."

Everyone patiently waited for him to finish the story.

"Yeah," Michael said, "you guessed it. Four."

"Yes!" Yesinia cried.

"That's my granddaughter," Darius laughed.

"How did you do that?" Markos asked.

"I sensed it. It just felt like the right thing to do," Sophia said.

"I should know better. She does that a lot when she plays cards," Michael said. "One time we were playing Texas Holdem with a group of friends at their home. These people took their gambling *quite seriously*. Sophia won $300 within the first 20 minutes, and one of the guys was so exasperated, he quit for the evening and left. After Sophia won the next hand, another guy asked why she made the choice to play the cards that she did. It just didn't make sense to him that she won. He was more than annoyed with her, but she simply told him the truth. 'It *felt* like the right thing to do,' she said. Let's just say I quickly feigned a stomach ache to get us out of there. And never again did we get invited to play cards with them."

"Do you win very often?" Lestari asked.

"Most the time I do, but I play very little. I like to think of it as beginners luck each time," Sophia said.

"So how much did you win at the blackjack table?" Lestari asked.

"Well, we don't usually bet very much when we come here, but you know, with the inheritance and all, we decided to splurge a little and play at the $15 table. I walked away with $300. Not bad for a day of fun!"

Michael looked skyward, "By the way, White Buffalo, if you're listening, we won't make a habit of gambling away our endowment."

"Forget that," Markos said, "if we ever decide to meet in Monte Carlo or Las Vegas, I'm sticking with you!"

"Michael, how did you do?" Darius asked.

"I lost right away, and after watching Sophia hit that 17, I went over and watched the lounge show."

"Yeah, he went to watch the girls sing and dance," Sophia said.

"Just because I'm on a diet doesn't mean I can't look at the menu," Michael said.

"When, at any time in your history, have you been on a diet, oh ravenous one?" Lou said.

"When food is mentioned, I will never win with you, will I?" Michael said.

"Nope! That's one of the reasons I'm here - to keep you on your toes," Lou said.

"Well, give me some ballet shoes and watch me twirl," Michael said.

"You'd better get yourself a tutu," Lou said.

"Mary, I asked you to keep an eye on her."

"I got her."

They grabbed the last available large table at the Fireside, and their food arrived shortly afterward.

"We need to discuss where we will meet next," Michael said, "and Sophia and I have what we think you'll agree is a masterfully brilliant, nay I say, genius level of an idea."

"How could we possibly say no to this?" Gaston said.

"Sophia and I are returning to Ireland soon, while I head up an archeological dig on the property we bought when we were there for our honeymoon."

"Oh, my," Darius said, "so far, I like the sound of this."

"Tell me about your project," Shoshana said.

"I was just about to say that I want you in on this. When we were looking over the property, we discovered the remains of a subterranean community, at least 2000 years old. Sophia has some knowledge of the place, so it will be even more interesting!"

"I'm in!" Shoshana said. "Any time there's something to uncover, I'll be there."

"It's on the western part of Ireland, not far from the Cliffs of Moher, the most popular visitor site in all of Ireland," Sophia said. "The Aran Islands are just off the coast, which is where those beautiful hand-knit sweaters are made. There are many sites to see near there - some are historical, along with boating, fishing, hiking, music, food, and the people are quite friendly and accommodating."

"Now you're talking," Markos said. "You won't be able to keep me from visiting the isle of green! I'm part Irish, you know."

"No you're not," Christofer said. "You're Greek. Remember?"

"I beg to differ, oh fellow Grecian one. Everyone is part Irish at some time or another."

"We're building a subterranean home on the property, built right into the hillside," Michael said. "I've drawn the plans, and the contractor is about to break ground as we speak."

"Why subterranean?" Anja asked.

"Markos and Christofer inspired us on the benefits of living in a cave home on Santorini," Michael said. "They're protected from strong winds – in that part of Ireland, the winds can blow up to 75 miles per hour - and being underground, they're naturally insulated, so they're very economical in power and heat consumption, and of course they naturally stay cool in the summer months. Interestingly enough, that part of Ireland has about 225 sunny days per year, so we will have solar panels and a wind turbine to create an energetically green environment. Even though it will be built into a hillside, it will also boast a bit of an Irish cottage flair, with lots of stone and slate. The surrounding grounds will be an enchanting garden."

"There will be plenty of bedrooms for all of you," Sophia said, "each with its own bathroom and fireplace. The house will have a big kitchen, of course, with a large dining area, a great room, library, and study."

"Sophia will have her studio over the garage, and next to it will be a separate studio apartment. Between the house and the garage will be a combination greenhouse and spa room - a dream of hers. It will also have exercise equipment, and an indoor fitness pool and hot tub. We'll have fresh herbs and vegetables year round, not to mention houseplants and flowers all over the place."

"Can't wait for that!" Sophia said.

"What about your cabin?" Gaston asked. "Didn't you just spend a couple hundred thousand dollars to renovate?"

"We'll keep the cabin," Sophia said. "We certainly don't want to leave it or Colorado."

"Thank goodness," Gaston said. "I don't know what I'd do if I couldn't come and ride in that delightful elevator."

Everyone paused and quizzically stared at Gaston.

"What?!" he said.

Sophia continued. "Anyway, Jameson, from the Riverside Inn, has a brother who is his chef. Aaron currently lives in Longmont, which is quite a distance for him to drive. So, he'll stay at the cabin as our caretaker."

"Why are you building such a large home?" Ananta asked.

"It could be that we'll be there for years. Shoshana knows how long these things take," Michael said.

"When we no longer live in Ireland full time, we may turn it into a bed and breakfast," Sophia said. "Our Irish tour guide was a man named Pádraig, who is a recent widower with no family. We're going to ask if he'd consider managing the place."

"So, what do you all think?" Michael asked. "In six months, it should be finished. We will get all of our finances in order by then. Chayton and Irina plan to have the foundation well under way, and we will make those developments part of our next gathering."

Chayton looked at Irina, who took a shuddered breath. They nervously laughed. "No problem," Chayton said. "It's only a few hundred million. What could go wrong?"

"We're all here to advise," Darius said. "And you can't be in any better hands than with the Rousseaus. That

Sebastien is an impressive young man, isn't he?"

"A bit overwhelmed with the lot of us, at first," Gaston laughed, "but we shall break him in."

"So, may we assume we're all agreed that Ireland is our next destination?" Sophia asked. The response was emphatically unanimous.

"This is so exciting," Anya said. "I have never been to Ireland!"

"Nor I," Lestari agreed.

Michael glanced over at the Ello sisters. Mary politely finished her meal, trying hard not to eavesdrop, with little success. Lou, on the other hand, was fading quickly from the champagne.

"Mary, my darling," Michael said. "Please forgive us for talking shop here. We certainly didn't mean to exclude you from the conversation."

"That's ok, sport, I'm keeping my eye on sis, here, to be sure she doesn't keel over."

"You know," Sophia said, "this group has grown fond of you two."

"Well, what's not to like? But, honey, you know the feeling's mutual."

"With the unexpected good fortune bestowed on us by our sweet White Buffalo, we're in a position to ask if you two and your husbands would consider joining us in Ireland."

"Get off it," Mary said. "Lou, did you hear that?"

"I can't feel my lips."

"Trust me," Mary said, "if she were here right now, she'd be as excited as I am. Do we really have to take the old men – no, I guess we should."

Everyone laughed. "Now, keep in mind we wouldn't expect you to work all the time, but as you know, this bunch loves your cooking. But we'd want you all to have time to sightsee and travel the countryside, courtesy of Apeiros."

Mary dropped the act and wiped a tear. "We'd love to, sweetie. Thank you all, so much."

"Well, that's settled," Gaston said. "I'm weary and ready to head back. Anyone with me?"

"One more thing, before you all head home tomorrow," Sophia said. "Although he'd never make a big deal out of it, my beloved Michael has finally committed to having hip replacement surgery this spring."

Many reacted with surprise. "I knew you walked funny," Markos said, "but I just thought it was your poor impersonation of that actor, what's his name, John..."

"Wayne!" several said.

"No!" Anja said. "Poor Michael has obviously been in pain for some time."

"When is the surgery?" Darius asked.

"We haven't gotten that far yet," Michael said. "I've been taking steroid shots to ease the pain in both hips every few months for more than a year, but they just aren't doing much good anymore. My doc said, when that happens, he'll put me in the shop for some body work."

"He made an appointment to see the surgeon next week, so we'll know more then."

"It's not a big deal," Michael said.

"It's hip replacement, you ninny," Gaston said. "It *is* a big deal."

"Okay, maybe it is," Michael said. "I have to admit the thought scared me for some time, but I decided surgery probably can't hurt more than the constant pain I have right now. It's just that I didn't think anybody my age should need a hip replacement."

"His physical therapist said he's seen many tall men who played basketball and football in their day have hip problems by middle age," Sophia said.

"I'd like to think of it as chronologically centered," Michael said.

"Take heart," Christofer said. "I have a neighbor who had one replaced, and he's in his 40s. He was a professional soccer player, and he's a big man like you. He also is now pain free and able to hike and climb without any problem – in fact, he completely recovered in just a few months."

"Well, when we meet in Ireland, he'll be in good shape, walking pain free without a limp," Sophia said. "I'll let you know the date, so when you all do the good work for the world, keep him in your thoughts and prayers for his healing. Bless the surgeon and the medical team, and keep me in your thoughts too, because I'll be his caretaker while he recovers. Now that he's committed to doing this, I think I'm more worried about his surgery than he is."

"Yeah, do keep me in your prayers," Michael said, "because for a few weeks, Sophia will be doing all the cooking."

"Oh, dear. I hope you don't die of malnutrition, my boy," Darius said.

"Thanks a lot, you all!" Sophia, said, laughing. "You know, I can make a mean toasted cheese sandwich and whip up a good frothy mug of hot cocoa!"

"Yep, that's your specialty, my sweet, but there's only so much brown food I can tolerate," Michael said.

"We'll keep you prayed up, for sure!" Chayton said.

CHAPTER Seven

Luciana tended Michel's arm once again, which was healing nicely, and she noticed his spirits seemed to rise above the grief of his many losses. "I enjoy getting to know my patrons - their history, and their joys. Tell me something about yourself, monsieur. What is it that brings you life?"

"Very well. I was one of nine children, born on December 14, 1503, in Saint-Rémy-de-Provence, France. My father was a prominent notary of Jewish heritage, but Nostredame was not always the name of my family. My paternal grandfather's name was Guy Gassonet, but attempting to avoid persecution, he changed it to Pierre Nostredame, meaning 'Our Lady,' following his conversion to Catholicism in the mid 1400s.

"My maternal grandfather, Jean de St. Rémy, tutored me in many languages, primarily Greek, Latin, and Hebrew. He also taught me mathematics, the celestial science of astrology, and Jewish mysticism, which is the ancient mystical interpretation of the Wisdom of Truth through the study of the Kabbalah, considered the soul of the Torah.

"When I was fourteen years of age, to earn my baccalaureate degree, I entered the Université d'Avignon, which is the papal enclave of Provence. I was there only a year before an outbreak of black plague forced the university to close its doors.

"For the next several years, I traveled throughout France, introducing new treatments for plague victims. I was quite different than my colleagues, who practiced bloodletting, the use of potions containing mercury placed on patients' robes soaked in garlic. When possible, I thought it best to relocate my patients from infected buildings in the cities where plague was prevalent, to sanitary facilities in the countryside with clean beds and open windows to let in fresh air. Their hygiene and diet increased by keeping their bodies clean, drinking only water that was first boiled, and eating foods free of grease and fat. It took much convincing the townspeople it was necessary to remove corpses from public areas to avoid further infection.

"In 1522, I resumed my education, attending the Université de Montpellier, one of the oldest of universities, established in 1289. However, at that time, my many years of experience as an apothecary prevented me from completing my education as a doctor of medicine, because an apothecary is a manual trade, but three years later I was licensed to practice medicine. I integrated my medical practice with my apothecary trade, using herbal treatments to aid my patients in their healing and comfort. One of my best remedies I developed from rose hips, in what eventually became the *Rose Pill*, which brought relief to those suffering from the plague.

"Having successfully treated and healed many patients of the plague, I became a celebrity of sorts, thus gaining substantial financial support from many fellow citizens of Provence. In 1531, I worked alongside a leading scholar and physician, Jules-Cesar Scaliger of Agen, in southwestern France.

"While living in Provence, I married a lovely woman. Within three years, we had two beautiful children, a boy and a girl. As I shared with you when I first arrived, my wife and children sadly succumbed to the plague when I was away treating other patients, which lead to the loss of my patronage. Not long after their deaths, my wife's family sued me for her dowry, which they won, and so that was another loss suffered."

At that time in history, the plague killed over twenty-five million people - up to 60% of the European population. Over the centuries, the plague claimed over two hundred million lives throughout the world, taking two hundred years for the European population to rebuild.

"In 1538, a few years after my family's deaths, I received a summons to appear before the Church Inquisition. To avoid charges of heresy, I again packed up my horse and promptly fled the south of France to find my way here, in Italy, with plans to travel to Greece and Turkey. Quite a journey it will be, I am certain..."

After Michel decided to remain at the inn for several days, Luciana asked for his assistance to move an armoire from her bedroom to another room in the inn. When they moved the large piece of furniture away from the wall, Michel noticed a gap on the side of the bookcase that sat a bit askew.

"What is this - a hidden door behind this bookcase built on a pivot? How I enjoy such intrigue."

"Go ahead, push on one side of the bookcase, and you will find that it leads to the attic." They carefully walked up the surprisingly solid narrow stairway to the upper level, which revealed a spacious room with a high-pitched ceiling.

"Such an incredible room - what are your plans for this hideaway?"

"This room will be solely used for my own private personal use. Here, I will rest under the stillness of the stars. My herbal treatments, healing concoctions, and some of my books will remain on the second floor. However, this will be my sacred sanctuary and my private retreat for meditation after a busy day of service to my patrons. Here, I can easily access the power of the eternal flame and the golden bowl, far from questioning eyes. I will finish the walls in earthly images that remind me of the grace, the glory, and the timeless realm of the presence of God, here on earth."

"I would be honored if you allow me to assist you in creating your sanctum sanctorum."

"I was hoping that you are willing to lend a hand."

"Very well then, if you will allow me, I will plaster the walls a gleaming white, ready for you to paint your frescoes."

Luciana began her murals along the base of the walls with paintings of distant mountain ranges at sundown, shadowed in dusty layers of violet. Directly above the crest of the mountaintops was the contrast of light golden tones, blending into a slight band of sage green that led to clouds in brilliant golds and coral tones, highlighted in fiery red lined clouds backlit by the sun. On one wall, brilliant sunrays filtered in from massive cumulus clouds far into the blue skies above, blending into the sunset scenes that flanked the images on adjacent walls. All around the room, above the spectacular sunset scenes extending up to the ceiling, she painted layered blues that perfectly blended into lavender and purple tones, extending to deep indigo skies overhead. Nighttime stars peeked out, far from the heavens, with sparkling starlight shining through, as if it were a moonless night. All the while, Michel sat mesmerized on the floor, watching her work without her noticing his attentions.

When her painting was complete, he helped her clean the floor to ready the room for furnishing.

"Will you help me carry these two Persian rugs up the stairs to cover the floor?"

"Of course. What else needs to be done to complete your new sanctuary?"

"I have a wooden canopy bed from India to assemble once we get it up the stairs."

They assembled the romantic bed, draping it in sheer coral and pomegranate-colored silks that hung from the ceiling down the opposite ends of the bed to the floor. From the inside of the high bed frame, she hung five Moroccan lanterns in vibrantly colored glass, varied in shape and size, which when lit would cast a romantic light on the cushioned bed below. Over the feather mattress, they placed layers of colorful quilts and an array of pillows in Persian and Indian Paisleys in shades of gold, peach, coral, pomegranate, persimmon, grape, lavender, a slight bit of sea foam green, and aquamarine. It was a room made for the romance of the heart - with colors and finishing touches that particularly appealed to Luciana's mystical feminine tastes.

"I feel like I am in the middle of a fruit bowl," Michel said.

"It is similar to a Kasbah from Morocco, yes?"

"I have not yet been to Morocco, but now I am intrigued to include it in my travels."

While she was painting, Michel took one of the small round tables from the tavern and sawed off the legs to knee height. He planed the tabletop until smooth and polished its surface with beeswax. They placed the table on the center of the plush carpet, surrounded with large pillows for comfortable seating. It was the perfect place for her golden bowl and the chalice with the eternal flame. Placed throughout the room were clusters of varied heights of wrought iron candle stands, holding her prized handmade beeswax candles.

Her mystical sanctuary was finished. Needing a few days to relax and enjoy her new haven, Luciana closed the inn for four days, placing a sign on the door reading "CHIUSO," giving the cook and her few servants four days off with well-deserved pay.

"Michel, would you care to join me for dinner this evening? I cannot thank you enough for all your help. Without you, I would never have completed this room in such short order. It truly is beautiful - absolute perfection. I will enjoy it for years to come."

"But of course, dinner will be the beginning of how we can celebrate. Tonight, let us initiate it together, yes?"

Suddenly shy, Luciana looked away from his obvious attentions. "Let us go down to the sea to bathe before the sun takes its place beyond the horizon. Afterward, we will return to share a meal, which I have already prepared." She led the way to the shore, Michel eagerly following behind her. For years, he rarely had time to do much else than tend the sick. Not wanting to seem too anxious, Michel quietly took a seat on the rocky ledge along the sandy coastline.

Mostly covered with heavily gathered floor length skirts and a big loose blouse, topped by a long apron, all he ever saw of her was her face, neck, hands, and forearms. She kept her long hair tied in a loose chignon at the base of her neck, covered by a thin silk scarf to keep the wisps of hair away from her face.

Little notice did she pay to his attentions as she

undressed. There on the shore, bathed in the golden colors of sunset, she first removed her apron and then her shoes, and untied the ribbons above her knees that held up her stockings. With the removal of her blouse, skirt, and under-garments, Michel witnessed the reveal of her extraordinary beauty. Never had he noticed her lovely body before. Always busy with the details of managing the busy inn, she worked constantly, so he was surprised to find that she was not worn and hard as expected, but instead her body was sensually soft and slender. She untied the scarf from around her head, as her waist-length chestnut hair trailed down in thick waves over her delightfully firm breasts that were beautifully proportioned to her height. Her legs were long and lean, as she sat on a rock and took a handful of wet sand to rub all over her feet, elbows, and hands, reveal-ing new pink skin beneath the weary worn parts.

Luciana waded into the cool water and watched Michel undress. In his mid-thirties, he was lean of body and well muscled, having spent the last years walking the country-side, administering healing to so many who needed his help. Luciana thought him a handsome man, with thick dark hair, brown eyes, and a full beard and mustache.

He waded into the sea until the water reached his waist, and then dove under the water and swam toward Luciana. He came up underneath, picked her up, and playfully tossed her back into the sea. She swam behind him and came up giggling as she jumped onto his back. She wrapped her arms and legs around his body, and they fell into the sea together. They splashed about and played like children until the sunset turned to shades of blue twilight, revealing starlight far to the edge of the world. They came onto the shore, dried off, and put on the clean clothes they brought with them.

Supper was ready, for while they finished preparing the attic, chicken and vegetables were cooking on the hearth. Up the stairs, Michel carried the tray of hot food, along with a freshly baked loaf of bread and churned butter, while Luciana brought two goblets and a pitcher of claret. They sat on the floor cushions at the table that Michel finished for the room, with the skylight door open above them. The indigo painted ceiling blended in well with the view of the starlit skies overhead.

For several years, Michel kept to himself, tending his many losses, in addition to keeping his distance from the Church Inquisition in France, which left no room for desire other than that of survival. However, sparks ignited between Luciana and him for the last several days while refinishing the attic. Very little was said between them, with nothing more than a fleeting glance, but the heat arose nonetheless.

Many considered Luciana a handsome woman - a refined beauty of great strength, dignity, and poise. Having fully run the seaside inn long before her husband died years before, she was tremendously independent, with a fine mind and good character. She did not need anyone in her life, but rather desired companionship for her own pleasure, and the pleasure she longed for was about to commence.

After the welcome meal, she took the dishes down to the kitchen to clean up. On her way back up the stairs, she grabbed two goblets and a pitcher of a new drink, brandy, brought to her by a patron from Holland. When she came into the room, Michel was sitting on the floor pillows with every candle lit, leaving a warm inviting atmosphere for their greater enjoyment.

He held a gift, wrapped in cloth. "Come. Sit with me. I have something to give you."

"Michel, when have you had time for anything but getting well?"

Luciana excitedly untied the hemp twine around the cloth. Inside was a carved wooden box.

"Oh, how beautiful," Luciana said. "Look at the exquisite hand-carving with intertwining circles that join at the middle. And the design on this clasp - it is Celtic, is it not?"

"Yes, you are well traveled, it seems," Michel said.

"Most of what I learn of the world is from my patrons who teach me without their knowledge of doing so."

Luciana pulled the pin that anchored the latch to the box and opened it to find a delicate hourglass held inside a bronze tripod frame, resting in deep blue velvet.

"How extraordinary," Luciana said.

On the inside of the lid was an etched silver plate that read:

I leave this hourglass of infinite time to Luciana Nervetti, a descendant of the Delphic Oracle, for her gift of vision, healing, and great heart. Its golden tripod is the symbol of prophetic powers. The glass, in the shape of infinity, holds the Greek marble sands of time, ever flowing, and never ending. I leave you with my blessing of apeiros, knowing you will continue to receive great gifts through the eternal, boundless, expansive love of God. I also leave you with my endless love and devotion, for we are forever one from this point forward.
Devotedly, Michel du Nostredame

She typically was not one to show much emotion, but his unexpected gift caught her off-guard. She sat in the candlelight, beaming with appreciation. It had been so long since anyone had given her a gift, much less something of such beauty and deep meaning.

"Oh, Michel, I am stunned." She smiled, radiant in the candles' glow. "How was it that you know that I am descended from the Oracle?"

"For one, you use a bowl in which you perform your readings, as did the Delphic Oracle," Michel said. "And for another, I too am her descendant. We know each other when in the same company, do we not?"

Luciana simply nodded, in awe of the hourglass as she turned it over, watching as the fine grains of sand fell through the narrow glass neck.

"This hourglass has been in my family for several generations, given to me by my grandfather. I had a propensity for being late for my studies, ever interested in what caught my immediate attention. He gave me the timepiece to help ground me, and I must say it helped in that way. Now, I want you to have it."

"But, Michel, this is a family heirloom. Would you not like to keep it - to pass it along to someone in your fam-" She caught herself, for he no longer was a father of two children. They were gone, along with his wife.

He cleared his throat to take time to pause. "You, Luciana, have brought me back to life again. That makes you and I united in the family of humankind, but more so because of our common ancestry that propels us onward through the purpose of our soul's calling. Please accept it."

"Thank you, Michel. This is a most generous gift that I shall forever treasure."

"Very well, then. The tripod is quite ancient. It contains the same etchings that are on both your bowl and the fiery chalice. I am certain they are of the same origin." He touched the engraving on all three pieces. "The hourglass is a manmade invention first noted in history back in the 1300s. The tripod was later designed to fit the hourglass, and I must say it is as if the two were made for each other from the beginning. There is something unique about the piece, which I have not yet discovered. Perhaps you will find it as you use it in your work."

On the table was a small stone box, carved from alabaster. Luciana removed the lid and pulled from it the amethyst amulet, which was already glowing. She held the chain in her hand, while the amulet turned in wide circles to the right. The intonation of attunement began, with all the sacred talismans joining in high frequency to reach harmony. The room lit up for a moment, as if the sun shined from all directions, leaving no shadows but only brilliant luminosity.

Nostredame's eyes grew wide. "You must tell me about the amulet. I have never seen anything radiate such light."

"This stone, like your hourglass, has come down the generations of my family. It attunes to pieces and locations of similar resonance. Obviously, the hourglass is one of these pieces."

"It is quite astounding and truly marvelous, as are you." Michel leaned toward her and placed his hand gently under her chin to lift her face to meet his. Luciana closed her eyes and opened her lips to join him in their first kiss.

Michel poured the brandy and made a toast to her, "To beauty, strength, and the heart of the healer." They took a sip and kissed again. He untied the ribbon that allowed her tresses to fall in waves down her back. He ran his hands through her long hair, watching the strands fall from his fingers while shimmering in the candlelight. She stood and placed her hand out for his. Backlit by the candlelight, he could see the silhouette of her curves through the sheer fabric of her caftan. They joined among the many pillows on the bed as he lay down beside her, bringing with him the brandy for their enjoyment.

He held her gently, feeling the curves of her body beneath the thin fabric. He leaned over and gently kissed her on her forehead, then her cheek, her chin, and down to her neck where it met with her shoulder. She laid her head back and moaned at the sensual pleasure.

She helped him remove his shirt, and then untied his breeches at the waist, dropping them to the floor. While lying on her side, he then placed his hand through the slit in the caftan on her bare leg and slowly moved it upward, pulling the caftan with it. He helped her pull it over her head, leaving them both naked in the golden candlelight.

In the sensual atmosphere of the sheer coral draperies hanging around them, they made deep and sensual love. As the hours passed, they drank the brandy, ate bread and cheese, and talked of their lives and their dreams. Much laughter and playfulness continued, along with more love-making until the sun rose in the east.

Luciana slept, wrapped in the quilts, her hair in soft tangles around her. Michel closed the door to the skylight and blew out the remaining candles, leaving only the eternal flame burning tirelessly in the chalice on the round table. He joined her under the covers, and they slept, entwined in each other until the sun was high overhead. For both, it had been years since they enjoyed the body of another, but neither had lost their touch. It was an evening they would not only remember, but one they would repeat many times...

CHAPTER
Eight

Unbeknownst to Sophia, Michael made reservations for them to spend ten restful days in Hawaii. He wanted to attend an archaeology conference in Lahaina, but they would first spend a few days on Kauai before flying to Maui, where, as luck would have it, they would observe a total lunar eclipse during their stay.

Before they left, Michael consulted with a highly recommended orthopedic surgeon in Denver, who confirmed it was time for a total hip arthroplasty on both hip joints, assuring Michael that replacing both at the same time was not uncommon, and in fact would hasten his overall recovery time. Michael and Sophia talked it over and agreed to schedule the procedure shortly after their return from the islands.

Travel day was the coldest day of winter in Colorado, during a day of extremes. They flew from Denver with temperatures of five degrees below zero, and arrived in Lihue with balmy sunshine weather in the mid 70s. Sophia marveled that from Denver's mile-high altitude, they traveled to sea level in less than seven hours. After retrieving their luggage at the baggage claim, they made a beeline to the rest rooms, where they changed out of their winter clothing and donned shorts and t-shirts.

The sun had already set by the time they drove their rental car to their condo, located on the north shore in the charming community of Princeville. While Sophia unpacked all their bags, putting their clothes away in the drawers, and hanging shirts and dresses in the closet, she noticed something scurry by. She stopped, moving only her eyes so she would not scare it away.

"Michael!" she called. "There's a lizard in here!"

Michael was already perched in a lounger on the lanai, listening to the darkened ocean and enjoying a tall, cold one. Only a volcanic eruption, or an empty beer bottle, was going to make him move. "Is he green and cute? Like he might want to sell you car insurance?"

She slowly approached and smiled. "He *is* kinda cute!"

"It's a gecko!" Michael hollered. "He won't hurt you - in fact, he's a little bug vacuum cleaner! It's like having our own personal valet!"

While Sophia appreciated wildlife, she preferred not to sleep with it. She grabbed a glass from the bathroom to capture the little guy and take it outside, but it wasn't going to be that easy.

Most of the furniture was made of bamboo. The nightstand was no exception. Pencil-thin bamboo pieces glued together made up the furniture, and the gecko was just tiny enough to fit in between the grooves, making it impossible to trap the little critter. When she tried to place the glass over it, the gecko easily slipped along the grooves just under the lip of the glass to another section of the nightstand. After trying a few times, she decided the little guy was quite frightened, so she stopped to consider the situation.

She took a deep breath and centered herself, asking her intuition what to do. She laughed at the thought that entered. *Why not? I'll give it a try.* Slowly, she bent over the nightstand, looking directly into the itty-bitty eyes of the gecko.

"You know, we are one," she tenderly said. She smiled as she thought, *this is ridiculous*, but she continued anyway because she believed it was true. Besides, she knew the power behind intention.

"Help me to help you, so I can take you safely outside, where you will have a much better life among the plants and flowers."

Immediately, the gecko jumped onto the floor right at her feet. It did not move. She was amazed! She took the glass and gently placed it over the tiny being, then slid an envelope underneath the opening, temporarily trapping it inside. The gecko jumped on the inside of the glass and hung on for dear life with its miniature suction cup toes.

Sophia carried the glass outside into the yard in front of the building, where there was a plethora of beautiful tropical bushes and trees. She saw bougainvillea, thinking the beautiful fuchsia-colored blooms would be a yummy taste treat for her temporary captive. She bent down close to the ground at the base of the bush and uncovered the glass. The gecko held onto the glass, not releasing its grip, even though she shook the glass several times.

At this point, Sophia questioned what she had gotten herself into, having already taken at least thirty minutes to capture the little critter and transport it to what she considered a gecko's paradise. Finally, she whacked the bottom of the glass, forcing the gecko to release its hold. She watched it scamper away into its new world, hopefully to a better existence than a dusty environment made of cinder blocks.

She came back in as Michael limped to the refrigerator for another beer. "I got him outside," she said.

"Who?"

"The gecko. I caught him and released him into a beautiful flower buffet."

"You *caught* the gecko? That's like trying to catch a sparrow. How'd you do it?"

"We talked it over and agreed he'd be better off outside, eating plants and flowers, so he jumped into this glass, and I took him outside."

"You talked it over," Michael said, opening his beer.

"You know me," she said, quite satisfied.

"Did he forget to tell you he doesn't eat plants? Only juicy insects, mealworms, crickets…?"

"Oh. No. He didn't mention that. How do you know so much about geckos?"

"I dig around in the dirt all over the world for a living. I know a lot about crawlies – especially the ones from which you should run away, screaming in terror."

Sophia gritted her teeth. "Should I know about any of those here?"

"Nope. Oh, a centipede or fire ant here and there, but this is paradise."

She looked out the window. "Well, I'm sure he'll find dinner sooner or later. It's better than him crawling up my leg in the middle of the night…"

This small moment left Sophia with much to think about. She could have saved herself some time and taken a shoe to the gecko, but that was not her. She was always one to save spiders, too. Occasionally, she would catch a fly and set it free out the doorway. Once, she had problems with ants getting into her home. She found their community not far outside the front door. So, early one morning she knelt down over the busy anthill and told them she would have to take measures that would not be beneficial for them if they did not stop coming into her house. She asked them to find a way to move on so this would not be necessary. A few days later, there were no more ants in the house, and their anthill was no longer outside the front door.

Sophia reflected on the gecko not letting go of the glass and just hanging on. It reminded her of herself. She thought of how many times she stayed attached to something when she really needed to move on, even though she could see something better on the horizon. There were times she did not give herself a chance to do what she would love to do because she was afraid to step out of her comfort zone. What was it about her that she would rather settle for less, remaining in mediocrity instead of moving on to something new and, most likely, even better? She was learning, if she did not make a voluntary shift by taking action toward her desires, she would eventually get the proverbial whack of the spiritual two-by-four, catapulting her into change, whether she was ready or not. This is how the universe worked. Either she chose to go gracefully, or more often than not, kicking and screaming along the way. Sometimes it was just too easy to get stuck in the melee of mediocrity and smaller thinking, and settle for less.

She had to remind herself that the ever-expanding universe is always conspiring for her good, eternally growing and becoming something greater within the upward spiral of evolutionary development. There was always something better beyond what she could see. If she could simply trust and allow, there would be less suffering in the thought that something should be different than it is. Then, she could more easily trust the process along the journey, which constituted adventure. That sense of exploration would gracefully move her toward that which called her to greatness.

Perhaps the thirty minutes with the gecko was time well spent, she thought, *for it made me take a better look at myself...*

They started the next day at the Kilauea Lighthouse, east of the condo across the bay. Much to their surprise, not far from the shore were two whales, breaching. For a couple of landlubbers, this was a sight they didn't want to pass up. The whales were making their way westbound, so Sophia and Michael returned to their condo for whale watching. Just west of their condominium complex was a path that led down to the secluded Sealodge Beach. There, they skinny dipped in the warm clear waters, sunning themselves on the beach with no one around. Afterward, they followed the whales, westbound from beach to beach, along the north shore Kuhio Highway, ending their day at Ke'e Beach, which was as far as the north shore road of Kauai could go. In addition to whale watching from the beach, the golden sundown gave Sophia ample photo ops to capture the distant mountains along the beautiful Na Pali coast.

The next day, they drove clockwise from Princeville, three-quarters around the island to Waimea Canyon, known as the 'Grand Canyon of the Pacific,' all in mountainous valleys of reds, golds, and patches of greenery. While the canyon itself was dry, stark, yet colorful, just to the north was the highest point on Kauai, Kawakini, elevation 5,243 feet at the summit of the inactive volcano, Mount Waialeale. Known as the second wettest area of the entire planet, with 450 inches of annual rainfall, it is covered in lush green forests. Kauai, known as the Garden Island, is the oldest island of the Hawaiian island chain, its beauty ancient and stunning.

After Sophia took several hundred photos, they left the mountains and Waimea Canyon, and returned to the southern part of the island, where they toured a beautiful coffee plantation. Hawaii, at one time, was known for its sugar plantations until it was discovered to be a perfect locale to grow coffee. Of course, they bought several bags of beans to take home, some for gifts, but mostly for themselves.

After such a long day of adventuring, Sophia slept well that night, returning to her dreams of Luciana and Michel...

CHAPTER Nine

Weeks later, Michel asked if Luciana would give him a reading. Of course, she accepted. Divination had become quite popular in Europe over the last one hundred years. He was curious about her use of the bowl, having seen it when he first came to the inn. Curiosity drew his interest, and he wondered if he too could divine the future, but he was not yet convinced that the water-filled bowl enabled her to do her readings.

They ascended the stairs to her secret retreat. Luciana lit all the candles in the room and opened up the skylight. They sat at the table as she poured fresh water into the bowl from a ceramic pitcher. She set the eternal flame directly behind the bowl so the firelight would reflect on the water. After she removed the hourglass that Michel gave her from the velvet-lined box, she placed it on the table. Her amethyst amulet began to ring out a tone of high resonance as a brilliant light filled the room. All was well.

Michel felt somewhat anxious. He shifted on his pillow, not quite able to get comfortable. "Before we begin, can you tell me why you look into the bowl of water to do your readings? Other seers performed readings using tarot cards, palm readings, and runes on my behalf."

"I am surprised that you ask," Luciana said. "You already know that the Oracle used a bowl to do her readings. You, a descendent of the Oracle as I am, must know why."

"I want to know why *you* use the bowl. What is it about the bowl that empowers you in *your* readings?"

"The bowl has no power without water," Luciana calmly responded. "Water, as you know, is the most powerful of all the elements. Water carries the life force for all beings, for all life on Earth, and without it, nothing can sustain or grow. Like Earth, our bodies are made mostly of water.

"Water symbolizes spirit and the soul. It connects us to the unknown, which is beyond what we perceive with our five senses. Water allows us to reach beyond the thinking mind, through the depths of consciousness, to that part of us which is the knower of all things. Think about the sea. What we see is only its surface, but what we know about the world beneath the ocean is very limited. Water is the only element constantly changing. It transforms from liquid to vapor, and to solid when frozen. It represents transformation of all life and its interrelationship.

"I feel most alive when I am near water. It is where I feel most at home. That is why my husband and I built this inn on the coastline. When I do a reading through water, I see beyond appearances into the possibilities - to the depths - beyond what the mind knows. It is as if the water within me connects to the most sacred part of another, joining us in unity."

Luciana invited Michel to sit closer. "Before we begin, let us invoke the angels and the Almighty to make this reading one that is spiritually directed," she said, following with a short prayer. Afterward, she opened her eyes and looked intently into the water-filled bowl. Past the flame's reflection, she peered directly to the inscriptions at the bottom of the golden bowl.

"What do you see for the remainder of my days?" Michel asked.

She took quite a bit of time looking into the bowl. He found himself entranced as well. The firelight reflection on the seamless bowl enchanted him for reasons he did not yet know. For a few moments, Luciana sat completely still as if in a trance, absorbing what she saw for his life.

"Soon, you will carry on with your travels along the Mediterranean, after which you will return to your hometown of Salon-de-Provence, in the year 1547. Not long after, you will marry a wealthy widow. I believe her name will be Anne. Together you will raise six children - three boys and three girls. She paused and took a deep breath to focus, for she could not allow her personal feelings to interfere with what she envisioned for his life.

"At some point you will Latinize your name, because many who obtain their medical license do the same. Perhaps changing it from Nostredame to Nostradamus will suffice. Your title of doctor will no longer be applicable, yet many will call you such. Instead, you will become involved in great beauty, for such a desire is far more prevalent than ever before, especially among the wealthy and the elite of Europe. Because of the quickly escalating cosmetic industry, you will shift your emphasis from medicine to the rising popularity of the cosmetic trade. Your calling to write will begin with two books on the medical sciences, and the making of cosmetics, which interestingly will include several cooking recipes.

"Over time, your years of study and achievements in the use of herbal healing treatments will change your interests to practices of mystical alchemy, but you must be wary in this endeavor. I invite you to find a private, hidden study where you can secretly utilize your mystic aptitude, hidden from prying eyes and overly curious minds.

"I see you using a candle to cast its light into a water-filled brass bowl similar to how I use my bowl with the chalice. The difference is you will add herbs to the water to further aid you in your visions. In this, you will continue the tradition of your ancestor, the Delphic Oracle, who also saw her patron's future while peering into a bowl filled with sacred spring water. As you look into the water-filled bowl, you will invoke mystical visions that will bring inspiration to your writing, but take heed - no magic is for your use.

"Around the year 1550, you will write your first almanac of local folklore, astrological information, and future predictions for the forthcoming year, including your prophetic visions of the distant future. I see you writing many published works of playful pieces, helpful to the common people - mostly farmers and merchants. As a result, you will write nearly a dozen almanacs, with several thousand prophecies throughout.

"Many will regard you a fraud, insane, and more likely, a servant of the devil, but most will consider your prophecies as spiritual inspirations from God. Some of what you participate in will relate to your heritage - the stars will lead your words, and people will follow. France will open its doors to you once again, most happy at your return. Your reputation will increase throughout France, gaining great renown and success from the almanac's publication, so much so, that prominent people and French nobility will request an audience with you to read their horoscope and future divinations. Your celebrity will spread from France to the European elite as well. I see that your prophecies will capture the interest of France's queen, who will invite you to the French court.

"Somewhere around the year 1555, you will publish a collection of long-term prophecies and predictions. What you later scribe will be vast and obscure verses written in a mixture of tongues, to protect yourself from religious persecution. These writings will detail hundreds and perhaps thousands of years in the future.

"Again, your ancestry lives through you, for you are descended from the Issachar Tribe - one of the lost tribes of Israel, known for their gift of prophecy. In I Chronicles 12:32, it reads:

...the sons of Issachar who had understanding of the times, to know what Israel ought to do. Their chiefs were two hundred; and all their brethren were at their command;

"The Issachar Tribe had the knowledge of time, and could interpret the word of God - teaching about God's divine messages. Hence, the purpose of this hourglass, given to you by your grandfather. If you are true to your heritage and live out the next decades of your life as your ancestors did, like them, you will teach the truth as you interpret it to be. Not only will your contemporaries follow you, but so too will royalty and those of high standing in all of Europe. Your predictions will affect the lives of many. Your word will be venerated for hundreds of generations to come.

"You are destined for greatness, Michel, but not without a price. Already, you have suffered great loss. Throughout the years, your health will suffer. You will live out your latter days in pain and physical challenge, which will eventually lead to your death. However, you will long outlive most of your peers."

The vision ceased. She looked into her lover's eyes with wide-eyed astonishment. Michel felt humbled by what she saw for his life. He took her hand in his and kissed it, knowing it would not be long before he must leave her.

She said nothing more that night. She was exhausted from the reading and saddened at the future she saw for him, for it was more about what she saw for herself, knowing he would not be included in her life much longer. She blew out the candles and crawled into bed. Michel lay behind her, his body wrapped around hers. The eternal flame cast its light on her lovely face as he watched her sleep. He did not want to leave her, but for some time he felt the calling to continue his journey, eventually to return to France.

They did not speak again of her vision for his life, for his leaving affected them both...

After Sophia awoke from her dream, she went to her third floor studio and library to research the history of Nostradamus, sensing the synchronous energy between herself and her ancestral grandfather. She found it interesting that one of Nostradamus' best-known patrons was Catherine de Medici, Queen of France, who was married to King Henri II. She was the mother of his ten children. In August 1556, Nostradamus arrived in Paris to meet with the Queen.

Not long after, he gave each of her children astrological readings, predicting that each of her sons would become king, and that she would outlive them all. His prediction was correct, with one exception - three of her sons eventually became the king of France, but one died before the age of two. Two of her daughters became queen - one of France, and the other of Spain. Some of his quatrains seemed to pertain to the royal family, specifically to Catherine's husband, King Henri II, himself:

The young lion will overcome the older one,
On the field of combat in a single battle,
He will pierce his eyes through a golden cage,
Two wounds made one, then he dies a cruel death.

Three years following Nostradamus' publication of the quatrain, King Henri was in a jousting match, when his young opponent's lance penetrated the king's golden visor, splintering into two shards. One piece pierced his eye, and the other lodged into his temple. The king lived ten days in excruciating pain, finally dying from infection at the age of 41.

Francis II succeeded his father to the throne at the age of 15, during which he married Mary, Queen of Scots. His reign lasted only two-and-a-half years because of his death due to an ear infection. Soon after Francis' death, Catherine de Medici appointed Nostradamus as Counselor and Physician in Ordinary to her son, sixteen-year-old King Charles IX of France, providing Nostradamus with a generous salary and many benefits of the French court.

For most of his adult life, Nostradamus suffered from gout and arthritis. On the evening of July 1, 1566, he told his secretary, Jean de Chavigny, "You will not find me alive at sunrise." The next morning, they found him dead, lying on the floor next to his bed. In his later years, the gout developed into dropsy, resulting in his death from congestive heart failure.

Obviously, Sophia's connection with Nostradamus had nothing to do with time or space, for nearly 500 years separated their three-dimensional worlds. Rather, it was a vital energy, as an instantaneous return to the collective heart and soul, that they shared.

Sophia couldn't wait until she returned to her dreams to find out more about Luciana and Nostredame, as he was known before his fame.

CHAPTER
Ten

Back in Colorado, Gaston and Darius were in a panic. For three days since Michael and Sophia left for Hawaii, Digit was nowhere to be found. The first day was no call for alarm, as Darius and Gaston surmised Digit was off pouting somewhere because Sophia and Michael had left. Sophia warned them that this might happen, as her furry little friend always recognized when someone was going away by the number of suitcases that suddenly appeared and were packed for a trip. The second day of Digit's disappearance raised a caution flag, however, because she wasn't known for missing a meal. Darius and Gaston conducted a cursory search with no success, but both agreed this extended absence would probably end no later than dinnertime. Now, on the third day, the boys were worried.

"Have you gone outside for any reason, accidently leaving the door open?" Darius asked.

"Of course not! It's three below and two feet of snow out there. I have no reason to traipse outside. And if I did suddenly vacate my senses and go out, I certainly wouldn't leave the door open."

"Ah, but if you *did* vacate your senses, why would you *not* leave the door open? It would only make sense, if indeed you had gone temporarily insane."

"Allow me the rephrase then," Gaston said, in an escalated state of annoyance. "Being of sound mind these past three days, I know to a degree of complete certainty that I *did not* go insane *or* outside, so logic dictates that I subsequently *did not* leave the door open. Do you have any better ideas, oh wise one?"

"There is no call to get snippy with me. I'm just trying to think of where she could have gone."

"I am *not* snippy."

"Well, you're not on the higher side of life, that's for certain."

"Can we dispense with the semantics debate and find Digit, please?"

"If we lose Sophia's cat," Darius said, "how will we ever face her?"

"She can't be lost. She must be here somewhere."

Darius nervously shook his head. "She hasn't even touched the canned food we've put out for her. It's all dried up in her bowl. I did go up and look in Sophia's studio."

"Good lord, were you even able to get the door open?"

"She could be anywhere in there and we'd never find her. It's a mess of boxes, bins, shelves, and stacks of canvases. I looked around as best I could, and then I shut the door so she couldn't get in – or out. If she's there, we'll find her."

"Wait a moment! The litter box! Have you checked it?"

"No, that was your responsibility."

"*My* responsibility?" Gaston said. "I don't recall agreeing to any such arrangement."

"Well, go check and see if she's been there."

"Me? Why don't *you* go check?"

"Oh, for God's sake, come along," Darius said. They walked through the kitchen to the mudroom. "Now, go in there and have a look to see if she's made any deposits."

"Me? Why don't you go look?"

"Because I am older than you and more susceptible to – uh – cat diseases."

Gaston shook his head and grumbled as he walked into the mudroom while Darius stayed outside.

"Oh, yes!" Gaston's voice boomed. "Digit does indeed live!" In a moment, he emerged with a plastic grocery bag full of the litter–packed evidence of Digit's leavings. He held the bag at arm's length, with his other hand holding his nose.

"Get rid of that!" Darius said.

"She's alive – and quite healthy, I'd say!" Gaston quickly took the bag to the garage and tossed it into a trashcan.

"Now we're getting somewhere," Darius said. "At least we have evidence that she hasn't escaped the house, but I would rest much easier if we actually found her."

"Dear brother, this is a cat we're talking about. We shall find her only when *she* determines that we are allowed to find her. I say, let's forget her and have a cocktail."

Darius simply stared and put his hands on his hips.

Gaston sighed. "I'll search upstairs; you look down here."

"You just want an excuse to ride the elevator."

"I have to say, it's not as much fun with everyone gone. You're the only one to ring the emergency bell for, and that doesn't give me much of a thrill." He walked into the elevator and pushed the second floor button. The doors closed as the two gave each other a patronizing look, complete with one theatrical eye-roll each.

The elevator slowly hummed into action, and a second later, it came to a halt and the emergency bell rang.

"Stop that!" Darius hollered.

All was quiet for a moment, and the elevator remained still.

From somewhere in the bowels of the cabin, Gaston's voice echoed. "Uh-oh."

Darius curiously looked up. "What?" he called.

"It's not moving!" Gaston yelled.

"Did you push the button?" The emergency bell rang. "Not that one! The floor button!"

"Which floor button?" Gaston called.

"Any one! There are only three! Try the second floor button!"

"I pushed it and nothing happened!"

"Try the first floor!" The emergency bell rang. "First floor! First floor!"

"Nothing!" Gaston called.

"Now you've done it! You lost their cat, and now you broke their elevator!"

"I lost their cat? I may have broken the elevator, but I most certainly did *not* lose their cat! In fact, the blasted cat isn't lost, and if you'd agreed to have a blasted cocktail instead of continuing this blasted cat search, I wouldn't be stuck inside this blasted elevator!"

"Alright," Darius said. "Okay, blasted one! Let's just be calm and reason this out!"

"You can be calm! You're not the one stuck in the elevator!"

"Is there anything on the panel that instructs you what to do if the elevator stops between floors?"

"Yes! It says 'Ring Emergency Bell!'"

"No! We already know that doesn't work! Now think!"

"I'm thinking!...."

"What do you suppose White Buffalo would have done in this situation?" Darius asked.

"Well, after he stopped laughing, he would have told me to wait a moment, take a few breaths to center myself, send a prayer to the Great Spirit for guidance, and then try the floor button again!"

"Well? You have nothing to lose!" Darius awaited the silence and patiently watched the elevator doors. In a moment, the elevator hummed back to life and delivered Gaston to the second floor. "Hallelujah!"

Gaston called back through the walls. "Great Ska-T! Wouldn't White Buffalo appreciate that!" Gaston exited on the second floor, and after a long moment, he called out, "Oh, Darius?"

"Yes?"

"I forgot why I came up here!"

"The cat, you imbecile!"

"Oh! Yes!"

The search continued for 35 minutes. Gaston finally came back down the elevator without incident, or Digit, and met Darius in the great room. "I searched high and wide for that little vixen. I went through every room, clothes closets, hall closets, and I even looked in the bathtub."

"I searched the study, the library, and the mudroom. I even looked in the washing machine and dryer," Darius said. "I also checked inside the kitchen cabinets, just in case. The rest of this floor is open space. Where in the world could she be?"

"I don't know. Let's have a cocktail."

"Is there a crawl space or cellar in this cabin?"

"Dear brother, this is a cat. A cat! She'll show up when she is good and ready. Now, we have a lovely pot of Ello chili simmering on the stove. Let's take a break and have a cocktail in front of the fireplace before dinner."

"I should call Sophia."

"No!" Gaston said. "There's nothing she can do, and you'll ruin her vacation. Besides, they will think we're too old and irresponsible to care for Digit – and their home - and they'll stick us in a nursing home."

"What? That is ridic-"

"Put down your phone," Gaston said. "We'll probably find Digit hiding in plain sight."

"I have an idea," Darius said.

"Does it involve and easy chair, a roaring fire, and a nice single malt?"

"Why don't you use those powers of yours, and do that voodoo that you do so well," Darius said.

"My dear brother. You're not going to stop, are you?"

"I'll get some of Sophia's talismans to help out."

Gaston sighed and followed Darius to Sophia's altar. He retrieved her golden bowl and the fiery chalice and took them over to the coffee table. "I'll say this – if we break one of these, it will be off to the nursing home for certain."

"Be careful."

"I don't know if these will work for me like they do for Sophia."

"I believe it has to do more with your intent. I do know they won't work for someone with nefarious intentions. It can't hurt to try."

"Well," Gaston said, "since we're just looking for a shiny little black cat, and not Al Capone's secret vault, I'm sure the gods won't mind." He took a few breaths to clear his thoughts. Then, while looking into the bowl with the firelight reflecting into the water, he inquired of Digit's whereabouts.

"The first thing that comes to mind is to look in the kitchen pantry. Go inspect it, will you?" Gaston said.

Darius returned with the bag of dried cat food. "This was on the floor with a hole in it. There's cat food all over the floor of the pantry. She's been eating this, the little sneak."

"Very well, now I'm getting the message to look up." They both looked up into the high ceiling rafters. "Now, my intuition is telling me to turn on all the table lamps, then look up again." When they did, directly overhead they saw two tiny golden eyes looking down at them.

"There she is!" Darius cried.

"You little critter, how did you get up there?" Gaston said. "Okay, now we have a good excuse to ride the elevator to the second floor."

They scurried into the elevator, and Darius edged in front of the control panel. "Don't you touch. I'll drive."

"Two, please," Gaston said.

The elevator opened, and they walked out to the hallway that overlooked the great room and leaned over the banister. "There she is," Darius said, pointing at the rafter where Digit sat, watching.

"Here, kitty," Gaston said.

Unimpressed, Digit smugly looked at the boys, blinked, and calmly looked away as if purposely ignoring them. And she probably was.

"Look at all those tiny paw prints all over the rafters!" Darius said.

"We must give Sophia a scolding about her housekeeping."

Darius dug into his tweed jacket pocket. "Here, I brought something that might lure her." He pulled out a bag of cat treats. The rustling sound got Digit's attention as she turned around to face them. Darius poured a few treats into his hand. "Good lord, these smell strong – like the docks back home."

"She has a much better sense of smell - and look who's coming to get a goody!"

"Look at her, walking that beam like a model on a runway," Darius said.

At the end of the beam, Digit casually jumped through the baluster and onto the floor at their feet. Darius rewarded her with the treats and then picked her up and handed her to Gaston. "Here, take her downstairs. I'm going to fix it so we will have some peace of mind until Sophia and Michael return."

He took the elevator to Sophia's third floor loft studio and gathered as many blank canvases as he could find. Then, all around the balustrade on the second floor, he laid the canvases end to end to block Digit's access to the rafters.

Gaston looked up from the great room. "Say, now that's an idea."

"She can't get to the beams now," Darius said.

"Bravo! Now, may we please adjourn to the fireplace?"

"On my way!" Darius rubbed his hands together and took one last look at his anti-cat wall against the railings. He entered the elevator and pushed the '1' button. On the way down, a grin crawled across his face and he hit the emergency button.

The bell rang, and Gaston looked up from the bar, where he poured the cocktails. "Very funny!" he said. "Come on down now!"

He finished pouring and curiously looked at the elevator doors. Nothing. From the bowels of the cabin walls, he heard Darius' voice echo.

"Uh-oh..."

Chapter Eleven

Sophia awoke quite unhappily to a rooster crowing just outside the window. She opened her eyes just long enough to notice a pink hue in the room. So, instead of a couple more hours of beauty sleep, she grabbed her camera and walked outside to capture photos of the most stunning dawning of the new day. Never had she seen such pink skies, from shades of fuchsia, to watermelon, and pink coral. As she looked to the north, the skies turned from pink tones to lilac and lavender. After the sunrise, she joined Michael on the lanai, drinking their morning coffee as an albatross flew close by around the edge of the cliff.

"Goodness, there are roosters everywhere," she said, noticing their colorful plumage as cockerels strutted about.

"The whole island is overrun with them. The Polynesians initially introduced them to the islands as a source of food. They've had the run of the place since they don't have any natural predators."

"They're quite beautiful, crowing at early hours, of course."

"I read, despite their charm to the tourists, they're quite a nuisance to the locals. There was a hurricane here in 1992, which set thousands of hens free and put the roosters on a mating spree. It increased the number of feral chickens and roosters already crowding the island."

Roosters, albatross, geckos, Sophia thought...what was next?

That afternoon, they stayed at the condo because of a heavy rainstorm, but their time was not lost, for after the storm ceased, a complete rainbow glowed to the northeast over the Pacific Ocean. They completed their last night on Kauai with a moonlit, star-studded walk from Princeville to the cliff above Hanalei Bay. Although the area was well populated, it seemed they were the only ones out that night, watching billions of stars, unimpeded by city lights.

Sorry to leave their favorite island behind, they flew to Maui early the next morning so Michael could attend his archeological conference in the afternoon. That night, they looked forward to viewing the total lunar eclipse from their oceanside condo, but with a massive storm brewing, they weren't sure they would see anything but rain. Sure enough, a violent tropical storm passed through the islands with a deluge of pelting rain that came in layers along with hurricane force winds. Palm trees on the condo property bent nearly parallel to the ground. Their fronds slapped together in deafening clashes, in concert with the waves of the high tide that crashed on a colossal boulder not 20 feet from the building. Sophia's senses were in overload from the violent energy of the storm.

Typically, they would stay inside, not bothered by the weather, but that evening they did not want to miss the rarity of a full eclipse. For hours, they sat wrapped in blankets on the lanai, waiting for a glimpse of the silvery-white moon turned to red in the earth's shadow. The wall of the lanai provided barely enough protection from the torrential rain coming from the north. Occasionally, the downpour ceased as a portal opened into clear skies above, which revealed the moon in one of its stages of transformation. The downpour came again, and the clouds hid the moon once more. Sophia and Michael awaited the eclipse to show itself, hoping they wouldn't miss the remarkable opportunity.

At one time, Michael looked over at Sophia. "You look like a scared owl, wrapped in that blanket from head to toe." She just looked at him with nothing to say. Her face was wet and her eyes wide, evidence of her awe at the storm's power.

Finally, the wait paid off. At 3:24 a.m., the clouds opened and the storm ceased for only a brief moment. In the midst of sensory overload, they found themselves rewarded by a slight and fleeting glance of the eclipse. The moon, then completely shadowed by the earth, glowed in an eerily mysterious shade of blood red. On the horizon, the ocean reflected millions of diamonds of the moon's red light. Both she and Michael were more than satisfied with the grand exhibit, leaving them in absolute wonderment at its finale.

Sophia, being a sensitive soul, was over-stimulated by the evening's events. It was past 4:20 a.m., and she was restless. Finally in Michael's arms, she drifted off to sleep. She was not surprised as she returned to a dream about Luciana and Michel...

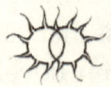

Several days passed as the romance of Luciana and Michel continued, but the shadow of his impending departure loomed over Luciana. She already felt the loss of his company, for it would not be long before he took his leave.

One evening, during a lull in the conversation, Michel asked, "May I use the golden bowl to do a reading for you, my love?"

"Of course! I have not had a reading since I was quite young."

He followed her directions, lighting candles and placing the eternal flame behind the bowl to reflect its light on the water's surface.

"Before you say a prayer to invoke your ancestral powers of insight, center yourself, knowing that you are a servant of the Light," Luciana instructed. "The reading is not about you, for your power lies in being the conduit, the channel through which the wisdom of God will flow easily through your mind and form your words."

"Do you have a particular inquiry, my love?" he asked.

"Please tell me what you see for my future."

He looked into the bowl and relaxed his eyes until the outer circle became two, joined at the middle, like the symbol on the box containing the hourglass. He did not blink, nor adjust his gaze, as visions in his mind began to come clearly into view.

"I see two children, a boy and a girl, who will come to you at the same time. Both children will grow to be prosperous. As the boy becomes a man, he will carry on as an innkeeper and will take his trade to Hibernia. The girl will be a healer and will raise her family in France. You will help both of your children develop their own powers of sight, but your daughter will possess the gift in far greater ways than those who have preceded her. To her, you will pass on the amethyst, the chalice, and the golden bowl. The box with the hourglass, and your aquamarine ring will go to your son. Your daughter will carry on the Oracle tradition to many following generations.

"You will follow your inner guidance, which is the Holy Spirit that lives within you, for it is the most powerful way to live," Michel said. "In returning to this knowledge of your being, you will be true to the God that lives within you. Living in this way of simplicity will empower you to bypass unnecessary sorrow."

He looked at her and smiled, for he could see a life that would be well lived. "As a shining beacon for all who surround you, you will live in peace when chaos encircles you. Harmony will be yours when the world is at odds. Vibrant health will continue to be yours, because you will instinctively know what to eat, what herbs to ingest, and how to prepare the right tonics and ointments to heal and maintain your mind and body. Of course, you will do this well for those you serve, but only if you first care for yourself. All your needs will be met, because you will live in gratitude for what you have, and as a result, you will naturally live an opulently abundant life.

"The love and compassion you have shown me will magnify as you continue to serve others from the heart." Michel took her hand in his, brought it to his lips, and gently kissed it. "Living in this way of balanced truth and order will bring you tremendous joy, for you will recognize beauty when others cannot see it. Those who are self-concerned can only see what it is they do not want in their lives, seeing what is wrong with others, with life, and with themselves. The grace of God will be your reward as you live in the Sacred Way of the Heart. If you raise your children with these principles, they will pass them along to those they serve, and to the generations that follow.

"Far beyond your life, I see a light-haired woman by the name of Sophia. She is your descendant who will live across the sea in the New World. With her are twelve others, all who are teachers of the Great Mystery. Sophia and three others of the thirteen will be your descendants. One of them - a sage with a very old soul - will be her greatest teacher. His people will be caretakers of the golden chalice for three centuries before he passes it on to Sophia.

"Here in Genova, a similar group of twelve, called the Order of Apeiros, is seeking the wisdom and grace of an esteemed thirteenth member. Luciana, you are to join them. This ongoing sacred assemblage of sages has been in operation for centuries. Your union with this group will establish its heritage, which will re-generate for centuries to come.

"To your children, you are to bequeath the five talismans - the bowl, chalice, amethyst, ring, and hourglass, with the understanding that they are to pass them down through the generations, eventually to arrive in the full possession of Sophia.

"The aquamarine ring protects you, the wearer, from harm, in which you may safely venture throughout the world, knowing that protection is yours in all your endeavors. Naturally, you will find the twelve others that possess the aquamarine ring similar to yours. These people are an assembly of souls who gather to do their good works in the world. When together, your rings emanate a powerful radiance that shifts the energy in the location where you join in unity. Each year, in a different locality, that shift shall support the forward change of the earth and her inhabitants.

"The chalice of the eternal flame cleanses, renews, and enables you to become instantly cleared of all that you wish to release. It represents energy, power, passion, and creativity - ever lighting the way to new adventure. As the eternal flame shines its perpetual light upon the water of the golden bowl, revelations will emerge beyond time and space.

"The hourglass holds sands of quartz crystals, representing the power of the earth. When used with the other golden objects, it shall take you far beyond time and space, into worlds without end. The sands of the hourglass will ground you in your readings, allowing you to enter other worlds for an hour at a time. When the sands run out, you will safely return to the present. It is best to conclude your dealings long before the hour concludes, so you will not leave behind unfinished business.

"The golden bowl, holding sacred water, enables you in your prophecies as a seer, revealing both the wisdom of the world and beyond. As you saw for me in my reading, water is a symbol of transition as it moves from a liquid state, to solid, to vapor. It represents reflection, clarity, intuition, and life itself. If this is the only talisman you use, you will achieve wonders, but this bowl used with the other talismans... wait to be astounded.

"The amulet pendulum represents air and motion, used to aid you in determining the best course of action for any given occurrence. The amulet's authority and power will increase as you become comfortable with its use. As you hold the crystal in your hand, it will illuminate wherever you are in alignment with God, resonating with all the elements and bringing them into synchronicity. You may also ask questions, or make affirmative statements, and the amulet will let you know their truth, for it will turn in the direction of your soul's resonance. It is a very powerful tool that will save you from needless regret, assisting you with decisions of great significance and consequence.

"As you attune with the talismans, what you will achieve shall be wondrous beyond your imagining. With them, you will be a master practitioner of the elements, which will assist you in serving the earth and her inhabitants, as was their purpose when given to us by the Star People. There will be a time when all humanity will join with these beings, for your souls will evolve to dimensions far beyond the realm of this earth. You and your descendants are to pave the way.

"Other talismans will emerge over time. Their union with these five will create power and knowledge beyond the imagination, which will increasingly empower you to perceive the unseen. Your awareness of other dimensional fields will become manifest, allowing you to Know Thyself, which was the purpose of the Oracle of Delphi in knowing the wisdom of the god Apollo - knowing herself, and therefore *knowing* for those she served.

"Additional talismans will also come to Sophia, as well. All these used together will assist Sophia to become the most powerful of all Oracles. She will commune with the entities and the angels, with those who dwell beyond the place of here and now – with God, the creator.

"Sophia is destined for great things, living from the same principles that are also your calling. Reach out to her, for time and space are truly irrelevant in the greater way of life. She will know that it is you, for she will seek out who you are, and your life's experiences will teach her who she is. So choose well when you seek out the father of your children, for his seed will reach far into the future."

Luciana placed her hands on her belly, for she already knew who the father was. She was certain that she was pregnant, and if what Michel was saying were true, she would soon give birth to twins.

"You will live to a very old age, while maintaining your independence," Michel said, continuing her reading. "When you no longer desire to live here in Genova, you will successfully sell the inn. Then, you will travel to live happily with both the girl in France and later with the boy in Hibernia, until it is time for you to leave this world. Your legacy will live on - both the legacy of your trade as an innkeeper, but more so that of healer, seer, and visionary. So much more than we can ever imagine reaches out to touch others. Living fully and consciously will serve generations to come."

He finished and was taken aback by his first reading that came through easily on her behalf. All he could do was smile at Luciana. He took her hand in his, drew her to him, and kissed her deeply and fervently. Tears rolled down her cheeks, for she believed what he saw for her. Although he would no longer share her life, all would be well.

That night, they laid in each other's arms, their bodies entwined in their lovemaking. It would be the last time they shared themselves with the other. Although they both realized it, they did not speak of it. They emerged into a depth beyond the human realm, experiencing the eternality of their souls.

The next morning, Michel said his goodbyes. Before he mounted his horse, he held Luciana in his arms and kissed her. She did not want him to leave, for never had she felt such closeness to another, sharing body, mind, and soul, but even then, she knew their time had ended.

"Goodbye, my love. I will forever remember you," he said, tenderly caressing her face and trying to memorize every detail about her. Thank you for the generosity of your heart - for it healed my every wound. Your teaching me how to *see* through the water-filled bowl will take me to newer dimensions for those whom I serve. The love I feel for you will never fade. I have one last item to leave with you before I take my leave." Michel handed her a small leather pouch.

Luciana tipped the opening of the pouch toward her hand, revealing what looked to her like a metal skeleton of a shell.

"This was a gift from my paternal grandfather, who possessed an understanding of mystic ways. It is a golden cast of an ammonite, the ancient ancestor of today's nautilus. This cast is from the same golden metal of your bowl and fiery chalice, and I suspect these golden objects in your possession are older than humankind.

"The ammonite represents the ethereal plane of infinite expansion - the never-ceasing continuum of life. It will enable your continual growth and evolution through your many lifetimes to infinity, into the eternality of the ever expanding universe. That which needs release eventually disappears, because it is no longer of importance. When my grandfather gave this to me, he said I would know to whom I should pass it on when the time came. I knew it was you when you approached me the first day I came to the inn.

"So, my dearest Luciana, I pass on this piece of infinity to you, for it completes the representation of the elements through the talismans in your possession. Use them wisely, for they will render you more powerful than you can imagine. However, I must emphasize, yet again, you are the temporary custodian of these pieces. In higher consciousness, you will bestow them to your successors for the eventual possession of Sophia. It is she who will learn to utilize their collective power for the greater good of the world."

He gave her one final kiss upon her tear-stained cheek before mounting his horse. As he turned to leave, he reached down and handed her a leather pouch of gold florins, which would leave her in substantial comfort for years to come.

"Mon Dieu... je vous aime!" Luciana said. "Thank you, my love. Go with God, and be well. Your love will stay with me, as it shall grow over the years. Your legacy already precedes you, Michel."

Luciana never revealed that she was with child, for although she fell deeply in love with him, she knew he was destined for greatness in France. She did not want to burden him with the obligation that he should remain with her, knowing that she made the best choice for all concerned. Luciana would flourish, for she and her children would be well and happy. Of that, she was certain...

Sophia no longer questioned her ancestral connection with Nostradamus, which came through both sides of her family by Luciana's children. It was evident that Nostradamus understood much more than the average scholar of his day, and Sophia had a feeling that she inherited a good portion of his clairvoyant and precognitive acumen.

Sophia emerged from the dream of her ancestral grandparents feeling strengthened by their legacy and empowered by the fact the DNA of so many astounding people of history coursed through her veins. She realized that she stood on the shoulders of giants. From that vantage point, Sophia understood she had greater opportunities to accomplish her dreams than that of her ancestors, because she was free from the limitations of their time.

In this, she realized yet again that who she was, was more than her ancestral roots. She was the collective whole of not only those who went before her in linear time, but within the dimensional framework of everything in existence. Whatever her need, all she had to do was ask with sincerity, and the answer would come in ways beyond her imagining - by reading a simple passage in a book, through a conversation, or perhaps someone with the knowledge she needed would then appear. She simply had to open up to the endless possibilities that already existed, and trust. It was simple!

In essence, Sophia was here to do what she loved and share it with the world in ways her ancestors could not, for some of what Sophia dreamt of doing was far beyond the mindset of those in her history. So now was the time - not somewhere in the future - but now. Sophia was beginning to understand that she simultaneously existed in countless dimensional fields. As with any realization for herself, she also knew the same for all of humankind - for all beings in the world, and beyond the earthly domain.

CHAPTER
Twelve

Michael attended his conference in Lahaina until it ended in the early afternoon. He made a quick exit because he wanted to go snorkeling. This was the first sunny day since their arrival on Maui, which typically made for good viewing beneath the sea. While Sophia waited for Michael on the beach, she became entranced in her photo taking of the ocean waves along the shoreline. Evidently triumphant, Michael returned to the shallow waters after an hour, rolling up onto the shore in his snorkel and fins and excited to tell Sophia of his underwater sightings.

"The water is usually clear," Michael said, "but the storm last night washed all the silt and sand down from the mountains and made the water murky. The rich colors of ocean life were not visible."

"That's disappointing," Sophia said. "Did you get to see *anything* interesting?"

"The water was so muddy, all I could see were a few fish, but something wonderful happened. Instead of swimming around, I decided to stay still and wait to see what might show up in front of me. You know – it's very cool to completely relax and float in the ocean and take in the sights and sounds. Within a few minutes, this beautiful adult green sea turtle swam past, right in front of me, close enough for me to touch."

"Did you touch it?"

"Nah, I didn't want to startle him. He just meandered up, and we looked each other over, and then in a minute he went on by, looking for his evening meal of sea grass. He was almost as long as I am tall. I had no idea they were so big. I've never seen a turtle in the water up close like that before."

"Staying still, huh?" Sophia said.

"Yeah, you see a lot more that way, even in murky water like that. You know something else interesting? I have no pain in my hips when I'm snorkeling."

"That's the healing power of water, don't you know. It's also the power of living in the present moment. I think it means we have to come back here more often, don't you?"

"Yeah, twist my arm. I love this place! Hawaii's closer to paradise than anywhere else in the world. Except for the hurricanes. And the volcanic eruptions. And the occasional tsunami."

"And the centipedes – don't forget the centipedes…"

The following day, they drove the narrow road up the emerald green velvet mountains of West Maui. Lush from far more days of annual rainfall than sunshine, that part of Maui has nearly the same amount of rainfall as Kauai. From there they decided to be adventurous and tackle the Kahekili Highway, Maui's infamous and far more dangerous cousin of the popular Hana Highway on the southern shore. While the Hana road has an abundance of switchbacks, endless and exhausting turns, and adrenaline-inducing blind curves, Kahekili is simply a nightmare of heart-stopping, snaking turns, sheer cliff drops, and narrow passages barely wide enough for one small car.

"The Hana Road is packed with tourists, and it's a long

all-day drive. Besides, it's for sissies," Michael said, obviously kidding. "Kahekili is for stupid people from Colorado who think they've already driven every possible terrorizing mountain road."

Sophia, not a mountain road rookie by any means herself, was undaunted. "Sounds like our kinda place. Let's do it!"

The road was sometimes only a one-lane dirt road around the northern edge of the island. At one of the stops along the road, hundreds of feet above the sea, they stood on the muddy cliff and looked directly over the edge to view massive waves, several stories high, crashing into the cliff walls below.

Later, while driving through a field, they came across eight baby pink piglets running wild next to the road. One kept Sophia's gaze as she took several pictures of them clustered together. That part of the island was less inhabited and stunning in its natural beauty of complementary colors of rich red soil, and foliage in multiple shades of verdant green. A local elderly Hawaiian woman trailed behind the piglets, apparently tending them.

Michael smiled and rolled down the window as he slowly drove by. "Not much different than herding cats, is it?" he said, fishing for a native smile.

The woman said nothing and glared with a look that might kill.

Michael closed the window as he drove on. "Oh...kay."

Sophia giggled. "Maybe she doesn't speak English."

"Oh, I think she spoke it very well – like 'Get lost, *haole*.' Some of the rural locals aren't too fond of tourists. Can't really blame them, though."

"Yeah, but look at us. What's not to like?"

Other than when he drove the one-lane roads along the steep mountainside, Michael remained at his quiet peaceful tempo. His grounded nature caused him to be comfortable in most settings, just being present in the moment. However, his typical calm demeanor became unnerved as he drove along the narrow dirt road. The cliff's edge that dropped hundreds of feet below to the rocky shoreline was sometimes only a couple of feet from the side of the car. Sophia knew in times like these just to be quiet and open her window so his venting would quickly disburse out into the open air.

On two occasions, they met an oncoming vehicle and had to negotiate a solution. The first encounter offered no other alternative but for the two small sedans to very slowly and gingerly pass, their doors just inches apart. The second encounter was with a pickup truck simply too large to share the passageway. Michael waved to the other driver to indicate he would back up fifty yards to a wider spot, where the pickup had room to go by. Unlike the woman pig herder, the local in the truck was very friendly, and he gave a grateful wave as he passed.

All over the rural parts of Maui, tiny huts sat along the roadside with items for sale, like freshly baked banana bread, bags of shelled macadamia nuts, papaya, guava, and other fruits, with an honor box for people to leave money for whatever they took.

"Let's stop and get some banana bread. It's probably delicious," Sophia said.

After the grueling drive though the mountains, Michael was grateful for the break, where he could stretch his legs and un-cramp his aching hips. The asking price was $5 per loaf, and Sophia left a twenty-dollar bill for bread, a bag of salted macadamia nuts, and a bunch of lavender tied with a ribbon. *Not a bad deal*, she thought, and she was right, the bread was just what Michael needed to get back into a pleasant mood again.

The vistas of both the sea and the lesser-known parts of Maui left them with a sense of connection to the beauty and wonder of nature. They returned to the condominium with a greater appreciation for the world's wonders. Perhaps it was partially because the drive had a bit of danger, and they both returned feeling grateful for the preciousness of life.

Their view from the lanai overlooked a small section of the Pacific known as the Au'au Channel. Au'au meant *to take a bath*. This 8.8-mile-wide stretch of ocean is only 108 feet deep, bordered by the islands of Maui, Lana'i, Moloka'i, and Kaho'olawe. It is known among the locals as the 'Nursery,' for more humpback whales are born there than any other part of the Pacific Ocean. The warm calm waters, one of the most protected areas of the ocean, invite the whales to travel each autumn approximately 3,500 miles from the Alaskan seas. In Alaska, they feed during the summer months on the rich marine life, which sustains them for their annual cyclical voyage back to the Hawaiian Islands.

After being on island time for a few days, Sophia finally slowed down from her typical fast pace to the gentle rhythm of the island, joining in its splendor as her awareness opened up. This was one of her lessons from the afterlife, to be fully present in the here and now so as not to miss anything. Instead of speeding up, she slowed to the pace of nature - similar to the way Michael snorkeled - staying still and allowing the sights to reveal themselves. She became the observer, the witness, being in the moment of here and now, and interestingly enough, she found that life at that pace allowed her to observe even more.

As Michael likes to say, "It's right in front of you." In this case, he certainly was right. After dinner, they sat on the lawn, enjoying an evening cocktail, and before she even saw them in the distant waters, Sophia felt the presence of the whales, miles out into the sea.

"Look out there! I just saw a whale breach. And look at the spinner dolphins around it! Oh, Michael, how amazing - aren't they magnificent?"

"We should take a sundown cruise to get a little closer," Michael said.

"What would you think about a romantic dinner cruise on a sailboat?"

"Next time, let's plan on it," Michael said.

They watched the whales and dolphins as shades of indigo seas on the far horizon blended into layers of aquamarine blue in the forefront near the sandy shore. The water's constant flow of never-ceasing ocean current repeated its fractal patterns, eventually breaking at the coastal edge. Sunrise backlit the high tides, which revealed opaque sea foam greens, with crashing waves of white frothy foam brought to a halt by the ancient twenty-foot black volcanic boulders that bordered the perimeter of the coastline, standing like dozens of sentinels protecting their territory.

The next morning, only a stone's throw from the edge of the property, green sea turtles peppered the aquamarine waters backlit by the sun. They rode the waves to the island's edge, where they came at dawn and dusk to feed on the tender sea grass that grew at the base of the megaliths. With the turtles that were visible, Sophia and Michael could only imagine the number of turtles below the sea. Their shiny domed shells reflected the early morning sun's rays as they bobbed above the water, diving to partake of their morning feast.

On one of the last days of their trip, they drove to the mythical surfer's paradise, aptly nicknamed "Jaws" on the north shore of Maui, known for some of the best and most dangerous surfing in the world. They watched surfers navigate waves reaching fifty feet, which was unfathomable to Sophia. Michael had surfed many times before, especially in Australia, but Sophia had only tried it once on Oahu without much success.

"What do ya say, sport," Sophia said, grabbing Michael's arm. "Are you game to rent a board and try your luck?"

"Oh, yeah, but first I think I'll drive into town and jump off a ten-story building to warm up. Look at those waves! But I *am* reminded of when I surfed with my buddies in Australia. One of my friends was tall, like me, but he was a big bear of a guy, fur and all. His name was Thorndyke Finster Van Buren, but we called him Bubba."

"Thorndyke Finster Van – how the heck did you get Bubba out of that?"

"He always joked that his Neanderthal ancestors passed on to him the hairy gene. He just looked more like a Bubba than a Thorndyke. I mean, really, look at all those guys out there with only hair on their heads. This guy was a living sweater, all year around. In the winter months, he wore a sweater over his natural wool, with tufts of hair peeking out from his shirt collar and around the ridge of his cuffs."

"You know, the last time I was in Hawaii was during my freshman year in college," Sophia said. "One afternoon, I was sunbathing on Waikiki Beach with my friends, and I got the bright idea to rent a surfboard for an hour and take it out for a spin by myself. That time of day was when the tide was ebbing away from the shore, and I didn't take any lessons, so I didn't really know what I was doing."

"Not one of your better ideas, I'm guessing," Michael said.

"No. The gentle tide kept pushing my surfboard farther away from shore to the point that I was farther out than the Hawaiian outrigger boats that take people out for a tour. The pink Royal Hawaiian hotel appeared about an inch tall from my vantage point, and Diamond Head looked like a small hill in the distance."

"My God, do know how dangerous it was to be that far out?"

"I was learning fast, yes. No matter how hard I paddled, I couldn't fight the tide, which kept taking me farther out onto the ocean. The water looked shallow enough, with clear blue waters and clusters of volcanic rock, but all I could think of was the *duh-duh-duh-duh-duh-duh-duh-duh* soundtrack, and a massive shark stalking me from the depths below. I was starting to panic, and I knew that unless I got off the surfboard and tried swim with it toward the shore, I would most certainly be washed out to the open ocean. So, I got into the water and held onto the surfboard with my left arm, and I kicked the entire way toward shore until a few waves were strong enough for me to hop back onto the board and paddle the rest of the way in."

"Wow, you've never told me that story before."

"Didn't really think about it until now. You know, when you're young, you think you're invincible and nothing bad will ever happen to you. When I got back on the beach, my friends asked where I'd been for the past three hours. I was fine, other than a major sunburn, but I admit I was humbled when I started thinking about how much danger I was in. Other than imagining a shark looking to take a big bite out of me, I didn't feel any true fear while I was out there. Maybe for a moment I did imagine myself eventually washing up on another island, but when I decided to slide off the surfboard and start swimming back toward the beach, I never doubted that I would get back to shore. Not once did I consider that I would die out there."

Sophia shook off the brief recall as she stood watching the fearless surfers navigate the waves.

"Well, I for one am glad you didn't drown. Otherwise, I'd be sitting here, watching these surfers and thinking – I wonder whatever happened to my old girlfriend."

Sophia laughed. "You probably would have read about me, or rather, the lack of me in the daily news..."

Last on the day's agenda was a road trip to the top of Haleakala, meaning 'House of the Sun.' The weather, however, was typically unpredictable, and it looked like it might rain.

"I don't know if it's worth going," Michael said. "The peak is cloaked in clouds, which will hinder the view from the summit."

"It's our last opportunity to make the drive this time around, so why don't we go anyway," Sophia said.

On their way up the mountain, they drove past a lavender farm in full bloom and later through the eucalyptus forest, rolling down the windows to breathe in the potent, crisp aroma. About halfway up the volcano, they drove through thick grey clouds. Michael could only inch along at 10 mph, when suddenly the clouds broke. "Whoa!" was all they could say in unison, exclaiming their immediate surprise when gorgeous colors and textures of tundra plant life unveiled from beyond the thick mist.

"Just wait. You're about to see something even better," Michael said. He drove just above the tops of the clouds and stopped the car. Several rainbows surrounded them, casting a magic mist on their skin. At the 10,000-foot summit, far above the clouds, the sun shined brightly on the stark, yet beautiful volcanic landscape that looked like the moon's surface, except in full color. Far to the southeast, the clouds cleared with a view of the Big Island of Hawaii. Their time of rejuvenation was complete.

Chapter
Thirteen

"So what did the surgeon say?" Darius asked.

"He suggested that I do a double hip replacement," Michael said.

"Both at the same time?" Gaston asked.

"He said both hips have deteriorated badly and should be replaced, otherwise I'll have one good and one bad, which leads to more problems. My alternative is to have one done, recover for eight weeks, and then go through the whole ordeal again with the other. When he put it that way, it makes sense to get both done in one procedure."

"That just sounds like a tremendous strain on you," Darius said.

"He recommends it because I'm still young and healthy, and I should sail right through it without a problem."

"Easy for him to say," Gaston chuckled. "He won't be laid up and unable to walk for weeks."

"That's not what we're told," Sophia said. "In fact, we've been to a seminar that tells us they'll have him up on his feet and walking with a walker within hours after the surgery, and he'll only be in the hospital overnight. They said he'll be walking unassisted in ten days, and be quite mobile within six weeks."

"Remarkable," Darius said.

"It will take about six months to return to full mobility, and a year to return to optimal health," Michael said. "The thing is I just can't get over that my surgeon looks like a giant teenager. He's about 6'8", with legs five feet long, and he's only about twelve inches wide."

"You're taking issue with his size?" Darius said.

"Not really. It could be that I'm a bit jealous. It's just that he's so young - or maybe it's that I'm not as young as I used to be. I mean, I'm letting a giant Opie Taylor cut me open here."

"Maybe that's part of his shtick, to maintain his surgical expertise - youth plus skill equals awe," Darius said.

"Well, I'm going through with it, jealousy and all. This kid seems to know what he's doing."

"Thanks again, you two, for staying here while we were in Maui, but if you could be here during his recovery, I would so appreciate it," Sophia said. "It would give me a diversion from being a nursemaid."

"We wouldn't miss seeing Michael and his new zipper hips," Gaston said, "but I must return home to New Orleans for a week to check on the shop."

"I know everything is running well with the company, but I want to check on the plantation, as well," Darius said. "We arranged to have a car take us to the airport. We fly out tomorrow afternoon, but we'll be back in time for Michael's big day..."

The surgery took place two weeks later. Darius and Gaston sat with Sophia in the hospital cafeteria during Michael's surgery, engaged in a lively debate over whether cheesecake is really cake, are cats preferable to dogs, and which was more grammatically correct: 'I could care less,' or, 'I *couldn't* care less.' This went on for the entire duration of Michael's surgery. Other than a few eye-rolls, Sophia didn't weigh in on the debate. She instead immersed herself in a novel about the Scots Highlanders. After two hours, the surgeon came out with the good news of both successful hip replacements. Michael was now in recovery and coming out of the anesthetic.

"How is he doing?" Sophia asked.

"He's almost his usual self already," the doctor said. "He asked who I'm taking to the prom this weekend."

Sophia laughed. "I'm sorry. I told him to stop with the youngster jokes."

"I'm used to them now."

"Thank you, Doctor. I do hope you gave him the best hardware available so he doesn't have to do this again down the road," Sophia said.

"It's the best titanium available – so good in fact that he'll be setting off airport security alarms for the rest of his life. The nurse will come to get you in a few minutes, and she'll take you to see him in recovery."

All three briefly went into the recovery room. Michael's eyes were open, but with all the drugs in his system, he certainly wasn't entirely there. His attending nurse stood over the bed, adjusting Michael's IV line and reading his vitals on a monitor next to the bed.

"Michael? My name is Joseph. I'm your recovery nurse. How are you doing?"

"I'm ready for my M&M's," Michael said.

"I guess he's back to normal," Sophia said.

"You'll have to wait a few for those," Joseph said, chuckling. "I want to get you a little more stable, and then we'll take you up to your room."

"M&Ms stabilize me, Joe," Michael said. "That, and my wife."

"Oh, he just said that because he thinks I don't know he saw us come in."

"Oh, hi, honey," Michael said. "Have you met my wife, Joseph?"

"Dear me," Darius said, "the boy is still a bit daft."

"He's doing great," Joseph said. "It takes a little time to return to our planet, but he'll be here in a few minutes."

Sophia kissed Michael on the forehead, and she placed one hand on the top of his head, and the other on his heart, extending him healing energy.

"Good lord, what a ghastly green - he certainly looks dead," Gaston said.

"Uncle?" Sophia said, glaring.

"Lovely bedside manner," Darius grumbled.

"Hey, Joe?" Michael said. "Either the room's beginning to black out – or I am." His eyes started fluttering.

"Okay, Michael, I'm going to increase your IV fluids," Joseph said. "You lost a lot of blood during the surgery, and you're a little dehydrated. There. How do you feel now – better?"

"Who?"

"You, Michael. Are you back with me?"

"Where are those M&Ms?"

"Honey," Sophia said, "I'll bring your M&Ms up to the room when you get there."

"Oh, hi, babe. When did you get here? Gaston! Darius! You're here, too? This calls for a Bohannan..."

"Positively daft," Gaston whispered.

"Ma'am," Joseph said, "he's going to be here for a few hours, but I promise he's in good hands. You might want to take a break and get a bite to eat. I'll text you when we take him to his room..."

Once Michael was in his room, Sophia showed up with a super bag of peanut M&M's. She left Darius and Gaston down in the waiting room to try to figure out how the coffee vending machine worked, which she surmised would take a good 45 minutes.

"Oh dear, you still look kind of green. I'm going to order you a hamburger from room service. You need some protein."

Although indeed a pale olive green, Michael was more alert and sitting up in his hospital bed. He dug into the M&Ms. "That sounds good to me. I'm famished."

"How are you feeling? Are you in pain?"

"They said I lost a lot of blood during the surgery. I hope they can find it."

Sophia picked up the phone and rolled her eyes.

After he ate, Michael's senses came roaring back. His mind cleared, and he felt well enough, when the orthopedic nurse came in with a walker, to take his first stroll on the new hardware.

"Now, you're sure it's ok to walk?" Michael asked.

"Absolutely," the nurse said. "You don't have those gnarly hip joints anymore. You're gliding on pure, smooth metal hardware. You just have to be careful not to strain your incisions – so no ballet or high jumping for now."

"How old are you?" Michael said. "What – fifteen...sixteen?"

"Michael..."

"Thanks, but I'm thirty-two," the nurse said.

"Oh, jeez..."

After a surprisingly restful night in the hospital, Michael passed all the required walking and balance tests to earn his release. The surgeon stopped by around one o'clock and pronounced him good to go. Sophia arranged for a private ambulance to take him back up to the cabin, for sitting in a car during the long, three-hour drive up the winding mountain roads wasn't advisable. Sophia rode with Michael, and Gaston and Darius drove the SUV. They got lost for an hour, but they finally found their way home.

Michael was resting comfortably upstairs when they finally arrived.

"Did you have any trouble getting our boy up to your room?" Darius asked.

"Not at all," Sophia said. "I'm so glad we decided to put in that elevator."

"Thank God it's working," Gaston said.

"How's that?" Sophia said.

"Nothing," Darius said. "Now, what can we do this afternoon to help?"

"He's should be pretty quiet the rest of the day. I'm just utterly exhausted, so if you don't mind taking charge of dinner tonight, I'm going to take a nap. The Ello sisters packed our freezer with ready-made meals, all labeled, so all you have to do is take something out and heat it up."

"Consider it done, my dear," Darius said, kissing her on the forehead. "You go have a good rest."

"Just look in on Michael now and then. He's still a bit loopy from the painkillers, so I told him to give you a holler if he gets up to go to the bathroom."

"Oh dear," Gaston said, "does he need any help to – you know?"

"No no!" Sophia laughed. "In fact, he can walk with the walker quite well, and do his business alone, but I'd just feel better if we stand by for at least a day or two until he's more sure on his feet. In fact, the doctors say it's important he walks frequently to keep the circulation in his legs."

From his first day home, Michael walked all the way to the elevator, rode it to the first floor, and then walked to the dining room to eat his meals. He was entirely spent after those simple chores, but within a week, he was taking several laps around the cabin, often without the walker, and regaining his strength every day. He even refused the narcotic painkillers after the second day, saying he preferred the pain over the mind-bending effects of opiates. Opting for over the counter pain remedies was an adequate substitute, he said, because his current discomfort was amazingly minimal to the pain he experienced in his hips over the last five years.

In two weeks, he could walk unaided, and his surgical scars were nearly healed. In a month, he walked without any trace of a limp and often opted to use the staircase at home to regain strength in his legs. His doctor cleared him to begin a stationary bike exercise program, and other than postponing any ski trips or golf games for a year, he was cleared to resume most any other low impact physical activities at his own discretion. In all, Michael's hip surgery was a resounding success...

Several months passed since Michael's surgery, and he was ready for a trek to South Dakota. It was a warm and beautiful spring day in early May, with clear skies to the west. Per White Buffalo's wishes, Michael and Sophia drove to the Black Hills to scatter his ashes in the land of his people. Following the stories of his youth, they did their best to find the location where Wichahpi, White Buffalo's mother, had her first vision quest. It was there that she saw, several years before his birth, a blonde-haired, blue-eyed boy, who would grow to be a spiritual warrior for the

Lakota nation. She also saw that her son was an incarnation of Crazy Horse, carrying the famed Sioux warrior's spirit with him throughout his days. That was why it was so important to him to have his ashes returned to the Black Hills.

Before they scattered the ashes, Sophia and Michael smudged themselves with the smoke of sage. They both said a few words to the Grandfathers, in honor of their beloved elder.

"Great Spirit, we leave you the earthly remains of your grandson, Tatanka Ska," Michael said. "He was a kind and humble man, in service to all people, protecting the history and the ways of the Lakota. He is now one of the Ancestors, whom we will always remember. Goodbye, my beloved elder."

"Great Spirit, Tatanka Ska - White Buffalo was like a grandfather to me," Sophia said. "I thank you for presenting us with the life of such a great spiritual warrior. He was an honorable man who loved well. How could anyone be of greater service than he? The love he extended to me, I will pass on to all those whose lives I touch, and in that way he will continue to live on. All I ask today is that the rains come, so that his ashes become part of the mountain. Here, he will remain in the place where his mother first saw the image of who he would become. Here, high on the mountain, his spirit will rise above all else in the world, continuing to bless those on Grandmother Earth. We will always love you, White Buffalo. We leave you in peace. Aho Mitakuye Oyasin!"

Just as White Buffalo's ashes scattered to the wind, seemingly from nowhere, a light rain fell from the cloudless sky. "Thank you, Grandfathers. Thank you, Great Spirit!" Sophia said with tears in her eyes.

It would be a couple of weeks before they departed for Ireland, and before they drove home to Colorado, Sophia had a weekend art show in Kansas City, Missouri. The show was a success, Sophia selling many of her paintings, but she most loved sharing with the people who came into her booth. It had been some time since she did a show, which sparked the idea to participate in some art fairs during the time they lived in Ireland.

On their way home, they drove along I-70, through what recent technology brought to Salina, Kansas - wind farms of hundreds of enormous white bladed energy producing wind turbines as far as the eye could see. It was mesmerizing to watch them turn, some in sync, and others turning at their own pace. Beneath them were herds of grazing cattle, oblivious to the massive blades revolving overhead.

The Midwest truly was the heart of America, where the wide-open fields yielded grains for the world. That time of summer, row after row of green, gold, and Indian red crops were not yet ready for harvest, but promised acres of plenty for the time soon to come. In between the miles of farmland were small towns, with people dressed in jeans and boots, driving big pickup trucks, who worked hard to the bone from dawn to dusk. Only a few weeks to plant in springtime and the same for harvest were controlled by storms that had no preference for the well-being of the rancher or farmer.

Winters were brutal, with whiteout blizzards and sub-freezing temperatures threatening livestock. Summer was no better, with extremes of hot and humid air and tornados that could rip up in a matter of minutes. It was a life controlled by the elements, mostly weather - either not enough rain, leading to drought, or too much, causing floods. It was a life of hard work, a little bit of luck, and an abundance of prayers.

As they approached the Kansas/Colorado state line, both Sophia and Michael couldn't help but notice menacing dark gray skies on the western horizon. That time of year was volatile in the midst of the infamous Tornado Alley, but they had driven through many a storm in the Midwest, and they weren't too concerned.

They stopped at a rest stop, where over the dated weather alert intercom Sophia heard a raspy recording, warning travelers of stormy conditions brewing ahead. On her phone, her weather app showed a huge red mass directly to the west, indicating very heavy rain and high winds. Interestingly, however, Michael pointed out a clearing straight ahead. The radar showed that the highway seemed to cut a path between two distinct storm cells. They decided to drive on, and soon they saw the rotating mass of a storm about a mile south of I-70. This was an anomaly for them, not living in the part of the country where twisters were common, for this was not one of those skinny dust devils that sometimes corkscrewed across a mountain valley. This was a rotating, churning gray mass, several miles wide. Sophia got out her camera, but could only capture about a sixteenth of the storm. Above the roiling gray, she could see green, an ominous sign that they were on the edge of hail and possibly a tornado.

Suddenly, driving their high-profile RV directly toward a Kansas storm seemed a reckless notion, but they were now at the point of no return. If Sophia's weather app was accurate, the highway still cut a path clear of the two storm cells. Go forward or turn back and run – either way, there could be consequences, but Sophia clearly knew they should cautiously press forward. With faith in Sophia's intuition, and a little help from modern technology, Michael white knuckled it, driving past semi trucks at 70 mph in winds blowing at the same speed, not wanting to get caught anywhere near a semi in such a storm. The wiper blades turned fast, but they could hardly keep up with the pouring rain and marble-size hail, which added to the deafening sound. A frequent gust gave the RV a lateral shove, but Michael handled it and pushed on. Suddenly, several emergency vehicles with sirens and flashing lights sped past them so quickly, it seemed the RV was stopped along the side of the road.

As they approached an exit, Michael said, "What do you think - should we get off the highway here and wait it out, or keep driving?"

Sophia looked to the northwest and saw an abandoned Stuckey's roadside store with that distinctive roofline, and an offer of partial shelter under an old metal canopy where gas pumps once stood. She looked down quickly to go within for intuitive guidance, and the answer was immediately apparent. There was no fear, no emotion, just clarity. "No. Let's keep going."

"Yeah, a tornado would take that old shanty – and us - straight to Oz."

Sophia looked at the app again, noticing that the storm split even more now- red to the south, and red to the north, with I-70 right in the middle in orange and yellow. "It will be dicey going through the lighter stuff, but I don't think things are going to be very good around here in a few minutes. If we push forward through this thing, I think we can shoot the gap right past the worst of it."

They continued on, at that point directly north of the twister, when Sophia looked up through the passenger window. In the dark gray skies above, a churning black tube, clearly a tornado, rolled right overhead. She didn't say a thing to Michael. He had enough on his mind, but she quietly had a brief word with God right then.

The air pressure and power of the storm had a heavy tension about it, causing Digit to coil tightly in her cat carrier. Sophia checked to be sure the seatbelt held it snugly in the rear seat. Sophia wished she could curl up inside the carrier with Digit. Her tiny four-legged sage of a cat always made her feel better. As they drove to the west end of the storm, directly ahead in the far distance, they saw a phenomenal sight - in the midst of dark gray clouds was a narrow window of puffy white clouds and blue skies.

"Yeah, baby," Michael whispered, "there's that passage we're looking for."

That small ray of hope diminished a bit, however, as they soon approached the emergency vehicles that passed them thirty minutes earlier. In the median was a semi-truck folded like a sandwich around a brand new pickup truck. The driver of the pickup was most likely injured, for the truck was certainly totaled. Sophia and Michael sent their blessings to all involved, and counted their own blessings while they were at it.

It was now apparent the light at the end of the tunnel was fortunately not an oncoming train. With each passing mile, the sunlight grew brighter through the clouds, and the rain fell gentler. The danger now passed, Michael theatrically pried each stiffened finger from the steering wheel to evoke a needed laugh from Sophia.

After the laugh, Sophia blew a titanic sigh. "*That* was intense, I don't mind saying."

Michael agreed. "I want to officially declare that I absolutely *did not* have any fun in the last hour. This made that mountain road in Maui seem like a stroll in the park."

Sophia checked the cat carrier and found Digit on her back, sound asleep. "We're good now. But I sure pray for all those people back there…"

At the next exit, they stopped to get a bite to eat. Sophia looked at her app again. The two storms indeed had merged right where they had driven a half-hour before. The storm went on to wreak havoc in Missouri, spawning tornados around Kansas City, and as far east as St. Louis. She silently gave thanks for their safety, knowing that when she made an inquiry of her intuitive guidance, she always received the right answer for the circumstances at hand.

Six hours later, they were so grateful to be safely home again…

CHAPTER
Fourteen

The next week after their homecoming, Sophia and Michael took it easy, and Darius and Gaston returned so they could travel together to Ireland. Sophia caught a cold when they were out of state, and it held on for too long. Michael came in handy under those circumstances, because it gave him reason to make his special Seamus-Riordan Chicken Soup. After dinner, they had coffee on the deck, enjoying the first warm spring evening of the year. Michael held Digit, who loved the breeze that carried varied scents of the outdoors. He didn't dare let her loose because of the numerous wild mountain critters running and flying about that could make a quick snack of her.

Suddenly, and without warning, Sophia blasted out her famous gargantuan sneeze, and everyone jumped in utter terror.

"Good heavens!" Darius cried as he spilled coffee in his lap.

The dog next door began to bark, and birds flew from the trees.

Michael cried out and pulled Digit's extended claws from his arms and chest. He scurried to put the startled cat back in the cabin, while Darius danced a two-step and dabbed his scalding hot, wet trousers.

Gaston held his heart. "I must say I never have grown accustomed to that."

"You can't," Michael said, pressing a napkin to his bleeding arm, "it's like living next to a munitions plant." He looked at Sophia, who wanted to laugh, but couldn't speak through her impending sneeze face. "Stand by, incoming!"

The second was just as powerful as the first, but the boys were ready for this one. The dog next door barked louder.

"Oh...I'm so sorry." She quickly retrieved a tissue and tried to suppress any further explosions.

A loud voice called out from the neighbor's house next door. "God *bless* ya!"

Everyone had a good laugh. "Thank you, Jim!" Sophia called back.

"Extraordinary," Gaston said. "How do you do that without losing your voice?"

Sophia sniffed and dabbed her nose with a tissue. "I try to give a warning, but sometimes they sneak up on me. This darned cold..."

Having been under the weather for a few days, Sophia slept a lot, finding herself easily slipping into another lifetime through her dreams...

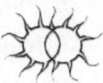

In the long summer days of the early fourth century, Laurinda lived within a small community of people along a hillside in western Eire. Barefoot in the lush green grasses, she and her friends explored the next bit of excitement as their feet became a bright shade of green, for life was a joyous adventure. As they explored about, the dense forest held a strange and mysterious phenomena. Along the edge of the deep black loughs were never-ending, nameless places to discover wonders that kept calling the children to return. From views of the high cliffs that faced the dimming of the day, Laurinda peered out over the sea to the far curve of the horizon. She imagined far distant lands beyond, beckoning her to places of wonder. Yet, the shore brought her peaceful stillness not available anywhere else in her mystical, magical world. Many tales told by her father around the fire at night spoke of ancient people in lands foreign to her young mind, known only to her imagination. Steeped in possibility, nothing stopped Laurinda, and nothing seemed unattainable to her wide-eyed wonder and wily ways.

For hundreds of years, several families lived along the hillsides in elaborately constructed subterranean homes of interconnecting rooms, fortified with walls of stacked stone, and mortared with a mixture of mud, ash, and grass. They were cool in the summer, and warm enough in the winter with a central fire. Wood framed doorways and windows held coverings of deer hide to keep out the cold and rain. Ceilings held tightly fitted mortared branches topped with layers of sod to keep out the elements. From uphill, all one could see were undisturbed rolling hillsides, for the grass-covered roofs of their hillside homes blended with the surrounding natural foliage.

Laurinda's mother, Magda, was a woman of exceptional mind, extraordinary artistic talent, and feminine beauty. One of her specialties was the well-crafted colorful clothing she made from woven dyed wool and linen. Some 20 suns earlier, Magda captured the heart of Lon, Laurinda's father. He, like his father and grandfather before him, was now the Archdruid, the highest-ranking Druid in that part of Eire, known at that time to Greeks and Romans as *Hibernia*.

Druids did not believe in personal gods, but instead saw the gods' presence in all things. Nature was both divine and sacred, as they held respect and reverence for all beings with no individual more or less important than another living creature. They believed humanity was only one part of an expansive family of life, not superior in standing among all who inhabited Mother Earth. As a peaceful people, they practiced mercy and leniency when they gathered with other communities, while honoring each other's ways.

The Druids of Eire, at that time around 300 C.E., observed the natural world as a part of the universal wisdom, believing everything was connected in a continual spiral of life. Their understanding of nature's cycles of the sun, moon, and stars determined what they did and how they lived. If they were in harmony, they believed that the gods, in turn, rewarded them in prosperous ways. Contrarily so, if they were of a discordant nature, the effect would be one of dissension and disappointment at the very least. Therefore, the Druids did everything they could to appease the gods, honoring Mother Earth, her inhabitants, and all of life. Among their many gods, they revered the sun, the moon, the stars, the skies, the seas, and all of life therein.

Druids were scholars among the ancient Celts. They were bards and teachers. Later in history, they became priests and priestesses, judges and lawmakers, practicing logic and reasoning in combination with the laws of Nature herself. They worked together within the community, more concerned with restoring justice, rather than seeking vengeance for an offense.

Lon was a well-respected bard who told tales of the Druids' ancestry through wisdom, song, and storytelling. Through mystical revelation and ancient verse, he expressed their philosophical reverence for the stars, the heavens, and all of nature. Druids had no written language, so at the very least, Lon's powerful storytelling passed on their history with an entertaining tale or two, sometimes of love and romance. He told extraordinary accounts of myth and legend, in which rapturous revelations oftentimes transported the listener beyond conditions of illness to healing.

Above all, Druids sought the enrichment of wisdom and love. They were a culture that displayed love for the beauty of nature, extending into the Eternal with a spiritual sense that assisted them in every aspect of their days and nights. They possessed a sensual beauty that incorporated the spiritual world with all of Mother Earth. Their artisans and craftspeople were among those most highly honored. Music and dance, drumming, and song occurred not only in ritual, but also in celebration of everyday life. They were intelligent, joyous people, who loved life with great passion.

The Druids' love of trees, especially the oak, was vital in the same way they viewed animals as sacred beings. They revered stone, fortifying their homes with stacked stone walls, and they made use of the stone circles of their ancestors to worship the gods. Three thousand years before, the people of Eire were part of the mound culture, which existed throughout the world. A thousand years later, they erected standing stones in circles and pathways. The human body and sexual act was not only sensual to them, but considered sacred. Every aspect of the Druid life reflected balance of the whole of their humanity, Mother Earth and all of nature blended with the sacred and divine.

Community was the overriding principle to the Druids, as they cultivated love in their relationships with one another. They celebrated life with a fundamental respect for all living things. Their reverence for nature encouraged them to love the land, the earth, the seas, the stars, and all beings upon the earth. Traditionally, the Druids were a people that practiced reason and equanimity as peacemakers. Their artistry was the truest celebration of their love for life.

In their belief of Eternality, the soul lived on, either in human form, or in an animal. In between each life, the soul remained in the realm that bridged humanity with the spirit world, where one could also travel in one's dreams in a contemplative, meditative mindset within an altered state or trance. They believed that by living a number of lives on earth, one developed the soul-qualities to their fullness of wisdom through love.

In the early 5th century, after Christianity came about in Eire, Druids evolved from bard and philosopher, to the poet, writer, and musician. The lover of ancestry became the historian. Lawmakers and judges became politicians and members of Parliament. Yet, the pure heart of the artisan remained unchanged...

Laurinda was nine suns old, only a few suns from her prime. She was the second daughter of Lon and Magda, and her elder sister, Gona, was three suns older than she. Laurinda possessed azure blue eyes with long flowing red hair lit with gold, like that of the great beauty of her mother.

Gona was once a dark-haired, green-eyed beauty, but ill health made her age prematurely. Early in her young life, her body began to bend in unnatural ways, leaving her disabled and immobilized with pain. Almost daily, she suffered from seizures that left her exhausted. Deep into the hillside, at the back of their home, Magda and Lon built Gona a special room, where she would less likely injure herself when she experienced her tremors.

The two girls could not have been more different from each other. Laurinda was a lighthearted youth, who possessed gentility with a great love of nature, true to the Druid culture. She was kind and caring to all beings. Gona, however, was contrary to Laurinda in most every way. Some thought Gona a malevolent conjurer because of her invasive nature and insensitivity, vulgarity, and malicious manipulations. They believed her convulsive seizures were evil spirits that possessed the young woman's body and mind.

Laurinda loved her older sister, hoping she would soon heal from her maladies, but Gona did not return her younger sister's affections. In fact, she despised Laurinda, and out of hatred and jealousy, Gona spent much of her time conjuring up ways to rid herself of the young redhead.

Advancing in years, Lon was 36 suns in age. Another ten suns and he would most likely move on into the spirit world, so it was time to find his successor. No one was a better choice than his younger daughter, Laurinda. Her dedication to those of the community, and love of the earth and all of nature made her the perfect person to become a Druid priestess. Although she was quite young, Lon began her training, finding that his teachings came easily and naturally to the child. To his surprise, Laurinda also possessed the gift of storytelling, having learned well from her father.

By the time Laurinda was thirteen suns, her father felt she was ready for her initiation, which would make her the youngest Druid priestess in the history of their people. The event took place in the stone circle, located in a clearing at the center of the oak forest, a distance downhill from where they all lived in community. Everyone was present, with the exception of Gona, who suffered a seizure earlier in the day. She was exhausted, and she remained at home to rest in her room.

Members of the community came in celebration and laid flowers on the circle's edge as an offering of their love for Laurinda. Inside the stone circle, they chanted, drummed, and danced. The reverberation of their merriment echoed off the tall standing stones, creating a powerful ecstatic energy that caused them to shift into an altered state of consciousness.

Lon, as the Archdruid, the highest order of Druid High Priest, wore his crown of gold and dressed in a long robe of finely loomed white wool. He reverently entered the stone circle and stood still at its center. When Lon felt the energy rise to a level of blissful joy, he raised his arms out to his sides, his long white sleeves draping toward the ground. With this gesture, he welcomed in the peace of the oak forest as everyone fell silent. On his right, Magda joined him, taking his hand. Laurinda entered the circle, dressed in a gown of sage green, her red hair falling to her waist in a mass of wavy curls highlighted by the golden kiss of sunlight. A radiant and rare flower of the forest, she gracefully walked up to her father and placed her right hand in his left, taking notice of the gold ring on his forefinger given to him by his father when Lon became the Archdruid. The community clustered closely around them and grew still.

Lon glanced around at his people. "We are all blessed this day to welcome the gods in song and celebration. We offer this bowl filled with the fruits of the forest for the *Daoine Sídhe* - the fairie people - who live in this sacred wood. They come from the Tuatha dé Danann, the wise and beautiful goddesses and gods. We welcome them all, for the sun will soon set, and they will then make themselves known."

Magda placed the bowl of fruit as an offering at the stone altar in front of the tallest standing stone. From there, she took a small bowl of oil and stood to the side of her husband. Lon took Laurinda's hand and pulled her in front to face him. He dipped his finger into the oil and gently placed it at the center of Laurinda's forehead, then cupping his hands over the top of her head.

"I call upon the gods of the earth, sky, and waters to infuse you with their ancient wisdom and power. With this oil I anoint you, which now sets you apart from the girl you were yesterday to the woman you are today, for you have been chosen as our Druid priestess.

"Today, you are here in this sacred circle to join with the gods, who are everywhere, in everything, and all powerful, meaning that you are included within their realm of being. Nowhere can you be where the gods do not exist. Laurinda, everything about you is sacred, but it is up to you to realize this truth, for only then can the gods fully activate their power *through* you, into your thoughts, as your words, and through your actions. You will then be the sacred vessel by which you will serve your people and all who reside on Mother Earth.

"My daughter, you are to stand tall as the oak tree facing the heavens, with your head held high while rooted deep into Mother Earth. The sands along the sea call you to them, for the ocean's waves will soothe your soul when your mind and heart are weary. Cast your sight into the heavens, for the stars will guide you to worlds beyond your awareness of Mother Earth. The sun will bring you the warmth of day, and the moon will wash over you in the mystery of night's shadows.

"Come and join the gods within this sacred circle of stones. Ask for their guidance, and accept it with expectancy, knowing that the gods are already providing you with answers to your every question, for the answers are always before you. Be patient, wait for their direction, and make it welcome by trusting that it is so, and so shall it be. Keep in mind that you may need to shift your perspective to understand that what you are seeking is also seeking you. Follow the wisdom of animals, for they naturally know the ways of the gods. Their patterns will teach you how to live well.

"The life you live is sacred. It will affect those who shall live many turns of the sun beyond your time here on earth, and so take care in your thoughts, the words you choose, and the measure in which you take part. Your children's children and their seed, far into the future, will know your name, leaving our people's history on their breath and in the tales they pass to their lineage.

"Laurinda, you are a daughter of Mother Earth, of the stars and the seas, and you are a child of the gods. The color of your hair, your blue eyes, and your fair skin is a physical reflection of the Tuatha Dé Danann - the ancients who once lived on this island home. They live in you, as you. You came from their essence, and to them you will eventually return.

"Remember, you are always safe when you live in the present moment, for it is there where you are in the full embrace of the gods. Bear in mind, your calling can be easy and graceful if at first you smile and then breathe. Breathe deeply, my dear, remember to breathe in the breath of the gods, for they will guide your every step when you do.

"Soon, you and I will travel to the far east of Eire, where your first task as a Druid priestess will take place at the Tulach - the Great Mound - on the day we welcome the sun to join with Mother Earth - the Celebration of Light. There, among all of Eire's Druid priestesses and priests, you will welcome in the first dawning day - the promise of life."

Lon removed his elaborately designed gold torque with interwoven spirals in which two large cabochon emeralds were set into the terminals. He gently placed it around Laurinda's neck. She placed her hand on the torque, feeling its weight representing the influence and responsibility she was about to assume.

"For countless suns, each Druid priestess or priest of our people has worn this golden torque, each as a seeker of love and a revealer of truth," Lon said. "The emeralds in this piece are ancient crystals, used for their power of intuition. They will assist you as you hone your prophetic abilities, foreseeing the vision of all that is before you. You are to wear this in remembrance of your service to the gods, to the heavens, and to Mother Earth, who houses all beings.

"And in representation of the authority, honor, and truth in which you live, I place this intricate crown of gold upon your head, for its circlet is symbolic of your never-ending immortality. Laurinda, I now declare that today and forevermore, you are eternal - *Síorai*."

"Síoraí!" The community cheered with joy.

Lon kissed Laurinda on the forehead as Magda joined them. They held each other in a deep embrace, but unbeknownst to her family and the community, Gona had been standing out of sight in the forest behind a large oak tree, watching the ceremony and festivities. She seethed with jealousy at the outpouring of love toward the one she most hated.

As if in direct contrast with Gona's loathing, all who gathered inside the stone circle immediately roared with delight in celebration of their newly appointed Druid priestess. The commencement of drumming, song, and dancing reverberated throughout the forest of mighty oaks, quaking their golden brown leaves in the turning of the season as their acorns dropped to the ground. Ash trees changed from shades of green, to gold, to red, then maroon. Berries ripened, ready for the picking, while the tastes and scents of autumn welcomed all those in celebration of the season's harvest bounty. The community continued to celebrate long into the night with a harvest feast and the endless flow of honey wine until all quieted down. All the while, Gona remained hidden in the forest.

Eventually, as everyone fell asleep, Gona anxiously awaited the moment to stalk those slumbering or too inebriated to know she drew near. She skulked around dozens of sleeping bodies until she found her sister curled up asleep in the arms of young Balogue, Laurinda's true love. The sight ignited Gona's fury even more.

With both hands, Gona picked up a large rock and raised it high above her head. She cried, "You have taken my man! Balogue belongs to me, and for that, you shall be the shortest-lived Druid priestess, with your only act of service being that of your death!"

In full fury, she attempted to throw the rock down upon her sister's head of golden-red locks, but she suddenly seized up in her all-too-familiar convulsions. In a loud groan of frustration, Gona awoke Laurinda, who for the first time realized her life was in danger at the hand of her sister. Laurinda quickly scampered away from her malevolent sibling before the rock fell from Gona's hands, greatly disturbed at the realization of her sister's malicious intent.

Balogue lunged at Gona and grabbed her by the legs, knocking her to the ground, while she shuddered, unable to move.

Leaning over her, Balogue said in no uncertain terms, "I am not your man, and never will I be!"

Balogue and his brother, Sedu, carried Gona uphill to the village and placed her in her earthen room. They blocked the entrance, and Sedu stayed behind as a guard. Balogue returned to Laurinda, who waited with the others in the forest.

The punishment for one who attempted to take the life of another within the village was harsh. If Gona had injured Laurinda, death would have been her sentence. Laurinda's life was clearly at stake, so Lon, Magda, and the elders spent the following day discussing alternatives for Gona, who had become more than they could manage. They had to decide what to do before Lon left for the Tulach with Laurinda, for Magda could no longer manage her eldest daughter, now sixteen suns old.

That same day, Gona had no idea of her fate and believed she was the only one in the family who was happy. In her twisted mind, she believed Laurinda would soon take her leave across Eire for the several turnings of the moon. She hoped providence would take its toll on her sister while she was away, and she would never again return to the land of the cliffs. With Laurinda out of her life, the delusional Gona believed Balogue would then be hers forevermore.

Lon and Magda, in council with the village elders, came to a consensus, arriving at the difficult decision to banish Gona to the largest of three islands off the coastline, west of the land of the cliffs. Only a small group of sturdy people lived there, where the savage weather was unforgiving. There, Gona would remain in exile for the remainder of her days. She would never return to her people, for coming back to the mainland was almost impossible for a strong man to row a boat, much less a slightly built woman with physical infirmities. With her disabling seizures and the increase in her contorted, gnarled body, Gona could not do much more than dress and feed herself. Magda was heartbroken, but her daughter's banishment was more forgiving than if Gona remained in the village. The well-being of Laurinda and the community was at stake.

Until they could take Gona to the island, she remained confined, guarded by two of the village men. During those two days, Laurinda stayed with Balogue and his family, where Gona was unaware of her sister's whereabouts. Likewise, Laurinda was not privy to her parents' decision to exile her sister until Gona was long gone. The following morning, three men from the village went with Lon to take Gona to the small island. She was in great resistance to go, but they held her still so her mother could reach out one last time to her eldest daughter.

"Gona, my daughter," Magda said, "I have always loved you so, and even though it is not possible, I wish I had the power to take your gnarled body as my own, and give you my healthy body in return.

"What I do know is that we are always at choice to love, and when we do not choose love, we are often reminded in many ways how to return to love, yet again. However, my daughter, because over and again you choose hate instead of love, we can no longer allow you to live in our community. But please know I have always wanted the best for you. I have packed for you several tools. There is food here, which will last for many passings of the moon. We are giving you most of our winter food stores in bags of grain, root vegetables, and dried meats, for I cannot leave you without means for survival. All of your clothes are in this bundle. Here, take my winter boots as an extra pair."

Magda removed her fur-lined deerskin boots and stuffed them in the bundle among Gona's clothes. She took off her heavy woolen cloak and wrapped it around her daughter's shoulders. With tears in her weary eyes, she fastened the cloak at her neck. Magda stood barefoot and shivering in the cold winds as she said her last words to her eldest child.

"May the gods surround you with all you need to live well, my daughter. May they bestow upon you full healing of your body, mind, and spirit. My heart will extend to the heart of you, for you will remain the first child of my body."

She took Gona's face in her cold hands and kissed her forehead before Lon placed his resistant daughter over the back of the horse. As they left, Gona had a few last words to say, none of which was in gratitude to her mother for her sacrifice of food and clothing.

"You tell my sister it is good that she is not here to bid me farewell, for she would hear me wish her nothing but ill will! Every day, I will conjure up the greatest of evil, of which this community thinks I am capable, and I will think them upon her. To the end of my days, my task will be to bring her to ruin!"

"You are fortunate that you were not put to death because of your poisonous ways," Lon said. "We give you a chance to survive, whereas other villages on Eire would have no mercy for you. Your mother gave you the best of her winter clothes and most of our food, and you have nothing to say except vile words for your sister. No longer will I call you my daughter. You no longer exist in my mind and heart. You are banished - no longer do you belong to our people." He then directed the men, "Come, let us be gone, for it is past time to leave."

Lon and the others swiftly took the defiant Gona on horseback to the shore, where a small boat awaited them to row with the tide...

CHAPTER
Fifteen

When they landed at Shannon Airport, Pádraig was waiting to drive them to their new home. "Well, if it isn't my favorite Americans. Welcome back to Ireland!"

"Pádraig, it's so good to see you!" Sophia said as she gave him a big hug.

"Michael, me boy, you old son of a sailor!"

"Faith and begorrah! Top of the blarney to ya!" Michael said. They shook each other with a hug and a laugh.

"Pádraig O'Hannigan, I'd like to introduce you to my grandfather, Darius MacPhaidin, my grand-uncle, Gaston Delacroix, and this is Digit." She raised the cat carrier to face Pádraig.

"Gentlemen and kittycat, it's my pleasure." Pádraig extended them a hand.

"We've certainly heard so much about you," Darius said.

"Well, I hope ya give me a chance to redeem meself. Michael, I see you're without your limp. Sophia wrote that your surgery was a grand success?"

"I'm doing well, thanks. I have another six months before I'm at my best, but no complaints here."

"Well, we'll see if the new hips are prepared for your archeological pursuits!"

"I take it that you're still interested in helping out at the dig?"

"You bet! I'll be puttin' all my years of teachin' history to the test," Padraig said. "Sophia, darlin', I've attached a good-sized trailer to the car for all your luggage. Last time, you brought enough with you to last a year, and being that you'll be here a good while longer, I assumed we'd need more than the boot to carry all your many necessities."

"A wise man, you are, Pádraig, an astute man indeed," Darius said.

"The airline charged a small fortune for all the extra stuff," Sophia said.

Gaston agreed. "We hired a small van to take us to the airport, and I dare say we barely fit everything in."

"Hey, I'm worth it! Need I say more?"

Pádraig motioned for them to follow, and they began to walk toward the airport exit, leaving Michael to tend to the large baggage cart. He rolled his eyes and dutifully pushed the heavy cart behind them. "Yeah, don't worry about old Mikey's hips. He's fine. Nothing ever changes around here…"

"So, you're Sophia's grandfather and uncle, are ya now? You don't look like brothers."

"Thank you," Gaston said.

"Gaston's sister was my wife, now gone for many years," Darius said.

"I empathize. I too am widowed. So, have you two ever had the privilege to travel with Sophia, here - especially when she's takin' pictures with that camera of hers?"

"Oh, yes," Gaston said.

"Every turn around the bend, we stop, which means it takes us *at least* twice as long to get to where we're goin'. So, to prepare meself for your time here, I put new brakes on the car. And... I've also had me blood pressure checked, so when she yells to stop, causing me heart goes sideways, I won't stroke out."

"Have you heard the sneeze?" Gaston asked.

"No, but Michael warned me before to beware."

"Dear Sophia is one of the few people I know who lives with such passion," Darius said. "She's definitely added a lot of adventure to my life, just wondering about her next escapade."

"Oh, it's *the* sneeze, is it?" Sophia said with a giggle. "Alright, enough about me."

"What have we here?" Pádraig said as he took notice of what Sophia was carrying. "That leather satchel must date back hundreds of years."

"It does," Sophia said. She smiled and opened it ever so slightly to reveal the soft eternal flame glowing inside.

Pádraig's eyes widened. "What in the world?"

"It's one of the many riddles and conundrums about Sophia," Gaston said. "Maybe over time, you'll come to know more about her mystery once they're settled in. Just you wait!"

Pádraig's confusion reflected in his eyes. "But what – who – how did ya pass that through security, lass?"

"Let's just say our Sophia has a way of transcending time and space," Darius said.

"Aye, do ya think?" Pádraig said. "There's no doubt in my mind that Sophia is certainly a lass of the Old Irish, possessing shall we say *special* powers? I wouldn't be surprised if she were the Fairy Queen herself. I can't imagine her with any animal other than a black cat!"

"I didn't think it would be any different," Sophia said, "but I'm so glad that you'll have no problems getting along. But if we want our travels to be filled with that extraordinary Irish enchantment, I must first put on my pointy black hat. Then I'll dig deep into my mystical carpetbag to retrieve my magic wand from its deep recesses."

"Aw, go way outta' that! You are a witty one, aren't ya?"

"If you don't mind," Sophia said, "we'd like to first stop at our new home to take a quick gander at the progress. Afterwards, you can take us to Hailey's Cottage, in Doolin, where we'll be staying while we wait for the shipment of our furnishings from the U.S."

"And what, pray tell, is wrong with our Irish furniture?" Pádraig asked.

"What? Because we are having our antiques shipped from the States?" Sophia asked.

"That's right," Pádraig said.

"No, it's not that," Sophia said. "Gaston owns a wonderful antique store in New Orleans. So, most of the antiques for the house come from his shop. I've already ordered everything else we need for the kitchen and bathrooms from here, in Ireland - and there are eight bedrooms, nine bathrooms, and a separate apartment off to the side. So, Ireland's economy will get a bit of a boost from all of our purchases."

"In all of God's green earth, why do you need eight bedrooms?" Pádraig asked.

"In a couple of weeks, we will be hosting our nine other friends, who come from all over the world. The thirteen of us get together every six months for a few weeks. By the way, we want to hire you to give them a tour through the country. You may have to hire another driver or two."

"Aye, that won't be a problem. But I'm curious - for the other 49 weeks out of the year, what do you plan to do with all those rooms?"

"We have a grand plan. We'll let you know, once we're settled in..."

On their way to County Clare, Pádraig asked, "So, Hailey's Cottage... I assume you made arrangements with the owner, Hailey O'Donnell?"

"Why yes! Do you know her?"

"There's not a man in western Ireland that doesn't know Hailey O'Donnell, for she's dated everyone who is single, and probably a few that are married."

"Oh my!" Sophia laughed.

"Never have I known such a woman. She's notoriously known as Hailey, Who Can't Get a Date."

"Wait," Michael said. "I thought you said she's dated every man in western Ireland."

"Indeed, but they're like hen's teeth for her now."

"I see. One and done, is it?" Michael said.

"Aye, that's a good way of puttin' it, boy-o."

"She seems like a friendly enough woman," Sophia said. "We've talked back and forth several times, mostly by email and text. She wanted everything to be right for us while we stay there."

"That doesn't surprise me. She's a stickler for details."

"Being that you're from western Ireland, does that mean that you've dated her?" Sophia asked.

"Yes, I'm one of the many who've fallen for the legendary Hailey, Who Can't Get a Date."

"What's so bad about her?"

"Don't get me wrong, she is a beautiful lass," Pádraig said. "And at first, ya can find her quite charming. But after conversin' with her a wee bit, ya find the lass simply can't be pleased. Nothing is ever right. A sincere compliment is always deflected with a reason why yer wrong. Hailey, yer hair looks lovely – no, it isn't he proper shade. Hailey, I love your dress – oh, this old thing? Hailey, I admire your home

– nah, the plumbing has a leak. Oh, and then the supper – ordering included twelve to seventeen special instructions to be delivered to the chef, and then she returned her food because the steak wasn't cooked properly, her drink wasn't fruity enough, and the chocolate cake was too dry.

"She had to point out that I missed shaving the whiskers right under my nose, and that I needed to trim the hairs in my ears. When I delivered her to her door after our date, and lied that I had a lovely evening, she said, 'yes, but we're due for rain tomorrow.' I never felt so small than when I returned home after a date with Hailey, Who Can't Get a Date."

"I see," Sophia said, glancing back at the boys and raising her eyebrows. "I believe your experience-"

"She forever calls attention to herself because her hair isn't proper - it's too long, too short, not thick enough, too much curl. I can't assure her enough that she is a fine woman, just as she is. Her clothes don't fit right, or she chose the wrong style or color for the occasion. Oh, and the personal observations - the gentleman at the other table was too skinny, the woman's shoes didn't go with her clothes. That woman's hair color was too harsh - and Hailey should talk - she dyes her own hair the color of an erupting volcano!"

The car fell silent for a moment. "Yes, well I can see-"

"She makes herself up with false eyelashes and makeup so thick, she must have to remove it with a trowel. Every week she goes for a mani/pedi, with nails so long you don't dare let her touch you anywhere you don't want to be impaled. They're actually called claws, or talons, or something of the like. Your cat's claws, like tiny fish hooks, are less offensive. Aye, she'd be a terror in a balloon factory, no less. And let me tell you about the discussions of her possible liposuction! Do ya want to know about liposuction? Because I now know all about it! She's let me know just exactly how they basically vacuum out the fat cells from whatever part of her body she wants to be permanently fat-free. Tell me, would you fancy a bowl of bangers and mash after you heard that?"

"No, I-"

"And the collagen treatments that make her lips plump – that came up nearly with my bread pudding! She could compete with a camel. Then, on the way home, the Botox shots, of poison no less, so she won't appear to be as wrinkled, but when she smiles, there's no life in her smile."

The silence lasted a bit longer this time until finally broken by Gaston. "Pádraig, I believe you'd feel much better if you didn't deny your feelings and tell us what you *really* think about this woman."

The car erupted in uproarious laughter, Pádraig slapping the steering wheel.

"Get it off your chest, lad!" Michael said.

"Aw sure look it, aren't I acting the maggot!" Pádraig said. "I'm sorry, I mean no harm to the woman, don't get me wrong. Sure look it, she could be a naturally beautiful woman, and she is intelligent and often a real craic, but because she's so insecure, nothing is ever right, no matter wherever she goes. Perhaps we should call her instead, Hailey, Who Can't *Keep* a Date."

"I'm assuming that she doesn't know you call her that," Sophia said.

"She's oblivious."

"I'll be sure not to spill the beans..."

CHAPTER Sixteen

Sophia and Michael's new home was furnished just in time for everyone from Apeiros to arrive. The Ello Sisters arrived early to prepare all the meals for the group. After everyone settled into their rooms and took time to rest a bit from their long journeys, they met for dinner and drinks to catch up since they last gathered six months earlier.

"Please join me as we raise our glasses to White Buffalo, our friend, brother, our blood, and our sacred sage. His memory we will never forget," Gaston said, as they all raised their glasses.

"He would have loved being here in Ireland with all of us," Darius said. "So, let us all catch up with what we've been doing for the past six months. I would imagine we've all made the legal arrangements for our newfound wealth, thanks to the generosity of White Buffalo?"

"Chayton and I moved to Taos a few months ago," Irina said. "We bought a small ranch not far from town."

"We have a dog we named Blue Feather," Chayton said. "'Feather' for short, because his fur is a wispy blonde, and he's very grounded, like White Buffalo."

"Wouldn't he love to know you named your dog after him," Gaston said. Everyone laughed. "No, seriously, he would be honored."

"We wouldn't have named him that if we thought it would offend the spirits," Irina said. "We also have two cats, and a donkey with the sweetest face who loves being loved. Our mother goat just had the cutest little kids, filled with playful energy. I love that they're called kids. If I'm tired, I go outside and spend some time with them, and they fill me with laughter that invigorates me. It is such a welcome change from living in a metropolis for my entire life. I love the wide open spaces, the clean air, and the quiet. And the stars - ah, they simply take my breath away."

"I love Taos, its history, the artistry. It is a magical place," Sophia said.

"Yes, I immediately felt at home. It's a good thing we have the stillness about us, because we've been busy setting up the directions from White Buffalo's bequest for what we are calling, the *Tatanka Ska Foundation*."

"That's a perfect name!" Ananta said.

"Indeed!" Gaston said.

"If I may go next," Ananta said. "I've been about my job, day by day, as the chef for His Holiness the Dalai Lama. Recently, he requested that I meet with him in his office. If you remember, I briefly spoke with him before, but haven't since."

"Oh, my goodness," Irina said. "How exciting!"

"I've never had the opportunity to have an audience with him, at his request, so I was very nervous. He's certainly a gentle man, as one would expect, but the power he exudes is a supremacy that comes from his inner peace within. It is a palpable authority, not one of force, but of spiritual strength. I must say, I aspire to be the same in all I do."

"What did you discuss with him?" Sophia asked. "I'm afraid I would be tongue-tied!"

"When I met with him, he first complimented me on the meals I prepare for him and his guests, by which I was quite honored. It came to his attention that I am gone from my position for at least two weeks at a time, twice a year, because the meals are noticeably not as appetizing during that time. That was why he asked me to meet with him, because the answer he received from his assistant caught his attention, and he wanted clarification. For over an hour, we had a conversation about the Order of Apeiros and the work we do in the world."

"How wonderful!" Lestari said.

"We briefly talked in passing about Apeiros once, but this time I had a chance to elaborate. It was like talking with my best friend. He was so interested, so much that he invited us all to meet with him in Dharamsala!"

"Oh my!" Darius said. "There could not be any other person that I would rather meet than the Dalai Lama."

The room pulsated with conversation at such an opportunity.

"When can we meet with him?" Sophia asked.

"As soon as we can make the arrangements, even if it means we take time from our gathering here. His schedule is quite full, as you can imagine, but he specifically said he will accommodate us just as soon as we can arrange our visit."

"Let's go tonight!" Markos said. Everyone laughed. "Leave the dishes – we'll clean up later!"

"And the best thing is, I will cook a grand meal for all of us!"

"Oh, this is splendid!" Darius said.

"Ananta, how can we ever thank you?" Irina said.

"This is my honor," Ananta said. "I have the contact information for his assistant, who is a very kind and accommodating man. I will contact him in the morning. Oh, by the way, Michael, I did prepare a Bohannan for him when he was entertaining some Americans for a luncheon."

"Aw go way outta that, as my ancestors would say!" Michael said with a thick Irish brogue. "Seriously, you made a Bohannan for the Dalai Lama?"

"He loved it, and he asked that I put the Bohannan on his list of favorites. I told him that when we meet with him, I would introduce him to its creator."

"Well, I would never have believed that I would someday be talking with the Dalai Lama about a sandwich," Michael said. "My great grand uncle, Liam 'Boom Boom' Bohannan would have been so proud."

"Boom Boom?" Chayton asked.

"He was firefighter in a Hazmat unit for FDNY."

"Ah, you may have to share a few stories about him sometime," Chayton chuckled.

"Ananta, while you still have the floor," Markos said, "some of us know very little about who you were before you joined Apeiros. Would you tell us a bit more about your life?"

"Let's see, what kind of story can I invent that will be more interesting than who I really am?"

"Oh, come now, my dear," Darius said, "much too modest for the Dalai Lama's personal chef!"

"Alright." Ananta thought for a while, looking off into the distance with her large, dark brown eyes. She sat back in her chair, crossing her long lean legs, and gracefully holding on to the stem of her wine glass with her delicate fingers. "As you all know, I was born in Punjab, India, bordered by Pakistan to the west, and to the southwest of Himachal Pradesh, where the Dalai Lama lives in

Dharamsala. I lived in Hoshiarpur, a large city, located in the northeast part of the Indian state of Punjab.

"I was an only child, much to my mother's disappointment. She loved me, but wanted more children, which I always found interesting because she spent very little time with me. To her, I was more of a possession than someone to love. My mother was a beautiful woman, who was tall, lean, and elegant. One of the things I remember about her most was that for work, she dressed professionally in a suit, and always wore her thick black hair tied up off her face. But at home, she let her hair down, where it fell loosely to her waist. And while barefoot, she often wore a colorful saree."

"You must possess the same features," Markos said.

"I do look a lot like my mother, but she had an erudite air about her. I appreciated her good mind; however, she was almost untouchable. She lived with rules, logic, and reason, and very little feeling, and I imagine it was necessary for her to be that way, because she was the hospital administrator at Maheshwari Hospital. As you might guess, she was tremendously successful in her career.

"My father was a fine-looking man, with thick black wavy hair and a silver shock of hair, as if he had been struck by lightning on the left side of his forehead. He was very fit, because he walked most everywhere. I remember watching him when I was small, thinking that someday I would find a man to love who would be just like him. I suppose that is the wish of most little girls who have good and loving fathers."

"What kind of work did he do?" Sophia asked.

"He was a well-respected medical doctor, and was much more spiritual than my mother was. After a day at the clinic, he would walk home, eat dinner, and then spend an hour in meditation about eight o'clock every evening. He did this most every day, long before I was born. I suppose you could say I was a spoiled child."

"I would never think of you as spoiled," Irina said. "Your demeanor is one of humility and grace."

"Oh, thank you, but I say that because I had more than most children in India. Because of my parents' wealth, I grew up with everything provided for me, with the exception of little support from my mother to hone my intuitive gifts, but I had a good life growing up.

"From the time I was old enough to talk, I could speak of future events I saw in my dreams, or from visions that came to me naturally. I would sit at the breakfast table with my father, telling him what outfit my mother would be dressed in to go to work, right down to her jewelry. She would walk into the kitchen to eat before leaving for work, and my father typically burst out laughing, because most of the time I was right.

"Before I was of school age, I would go with him to his clinic. I sat in the waiting room, and I could look at a person and know what part of the body was ailing them, often knowing what habits they needed to cease in order to heal. One bit of logic I knew was that whatever they were doing when they got sick, if they ceased the habits and patterns of their thoughts at the time of their illness, they oftentimes got well. I would tell my father what I thought, and often he passed along some of my thoughts to his patients, not letting on that his five-year-old daughter said so, of course. My medical intuition helped him diagnose his patients much faster and with greater precision than many of the tests he normally used. Let's just say he liked having me around the clinic."

"I should think so," Darius said.

"And what a credit to your father that he respected your intuition, despite your age," Markos said.

Ananta smiled as she peered into her past. "Out in public with my mother, I would tell her what I 'knew' about the people around us, from the simplest things like - this man was about to sneeze - and then he did. That woman who just walked past us with her food tray was about to trip and spill her food all over the man seated at the table in front of her - and she did. I also knew serious, sometimes complicated details that no one could have guessed. One time, when I was with my parents at a wedding, I knew that the woman my mother was speaking to had a daughter who was seriously ill with leukemia, but no one knew just yet. Weeks later, the little girl's illness became known. My being an intuitive caused my mother much distress."

"I simply don't understand why," Irina said.

"She was a woman of science. She thought that mystic abilities were unsubstantiated and largely in the realm of charlatans. She didn't want to *know* things about people, particularly coming from her daughter, from whom very little could be hidden. As my intuition became more insightful, my mother distanced herself from me even more. Although my father was a physician, also of logic and science, he encouraged my spiritual nature.

"Where I'm from, grandparents live with their son or daughter, but my mother and paternal grandmother did not get along at all. So, my father thought it best to buy his mother her own flat. That worked well for me, because I spent most of my weekends and every summer happily with my grandmother. There in her home, every morning, I would cross the threshold of the plant-filled sunroom, always noticing the small water garden gurgling among the plants. I think they liked the laughing waters, because the plants around seemed to thrive even more than the other plants in the room, which were doing quite well as it was. Immediately, I could feel peace and great love. No matter what was going on with me, life just got better.

"There, my petite little grandmother would be on the floor, sitting on a cushion, saying her prayers. She chanted the Guru Gita, a Hindu scripture, a devotional prayer to awaken the remembrance of the light within. She counted her mala beads and read aloud from the Bhagavad Gita her singular focus always on the Divine. She chanted Buddhist mantras, and spoke aloud Buddhist meditations. She taught me about the life of Jesus, not about his death, but about who he was - his faith, how he healed and treated all people equally - how he loved. This is how she helped me develop my mystic ways - by teaching me about Jesus, the Buddha, Rumi, Tagore, and so many more who lived the mystic life, which let me know that I was in good company.

"One thing that stays with me was she kept a tape player of beautiful devotional music playing in the background during her meditations when she cooked, cleaned house, and during meals. When I gave her a CD player with a collection of her favorite music, you'd think I gave her the moon. She was so appreciative of anything I did for her. My vibrant 'Dadi,' which meant she was my paternal grandmother, was also a wonderful cook. She taught me how to trust my intuitive nature when cooking with most every fruit and vegetable I could find. Even when I was in my later years of primary school, I towered over her. My tiny, but mighty Dadi encouraged me to trust which spices to use and when to use them. Thus was the formulation of my start as a chef."

"How did you become a member of Apeiros?" Chayton asked.

"Like everyone else, I was recommended to join by another member. White Buffalo met my grandmother in Hoshiarpur during his travels. She sat in the front row of one of his lectures. He couldn't help but notice this bright and shining light that beamed in front of him. During the book signing, he asked her permission to meet with her for tea the next day. White Buffalo later told me that he sensed he had to find out why the Grandfathers were whispering in his ear to engage her in a deeper conversation. Immediately knowing that this conversation would be one of importance, she invited him to her home the next day for more privacy.

"The evening before they were to meet, she spent much time in meditation, seeking deeper guidance about the next day's meeting with the mystical Native American. She woke up in the middle of the night from a dream, knowing it was very important that she introduce me to this man. The next day, after she mentioned the strong intuitive nature of her granddaughter, they talked for hours about me. White Buffalo later told me it was at that moment that he was certain of the Grandfathers' insistence to meet with her.

"Dadi encouraged him to delay his next day's flight for London so he could meet me. As usual, two days later, I came to my grandmother's home to spend the weekend. Unbeknownst to me, she invited him to dinner, because she didn't want to influence me in any way. She wanted my introduction to White Buffalo to be genuine and natural. Of course, I found him to be more than charming. He was a gentle, humble soul, rich in wisdom, and such a wise sage, just like my grandmother. I felt right at home with him, trusting him immediately, realizing I knew him in another life, and another time.

"The next day, he had to leave for a speaking engagement in London. I just thought I had met an interesting Native American mystic, and didn't think much more about it, but about a month later he called my grandmother and me, knowing I would be visiting her for the weekend. He invited me to attend the Order of Apeiros in Banff, Alberta, Canada, to be held three months later.

"Meantime, my grandmother talked with my parents, after which White Buffalo called them and introduced himself, explaining about the Order of Apeiros, and why he chose me to be the next new member of the group. Up to that time, I had never been anywhere else but India, but White Buffalo graciously paid my way. My mother was suspicious of his intentions, but my father was certain about this trip, sensing that the organization itself would be for my benefit. My father told me, since I was quite young, that my gifts must be used throughout the world, and that staying in Punjab would stifle my passion for life. My grandmother couldn't have been happier. She already had many dreams of the life I would lead. She recorded them in a journal to give to me, and most of them have come true, with more to come.

"From what I know, I was the youngest member, joining the Order of Apeiros at the age of sixteen. Dadi and White Buffalo remained good friends over the years, with him having visited her two more times. Later, she told me they talked on the phone a few times over the years, but occasionally they wrote to each other about me. The majority of their communications entailed their spiritual commonality. She passed shortly after he did, about five months ago. I like to think they are still enjoying their souls' connection, perhaps sharing an Indian meal together, either her type of Indian cuisine or his - it doesn't matter."

"How did you end up working in Michigan?" Yesinia asked.

"My mother wanted me to attend university at Takshashila, the world's oldest university, which, by the way, was operational before the time of the Buddha, but my interests were not in strategic affairs, public policy, nor governance. I think she thought by placing me in a program opposite of my intuitive nature, all that woo woo would be educated out of me. Instead, I attended Punjab University for a couple of years.

"Later on, after many an argument with my mother, my father agreed to send me to one of the best culinary schools in the United States, Kendall College of Culinary Arts in Chicago. Going there was one of the best decisions I ever made. My father, a kind and selfless man, said that certainly, he sent me there for my benefit, but mostly it was for his own." Ananta laughed. "Wedging half the globe between my mother and me finally brought him peace of mind. In three years, I graduated with a Bachelor of Culinary Arts. One of the benefits of the school was its career placement program, which helped me get my start in a small, but fine Chicago restaurant.

"I was already a member of Apeiros, which, at the time, met once a year for two weeks. I only had a one-week vacation in Chicago, and needed to find another employer that would allow me to leave at least two weeks out of the year. About a year later, I was hired as the sous-chef at the Inn at Saugatuck, on the west shore of Lake Michigan. It was there, when I took over for the executive chef, who was ill. As most of you already know, the assistant to the Dalai Lama came there for dinner. He was vacationing in Chicago at the time, when lucky for me, a friend of his took him to Saugatuck for the weekend. And you know the rest."

"I'm embarrassed to admit I don't know much about Hinduism," Michael said.

"Well, scholars believe it is the oldest religion in the world, at least 4000 years old. We could be here for hours as I explain the roots and customs of Hinduism, but for now it is the 3rd largest religion in the world, with about a billion followers. Unlike other major religions, Hinduism has no founder and no common doctrine, having developed over millennia. It teaches that Truth is eternal, as the essence of the universe and the only reality. Hindus believe in thousands of gods and goddesses that contain a part of Brahma, as the one true God, which is formless, infinite, all-inclusive, and eternal. Brahma is each being, and within each object, which transcends everything in the universe, and is the essence of each soul, which has no beginning and no end, and is divine. The purpose of life is to become aware of that divine essence. Hindus believe that the soul may reincarnate in another body, depending on one's karma. If the soul realized the true nature of reality, it may become one with the Brahma, the 'One.' I would like to believe that my father was such."

"I guess maybe I've had a bit of Hindu in me without knowing it," Michael said.

"Are your parents still alive?" Anja asked.

"No. They both passed away just weeks apart when I was working in Saugatuck. For any of you who have lost both of your parents, you would understand. I had no choice but to start completely over and begin again, feeling like an orphan. I reinvented myself in Dharamsala, and I suppose that is one reason why the universe opened so many doors for me.

"When my father died, I never realized, until then, how much my mother loved him. He had been about his regular routine of working at the clinic, walking home for dinner, followed by his regular meditation hour. When he didn't come out of his meditation room, my mother went to check on him. He was slumped over on his cushion, having died during his meditation. I miss him so, but I can't imagine a better way to go."

"Oh, Ananta, I'm so sorry," Sophia said, reaching across the table to grasp Ananta's hand.

"Thank you. It was a little over a year ago. He remains in my memory, as if I just saw him yesterday. When I heard the news, I left as soon as I could, and being that it's such a long trip, my father's body was cremated before I reached Hoshiarpur. In Hinduism, a body is cremated within 24 hours. His ashes were then scattered in the Ganges River, a most sacred body of water. Mourning tends to last from ten to thirty days after death, but my mother grieved his loss so deeply, she died in her sleep three weeks later."

"Oh, my," Sophia said.

"Sadly, I understand how many losses in such a short time can be overwhelming," Darius said.

Ananta raised her hands toward them. "Thank you, but you know, I was actually happy for her. She was so lost. They were a balance for each other, and without him, I think she felt completely empty."

"None of us knew about this. Why didn't you tell us?" Darius asked.

"White Buffalo knew. My parents died shortly before we all gathered in Colorado. Sophia, you had just found out about your parents and their deaths, and I thought what you were going through was far more emotional than what I was dealing with. Even though I missed them, I was quite happy for my parents. White Buffalo did spend some private time with me during that trip, which helped immensely. Being with all of you was good medicine, as he would say. Plus, I had just been hired to work for the Dalai Lama, and I was overwhelmed from all the change. So, I just kept it all to myself. I have to say, it is good to tell you about it now, though."

"We're honored that you shared it with us," Lestari said, and everyone agreed.

"If I understand correctly," Sophia said, "your grandmother was still alive when your parents passed on?"

"Yes, Dadi was still living and coping with her own grief for the loss of her only son. Fortunately, being that I had moved to Dharamsala, I was able to travel to Hoshiarpur as often as possible, whenever I had two or three days off to spend time with her. She died shortly after White Buffalo passed. It could be that Dadi felt her purpose was complete. She's the one I miss the most. I must say, my heart is still healing."

"Oh, my dearest girl, you're feeling the loss of three loved ones, all in a very short span of time." Gaston put his arm around her as she laid her head on his shoulder with tears welling in her eyes. Ananta then left the table for a brief respite and went outside to get some air.

CHAPTER Seventeen

They all took a break, cleared the table of all the dishes, and then sat in the great room in front of the burning fire. Lou Ella brought in a tray of cups and a fresh pot of Barry's Tea that she found in a charming little shop in the village. She then surprised everyone with a lovely Irish teacake she baked from a recipe Pádraig gave her.

Michael took his turn. "Well, as you all know, I've been healing from my double hip replacement with the help of my lovely nurse, Sophia."

"A full-time job, I would imagine," Markos said.

"It wasn't so bad. He was a good patient," Sophia said.

"Uh huh," Michael said. "The poor girl was utterly exhausted, waiting on me, helping me in and out of bed, keeping track of my meds, and wrestling those damn compression stockings on and off my legs."

"They were quite a struggle, especially since Michael's feet are extremely ticklish - I'm talking really squirmy," Sophia said, "but it only lasted a few weeks before he was up and dancing the meringue. And my sweet grandfather and grand uncle pitched in around the cabin and made our lives so much easier."

"I did most of the work," Gaston said.

"Oh, yes," Darius said. "Stoking the fire all day and feeding the cat. You must have been utterly spent."

"Since I now have your full attention, I'll go next," Sophia said. "Michael and I took White Buffalo's ashes to the Black Hills, as he requested. We did our best to find the place where his mother, Wichahpi, had her first vision quest. It was where she saw a vision of him, long before he was born. It was a very spiritual experience for us. Afterwards, we drove to Kansas City for an art fair, where I sold some paintings, and Michael fully regained his strength on Bar-B-Que, morning, noon, and night."

Michael shrugged. "What can I say? Doctor's orders. I gained ten pounds."

"And now you have good hips to exercise it off," Chayton said.

"The trip sparked an idea to participate in an art fair or two here in Ireland," Sophia said. "It's been a couple years since I've done that, and it felt good to get out there again. But on our drive home, we had a bit of excitement when we drove through a tornado at the west end of Kansas - or I might say, the tornado split in two as we drove through it. I felt like Dorothy, without her red slippers."

"I take it there was no Wicked Witch of the West flying around?" Shoshana said.

"Some people think I'm a witch, so maybe it was me," Sophia said with a laugh.

"That's only because people don't understand who you are," Shoshana said.

"If I lived three hundred years earlier, I would have burned at the stake, and we wouldn't be sitting here by the fire," Sophia said.

"We know who you are, and that's all that really matters," Irina said.

"Thank you, Irina, you're sweet to say such a thing. The same is true for all of us. Sometimes, we can't see ourselves within our own framework, but I have to say, when I get such reactions from people, I remember some of White Buffalo's generous wisdom that he left with me. *We see with the eyes of our focus. We hear with the ears of our beliefs. We feel with the heart's willingness. The closed heart opens no doors, but the heart that is open connects with the universal wisdom of love.* When someone reacts negatively toward me, I know their response is not about me, but it is from their own experience - their own perspective. My highest intention is to be at my best, to silently send them love, and then let it go."

Darius chimed in, "Speaking of letting go, we joined Sophia and Michael in Colorado before we flew here, but Sophia had a cold. If I didn't know better, I would think she took some lessons from the tornado they drove through, because this petite little granddaughter of mine caused quite a stir one evening out on the deck."

"Oh, brother, here we go," Sophia said. "It was just a sneeze!"

Everyone laughed. "Michael told me about your sneezes," Markos said.

"He tells *everybody!*" Sophia said. "He even warned the mailman."

"Dear God, I thought I would have a heart attack," Darius said.

"The dog next door started barking, and a flock of birds flew from the trees," Gaston said. "Digit leapt onto Michael's chest and nearly clawed the poor boy to death!"

"Okay, I give," Sophia said, giggling. "I do have to say that the deck was literally a bloody mess, with Michael bleeding all over the place. Digit's claws dug into his chest like thumbtacks on a cork board, all from a sneeze from li'l ol' me."

"I'll just say this," Michael said, "if we decide to visit Italy, we aren't going anywhere *near* Pisa."

Darius laughed with everyone. "Now, I don't know if this is true or not, but legend has it that her sneeze can make fine crystal ring."

"Next time, at the dining table, let's blow some pepper her way to test that theory," Markos said.

"We'll have to pass out the ear plugs as an appetizer beforehand," Michael said.

"Okay, enough," Sophia said, giggling. "Grandfather dear, I think a change of subject is appropriate right now. Will you please rescue me and fill us in on your news?"

"Yes, Gaston and I *do* have some news. We broke ground for our new boutique hotel in New Orleans a few weeks ago. The architect's plans are quite spectacular, with details we were surprised to discover. The finished building will be stunning, with Gaston's antiques and fine decorations displayed throughout. We hope to have it up and running in about a year."

"What is the name of your hotel?" Yesinia asked.

"We decided on a simple, but elegant name, *Auberge*, which means 'inn.' Our ancestral grandmother owned a seaside inn in Genoa, Italy, in the 16th century. Her son later moved to Ireland, taking the business with him. The innkeeping business was passed down through the generations to me. Auberge will be under Delaney Hotels, but this is the first boutique hotel in the chain. Gaston and I will share ownership."

"Business partners," Michael said. "Wouldn't you love to be a fly on the wall when these two get together at a board meeting?"

"Yes," Gaston said, "we expect a mass exodus of resignations, but somehow we'll manage."

"Oh, how White Buffalo would have loved to be a part of your venture," Sophia said.

"He'll be a silent partner, dear," Darius said with a wink. "Unlike Gaston, here."

"How is it that you have so many antiques, Gaston?" Yesinia asked.

"My father developed an affinity for buying and selling antiques when he was no more than 20 years old, for he inherited his impeccable design taste from his mother, and a strong business acumen from his father, François and Jocelyn Delacroix."

"Oh, the *Titanic* survivors, yes?" Yesinia said.

"Indeed. I inherited the business from Papa, so together we've accumulated antiques for well over 80 years. It goes without saying I have a few sticks of furniture, if you need a nice Louis XIV coffee table."

Sophia laughed. "You should see his warehouse full of antiques. It's a collector's dream."

"I also have interesting pieces from all over Europe, Egypt, and Mexico as well. I'm constantly buying many 'new' items to sell. I don't think I'll ever run out. In fact, I'm overrun so much that I've filled up my home, as well."

"Your home?" Sophia said. "You mean your apartment above the shop? You have antiques stored up there?"

"No, I have a house that is also filled to the rafters."

"You never told us about a house," Sophia said. "Until now, I never gave it much thought about where you live. You spend so much time at Darius' plantation. I always assumed that you live in the apartment above your shop."

"I spend quite a bit of time there," Gaston said. "In fact, my sister Lianne and I grew up in that apartment. Papa and

Mama owned the building. But I have a house on the far outskirts of New Orleans."

"Oh, this is good! You'll enjoy this," Darius said.

"Tell us about it," Sophia said.

"It's haunted," Darius said.

"What? How exciting!" Sophia exclaimed.

"It's *not* haunted," Gaston said. "At least, not so anyone would notice – I mean, it's not something out of a Charles Addams cartoon."

"And it was a brothel," Darius said, bobbing his eyebrows with a grin.

"What! You ran a brothel?" Markos asked.

"Wait a minute! I most certainly did *not* – at least –"

"Pray tell! Come on, don't keep us guessing any longer," Michael said.

Gaston sighed. "May I conduct this narrative please?"

"Oh, we're all ears," Sophia said.

"You would love it, Sophia. It's a beautiful Antebellum Greek Revival home, built in 1836, with six large, three story Corinthian pillars that border the front entry of the wraparound porch. On the second floor is a grand veranda with wrought iron railings as an extension of the three largest bedrooms located at the front of the house, for those sultry nights when the house is too warm. There are ten bedrooms in all. Back in the day, before the Civil War, the house was far outside the city... and for a good reason, I might add."

"Why haven't you invited us out to see it?" Sophia asked.

"Well, when you and Michael have been in town, it seemed we were engaged in many other things. As I said, it's rather cluttered with more antiques than I know what to do with. But don't fret, you'll inherit it someday, and then the two of you will have the joy of not knowing what to do with everything. I am such a packrat."

"Inherit it all, huh? Well, that's intriguing and terrifying at the same time, but do tell us more," Sophia said

"Yes, skip to the brothel part," Markos said.

"I'm getting there. It is not unlike Darius' plantation house, with ceilings fourteen feet high. There are crystal chandeliers, the most elegant one in the foyer. There, you can climb the curved dual staircase that leads to the second and third floors. For formal entertainment on the main floor, you will find a beautiful parlor and an impressive library with a central fireplace for more intimate, private conversations. The formal dining room can comfortably seat twelve. As with so many Antebellum era homes, the large kitchen is located in a separate building behind the house, accessed by a breezeway."

"And..." Markos said.

"And... it wasn't a brothel when I obtained it, nor is it now!"

"Weee're listening," Markos teased.

"I love this," Darius said, sitting at the middle of the table, enjoying the ping pong match of a conversation.

"Was it ever a plantation back in the day?" Sophia asked.

"You *could* say it was a place where many seeds were planted," Gaston said.

"You Americans have expressions that don't make sense sometimes," Yesinia said.

"And yes, indeed, for over 130 years, my home was a brothel."

"Oh, this is just too good," Michael said.

"What is a brothel?" Yesinia asked.

"It was a place where gentlemen went for a bit of

hanky-panky," Gaston said.

"What's hanky-panky?" Yesinia asked.

"Boffing…dancing in the sheets," Markos said.

"How about, rumbusticating?" Darius said.

"Shaboinking is a good one," Sophia said.

"There's always scrogging, or a little slap and tickle," Christofer said. "Say, that gives me an idea!" He grabbed Shoshana and tickled her ribs.

"I've heard it called chesterfield rugby, like they say in jolly old England," Shoshana said, laughing while trying to wiggle away from Christofer's teasing.

"One of the best American references to such a thing is, the joint session of Congress," Darius said.

Everyone was silent, grinning and waiting for Yesinia. Gaston, for once, just sat back and was entertained by everyone else letting loose.

"Oh! Okay, I understand," Yesinia said. "In Spanish, we say, mojar el churro."

They all laughed and raised their glasses to that one, first pausing so they wouldn't choke on their wine.

"So, you lived in a brothel - please continue," Markos said.

"I prefer 'Gentleman's Club.' And I did not *live* in the brothel. Prior to my owning it, it was a gathering place where men of high standing socialized and met for business purposes, not just for the ladies' attentions. Many well-known men of prominence made important decisions there that affected business, politics, and foreign relations. At the time, the large dining room held five, four-top tables for more private conversations."

"How did you come to own it?" Irina asked.

"In the mid 1960s, a few years following Dominique's death, I had saved enough money to move out of my mother and father's apartment and buy a home. Coincidentally, just about that time, my great aunt Margaux passed away, leaving her legacy to Lianne and me. Margaux was my grandfather François' sister, and she had no other heirs."

"Oh, so she came to New Orleans, too?" Sophia said.

"Yes, in 1913. World War I was brewing on the horizon, and François and Jocelyn convinced her to escape the growing tension in France and come to America. Grampa was always a bit embarrassed about his older sister's profession, but she was quite successful at it. By the time she died, her estate was not remarkably large, mostly cash of course, but it did include the mansion, which was free and clear. Darius and Lianne understandably couldn't allow the Delaney Corporation to have any association with a former house of ill repute, so they took the cash, and I took the mansion."

"Did you maintain the business, as your aunt had done?" Christofer asked. "Madam Gaston – it has a nice ring to it."

"I most certainly did *not*." Gaston rolled his eyes at the teasing laughter. "Thankfully, Margaux grew weary of the constant pressure from local authorities and the IRS, not to mention threats from organized crime, so she retired in the late 1950s and led a lovely, less notorious life until her death a few years later. The house was falling into disrepair after her health began to fail, so when I inherited it, I began to rehabilitate both it and its seedy past reputation."

Sophia rubbed Gaston's shoulder. "I think we're all relieved to know my grand uncle and our cherished member of Apeiros is not a-"

"Please, dear, don't say that word," Gaston said.

"I was going to say proprietor of erotic pleasures," Sophia said.

Gaston smiled. "I know you're having fun with me, but in all seriousness, I am not terribly proud of my home's legacy, for its dark side is contradictory to what we stand for."

"Indeed," Markos said. "I hope my kidding was taken in fun, Gaston."

"Of course, my friend," Gaston said. "If we can't laugh at ourselves, we're the only one not in on the joke."

"Well put!" Michael said. "But we're not letting you off the hook yet. Please tell us more about this interesting home of yours."

"I must say, the house is lovely. In her heyday, Margaux kept the house and the grounds well maintained by employing in-house caretakers, who were gardeners, carpenters, and electricians. Each of them was also cross trained to protect the premises and the grounds."

"Today, they're called bouncers," Sophia said.

"I prefer to call them guardians," Gaston replied, "because they kept people like Algernon Gillette out. Her idea for the business was not solely about money, but rather, she created a successful enterprise for worldly leaders, the erudite, and the elite. This was no cat house, like those in the city."

"Ok, wait a minute," Sophia said. "I'm doing the math here. When we first met, you played your riddle game and gave me the golden bowl, pendulum, and hourglass. And you said they had been passed on to your father by an elderly aunt who told him they were meant for the *right* person to come along and claim them."

"You have a good memory, my dear," Gaston said. "Papa passed them on to me with the same instructions."

"I knew there was an interesting story not yet told about the mysterious aunt. So, I heard you before, but I'm just now getting that Madam Margaux was the sister of François."

"Yes, Margaux Delacroix."

"Now wait another minute! Darius, you told me that Gaston's aunt's great, great grandfather was the physician during the Civil War, to whom all the talismans were given, in trade for his services for his wife who died during the childbirth of her baby girl."

"That's right. I'm amazed that you remembered all that," Darius said.

"At the time, you hit me with so much information, I couldn't help but write it all down to make sense of it later," Sophia said. "So, how could it be that both Margaux and François came to New Orleans in 1913, where their ancestral grandfather just so happened to be from the same area, serving the same family that François would marry into sixty years later?"

"What can I say? It's a small world," Darius said.

"Or, as Grandfather liked to say – kismet!" Gaston said. "Actually, their ancestor sailed from France in the 1840s, after he earned his medical degree in Paris. When François and Jocelyn settled in New Orleans, François was surprised to find relatives who had lived there for 80 years. Margaux, however, was the one who established a close relationship with the family, hence her eventual attainment of the talismans."

Michael whispered to Christofer, "This family should be required to publish a genealogical syllabus."

"Did she possess mystical powers?" Sophia asked.

"Margaux dabbled in the mystical realm," Gaston said. "Her services were not just for men, but for women's enjoyment as well, with tarot card readings, palm readings, readings of tea leaves, séances, and a bit of voodoo folk magic. You might remember the crystal ball we used for your séance. That originally belonged to Margaux. As you might expect, with such a business as hers, her catchphrase was, *le bon temps rouler*, let the good times roll."

"I thought that was a B.B. King song," Michael said.

"Yes, he and many other great artists sang that song, but *le bon temps rouler* was a French Cajun phrase associated with New Orleans and Mardi Gras long before it became a song, which, by the way, was written by a jazz singer from New Orleans named Sam Theard."

Michael sang, "Let the good times roll..."

"Don't help," Gaston said.

"What a colorful woman Margaux must have been," Sophia said. "I imagine the house was beautifully furnished with pieces like those in your shop."

"Yes, as a matter of fact, that is how my father began his business. Margaux had a penchant for decorating, and she owned a storehouse of antiques, which I now own, including acquisitions, some from hundreds of years ago. She often changed the furnishings in the house, accessorizing it with 'new' pieces to give it a fresh ambience, so her clientele would find it constantly appealing in its southern charm. She collected far too many antiques over the years, so my father opened the shop on Royal Street and filled it with some of her excess furnishings and accessories. Little did you know that many of those pieces came from such an establishment."

"I knew each piece had a history, but not *that* kind of history. Are any of our furnishings from there?" Sophia asked.

"Oh, yes. In your master suite at the cabin, the bed frame and the charming little chair that folds up inside the hinged desk came from one of the more exclusive rooms, plus several of your dining chairs were from the dining room, while some sat in the bedrooms. As you now know about psychometrics, furniture and accessories can hold the energy of those who used them. I just have to touch one of the pieces, and the imprinted memories come easily to me."

"Ah, is that why Darius said it's haunted?" Lestari asked.

"No, he said it because he has a proclivity for hyperbole, but my house has more history than some in the South. Naturally, because I'm a medium, I believe ghosts and spirits still reside there."

"I expect that you must not be able to get much sleep," Irina said. "No matter what you touch, you tap into layers of history and tales that just won't stop. There couldn't be anyone better suited to live there than you, since you're a medium."

"I'll have you know that I bought a brand new bedroom suite for that reason alone, because I only wanted to spend my time with women of choice, and not spirits that were one-hundred and thirty years old."

"That would be Markos' territory," Christofer said.

"No," Markos said, "I have a rule not to court any woman who does not have a pulse, or whose name is Hailey Who Can't get a Date."

"Hey, Michael," Sophia said, "segueing uncomfortably from the Hailey comment, we're going to have even more fun now that we know how our bed has been put to use. That little hinged table in front of the window has a steamy atmosphere about it beyond its clever design. Maybe I should get a red scarf to drape over the lamp that sits in front of the window. What do you think?"

"Let the good times roll, baby!"

"So Margaux must have left you with some interesting stories of intrigue," Christofer said.

"Oh yes, and I don't mind saying, as a young teenager, my blood pressure often arose at the very thought of another tale. I suppose her story began in France. Margaux managed a successful cabaret in Paris, but it was late 1913, with the war looming in the near future. She decided to play it safe and leave France to join François and Jocelyn in New Orleans. They were just getting their start in the city. Margaux was quite lively - you know the French - when most women in America, particularly cultured southern women, back in the day were quiet and demure. Very few women worked for a living, but Margaux was neither married, nor dependent upon anyone else. She was going to live well on her terms, and that was all there was to it.

"While sailing to New Orleans on a passenger liner from France, she won the brothel in a poker game from a man who had too much to drink and was unable to outsmart the clever Margaux. She quickly upgraded the establishment from one that served anyone who had money, to one of Parisian style and class, where only wealthy, refined, and cultured intellectuals could gather. She called it *Maison de Fleur-di-Lis*, with each woman in its employ named after a flower. Some of their spirits have introduced themselves to me throughout the years. So far, there is Delphine, Azalea, Marguerite, and of course, Lily."

"Why 'of course,' Lily?" Irina asked.

"'Lis' means lily. Maison de Fleur-di-Lis means the 'mansion of the lily flower.' Some other spirits I have gotten to know are Jacinda, Belladonna, Camellia, Jasmine, Magnolia, Veronica, and my favorite of them all, Zahara."

"Why is Zahara your favorite?" Anja asked

"Perhaps it is because she reminds me of my

Dominique, with her long ebony hair."

"Maybe it *is* Dominique that comes to you," Anja said.

"I've often wondered, but Zahara possesses green eyes and mocha skin - a mesmerizing combination. Her presence is not the same as my sweet dark angel. I would know if it was Dominique.

"Margaux was what they termed, back in the day, a handsome woman. She was a slender, tall, dark blonde, with striking blue eyes - as much a feminine beauty as her brother, François, was of masculine magnificence. She was elegant and graceful, yet highly spirited. An astute businesswoman, having managed the cabaret for years, her greatest ability was managing people well in all aspects of her business. All it took was a look in her eye to be very persuasive without a word spoken. She, more than any of her flowers, caught the attention of many possible suitors, but I only know of one significant tale involving her personal life.

"In 1932, the Prohibition era, Maison de Fleur-di-Lis was a popular place for the unlawful drink. Margaux had a contract, if you will, with the local authorities. They would look the other way in trade for a bit of the take."

"Did she have any racy beaus of her own?" Sophia asked.

"There were a number of politicians and people of fame that frequented Maison de Fleur-di-Lis, but Margaux operated under a very strict code of confidentiality. To her dying day, she never revealed names of her clients – not even to any of us – but she sometimes tantalized us with references to famous politicians, writers, journalists, and artists. In fact, she did reveal that she once had a love affair with a very famous movie star."

"Oh, now I'll lie awake all night wondering who it was," Sophia said.

"He was well-known and very handsome, according to her. His profession kept him occupied, especially when he first began his acting career. When he was in New Orleans, she arranged for romantic nights on one of her yachts, either on the Gulf of Mexico, along the Mississippi, or on Lake Ponchartrain. Sometimes they went for an exciting day of fishing on the Gulf, taking a picnic lunch and their favorite libations. They would go to the French Quarter to dine at a private bistro, and afterwards they enjoyed an evening of Dixieland Jazz on Bourbon Street, which was relatively new at the time. Occasionally, cocktails and dancing at an exclusive speakeasy was on their agenda, ending their evening at one of New Orleans' finest hotels. They did their best to keep their business out of everyone else's business."

"It sounds like their relationship was something like a Hollywood movie back in the day - a classic tale of romance," Sophia said.

"I do think he loved her, and she certainly loved him. She said he was the strong silent type, and she, being full of *joie de vivre*, would have been a good complement to him. I think they must have made a good pair. But, being in the business she was in, their relationship couldn't be public. He married a couple of years afterward, and then had a family. That was when their relationship changed from being lovers to friends - at least that was the story she always told. Perhaps she was protecting his reputation.

"Over the years, on occasion, they would reunite for a short time, developing a lasting companionship. He outlived her by twenty years into his nineties. She truly loved the man, once telling me she never again gave herself to another. I suppose, in the long run, their friendship was far more cherished than that of a short romance that died on the vine - a story adding to the compendium of the heart."

"Gaston, you never fail to astonish," Sophia said.

"I know, dear..."

She laughed. "You're always coming up with intriguing new tales about our family! I suppose I shouldn't be surprised that the sister of François was an equally fascinating person."

Gaston smiled as he continued. "Margaux made the best of her Hollywood romance gone awry by establishing herself as an exclusive concierge of romantic interludes for the rich and famous. Soon there were regularly scheduled two-night romantic outings on one of her yachts, including cocktails, a catered meal, with a choice of delectable desserts and champagne. She developed a good reputation with New Orleans' finest restaurants and nightclubs, making reservations for her clients at their finest tables, with the best of service. She even arranged travel plans for her clientele, creating a full-fledged business for the pleasure of her clients, which ensured a constancy of repeat business.

"One of the more juicy and prominent tales about the brothel, long before Margaux's time, was during its early days in the 1840s - a man named Maximilien Charbonneau, who was the French Minister of Finance to King Louis Philippe I. Monsieur Charbonneau was a man of expensive tastes, who enjoyed the finest of offerings at such establishments - the best bourbon, the richest foods, and the finest of women. He had returned, yet again, to the brothel after having been there every night for well over a week. Quite inebriated, he found himself in a heated argument with another gentleman, also a regular, both of them competing for the attention of Lily - the most desirable of all the flowers. The argument turned to a duel, which commenced immediately on the lawn just before sundown.

"Quite a tall man, Monsieur Charbonneau was also of enormous circumference, but that did not impede his efficacy to duel with his French revolver. After fifteen paces, he turned, aimed, and with a single shot, he deftly injured his opponent, purposely shooting him in the thigh. Because he was a representative of France, he could not allow his reputation to come to ruin because of a death. Maiming was one thing. Murder was another. He could do most anything else, as they say, with wine, women, and song, but never could he purposely kill another.

"So, having won the duel after a week of nightly participation in the best that Maison de Fleur-di-Lis could offer, Monsieur Charbonneau extended himself to his limits and died of a heart attack in the company of none other than Lily. It was certainly an unfortunate affair for New Orleans, not only because of the loss of a foreign dignitary, but being that Monsieur Charbonneau was a man of great girth, he crushed the petals of Lily, the establishment's finest flower."

"Oh, poor Lily! What an awful way to go!" Sophia said.

"Yes, it was a shame."

"I imagine they were 'hard pressed' to come up with a cover story for old Maxie's death," Markos said with a grin.

The room filled with a collective groan.

More than ready to complete his tale, Gaston smiled and said, "Well, to this day, one of the spirits in the house is a very large spirit who fills the room with both his presence and size. When he makes himself known, I sometimes hear the final exhale of a woman, and then I smell the sweet scent of lilies."

"I'd love to visit your home sometime," Sophia said with a big grin. "You never know, it might spark some pleasurable excitement for us, Michael."

"Le bon temps rouler, mon chéri," Michael said, looking into Sophia's eyes and kissing her lightly on the lips.

"You are welcome any time," Gaston said. "Your presence will add great beauty to my bouquet of flowers."

CHAPTER
Eighteen

On the same note of new businesses, our idea for the replica of Akrotiri on Santorini is on hold," Markos said.

"Oh? Why is that?" Gaston asked.

"There are many government regulations we have to tackle before we can proceed. So, while Christofer was handling the legal matters, I decided to spend some time traveling through Europe. I went to Italy, Switzerland, Austria, Czechia, Germany, France, Spain, and Portugal, and then flew here from Lisbon."

"Did you travel with a tour group?" Yesinia asked.

"No, I first flew from Santorini to Athens, then to Rome, and stayed there for several days. From there, I rented a car and drove, staying where I wanted for as long as I desired. I met some wonderful people all along the way."

"We should do that as a group in a tour bus, like we did in Colorado," Anja said. "Another gathering could be from coast to coast through Canada by rail. Ibrahim and I just returned from the same trip. We took a luxury train. The food was good, and the accommodations were quite nice, and the scenery - so beautiful and constantly changing.

"We usually sell our products at fairs across the United States, but this time we spent our time sightseeing and bought many items along the way. Then we shipped them back home for our community to reproduce. We actually enjoyed ourselves for a change."

"I take it that you didn't invite Bintou to join you," Irina said, and they all laughed.

"No, Bintou never travels with us. She likes to stay at home in Senegal and run the business, which I must say that she is quite good at. Let us just say that Bintou and I keep our distance. She likes to be in charge, but I am not one that she can control, which does not make her happy. Ibrahim works very hard to keep her away from me. She can be, I might say... difficult at times."

"Tell us, Anja," Irina asked, "do you ever get tired of selling your products at craft shows and fairs?"

"Yes, it is very tiring. Sophia would understand, because we have to do all the packing, shipping, and preparation before each fair. We have to arrive early, between six and seven a.m., to set up the tent, displays, and all the merchandise so we are ready to sell by nine. The most tiring part is we must be *on* for whoever is in the booth, which means most of the day, because it is often-times filled with lookers and buyers. At the end of the day, we must put everything away for the night. It is at least a twelve-hour day. We start over the next day until we tear down at the end of the fair."

"Have you ever considered hiring extra help?" Markos asked.

"As a matter of fact, we are now making many changes in our business. We started an online store on our website, which is doing quite well. My nephew is, what you say, a techie? He designed our website and connected us with Amazon and some other websites that sell handcrafted items, which has made our community busier than ever. We now have five employees that take care of shipping and handling. With all the changes, Ibrahim and I may no longer need to sell at craft fairs, meaning that soon we may have four properties to sell in the U.S. and London."

"That's a big change in your business," Markos said. "Will you then live in Senegal, or elsewhere while running your business remotely?"

"That I cannot answer right now," Anja, said. "We will always call Senegal home. Bintou is there, of course, with other family members and our community. We do enjoy living in different places, and perhaps there will be some other place to call home. All I know is that one good decision will lead to the next, and all will work toward what is best for us."

"Tell us more about yourself. I don't know much about your history," Christofer asked.

"I will try to make it short, but to begin with, I had a good life growing up. I was the youngest of five girls, raised by my loving mother and maternal grandmother. Before I was born, my father moved on. I never knew him. We lived in southeastern Senegal, between Tambacounda and Niokolo-Koba National Park, a World Heritage Site. It is a woodland savannah, famous for its wildlife. There are lions, elephants, hippos, chimpanzees, water buffalos, leopards, African wild dogs, baboons, many species of monkeys, many birds and amphibians, too. From June to October it is rainy, and it is dry from November to May.

"We were what you call dirt poor, but we had no idea we were. The communities surrounding ours were the same, so there was no place to compare our lives with others. As far as we knew, everyone lived as we did. We lived in a thatched hut with a dirt floor. With a broom made from bundles of grass, my mother swept that floor every day, keeping the dust and insects to a minimum. We had no electricity, and did not even know such a thing existed. We lived by the waking sun and the sleeping moon.

"On one side of the hut, my sisters and I slept, side by side, on woven mats with blankets placed on the floor, while my mother and grandmother slept on the other side. In the center was a small fire pit for warmth and light when the sun went down. When we woke up, we straightened our mats and folded our blankets, making sure they were orderly for when we slept that night.

"We spent most of our time outside. We had very little. None of us even had shoes to wear. In fact, until I met Ibrahim, I never owned a pair of shoes. I *still* prefer being barefoot. From a variety of grasses, my mother and we girls made woven baskets of all shapes and sizes, and mats to cover the floor for sitting and sleeping. My grandmother made flatbread. We walked to nearby communities with her bread and our wares wrapped in a bundle placed on top of our heads. All day long, she ground the grains and made the dough, flattened it into something that looked like small thick pizza dough, then put it on a flattened rock that sat in the middle of the outside fire pit to cook. It was long, hot work. While she made the bread, we all sat around the fire, making our baskets and singing songs passed down through the generations, there in the part of Africa that time forgot.

"We girls could not wait for the night to take hold as we snuggled together and our mother and grandmother told us tales. Some of the stories made us laugh, and some made us cry. Many of their stories were fables with lessons learned, and others were about the history of our people. We always fell asleep with the tales woven into our dreams. We imagined life in the mountains and faraway places by the sea, in cities of ancient ways we had not yet seen."

"A life of carefree simplicity," Shoshana said.

"Mostly survival, but again, we did not think of it that way," Anja said.

"How did you meet Ibrahim?" Michael asked.

"It was my sixteenth summer when this handsome, tall man walked up as we gathered around the fire, making our baskets and flatbread. He was traveling through the nearby villages on a donkey to see if there was anything he could buy to sell through his community of craftspeople. My mother asked if he would like to join us for our evening meal. I locked eyes with him, and before I knew it, I was his traveling companion. It was not long before he acquired another donkey, because he gave me his as he walked alongside. At first, I thought the reason he selected me to travel with him was because I was tall and strong, and able to make more baskets to sell, but I later learned that before we left, he asked for my mother's permission to marry me."

"I suppose it didn't have anything to do with the fact that you're beautiful, stately, and elegant, not to mention hard working, and talented," Christofer said.

"Thank you - maybe," Anja laughed. "When we reached his community in western Senegal, near Dakar, we made wedding plans. My family came and remained with us there. My grandmother continued to make flatbread to the end of her days, but it was her character, her way that made her such an influence on me and my sisters."

"Were you Ibrahim's first wife?" Lestari asked.

"No, he was already married to Bintou for a few years. Even though Muslim men can have more than one wife, and actually up to four, she was not happy to share her husband with a fifteen-year-old, and I must say I do understand."

"Do you have any children?"

"No, we were not able to have children. That was one reason why Ibrahim married me, thinking it was Bintou that could not bear children, but it was him instead. That is why we were the ones to travel and sell the goods for years, because we did not have a family to raise."

"Tell us more about your being a shaman," Darius said.

"That was why I began to tell you about my history. I married into the Muslim faith, but I grew up with both my mother and grandmother, who were shamans. My grandmother's father was a well-known shaman, but because he did not have a son, he passed down what he knew to my grandmother, who already possessed the natural ability and demeanor of a shaman. She was quiet, and possessed a mystic air about her, as the observer of all things around her, but more so of things most of us cannot see or sense. She, in turn, passed on her knowledge to my mother and then to me. I am the only one of my sisters who became a shaman."

"I know very little about shamanism," Irina said. "I do know your calm presence is the quiet force needed for the type of healing work you do. Can you explain more of what you do as a shaman?"

"I believe that our ancestral spirits reside within us, even the ancestral spirits of the animals that we once were. In the type of shamanism I do, I take a person back to the origins of their inherent nature. In doing so, much of what has been locked up inside is released, and healing naturally occurs. Most people of the western world think what I do is supernatural, but it is *truly* natural for the miraculous to occur in commonplace events and happenings. In fact, that is when miracles happen the most. I am able to see beyond what most people observe, and because of that, I am able to reach deep places in people and animals that help them heal.

"The healing power of a shaman is where nature opens a portal for a spectacular shift, where one comes back into alignment. It may seem as inconceivable or not feasible to a westerner, but is more real than the 'reality' they know. What I do is shamanic medicine, which activates one's inner healing that is innate in everyone. My most important task is being a mediator for humans and their ancestors. Through ritual, I help remove the obstacles for healing to occur.

"I will take a person on a journey, for lack of a better term, to new territories, where all things are possible, where we rise above the world and any seeming problems, to an ascended dimension where the mystery is uncontested. In this dimension and mindset, we truly are unlimited in our body, mind, and spirit. In that dimension, all things are one. There is nothing to come between the entirety of the eternal and the wholeness of all beings gathered there in celebration, because they are the same thing. In that dimension there is no illness, there is nothing but love and pure awareness. If we remain there long enough, the higher energy becomes us, displacing anything lesser. It is like when clear water drops into a glass of muddy water, eventually displacing all the murkiness, in time you will have only clear water. In that place - that mindset - all is well."

"That sounds like where Sophia went in her near-death experience," Gaston said.

"Yes, I cannot help but think it was the same place, or at least the same state of mind," Anja said. "It is where we come to weave our connection with all beings. The more beings we include, the larger and stronger the healing network. You see, it is like the work that we do here, in Apeiros. When we heal one person, it has, what do you say?... a snowball effect, like an avalanche that gathers everything around it in its force of power. In one person's healing, it affects those around them, including their past lives, while altering their future as well. Our power truly only lies in this present moment of now.

"My grandmother and mother lived in the mystery, where their hearts were ever in awe of life and its wonders. Everything they did - all they experienced - they appreciated. Life for them was pure wonder and grace. Love always led the way in their healing practice, and compassion was at the forefront, as their intuition increased into the ethers of the sacred mystery on behalf of those they served. May I be like them."

"By all means, that you are, Anja," Darius said. "What a wonder you are. I, for one, would like to have you take *me* on a shamanic journey."

"We can do that. And one thing that becomes clear, when you understand the animal you once were, that is your animal totem. Some of us have many."

"So, because I resonate with deer, could it be that I once was a deer?" Sophia asked.

"What I know about you, Sophia, is that you resonate and attract most every animal and bird, for you are a very old soul, living at one time or another as each one of these beings. They come to you because they sense you are one of them. It truly is a gift."

"Well, I'd say we have some deep work to do in the future. I, for one, would like to know more," Markos said.

"It will be my honor," Anja said.

"Who introduced you to Apeiros?" Shoshana asked.

"It was Sophia's father, Patrick."

"Really?" Sophia said. "That's a surprise. I just assumed it was White Buffalo."

"No, Ibrahim and I were at an art fair in Santa Fe, and Patrick approached our booth. It was as if he sought me out, and we immediately had that soulful connection that we all feel in this group. We spent the weekend talking with him, and he invited me to attend Apeiros. I knew before he asked that I was to be a part of whatever it was he was doing in the world. The rest, as they say, is history."

"My, it seems I always have something new to learn about my sweet dad," Sophia said.

"Yesinia, what have you been doing since we last met?" Shoshana asked.

"We've had big changes, too. My brother and I were in a serious car accident when we were rear-ended by a large SUV that totaled my car."

"Are you okay? I *thought* you looked like you're not moving very well," Sophia said.

"No serious injuries, but we both suffered a concussion and whiplash. The trauma has had its way with my senses. I'm not completely here, I must admit."

"There's a great healer here in Doolin who might be able to help you. Let's call her tomorrow."

"I'm ready for an intervention. Not much has helped since the accident."

"When did this happen?" Sophia asked.

"About six weeks ago. Since then, we've decided to sell the travel business as it is. It can be quite strenuous. We've yet to decide what to do next. We certainly have time, but we both need to feel better before we make any big plans. The only thing is, White Buffalo left me his gift of the amethyst rosary to bless our travel business. I feel I'm not being true to the gift he left for me."

"Yesinia," Sophia said, "I know for certain that White Buffalo would not hold you to remaining in the travel business. He gave you the amethyst rosary, certainly because you're Catholic, but also in representation of the deeper meaning of the stone, which is purification, spiritual perfection, while creating a resounding shield of light around the body. His gift has greater meaning, now that you are moving on to something better, even though you do not yet know what that is."

"Sophia is right, dear," Gaston said. "White Buffalo would have been the first to encourage you to follow your intuition regarding this decision. He would tell you to follow your heart."

"Shoshana, we've not yet heard from you," Darius said. "Tell us what's going on in your part of the world."

"I have been very busy," Shoshana said. "I am so happy for several reasons. I recently received another grant to continue my work at Akrotiri, where the ancient people are like my family, and I am so pleased to continue my work there."

"That is good news! What is the other reason?" Ananta asked.

"Let me tell them," Christofer said, as he put his arm around Shoshana's shoulders. "I am the luckiest man to have ever lived, because my lovely Shoshana has agreed to marry me."

"Oh, how wonderful!" Sophia said. "Have you set a date yet?"

"If it's alright with you, we thought we would get married here in a simple ceremony," Shoshana said. "Neither of us have any close family that are living, but all of you are family to us!"

"Of course!" Sophia said. "What could be better than a Jewish, Greek, Irish wedding? We can have it here at the house, or outside on the cliffs. It's up to you. The Ello

Sisters can prepare all the food, and there's nothing like Irish music to celebrate with."

"Sounds wonderful! We'll make it simple and fun!" Shoshana said.

"Let's talk in the next couple of days to get everything planned," Sophia said.

"Lestari, what have you been doing since we last saw you?" Markos asked.

"I have had so much going on, but I'll tell you all about it later. I am getting very tired – no doubt jet lag. If you don't mind, I am going take my leave to get some rest."

"Of course," Markos said, standing and holding her chair as she got up.

"Good night everyone, and let me say, it is so good to be here with all of you. I've missed you!"

As Lestari left the table, Sophia went with her to see if she needed anything. She walked her to her room, when Lestari asked, "Tomorrow, if you could spare me an hour of your time, I would like to talk with you. I've been through so much lately, and I could use a friend."

"Of course. Why don't you sleep in, and then we'll take a walk by the cliffs and have a picnic. It's a beautiful walk."

"Thank you, Sophia, that will be just what I need."

Sophia returned to the dining room. "Is she okay?" Michael asked.

"She just needs a good night's rest. I'll talk with her tomorrow."

As the hour indeed was getting late, everyone agreed it was a good idea to call it a night. They bid each other good night, and retired to their rooms.

CHAPTER
Nineteen

The group gathered for breakfast the next morning. "What is there to do around here?" Irina asked.

"Let me give you a bit of history and suggest a few places you can visit that are nearby," Michael said. "Of course, there's Doolin, with lots of pubs and access to ferries that take you to the Aran Islands. It's at least a day trip, if not more - definitely worth taking. If you want to surf, Aileen's Wave can be thirty feet high at times, and you can also go diving in Galway Bay."

"Excuse me," Gaston said. "Did you say the wave is thirty feet high?"

"Would you like to rent a board? Each one comes with a complementary death or dismemberment insurance policy."

"How thoughtful."

"Nearby is the Burren. Interestingly enough, it has never been disturbed by the local farmers for over two thousand years. It's a karst landscape of glacial era limestone from 350 million years ago, containing one-percent of the land mass of Ireland, equal to 217 square miles. It contains caves, fossils, and rock formations - some of which are archeological sites. The most famous is Poulnabrone Dolmen, made of three standing portal stones covered by a large horizontal capstone. It is one of 172 portal tombs in Ireland, dated from 4200 B.C.E to 2900 B.C.E.

"In the Poulnabrone Dolmen, remains of 33 human bodies were found, many with severe arthritis. With them were several objects - a polished stone axe and other weapons, a bone pendant, pottery, and quartz crystals. From all the remains found among the portal tombs, it's evident that the people of that day suffered from hard physical labor and didn't live much longer than the age of 30."

"It sounds like a harsh environment," Christofer said.

"Yes, on the Burren, there's not a tree to be found, but instead you'll find alpine plants that grow next to Mediterranean and woodland plants, some of which are rare species. It contains acidic environments as well as alkaline. The wildlife there is diverse, from mice, rabbit, stoats, and hedgehogs, to fox, feral goats, otters, and mink. Of course, there is a wide variety of birds and bats, for those of you who have ornithological interests."

"That's for the birds," Gaston whispered to Sophia, who rolled her eyes.

"Another great place to visit is Doolin Cave, where you'll find the longest free-hanging stalactite in Europe, called The Great Stalactite; 23 feet long. They have a gift shop with some very nice pottery made from the glacial clay found in the cave."

"Where can we see a leprechaun?" Gaston said.

"Rent 'Finian's Rainbow' on streaming TV. And, by the way, don't ask Pádraig that question, or he might drop you by the side of the road."

"Perhaps I might at least be able to search for a four-leaf clover if he did," Gaston said.

"The Cliffs of Moher would be a nicer spot," Michael said. "They are just a half hour walk from here, which is especially beautiful at sunset. Sundown this time of year happens at 9 p.m. There are five miles of path along the edge of the cliffs for a good walk. Just don't go there when the wind is strong."

"Indeed, for I might find myself at the bottom looking up!" Markos said.

Laughing, Michael said, "There's one more place I think you'll find very interesting. It's the Ailwee Cave, a labyrinth cave system with underground lakes, bridged chasms, and underground waterfalls."

"Well, it looks like we have a day or two of fun in our plans," Markos said. "I'm game. Who wants to come along?" Most everyone joined him for the day...

Sophia went with Yesinia to see Saoirse, a healer from Doolin, to consult about the pain she was suffering from her car accident. After examining Yesinia, Saoirse gave her an osteopathic adjustment, and then followed up with acupuncture.

"I want you to take it easy for the remainder of the day. You'll be sore, but we got your spine and ribs back in alignment. Be sure to rest well and drink lots of water. Come back to me on Friday and I'll do some craniosacral therapy. It is very subtle. You'll be surprised at how effective it is."

"Can you tell me more about what you will do?"

"Craniosacral therapy is gentle energy work. You lay upright, fully clothed, on a massage table, while I hold your head underneath and slowly move it from side to side. I may gently shift your spine and your feet, but I don't always have to do that.

"One of my patients brought her son to see me last year. When Joseph was seven years old, he and his twin brother were in the back seat when their car was in a head-on collision. Unfortunately, the boys were not wearing seat belts.

His brother was instantly killed, while poor Joseph's body broke through the back window. It had been twelve years since the accident and physically, he appeared to be fine. He went through years of therapy in the attempt to bring him back to a functional state of mind and calm emotions, but nothing seemed to help. You see, the trauma of the accident remained in his body. Not knowing if it would be an effective treatment for him, I did one session of craniosacral therapy on him.

"The next day his mother called me in tears. I was worried that Joseph had a negative experience from the treatment, but I soon discovered she was crying tears of gratitude. She thanked me for giving her son back to her. That one session freed him of all that pent-up energy from the accident. He was happy and joyful, and within a day, the young lad had a whole new outlook on life."

"Well, my accident wasn't that bad."

"You would be surprised how much tension the body holds from all kinds of worries and concerns, not to mention physical traumas. This is very subtle work. I may apply slight pressure at the base of your spine, too. It is energy work. You might be amazed how good you feel afterwards. I look forward to helping you on Friday, Yesinia."

That afternoon, after Sophia brought Yesinia back to the house to rest, she took a walk with Lestari for the picnic lunch they planned. Sophia brought along her satchel with two sandwiches, some carrot sticks, two bottles of water, a couple of Y-ellos - the Ello Sisters' lemon bars - a box of tissues, and a book she sensed she would need.

They first sat on a hillside near the visitor center, along the edge of the Cliffs of Moher, and ate their food. "I appreciate you taking the time to talk with me," Lestari said.

"Any time, Lestari. What's on your mind?"

"It's my husband, Putu. We have had a difficult relationship for some time, especially since both of our children went to college. It has been a financial strain. Of course, now that is not a problem because of White Buffalo's generosity, but it seems we have little in common, with Gede and Kadek gone. I have this deeply enriching relationship with all of you of the Order, and he has his work with the World Wide Fund for Nature, but there's nothing that we have in common any longer."

"Sadly for some, when children leave the nest and parents lose that important thread that held them together for so long, they sometimes discover little else binds them."

"Since I returned to Bali six months ago, things have been even more difficult between us. I think Putu feels less important, because now I have all this money, and he is no longer the provider. I am sure his ego is wounded. Our children are not returning to Bali, at least for now. Gede has a good job as a computer programmer in India, and Kadek moved to London to pursue her dream of professional photography."

"That is something of which both you and Putu can be proud."

"Oh, yes, we are so happy for both of them." Lestari's lip quivered, and she held a tissue to her eyes. "So, to make a long story short, Putu and I finalized our divorce just three weeks ago."

"Oh, Lestari, I am so sorry. This is a surprise."

"I know it sounds sudden, but we have both been unhappy for several years. It's just something I didn't share with all of you – you understand – you keep hoping things will improve."

"It's such a difficult thing to go through," Sophia said. "I don't know your circumstances, but both Michael and I have been there in our own way. It is none of my business, but may I ask how are your finances, now that you split up? Financial matters are some of the biggest reasons for divorce."

"He was more than fair. He knew that White Buffalo left me the money to support what I am doing in the world, and he did not contest any of it."

"That says much about his character."

"Oh, yes, and of course, I took nothing from him, but now that I have so much more than he does, I paid off the loans for our children's educations, which was substantial. I also left him our home in Bali, now free and clear of any loans, along with most of the furnishings. Before I moved out, I had any needed repairs done to the house. He now only has the responsibility of his living expenses, which are minimal."

Sophia gave Lestari a hug. "And that says much about *your* character. How about if we walk along the pathway."

Lestari took a deep breath. "So, here I am a millionaire without a home. I rented a small furnished apartment until I decide where to settle permanently, but that is not the whole problem."

"I have all afternoon to talk, if need be," Sophia said. She put her arm around Lestari's shoulder. "Let's take that walk while you tell me more."

"A month after my return home to Bali from Colorado, Putu and I had one good night together. It's been a year and a half since we had been with each other in that way. We made love that night, and the moment he released his seed in me, I *knew* I was pregnant."

"Oh, no," Sophia said.

"You know how it is. We are so intuitive, we just know. And I was right. Here I was with a man that no longer loved me, nor did I love him. Every day was a struggle, and we had two grown children. Neither one of us wanted another child to raise, and that meant we would need to either stay together and be miserable, or raise the child in a broken home after the divorce.

"I was also concerned for my health. I am 42, and by the time the baby would be born, I would be 43. I was not sure that the baby would be healthy, especially since my emotional state has been steeped in anguish over our marriage for a few years. I've never had any difficulty with the topic of abortion, until it involved me. There are so many reasons people choose to do it. It is a personal decision that one should never judge. So, after several weeks, some of it in counseling, some in discussions with Putu, I had an abortion."

"Oh, Lestari - a divorce and an abortion within a couple of months... you've had a tremendous level of stress and strain. I imagine your heart feels like it's breaking."

Lestari began to cry. Sophia put her arms around her while she broke down and sobbed. Lestari's legs could no longer hold up. Sophia gently helped her sit on the ground.

"I have worked with so many women, and men, who have gone through abortion," Sophia said. "It is such an emotional decision, and until you go through one yourself, you never know the extent of what people experience."

"Putu and I made the decision together, but since then he has withdrawn from our relationship, which I don't blame him, but I don't know exactly how he feels now."

"He must face his own convictions, and unfortunately you both have to do that separately."

"I understand. I just feel so alone right now."

"Would it help you to know that I had one years ago, because my health would not allow me to carry the child full term?"

"You did?" Lestari said as her crying subsided.

"I may not have survived the pregnancy, and because of the medication I was taking, if the baby survived, she may have needed several heart surgeries. I couldn't afford health insurance, so the medical expenses would have caused tremendous stress, because I would have needed hospital care for the last six months of the pregnancy, not to mention all the surgical expenses for the baby."

"You were alone, too?"

"I was. The father did offer to help out, but we weren't married, and certainly not in love. We just made a mistake that so many young people make when they don't think about consequences. It was not a difficult decision to make for the baby's sake and for mine, and yet I struggled for a long time afterward. I couldn't go down the baby food aisle at the grocery store. Anytime I received an invitation to a baby shower, I found an excuse not to go. When I watched a movie and saw a baby held by a loving mother, I cried."

"Oh, yes, that is what I'm experiencing now. I'm not sure if it is second thoughts, or guilt, or – I just don't know what I feel right now."

"So much of the problem is that, out of fear of reproach, it's not something we can share. I told one friend about my abortion, and of course the father of the child, but no one else. There is still the political and religious right that holds the topic of abortion as dark and evil, and the liberal left that pretends abortion is no more emotionally significant than pulling a tooth."

"Yes, that's it," Lestari said. "I knew I could reach out to you about this, but I'm afraid to talk about it with others, even with some of my family, because I'm afraid of what they'll think of me."

"That's just it. There are millions of women and men caught up in a personal life altering decision amidst all the accusations and judgment, but let me say this, just about everyone I know has either had an abortion, or has a child, a spouse, a partner, or a close friend who did."

"Really?"

"Weeks before my abortion was scheduled, still not certain if I would follow through with it, I talked to many people, asking their thoughts on the subject. Because I felt guilty and wanted to hide the real reason I was asking, I told them I was researching a book on the subject. Some of them were good friends, and others were just acquaintances, but most of them broke down in tears, because they also made such a choice, or they were close to someone who did. For some, it was like a dam broke and their story came spilling out.

"Since then, I've read just about every book written on the subject by both sides, and the more I read about it, I know I did the right thing for me *and* for my child. I honestly do not regret my decision. I strongly believe that the soul of my baby will find the right parents who will love her and care for her just as she deserves. I also believe that someday I will know her, whether it is in this lifetime or another."

Lestari took a deep breath. "When I went through with the abortion, it was a logical decision - one strictly from my head. Now, I am dealing with the part of me that I did not allow myself to feel the pain of my decision at the time. Now, my heart is breaking. When I add the divorce to it, it emphasizes my failure as a woman. I did not know if I would be in the right mind to join you all this time around.

And last night, I certainly didn't want to share my sad story, especially with the wonderful news of Shoshana and Christofer's wedding."

"I'm so glad you came," Sophia said. "Over the years, you've heard of most everyone's challenges at one time or another. That's another reason we are all so good together, because we hold each other up when we need support. Always remember this, when you cannot believe in yourself, believe in my belief in you."

"Thank you. I *will* remember that. Even when I'm not at my best, I can believe in the good for others. So, that is a good reminder. I do know that I did the right thing, but why do I feel so empty?"

"You're grieving, Lestari. You have suffered two major losses in a very short time. First, let's talk about your marriage. Could it be the emptiness you feel is because you've let go of all the negativity you put your attention on all these years? That took up a lot of room in your mind and heart. Now that Putu is gone, your time and thoughts are not on how much you are struggling, and it has left you in a void. Vacant feelings are not easy, especially when you are starting over. Could it be that you are mourning the loss of the dream you had with him?"

"Yes, that is part of it, but those dreams died so long ago."

"The dreams still remain, because so many are innate in your being. They were there before you met him, and they still live within you. You may also be mourning the loss of the habits you had - the things you did together, or what you no longer shared - which is another void you are now filling with all things new. And what about Kadek and Gede? How are they handling this?"

"It has been difficult for them. Even though they are

grown and on their own, their emotions are divided."

"And so, add guilt to the grief you're experiencing. It's only human to feel personally responsible for your children's happiness, and now that they are adults, they will learn to deal with their feelings in their own way. Of course, you and Putu will be there for them, as you heal yourselves."

"That makes sense, but what I truly struggle with most is the forgiveness of my unborn child. Putu and I had very strong feelings about being good, nurturing parents to our children, and although I can't speak for him because we didn't talk about it, I think we both feel a sense of guilt that we put our needs and desires ahead of this child's."

"Then I invite you to speak to that very issue with Putu. An abortion is not a decision exclusive to women. I know many men who have struggled with these feelings of guilt and shame, too. You know the old concept about dealing with the elephant in the room – the large, obvious problem everyone knows about but don't want to discuss?"

"I don't know if he *will* discuss it."

"You might be surprised. At least, you'll never know until you try." Sophia pulled a book from her satchel. "Now, this is a little wild, but I have something to read to you from a book written for people like you and me who have gone through abortion. I brought it with me today. When I read it, it brought me to peace, and this final chapter brought it home for me. The book is called, *I Never Heard You Cry - A Compassionate Journey Through Abortion.*"

"You brought a book about abortion with you? How did you know? I didn't tell you..."

Sophia shrugged. "You know me, I'm an intuitive. You do the same thing too, in your own way. I just sensed it last night, when you asked to speak with me. The book tells seven people's stories - five women and two men - all of them different. It is written from a neutral point of view, staying away from political and religious opinions. Instead, it contains much heartfelt wisdom, some of it spiritual, that helps one come back home to themselves, particularly through self-forgiveness and gratitude. I'll give it to you to read. I think it will help, but I'd like to read the final chapter in the book, entitled, 'A Letter to my Daughter.' Is that okay with you?"

"Yes. Somehow I already know it will help me."

"That's a good way to think right now. Just stay open to what will bring you to your healing. It comes one moment at a time," Sophia said, as she began to read.

Dear Lanie,

I have given you the name of my mother, which was Elizabeth Elaine. Both names were originally Greek, and later, Irish. Elizabeth means, "My God is my oath." Elaine - "Light, torch, and bright." I interpret the combination to mean, "I am the promise of Divine Illumination." Both you and my mother have been beacons that illuminate my direction. In healing the past, the ship upon which I sail is the present leading to the destinations of my intended future.

Your grandmother, had you known her, was a beautiful dark-Irish woman with auburn hair and hazel-green eyes. In her prime, she was proud, intelligent, elegant, and stunningly beautiful. In my most fond memory of her, I remember her laughing until she lit up the room. This was rare. She had a dark energy. Growing up with my mother was an invitation for me to counteract that low vibration. So, in my writing I heal the memories of the past. This brings me to the center of my being, where I can live in forgiveness of her and for myself. I am then free to set sail upon clear waters.

I envision you as a vibrant, creative child, who has the same sense of beauty as your grandmother. I see you living from the reality of joy and creative expression like your grandmother did when she was at her best. I imagine you to be intelligent and wise beyond your years. You have what some know as being an old soul. You would love to learn. It would come easily to you. Everywhere you would go - life would be an adventure, and it would show up in miraculous ways.

Compassion of the heart would be your hallmark. You would have seen the universe through the lives of others with whom you are in company. You would have become a traveler, absorbing the atmosphere of your surroundings, taking with you every minute detail. It would have become a part of your being. Your charismatic nature would have invited the stranger into your circle, embracing life and reflecting the joy that you personified. Touched and changed, each would have been transformed as you expanded through the exchange of souls. Peace and love would have resided at the center of you. You simply would have been blessed everywhere you went as you radiated the essence of God to everyone you encountered.

I have come to you, in the form of writing, to let you know how very much you are loved by me. At the time I let you go, I thought it was safer for me to try to forget you. It was so difficult for me to admit that I had to release you. Now, as I honestly reflect my fears and failures, as well as my triumphs and achievements, I come to you with a transparent heart. Forgiveness and gratitude are the filters through which I clear the past. What results is the peace and harmony that I know is my birthright. It is time for me to open to the gifts of what this experience of abortion brings.

I know that, at the deepest level, you are aware of why I released you from my body before you could be my daughter. Even at the time, I sensed that I had your permission to allow me to let you go. It was the innate elegance of you that I felt as a great love radiating beyond the pain of the decision to have the abortion.

It was a decision that I had to make. No other choice was evident. The grief of the loss of you still resides deep within. This is why I am writing - to convey to you what I have done to come full circle in what has been my journey of atonement. The journey I have chosen - that of embracing all that has occurred - rides upon the mystical ship that supports my healing. The following is my voyage as I am returning, full circle, to myself again.

I never heard you cry. I have spent decades wondering what it would have been like to hold you in my arms - to rock you into a tender sleep. I never got to gently bathe you as an infant. There was no sweet scent of you as a baby - unlike any other scent. I missed the opportunity to dress you in beautiful dresses, and also in jeans and little sweaters along with tiny tennis shoes. I never got a chance to take care of you when you had to stay home sick from school - to bring you breakfast in bed, to pamper and care for you until you felt well again. I never had the opportunity to attend your school play, or to watch you in high school tennis matches. I did not hear about the sweetness of your first kiss. No graduation. No wedding. No grandchildren. No mother-daughter moments.

The only time I was a mother of any kind was during the eight weeks that you were in my body. In order to survive the decision that I made to let you go, I kept myself emotionally devoid so I could follow through with what I knew I had to do. I didn't even let you know that I loved you when you and I were together. I am so sorry that I was not present enough to let you know that you mattered.

I can tell you now that your presence in my life does matter to me. It has affected my journey ever since that day. No one has had the profound impact upon my life as you have. I thank you *deeply for your presence - for I continue to feel it with me each and every day.*

I think it is one reason, now, why I am so touched by the beauty of nature. It is part of my atonement, as I recognize the preciousness of all life. I had shut down for quite a while, but life just kept showing up to meet me with invitations to join with it again.

I did what was necessary to save my own life. Now, I formally ask for your forgiveness as I work through releasing myself from these shackles that have silently held me back. They are the worst of prisons - shame, doubt, and guilt. They are what held me back from anything that would propel me to my greatness, thus creating in me the belief that I do not deserve it. I felt I had no choice but to let you go. But how could I move forward if I did not allow you to come into this world as my daughter?

I am grateful to you for coming to me as an advanced being, and for choosing to come to me in the way that you did. I cannot help but believe that you knew, in advance, your purpose for being in my life.

I now choose a conscious life, a purposeful life, because I was not as conscious at the time we were together during those eight weeks. Consequently, I have made choices because of my experience of you, not in spite of it. It was that pivotal point when I changed my course to a greater destination beyond my cognition.

From what I have experienced since that time, which seems so long ago, I now know that love transcends all barriers. I know that I have many angels and guides that surround me. Perhaps I am, in essence, one of those for you, as you are for me. Through my experience on the multidimensional levels of life, I know the veil is thin between the numerous levels of consciousness. Love expands beyond time and space. So, I send you my love from the depths of my being. It kisses you on the cheek with tenderness, transcending all physical barriers.

There will be a day when we will meet. I will know that it is you who stands before me, for our souls know no separation. Until then, on behalf of you, I send my love to all beings as I see the God in them. I feel the essence of all children, as if they were my very own. I gaze into the eyes of every human: into windows of the soul, knowing that therein is the essence of God beneath the shell of the body's façade.

When I am filled with the peace of nature as it aligns with me, my body is straightened, as I stand grounded in the heart of God. I am then lifted into the ether of the vibration most high to its zenith. I radiate the light of God, and this is where you and I meet with all beings - where we meld together in oneness. The horizontal earthly realm, intersected by the vertical alignment of the spiritual, creates the axis point - the center of all power. It is here, in the center of being, where we have never experienced separation and never shall.

I thank you for what you continue to teach me. You have become me, as I have lived through what I know your spirit to be. In the oneness of our being, I am you, as well. From the depths of my heart, I send you my love each and every day, knowing that we are not without the other. I pass on to you what my father said to me just before he died... You are my precious, darling little girl!

- Your Mother

As Lestari softly cried, Sophia continued, "Lestari, the soul of your baby exists in the realm of eternality, where love resides fully. And since love is eternal, it is where we exist within this same realm of no time and no space. It is Absolute Awareness. The relative world of cause and effect does not exist in that dimension, and so there is nothing to forgive, for there is no darkness, no lack, only the infinite realm of the All There Is. Until you forgive yourself, you cannot be in that realm, for all forgiveness truly is self-forgiveness. You won't be able to rise above the situation and ascend to that realm where your baby's soul essence exists. If you can find some way to learn from what you have endured this year, and then live in gratitude for what these many experiences continue to teach you, you will then grow in grace. New life will emerge out of the circumstances that once caused you to spiral downward into the abyss of darkness. I promise, you will be happy again, with a new lease on life as you spring up from the ashes."

"Thank you, Sophia. I feel much better."

"We are all here for each other. You know... I have a great idea. Why don't you stay with us a while longer after the rest of Apeiros leave? It will be just Michael and me, and Gaston and Darius until they return to New Orleans to complete the final details of Auberge. I think the distance from Bali for a few months would help you heal. You can help us at the dig, which will be cathartic for you to get your hands dirty, digging into the soil."

"Let me give it some thought, but I think that such a change would be welcome."

"Another thing, I have to take Yesinia back to Saoirse, the healer, on Friday. She's going to do craniosacral therapy on her. I think it would do you some good, too. I'll tell you more about it on our walk back to the house. I have to walk to Doolin this afternoon to hand out our open house invitations to the locals, and also pay the band that will play for the party Saturday night. Why don't you come along?"

"Okay. Meeting some of the locals will get my mind off things."

"Did you bring White Buffalo's flute with you?"

"Yes, I take it with me everywhere. Why?"

"It's time to play it in public, now that you are single again," Sophia said with a smile. "You remember the story of the flute, don't you?"

"I do. If I play it in public, it will draw new love to me," Lestari said with a shy grin. "Maybe that's why I keep it with me…"

Three days later, Sophia took Yesinia and Lestari to see Saoirse. During the craniosacral therapy session for Yesinia, Saoirse held the back of her head and said, "My goodness, there is so much heat coming off of your body. I am sweating like a pig."

"I've often wondered if pigs really do sweat," Yesinia said. "What a funny thing to say."

"I don't know, but you're releasing so much energy. I can guarantee you're going to feel so much better in a day or two!"

The following day, Yesinia was elated. "Sophia, thank you for taking me to see Saoirse. I am so surprised that such a simple treatment can be so effective. I haven't felt this good in years. It's as if all the negative energies I didn't even realize were trapped inside me were released. I didn't even know it was there until it was gone. Everyone should get craniosacral therapy done. I can't wait to tell my brother about it."

After seeing the positive result on Yesinia, Lestari looked forward to going to Saoirse for the same treatment the next week…

CHAPTER
Twenty

Guests began arriving at Saturday's grand open house at 7, greeted by the green-clad Ello Sisters, who charmed, entertained, and delighted with delectable hors d'oeuvres and snappy patter. It seemed most of the village turned out, eager to get acquainted with their new American neighbors. Along with everyone from Apeiros, Sophia and Michael also invited Sophia's Aunt Lily and Uncle Colin, Michael's distant cousin Geoffrey O'Hara, Pádraig, and Hailey O'Donnell. A five-piece band played on the balcony with great vocal harmonies, including a guitar, fiddle, uilleann pipes, flute, and bodhran. A charming tenor sang Irish ballads and festive songs for everyone's enjoyment.

A variety of cocktails started the evening while introductions were made. Hailey made a beeline across the great room for Geoffrey and prepared to spin him in her web. Pádraig saw her coming and cut her off at the pass.

"Geoffrey O'Hara, I'd like to introduce you to Hailey, Who Can..." Pádraig stammered, "Hailey, who can, who can... give you ahhh... *a tour of the cliffs* while you're here."

"What are ya, boy-o, fluthered already?" Geoffrey said. "Pleased to make your acquaintance, Hailey, but I already know the cliffs well."

Hailey shook Geoffrey's hand, "I'd be happy to show you other points of interest in the area, if you fancy."

"What, did I just get off the boat?" Geoffrey said. "I lived here all me life – at least that's the plan. But thanks all the same."

"You're lookin' a fine thing tonight, Hailey," Pádraig said, elbowing Geoffrey.

"Oh, you must forgive me." She patted her hair and straightened her skirt. "I must be quite a sight. I made a haymes of meself before I came to the party."

"Makes no never mind to me," Geoffrey said, not giving her any slack.

"Oh...well, I must get meself a refill. If you'll excuse me."

"You're excused," Geoffrey said.

Pádraig's jaw dropped, just watching Geoffrey in action as Hailey skulked away with her tail between her legs. "You have to teach me how you do that!"

"Well, God knows ya spent a half-hour blatherin' on about her. You forget that I've been in the Gardí for nearly forty years. I know every trick of a woman who is gagging for it."

The two carried on for awhile, but were instantly silenced when Lestari walked by, dressed in a colorful, off the shoulder, floor length gauzy dress that followed her like a summer breeze. She didn't even know they were standing there, but both of their interests were piqued by her beauty and grace. Here, in front of them, was a petite woman with thick long black hair and warm golden skin, so contrary to the fair women of the Irish. She was striking - with poise that naturally spoke of her life force that flowed with equanimity in her every step.

"How's your drink, cuz?" Michael said, slapping Geoffrey on the back.

"What?" Geoffrey said, jumping from his fantasy. He

checked his Guinness. "I'd fancy another. This one suddenly got hot."

"Pádraig? Another Bushmills?"

"Thank you, lad."

Michael walked to the bar and found Hailey, Who Can't Get a Date had cornered Markos. "That's the funniest thing I've ever heard!" she said. "You're such a craic!"

Markos shrugged, "I'm a funny chap."

"Oh, Michael!" Hailey said. "What's the story? I can't thank you and Sophia enough for inviting me. Your home is lovely!"

"Thank you, Hailey. I hope you're having a good time."

"I am...oh, here." She brushed a crumb off his shirt.

"Oh, uh, thank you. Can I get you another drink?"

"Aye, if you will. I was just tellin' Markos here about the cliffs, and he suggested we might take an evening stroll that way after dinner."

Michael prepared the drinks. "He did, did he?"

"I said it sounded lovely, if only I was wearing the right shoes. Finding the right shoes is always a problem for me. So he said I could wear his. I said, 'what, you can't walk out to the cliffs barefoot!' And he said it was alright, in case he decides to jump! Isn't he an eejit?"

"Well," Michael laughed, "I'm... not sure."

"Oh, Markos, you have a little..." She rubbed her finger under Markos' nose. "Oh, sorry, it's a whisker. I thought you had a smudge. Oh, Michael, I can't drink this, would you mind fixing me another Jameson and ginger, and this time with just a wee bit less ginger?"

"Oh, not at all," Michael said.

"Well, if you'll excuse me, I must run to the jacks before dinner."

Michael and Markos watched her walk away as Gaston

approached to freshen his scotch. "You know," Gaston said, "this Hailey, Who Can't get a Date is quite beautiful and charming."

"In a terrifying sort of way, yes," Markos said.

"I for one don't quite understand why Pádraig ranted on so about her," Gaston said.

"I think it's the grooming," Markos said.

"You really invited her to take a walk later?" Michael said.

"Well, I haven't been able to get a date lately, myself, at least one who doesn't have blue hair..."

"Dinner is served, buffet style!" Lou announced. "Line up and come and get it, because we aren't coming to you!"

"This is quite an impressive delectable assortment of dishes, Lou!" Michael said.

"With your appetite, oh ravenous one, we pull out all the stops."

"You're never going to give me a break, are you?"

"You don't think just because I've traveled half way around the globe that I didn't pack my sense of humor. That is the first thing that comes with me."

"It's good that some things never change," Michael said.

"Except your boxers. Now go eat, drink, and be merry, before you faint from starvation."

After everyone settled in and began enjoying their meals, Hailey, Who Can't Get a Date waved to Lou, who just placed a basket of fresh baked rolls on the table.

"What's your problem, Red?" Lou said.

Michael's eyes darted around the table. "Uh oh."

"Sorry, my tea isn't quite warm enough."

Lou took her cup. "Feels hot to me, but I'll stick it in the oven, if you like."

"And while you're at it, do ya mind getting me a new cup?"

"What's wrong with this one?"

"I believe it's banjaxed."

"It's what the hell?"

Hailey laughed with everyone else, and she pointed it at the cup. "Sorry, the cup. You see?"

"She means it's broken," Pádraig said, rolling his eyes.

"Doesn't look broke to me," Lou said.

"Just a little hairline crack, you see?" Hailey said.

"It ain't leaking."

"But if it suddenly broke, I don't want hot tea in my lap."

Lou walked off with the cup. "Yeah, go ahead and spoil it for the rest of us..."

"What did she say?" Hailey asked Geoffrey.

"Have ya tried the bacon wraps?" Geoffrey said.

"Not crispy enough," Hailey whispered.

Lou walked back in, holding Hailey's new cup of tea with huge oven mittens, which brought the house down. "There you go, dear."

Hailey laughed, "Oh, sorry to be so brutal."

"Not at all," Lou said. "Can I get you anything else?"

Hailey lifted her plate. "If ya don't mind, my shepherd's pie could use a wee bit more ground pepper."

"Of course it could," Lou said. She dutifully walked Hailey's plate to the buffet table and ground more pepper, muttering under her breath.

Hailey smiled and looked at Geoffrey, who simply stared at her while he ate. Hailey looked around, and then whispered, "It really could have used a pinch more canola oil."

Geoffrey winked. "But we won't tell her, will we?"

"I'm old, but I'm not deaf!" Lou hollered.

Hailey shyly put her hand to her mouth and giggled. Lou brought the freshly peppered pie back and set it in front of her. "How's that, Shamrock?"

Hailey took a bite and nodded her approval. "It's perfect!"

"May I get Her Majesty anything else?"

"No no! Thank you so much, and sorry for the trouble."

"Not at all," Lou said, "you've given me a new appreciation for Michael here." She walked away, but first stopped and kissed Michael on the head.

Sophia took the floor. "I'm so interested to know some of the legends of the Irish. I've heard a bit about Tuatha Dé Danann, so I've asked Pádraig to fill in some of the details for those of us who are not from here. Pádraig, if you will?"

"Michael, if you could give me a refill to wet my whistle, please?" Michael poured him another Irish whiskey. "I'm going to stand as I tell you this tale, for it's a grand one, for certain. First, let me say I was a history teacher, not a mythologist, but I will do my best to tell you what I remember. The story goes that the Tuatha Dé Danann were a mythical race of god-like beings that invaded and ruled Ireland over 4000 years ago, and yet they ruled only for 200 years. I'll say that again because our Irish spelling is not pronounced as it may seem. 'Thoo-a day Du-non' means *the Tribes of the God.*'

"The Tuatha, or the 'Danann,' to make it easier, were also known as the tribe of the goddess Danu, a symbol of magic, poetry, craftsmanship, wisdom, and music. They came to Ireland on flying ships over a mist of fog, and some say in a cloud of darkness. They landed on Iron Mountain as darkness came over the sun, lasting for three days. On the other hand, legend has it they came in sailing ships, setting them afire once they set anchor near the shore. The flames and smoke warned observers on the land that they were here to stay."

"Burning their ships - that was extreme. What if they didn't like it here in Ireland?" Yesinia said.

"You have to remember they were gods," Pádraig said. "We have to assume that they knew what they were doing before they landed."

"If only I were as sure as that in all my major decisions," Irina said. "Life would be so much easier."

"The Danann possessed great intelligence and excellence of knowledge, for they were gifted with supernatural powers. They were quite a contrast to the small, dark natives of Ireland, being tall, slender, and impressively grand because they were so mighty and powerful. They possessed red or blonde hair, blue or green eyes, and pale skin that was almost white."

"Sounds like Vikings," Markos said.

"Vikings invaded Ireland in the late 9th century, nearly 3000 years later, but some believe that the Danann were originally from Denmark. Vikings were Scandinavian, and some of them *did* come from Denmark.

"As the story goes, the Danann High King, Nuada Argetlam, lost his arm in battle. A king could not be anything less than whole, so he had no choice but to step down from the throne. However, the physician, who was the son of Nuada, soon replaced his arm with a fully functional arm of silver, over which his skin later grew. With his health restored after seven years, he reclaimed his kingship, following the exile of his replacement, the oppressor Breas.

"The Danann brought with them four treasures, known as the Jewels of Eire. The first treasure was the Sword of

Light, first belonging to Nuada, the first king of the race. The keeper of the sword must have had helpers, usually animals with skills, a supernatural being, and a female servant. The Sword of Light was impossible to defeat, from which no one escaped once it was drawn against them. In addition, it was known as the 'glowing white torch.'"

"I saw that in a Star Wars movie," Michael said.

"Don't help me, lad."

"Sorry..."

"Now, 'Lugh's Spear' was known as 'the finest yew of the wood,' so named for the Danann's supreme warrior commander. The yew tree is a native evergreen in Ireland, which is long-lived, some over 1000 years old. Its wood and red berries are toxic, but it is thought to have magical properties associated, not only with death, but also rebirth and longevity. The Druids used yew to carve their wands and staffs. You may know about the burning of the yew log that brings in the new year."

"Isn't it *Yule* log?" Michael asked.

"It can be, dependin' on what century you're in," Pádraig dryly said. "'Yew' comes from the Old English word *giuli*, which evolved to 'yule,' the word we all know that's associated with the winter solstice, which of course leads us to Christmas and the new year, which embodies birth, death, and rebirth. Now, have ya learned a lesson about interrupting me when I'm pontificatin'?"

"I'm making a mental note of that," Michael said.

"Now, Lugh was a truthful king and the god of storm, sun, and sky. Lugh's spearhead was made from dark bronze and sharply pointed to a razor's edge. Attached was a rowan with thirty pins of gold. It was a long fiery lance, possessing magical abilities, able to burst into flames on its own, from which 'sparks as large as eggs flew' when the spear's heat took hold of it. The spear possessed many of the same qualities of the Sword of Light. The head of the spear was placed into a cauldron of mysterious magical liquid to prevent both the burning of the shaft and injury to the warrior holding it.

"Dagda's Cauldron was owned by Dagda, the father god, and one of Ireland's High Kings. Dagda was the god of wisdom, magic, architecture, strength, and fertility. He controlled time, seasons, crops, weather, life, and death. He always wore a cloak with a hood. Dagda symbolized generosity and bounty, ceaselessly providing food to the gods. The cauldron never ran out of food, providing overflowing sustenance to everyone. It had the power to bring the dead back to life and heal the injured, with the promise 'that none would go from it unsatisfied.' Some believe that the stone basin found inside Knowth, the passage tomb in Brú na Bóinne, is Dagda's Cauldron. The carvings on the side of the basin are purportedly a map of Atlantis.

"Lia Fáil, the Stone of Destiny, or the Coronation Stone, still stands on the Hill of Tara. Its cry confirmed the coronation of the rightful High King of Ireland, with its deafening roar heard throughout the land. Lia Fáil also awarded the king with a long reign, as well as reviving him if need be. At one time, the stone was broken in half and taken to Scotland, eventually ending up in the throne of the British monarchy, wedged between the legs, under the seat itself."

"Leave it to the monarchy to snatch up the good stuff," Markos said.

"We still have half of the stone," Pádraig said. "And because we no longer have any High Kings to rule, we don't hear it screeching out to us across the land. Tir na Nog, known as the land of the ever young, was the original home to the Danann. It was not about eternal youth and beauty, but it represented a passage of time. Tir na Nog stands still in time, while the mortal world passes by in an instant."

"A better solution than plastic surgery," Gaston said.

"Yes, but alas," Pádraig said, "let us say that you stay in Tir na Nog for twenty years, where time has stopped. You haven't aged a wee bit during that time, but then you decide to return to the human world. Those twenty years immediately catch up to you, and you wake up the next morning, twenty years older."

"A frightening thought," Gaston said. "That means I'd probably wake up dead. I prefer to take my aging one day at a time, thank you."

"The reign of the Danann ended following two battles with the Milesians, believed to be the first Gaels in Ireland. Some believe they were the Spanish. After their defeat, both sides agreed that each would rule half of Ireland, with the Milesians ruling above ground, while the Danann ruled below. Living in the Sidhe mounds, the Danann were shielded from mortal eyes by an enchanted mist, or cloak of concealment. Eventually, they were known as the Sidhe, Ireland's fairy-folk. And that was the beginning of the fairies, gnomes, leprechauns, and the many mystical beings here in Ireland.

"The Irish refer to the Sidhe as 'the gentry,' because they are tall, noble, and speak with a silvery sweet speech. The Sidhe are seen walking on the ground after sunset, whereas the sluagh Sidhe, the fairy host, travels though the air at night, known to take mortals with them on their journeys. Then there are the guardian Sidhe of most of the lakes of Ireland and Scotland."

"I'm not clear on where Dagda lived," Lestari said.

"In the Brugh of Brú na Bóinne, in the passage tombs of Newgrange, Knowth, and Dowth – I will take you there. Brugh means mansion, and because Dagda was big like a giant, he needed to live in a place large enough for his comfort. Dagda was the father of many children, to whom he left lands, with the exception of one son. His name was Aengus Óg, who forcefully took Brú na Bóinne from his father, wanting to live there himself. Aengus Óg was the love god of Irish mythology. He was extremely handsome. At all times, he was surrounded by four small birds that symbolized his kisses. He could woo any maiden, or evoke love for those in his company.

"There's a long story about one particular maiden, who came and went from his dreams. She captured the heart of Aengus Óg. The short version of the story was that it took the help of his father, who negotiated with other Sidhe leaders to find her. After three years, Aengus Óg and his love were happily joined for eternity, living together in Brú na Bóinne." Pádraig took a final sip of whiskey. "And that's enough about the ancient Irish for tonight, for I'm dry." Everyone applauded, as he took a bow.

Sophia asked the Ello sisters to bring in dessert for the other guests, while Michael showed the Apeiros members into the study for a quick meeting.

"I just couldn't wait to call you all in to give you some news," Michael said. "First, we hired Pádraig to lead you on the same bed and breakfast tour of Ireland that we took on our last trip here. Sophia and I still have some unpacking to do, and I have some details to attend at the dig, but when you return in a week, we thought we could all take a trip to England and Scotland, and we could conduct our business along the way."

"That sounds delightful," Irina said. The others agreed.

"We thought a visit to Britain's historic mystical places would be fun," Sophia said. "Of course, there is Stonehenge and Avebury Stone Circle, thirty miles from each other, built about the same time in the third century B.C.E. Puzzlewood is a mystical must see in Gloucestershire, as are the North Yorkshire Moors, and Glastonbury Tor, where supposedly King Arthur lay to rest in Glastonbury Abbey."

"Tintagel, on the north coast of Cornwall is quite interesting," Anja said. "I would love to go there. It's known as King Arthur's birthplace, with Merlin's cave on the coast beneath it."

"Let's put that on our list," Sophia said. "I want to see Canterbury Cathedral, in Kent. It is one of the oldest structures in England. I'm particularly interested in visiting Skara Brae, first built in 3180 B.C.E. on the Orkneys, the Northern Isles of Scotland, because they are subterranean houses."

"We can't go to England without a stop in London," Darius said.

"Indeed," Gaston agreed. "Wouldn't a grand evening at the theatre with dinner to follow be wonderful?"

"Well, there we have it!" Michael said. "How about everyone jot down some ideas of where you'd like to go, and we'll ask Pádraig to help us arrange a tour. And now, for the big news – Ananta, the floor is yours!"

Ananta laughed. "I just heard this afternoon that we have an audience with His Holiness the Dalai Lama scheduled in six weeks!"

"Oh! Can I come too?" Hailey quickly walked in. "I'll be happy to pay my own way. I've been saving for a holiday!"

Everyone froze in silence.

"Oh, I'm so sorry for barging in, but I was walking by and I couldn't help earwigging. Isn't the Dalai Lama grand? I'd so love to meet him."

"Well," Sophia said. And then, as if her mouth filled with cotton, she turned to Michael.

"You see," Michael said, and he turned to Markos.

"Don't look at me."

"Hailey, dear," Gaston said, "I'm sorry, but-"

Michael jumped in. "Hailey, you see, receiving an invitation to visit the Dalai Lama is like obtaining an audience with the Pope. Our group here, we had to make special arrangements-"

"I just made a right bags of that, didn't I?" Hailey said.

"Uh – I'm not sure what that means," Michael said.

"Sorry, here I am inviting meself, acting the maggot. What's a simple girl like me thinking she was good enough to see the likes of him? Sometimes I'm just thick as a plank."

"No, Hailey," Sophia said, "it's not that-"

"Not to worry!" Hailey said, her face crimson. "I was just coddling ya! I must crack on now! So sorry!" She quickly exited, near tears.

Everyone exhaled. Michael let his head drop. "Oh...man."

"Well," Chayton said, "*that* was awkward."

"Awful is the word," Sophia said. "Poor Hailey. I feel terrible."

"I'm such an idiot," Michael said. "Nothing like making somebody feel worthless with one sentence." He looked at Markos. "Why didn't you stop me?"

"Me? I wasn't exactly the epitome of diplomacy myself."

Darius agreed. "Should we say something – maybe apologize?"

"No," Ananta said, "at least not right now. If we run after her, she will just be more embarrassed. I'll speak to her privately later and try to explain."

"We hurt her feelings!" Sophia angrily said.

"Honey, nobody meant to hurt-"

"But we did," Sophia said.

"She just blurted in here and invited herself," Markos said. "She caught everyone off guard."

"Ok, yes, she's pushy," Sophia said, trying not to cry. "She obviously wants attention. But did you see the look in her eyes? There's a very wounded, yet wonderful woman in there. If you'd get yourselves out of your own way and drop into your hearts, it would be evident to you. This 'Hailey Who Can't Get a Date' business is not right, and I'll tell you guys right now, you will *not* refer to her that way anymore. Making fun of someone like that, or anyone for that matter, is *not* what we're about, and don't you think that I won't be having this same conversation with Pádraig, either."

She walked out, and the other women followed, leaving a room full of aptly scolded twelve-year-old boys.

"She's right, you know," Markos said.

"Of course she is," Gaston agreed.

Michael shrugged. "That's what makes Sophia, Sophia."

"When I make a colossal blunder like this," Markos said, "I'm reminded of an ancient Greek saying."

They awaited their wise sage to enlighten them. Gaston finally bit. "And that is…?"

Markos looked everyone over, and then he finally spoke. "Shit…"

Overall, the party was a smashing hit. It ended with dancing after they pulled the dining table off to the side. Some danced outside under the stars. Most of the women who were not dancing with a partner danced together, leaving some of the partygoers to observe from the sidelines. Hailey seemed to rebound from her earlier gaff. She appeared to have fun, in large part thanks to Michael, Markos, Chayton, and Christofer, who made certain she had her pick of dance partners throughout the evening. Even Gaston and Darius took a turn, much to Hailey's delight. In fact, as the evening wore on and everyone from Apeiros extended their friendship, they came away quite charmed by Hailey's intelligence and sweet personality, despite her slightly irritating penchant for fussiness.

Magic was in the air as twilight set in with the approach of midnight.

Despite her sadness, Lestari put it aside and enjoyed herself just watching everyone have a good time. Wherever she wandered, Geoffrey just happened to stand to her left, while Pádraig stood to her right, both towering over her. She was unaware of their attentions, but the two were well aware of each other with a heightened competition already brewing between them.

Even though they were tired, Sophia and Michael made luscious love late that night, basking in the afterglow of the party's success. As Sophia fell asleep, wrapped in Michael's warm arms, she had a smile on her face as she realized she was in the actual physical location of where she once lived in another lifetime. Here they were, having the time of their lives, as she remembered Laurinda and her people doing the same in the circle of stones. She fell asleep easily, returning to the life of Laurinda in her dreams...

CHAPTER
Twenty-one

Midwinter approached, and it soon would be time to celebrate the rebirth of the sun. Lon, Magda, Laurinda, and Balogue left by horseback, following the fire signals lit along the eastbound route for the Tulach, Eire's largest mound, otherwise known as a cairn, located on the far eastern side of the island. After many passings of the sun, while riding in perpetual wind and rain around mountainous regions, over rivers, and traversing around loughs, they arrived with two suns to spare before the celebration began.

Lon and Magda made the pilgrimage to the Tulach before, for the Celebration of Light, but Laurinda and Balogue, never having been there, were in awe of the massive ancient mound, seeing for the first time the 39-foot-high sod-covered mound, covered in white marble, granite cobbles, soil, and grass. Bordering the outside edge were end-to-end kerbstones, some of them twice as long as Laurinda was tall, with elaborate astronomically aligned stone carvings.

Previously built by the ancient Neolithic people of Eire, the 32-foot mound was higher than the tallest tree on the island. The internal passage floor was purposely designed with an uphill slant, and the undulating passage walls, lined with massive hard stones of greywacke, stood vertically, up to 6 1/2 feet high. Above the entryway was the roof box. For three days only, at the height of midwinter, a sword of sunlight entered through the roof box at dawn and traveled along the 62-foot passage, reaching the triskele - a carving of three adjoined spirals at the back of the central chamber - 20 feet high and 17 feet deep - allowing sunlight to dramatically illuminate the entire room.

The chamber itself, constructed of the same massive greywacke stones, overlapped in a corbelled spiral, creating the 20-foot-high ceiling of the chamber's interior. 1000 years after the construction of the Tulach, contemporary inhabitants erected 35 tall standing stones in a wide circle outside the mound.

The entrance stone, and the kerbstone directly its opposite on the northwest outside edge of the mound, contained a concave vertical line that separated the perfectly carved spiral designs on either side of each stone. The carvings to the left were large spirals moving toward the centerline, while the carvings to the right moved in the opposite direction. The vertical line of both stones indicated the tomb's alignment with light of the sun on the shortest day of the year, soon to penetrate the tomb's long internal passageway. The mound itself was surrounded around its exterior with 97 kerbstones, many of them elaborately carved.

It was evident to Laurinda and Balogue that the people who designed the Tulach were highly intelligent builders. The perfectly planned structure was a monumental feat, which would have taken generations to build. The design of its interior was constructed and aligned with the sun's rising on the shortest day of the year. In Laurinda's day, the Tulach was 3000 years old, still standing strong as if newly constructed.

The four stayed in the nearby village with many other wayfarers who traveled from distances afar. Much celebration took place with food, dance, and song in preparation for the ceremony at dawn. Because not many would fit inside the Tulach for the ceremony, a lottery took place, and Lon, Magda, and Laurinda were chosen. Balogue and the others remained outside, encircling the Tulach with the other Druids.

For the ceremony, Magda was determined that Laurinda look like the priestess she was. Months before her initiation, she wove her a white linen léine, a traditional long tunic with dramatic sleeve openings that fell to the ground, its hem and sleeve edges embroidered in saffron colored spiral designs with a saffron woven belt tied at the waist. She also made her a heavy fur-lined white woolen brat, a floor-length hooded cloak to wear over the léine for warmth.

Just before dawn, hundreds of druids stood in a circle, surrounding the Tulach and waiting for the sunrise on the longest night and shortest day of the year. Balogue stood as close to the entrance as possible to greet Laurinda when she emerged from the Tulach after the ceremony ended. Lon, Magda, and Laurinda joined the others chosen by lottery, and entered the Tulach's passageway, flanked by dozens of standing stones, which opened to a larger room with a domed corbelled rock ceiling overhead. A few druids held flaming torches to light the way as they entered the passageway. All who entered took a gift of food as an offering of gratitude for the Sun's return to longer, warmer days. Once inside, everyone stood still as the torch-light snuffed out, waiting in the dark stillness for the sword of sunlight to penetrate the passageway.

The Celebration of Light not only honored the sun returning to longer days ahead, but it symbolized rebirth. The light of the sun god would soon penetrate the dark-ened womb of Mother Earth, once again making new life.

The sun began to rise on the horizon as it entered the roof box over the Tulach's entrance, beginning its golden stream along the passageway into the interior chamber. It was not long before a dagger of light penetrated directly where Laurinda stood, facing the sun. She was a stunning sight with the vivid green emeralds on the golden torque around her neck, and the gold crown on her head of long golden-red hair in waves down her back. Lon and Magda stood several feet away. Instead of facing the sunlight, they turned to see the radiance of their daughter's ivory skin and her gleaming eyes of sapphire blue. She stood in all her glory, raising her arms to the heavens in the sun's light for the renewal of Mother Earth and all her inhabitants.

When the sun reached her, Laurinda felt a palpable inner shift occur, as if the sunbeam awakened something in her that lay dormant until that moment. She felt a powerful invincibility, and yet humbled by the sun's power. Words came from her mouth that were not her own. It was as if this new part of her, as a Druid Priestess, was speaking. The young woman she had known herself to be was merely a witness to her new and vibrant image of sovereignty.

"Welcome, great Sun," Laurinda said with a confident voice of one much more mature than her years. "We bask in the glory of your radiance as we stand here in the womb of Mother Earth, the greatest goddess of all feminine power. Here, we gather to celebrate as you penetrate Mother Earth, filling her with your light. Honored are we to witness how Father Sun and Mother Earth have joined, now fulfilled with light and life, until the sun takes its full turn, yet again.

"Here in the wings, we leave gifts of gratitude from the bounty of Mother Earth, saved from the time of harvest, when the day is as long as the night. We sing your praises, we dance in your brilliance, and we sleep well in the night's darkness with dreams of life flourishing in your golden rays, here on Mother Earth. We all celebrate your light as the days lengthen, for we greet each day with gratitude in our hearts. We honor you with our high yield of crops in the coming year, and with the birth of all new babes on this land, extending to the health and well-being of our children who will grow up to dance and sing for you in return for your gift of light and warmth. Great Sun, we thank you for your many blessings. We are so very grateful, knowing that in your light, each of us is also reborn as we are brought from out of the darkness to begin life anew, yet again."

Laurinda stepped aside, allowing the sun's light to reach the triskele. Magda beamed with pride. Not only did her daughter look like a priestess, but she acted as if she was one. Lon could not have been more proud. Laurinda would lead their people with the intelligence of insight, and with the humility of one already so very wise. She was like the sun, filled with brilliant radiance and the grace of knowing. His heart was full. Soon he would step down from his role as Archdruid with hope that Laurinda would take his place. Never would there be a doubt in his mind that he chose well to pass along his legacy to his daughter.

It was not long before the sun left the Tulach's passageway, as the Druids inside filed outside to join with the others who stood in a circle outside the mound. Balogue waited for Laurinda to come out of the entrance, and when she did, he noticed a subtle change in her. She was always beautiful, but what he witnessed now was a young woman of a sovereign radiance. She entered the mound as a girl, and she emerged a woman.

That night, everyone celebrated, feasting, singing, and dancing to the drums during the full moon. Meade and wine flowed ceaselessly, and the drums' beat awakened something in Laurinda that had been growing over time, especially when she was with Balogue.

Lon was in counsel with the other Archdruids. It was the only time of the year when the Druids gathered in such a large conference. Magda visited with many of the women she only saw when they returned to the Tulach.

Before their journey began, Balogue spoke with Lon and Magda about his intention to join with Laurinda. They were thrilled, and come spring, they would celebrate their union, providing Laurinda was in agreement with Balogue's offer.

"Would you care to get away from the crowd and go for a walk in the moon's light?" Balogue asked.

"Yes, thank you," Laurinda said. "I am weary of all the noise. It has been a day filled with celebration. I welcome the stillness."

It was a cold night. Balogue held out her brat, and wrapped it around her shoulders, pulling the hood over her head to keep her warm. They did not have to walk far from the village to find a rock outcropping that reflected the moonlight. There, they sat close to each other.

"Laurinda, I have something to ask of you. Since we were children, you have been my bright light, my radiant star. I cannot imagine living out my days without you by my side. Laurinda, will you spend the rest of your days and nights with me as my companion?"

"Oh, Balogue, no one can compare with you. Since we were small, you have been my true love. There is no doubt in my mind. Yes, I will happily join with you."

They kissed passionately, suddenly unaware of the cold. He removed a gold cuff bracelet, clasped it around her wrist, and tightened it to fit. "This belonged to my mother. My father gave it to her the night they decided to wed. Now it is yours."

"It is beautiful, Balogue. I will care for it until I pass it on to our son to give to his woman." Again, they kissed.

"When spring comes, we will marry, and the entire village will come to celebrate with us," Balogue said.

"That is perfect! I now have something else exciting to plan for."

Balogue then took her by the hand to the place where he lodged. Most everyone was singing, dancing, and drinking. He hoped they would be by themselves, and fortunately for them, they were. Lon and Magda saw them heading in that direction. They looked at each other and smiled.

For the first time, Laurinda freely gave of her body to Balogue. She was now of age, and the passion between them had been rising for countless cycles of the full moon. Neither of them wanted to wait any longer. They joined in rapturous union, intertwined in passionate lovemaking throughout the rest of the night. Finally, they lay blissfully sleeping in each other's arms until awakened at dawn by the stirring of others in the lodge.

After bathing, eating their morning meal, and bidding goodbye to many they had befriended, they packed their horses for the trek back to western Eire. The celebration was a time the four would never forget...

CHAPTER
Twenty-two

The next morning, Sophia sat next to Shoshana at the breakfast table. "How are the wedding plans going?"

"I don't know where to begin. I met with the Ello Sisters, who are planning a wonderful feast for all of us, but I just haven't done much else."

"Do you have a dress?"

"Yes, but it's not a typical wedding dress. I don't care for formal gowns, but I'm not sure that what I have is what I want to wear."

"Do you want some help?"

"Yes, in fact, I'd love it if someone would just surprise me with the entire wedding, and I would just show up. I do want it to be memorable for Christofer and me, but I spend my days digging in dirt. It's not my forte to plan all these wedding details."

"If you are serious, we could do that. You set the date and time, and just show up and we'll do all the rest."

"I was kidding, but the idea appeals to me. Wouldn't that be asking too much of all of you?"

Michael laughed as he walked past with his coffee mug. "You're talking to the Rembrandt of wedding planners."

"We would be helping you out anyway," Sophia said. "We have the place and the food already, and I'll order flowers from the shop in town, plus there are musicians all over the area. The group that played for the party last night would work well. We just want some good dancing music for everyone to have a good time. Oh, and we'd like to invite Lily and Colin, Pádraig, Geoffrey, and Hailey, too."

"Wonderful," Shoshana said. "I think Markos should marry us. He and Christofer have been close friends for years, and he's been a good friend to me, too."

"He's a perfect choice! Let's decide the date and time right now."

"How about a week from today?"

"Woah….kay," Sophia giggled. "A little short notice, but we can pull it off. We don't have any plans that day or the next. In fact, Pádraig's tour through Ireland will begin two days later. You could either join the group for the tour, or plan a honeymoon by yourselves."

"We definitely want to tour Ireland with the group. We have plans in a few months to go to Bora Bora, with those white sand beaches and emerald ocean waters. It is supposed to be one of the most romantic islands in the world. I want to go somewhere where I won't be tempted to spend my time with the Ancients, and Christofer can get away for a week from all of his business dealings."

"Okay then, that's settled. Why don't we hop in the car right now and go to a great dress shop in Liscannor. It's not far from here."

"Ooo, shopping! Lead the way!"

They grabbed their dishes and walked into the kitchen just as Christofer came in. Shoshana gave him a quick kiss, and followed Sophia out the door. He poured himself a cup of coffee and looked over at Michael, who busily perused his archaeological plans for the dig.

"Where are those two headed?"

Michael shook his head without looking up. "You don't want to know…"

That evening, Sophia asked Michael to join her on a walk along the Cliffs of Moher. During midsummer in Ireland, twilight occurred close to 11 p.m., so a two-hour stroll at 8 p.m. gave them plenty of time to enjoy the sunset.

"Last night in my dreams, I again returned to the life of Laurinda," Sophia said.

"What was your experience this time?"

"It's not only *what* I experienced, but *where*, and that's what I want to talk to you about. But please bear with me, because the gist of what I have to say won't make any sense until I'm finished with my long account of the details. I'm almost certain that the Neolithic people of pre-ancient Ireland were essentially more like humanity today at its best than we can imagine, especially in relation to indigenous people, who connect to nature while practicing their ancient rituals and traditions. So if you will - there's a method to my madness."

"I'm intrigued. Tell me more."

"Laurinda was initiated as a Druid High Priestess at the Tulach, at what we now know as Newgrange."

"Was it at the Winter Solstice, where the sunlight penetrates the chamber?"

"Yes, and I have a theory that adds to the common beliefs that Newgrange was a passage burial tomb, but I don't think that's what it originally was intended to be, at least not entirely."

"There *were* some human remains found there."

"Yes, there were many animal bones, and a few that were human, but *only* a few, unlike other passage burial tombs of history. Perhaps it was used for that purpose at one time, but I think the original purpose may have been far greater than a burial tomb."

"So what are your thoughts?"

"First, we must understand the mound was constructed by Neolithic people 5200 years ago, around 3200 B.C.E., 600 years before the pyramids of Giza were built, and 1000 years before Stonehenge. It is considered to be one of the oldest intact buildings in existence.

"Built on a ridge, the entrance faces southeast, so the sun enters the mound at dawn on the shortest day of the year, known to us as the Winter Solstice. The 62-foot undulating passageway slants slightly uphill. It is not a straight pathway, which was engineered purposely that way. I will explain why in a moment."

"Other than when we toured through it last year, I know very little about Newgrange, or the particulars about the Neolithic people that built it," Michael said.

"I'm glad that you find it interesting. I wouldn't want to bore you with all my thoughts."

"I *am* an archeologist, you know."

"Yes, but some people who are experts in their field, and you are literally such a man - digging about - those people don't appreciate a lay person's interference."

"You're not really interfering; you're teaching me your theory about the country we are now living in, being that you may well have insights into Newgrange beyond those in the know. So, perhaps you are the expert here. How do you like them apples, my sweet?"

"Thanks, I'll take that! And let me say that some may have a similar theory, but this is what I've gathered from the life of Laurinda, so far. So, let's get back to the structure. The roof box, built above the doorway, was the most important feature of the mound. Because the mound was built on a ridge, the roof box allowed the sunlight to enter at the level of the horizon at the breaking of dawn. Within minutes, the penetrating sun completely lit up the inner chamber. The sunlight that enters the doorway below the roof box does not reach that far into the chamber, because of the upslope of the floor. The location of the roof box is necessary for the sun to enter at the level of the horizon, to reach the back stone of the chamber. The building could only be designed and engineered by people that were clearly intelligent, sophisticated, and enigmatic."

"That's right," Michael said. "So many tend to think that Neolithic, or those of the New Stone Age, were people who wore deerskins, and clubbed their women in the head and dragged them by their hair. I don't remember exactly where, but archeologists found a human skull of the late Neolithic period somewhere near Stonehenge, where it was evidenced that someone had performed a successful brain surgery on that person – with stone tools, by the way, because metal tools had not yet been invented. A carefully chiseled triangle shape was wedged from the skull, and the interesting thing is, they could tell by examining the skull that the person survived. Archeologists think that a shaman may have helped by putting the patient into a trance before the surgery. They certainly were intelligent people."

"Who'd have thought they could do brain surgery, or know it was needed?" Sophia said. "But that brings one of my theories to point, which I will get to soon. It's clear they considered all the parameters of the finished building, long before they began construction. It may have taken them years to create such a complicated design. They had to engineer the mound on a hillside, with its passage, the doorway, the roof box, and the chamber with all the massive standing stones, or 'orthostats', and the kerbstones that created the structure, long before construction began.

"One of the reasons for the building was to create a connection to the heavens, to welcome in the shortest day of the year, what we know as the Winter Solstice. But, perhaps unknowingly, they also created a precise clock, where the light of the sun entered the building exactly as the sun rose above the horizon. In the time that the sunlight entered the chamber, to when the sunlight left, the people of that day could have then measured the speed of the sun, therefore being able to estimate and schedule other important events throughout the year. The precision of Newgrange was far more sophisticated than the Greeks' technology of the sundial at that time.

"The estimated weight of the mound is 200,000 tons, built mostly of greywacke, which is a type of sandstone, along with burnt soil, sea sand, white marble, and smaller rounded cobbles, six to nine inches in diameter. The passageway and inner chamber is built in a basic cruciform style, entering along the long passageway that leads to the inner chamber. The extensions at the sides each hold a stone basin that sits on the chamber floor. There also was a basin that sat below the back stone, now broken into pieces.

"Okay, so I'm going to explain in a number of ways what I think was the reasoning of the Neolithic people, their beliefs, and the mythology which later developed. They worshipped everything - the earth, the sky, the moon, the sun, the stars, and all life forms - human, animal, and plant life. They revered the seasons and therefore venerated the elements that made up the seasons - that of earth, water, fire, air, and spirit.

"First of all, Mother Earth is the greatest form of feminine presence among the elements, secondary is water.

Earth is cold. She symbolizes stability and stillness, groundedness, the material realm, potentiality and transformation, and most of all fertility. Earth is all about birth and death, where that which dies decomposes. The old gives way to new beginnings and becomes life yet again.

"Water is the element of emotion, wisdom, and the unconscious. Like earth, water is cold, and it is also moist. Water interacts with all the physical senses. It is the most powerful of all the earthly elements, always flowing and finding a way to move around or through any obstacle. Water is the life force of the planet, for over 70 percent of Earth is made of water, as it is with the human body. The tool of water is the cup, chalice, or cauldron.

"Fire is the greatest form of masculine presence, followed by air, both of which are warm and dry. Fire represents fullness, strength, activity, blood, and life force. Fire is purifying and protective. It consumes impurities and drives back the darkness. It is the most rarified and spiritual of the elements, because it lacks physical existence, and it has transformative power when it encounters other physical material. Some consider the implement of fire to be the sword or dagger.

"Air, also masculine, represents new beginnings, youth, increase, and creativity. Like fire it is warm, and it is also dry. It is the element of intelligence, creativity, and inventiveness. Air has to do with things that are growing warmer and brighter, as plants and animals that give birth to new generations. Its instrument is the wand, and sometimes the sword or dagger.

"The last element is Spirit, ether, or quintessence, which is Latin for fifth element. Spirals represent Spirit, as do spoked wheels. Spirit is the bridge between the physical and the spiritual realm - between body and soul. As above, so below, and within is the direction of Spirit, which is everywhere and eternal.

"Newgrange is made of all things of Earth - rock, soil, and sand, covered with grass. It is cold and represents the feminine - the potentiality of new growth, that of fertility. The sun, which is warm, represents strength, and the activity of the life force. It also drives back the darkness.

"So, it appears to me that the mound was constructed to represent Earth as feminine power of fertility, like that of a woman in full pregnancy. The mound's passageway is like the vagina. The extensions on either side of the chamber with its basins might just represent ovaries, with the chamber itself being the womb - all being cruciform in style - representative of the feminine power of life-giving birth. The basins may have been used for offerings to Mother Earth and Father Sun, representative of the ovaries offering of its eggs for life. The stone basin, which is now broken and located below the back stone, may have been representative of the culmination the masculine sun filling the feminine earth with its fullness, thus creating new life. And get this - Brú, of the Brú na Bóinne complex, of which Newgrange is the greatest of all the mounds, means 'womb.'"

Michael stopped walking. He curiously looked at Sophia. "That just gave me a chill."

"I know! Isn't it amazing!" Sophia said. "So, we have the earth, the most feminine of elements, penetrated by sunlight, the most masculine element of fire, on the shortest day of the year. The mound was brilliantly engineered by the upward slope of the passageway floor, along with the passageway's undulating walls of stone, so that the sunlight entering the roof box deeply penetrates the passageway like a narrow sword of light, first being only one and one-half inches wide. Within eight minutes, the light beam broadens to nearly sixteen inches wide, reaching the deep carving of the triskelion on the back stone of the chamber, at least that is what occurred when the mound was constructed. Today, the earth has shifted enough that the sun does not reach the triskelion. I have other thoughts about what the triskelion may have symbolized to the Neolithic people."

"I'm almost afraid to ask."

"We know that the human body and sexual act were not only sensual to the Druids, but were considered sacred. Every aspect of the Druid life reflected the wholeness of their humanity in balance with Mother Earth and all of nature - a blending of the sacred and divine. So, if this was true for people that lived here much later, why would it not be true for the Neolithic people, especially being that Newgrange and other nearby mounds at the time appeared to represent a woman in pregnancy?"

"I get what you're saying, but what does that have to do with the triskelion?"

"It may have represented what we call the G-spot," Sophia said with a smile and a spark in her eye. "When the sun hit the triskelion, it may have represented Mother Earth feeling her best self, shall we say, so that new life would be abundant."

Michael raised one eyebrow and blinked five times. "I'm getting a little hot."

Sophia laughed. "We might have to get a room, and soon!"

"Your theory has all the symbolism of a good Fellini movie."

"So, anyway," Sophia continued, shaking Michael back to reality, "the sun spills its seed of light, filling the chamber with its heat, joining the masculine and feminine, where the sun's warmth heats earth's cold, resulting in the promise of new beginnings, longer days of sunlight, and new life unfolding yet again. The sun's light then reduces back to a narrow beam before disappearing entirely after seventeen minutes have passed. This light effect happens for three days only during the time of Winter Solstice.

"But here's another thought about when the sunlight met the triskelion - the element of fire joining with the triple spiral symbol, is believed to have a couple of meanings. First, the triple spiral represents the three material domains of earth, air, and water. So fire, as sunlight, merges all four earthly elements together. Another belief of the symbology of the spiral is that it represents Spirit. In this case, the triskelion could mean something like Spirit, Soul, and Body – Spirit is the upper spiral, Soul is the middle, and Body is the lower spiral – all are connected, but I have yet another thought about the symbol.

"The upper spiral of the triskelion could represent the physical world, that of life as we know it. Secondly, the middle spiral could represent the ethereal world - that of Spirit, or Síoraí, and the third, lower spiral is the underworld - that of the ancestors, those now gone who precede us with wisdom. This blending of the three realms has been a common belief among indigenous peoples for millennia.

"Remember when Pádraig told the story of the Tuatha Dé Danaan at dinner the other night? Could it be that the Tuatha Dé Danann came out of the symbols carved into the stones, with the Milesians living above ground, and the Danann below, becoming the mystical beings of Ireland? The middle realm is the spiritual realm that is the glue holding all three realms together - what we call the soul.

"Now, we get to the Neolithic carvings on the stones, of which there are circles, spirals, arcs, chevrons, lozenges, radials, triangles, and triskeles, some of which we have no idea of some of their symbolic meanings. However, some were astronomically aligned.

"From the carvings of what are called lozenges we can see the 'X' in-between each one. Perhaps they represented sparks. Could it be the carving on the lintel over the roof box represented Lugh's Spear, 'from which sparks as large as eggs flew,' and the eggs are what archeologists call lozenges? Certainly, it's possible that the sun's light later became the mythology of 'the Sword of Light' being 'a glowing white torch that no one ever escaped once drawn against them.' That could be the promise of longer days of sunlight, extending into life-giving springtime. It's a different take on the story, but it could be interpreted that way.

"Then we have the three basins inside the chamber, specifically the one that is now broken at the base of the back stone beneath the triskelion. Originally, it may have been Dagda's Cauldron, having the power to bring the dead back to life, and 'that none would go from it unsatisfied,' representing new life, plenty, and bounty. That could have another connotation, as well. If the sun and earth join, creating new life, evidenced in the bounty of springtime crops, and the birth of children and animals, isn't that exactly what going from unsatisfied means? We know that the stone basin at Knowth, also in Brú na Bóinne complex, is believed to be Dagda's Cauldron. It too is at the head of the passage inside the inner chamber."

"Okay, all this makes sense," Michael said. "The mythology of the Tuatha Dé Danann didn't begin in its origins until 1300 years after the mounds were built. So the Sword of Light, Lugh's Spear, and Dagda's Cauldron wouldn't have been a part of the belief system of the late Neolithic people when they built the mound, but that part of Irish mythology developed later."

"Yes, exactly! It's possible that the people of Ireland, or whatever they called it back in the day, began the mythology of Tuatha Dé Danann, developing a part of their story from the carvings of the mounds and the sword of sunlight, because they believed that Danann were then the Sidhe, the spirit people that lived beneath the mounds. According to what Pádraig said, the stories of Dagda included the Brugh, known as his mansion, which is what we now know as Newgrange."

"It fits, doesn't it?" Michael said.

"I think so," Sophia said, continuing with her theory. "It is estimated that the mound took 30 years to build, about three generations of 600 people, which is what archeologists and scholars think was the population of the Boyne Valley at the time. It took 550 stone slabs to build the mound, all of them unquarried, meaning they had to find the stones lying around in the surrounding countryside, then transport them, most likely, on rolling logs for miles. They measured each one for the correct placement according to their master plan. The 43 orthostats, set vertically, that made up the passage were smaller, close to the mound's entrance, and they gradually increased in size, up to six and one-half feet tall toward the interior chamber. The kerbstones, placed around the outside of the mound, were from five and one-half feet long to nearly fifteen feet long, making up the nearly round mound's widest diameter at 280 feet.

"Many of the stones used in the interior, along with the kerbstones, were carved in advance with intricate designs before their placement, meaning some designs were carved on the base of the stone, as well as the side that faced the mound. A few were carved once they were in place, two of which are K1, the entrance stone, and K52, at the opposite side of the mound. Both were intricately carved with the use of sharp stones and antlers, but the most accurate carving in both stones is the vertical line carved into both."

"Why is that so interesting?" Michael asked.

"Because the vertical lines of both stones that are diametrically opposed across the mound align perfectly with the sun's light at Winter Solstice. It's my thought that those stones had to be placed before the mound was built, in order to carve the vertical lines so precisely. Every kerbstone was placed end-to-end, most of them positioned in a trough dug in the ground to fit the bottom of the stone. Alternatively, they anchored the kerbstone on top of the ground with rocks, so that the top ridge of all the kerbstones formed a clear line that paralleled the natural curve of the ridge that the mound was built on."

"I still don't follow why was it so important that the top edge of the kerbstones was parallel to the ground?" Michael asked.

"So, here's the part that I have not found in any of my research, yet. My theory is based on the belief systems of people around the world at that time. I think the kerbstones were created to represent an ouroboros."

"You think that the kerbstones surrounding Newgrange were meant to represent a snake? There are no snakes in Ireland. It's too cold."

"It's symbolic. There were no dragons anywhere on earth either, but many societies had dragon tales in their stories. Just hear me out."

"Alright, but your theory may be challenged by Saint Patrick."

"The story of Saint Patrick chasing the snakes out of Ireland is another story altogether, not believed to be in reference to actual living snakes. His chasing snakes out of Ireland represented the religious conversion of pagans 'old ways' to that of Catholicism in the early decades around 430 A.D.

"You know, more than I, that common belief systems across the globe created similarities in construction of buildings and ways of living, even though those societies were separated by oceans and masses of land, being an energetic shift in consciousness. The mound culture was just one example of this, having existed for 5000 years."

"Like the hundredth monkey theory," Michael said. "Once the hundredth monkey learned to wash the sand off its fruit before eating it, monkeys on islands across the sea, at the same time, adopted the same habits."

"Exactly."

"The same thing happened with cultural change for millennia, long before we could fly across the world by plane, or communicate via technology. Back to your point, however - why would it be so important that the kerb-stones look like a continual, smooth band around the mound?"

"If their idea of the kerbstones was only to support the mound, they would have simply been placed around the mound with no need for a clean, straight line on the top edge of the stones. In every major society during that time in history, the snake or serpent represented the creative life force, fertility, healing, rebirth and immortality. In Greece, snakes were worshipped as guardians of the Great Goddess's mysteries of birth and regeneration. In some parts of the world, snakes symbolized the umbilical cord, joining humanity to Mother Earth. You and I certainly can't forget the symbology of the Pythia – the oracle at Delphi, can we? Wouldn't it make sense that the Neolithic people would also symbolize the protective nature of the snake to guard and protect their well-engineered mound that represented one of their most revered gods, Mother Earth, who it appeared was clearly with child?"

"So why ouroboros?"

"Ouroboros is a snake swallowing its tail," Sophia said, "representing wholeness or infinity. Ouroboros also is the result of two opposing halves joining together, making a united whole. The kerbstones were divided in half, indicated by the carvings of vertical lines on K1 and K52."

"But how can you identify the stones as a snake swallowing its tail?"

"I know it's a stretch, but if you look at K52, at the left side of the kerbstone, it could be depicted as the head of a snake, because the upper portion is separated from the lower, appearing as the snake's mouth. There's even an indentation at the far left of the stone that could represent a nostril, and another indentation that could be the eye. The lower designs on the left side of the stone might just represent the scales of a snake. When we get home, I'll show you a photo.

"In some societies, ouroboros was inspired by the Milky Way, as a serpent of light residing in the heavens. It is a symbol of eternity and continual renewal of life, meaning All is one, One is All. Ouroboros is a totality of existence - the cyclic nature of the cosmos. These people were connected to the heavens' celestial patterns and cycles, as well as to Mother Earth. This building is evidence of that. Even some of the carving on the kerbstones looks like that of snakeskin - with diamond shapes, what they are now calling lozenges, and zigzags."

"So many of the carvings were spirals," Michael said.

"Spirals sometimes represent Spirit. They could also represent the cycles of the sun, moon, and stars, or the cycles of the seasons - and some believe earth, sea, and sky, but another thought is that the triskelion, being three spirals made of one line, could very well be another form of an ouroboros - the spiral of never-ending life itself. So, what's the bigger picture here? It's the trinity, which is Spirit, Soul, and Body. This, in my opinion, is what the triskelion symbolizes.

"Spirit, God, Higher Self – whatever people throughout history have called their divinity - is the Infinite Intelligence where we co-create and receive our inspiration and intuitive hits that seemingly come out of the blue. Soul is the truth of nature – the essence of humanity, animal, plant, and mineral – the invisible and eternal heart of all things in the universe. Body is the manifestation of Spirit as it moves through the Soul, coming into form. You certainly know this. In the physical realm, the triangle - a three-sided geometric form - is the strongest physical form in architecture, which takes us back to ancient Egyptians and the pyramids that still stand today. So, if this triangular form is so in the physicality of humankind, it is also exemplified as the trinity in the spiritual realm.

"It's my belief, as it is in many religions and indigenous belief systems today, that the trinity represents the strongest way we as humans can be our most powerful selves. Simply, as above, so below. What is Divine, becomes our eventual reality. When we combine spirit, soul, and body, it is the strongest way we in our humanity become our greatest selves. It is our natural way of being on behalf of our world for the greater good. And more so, these three powers, if you will, are ever moving, always regenerating – making new life while letting go of what is no longer in service to us. This, I believe, is what the Neolithic people intended when they built what we know as Newgrange, which still stands today. It's the triskele – the ouroboros – it's eternal and infinite in its regenerative power of life. It shows us the intelligence of these people – the Infinite Intelligence of their gods - is also a lesson of what our Source is today. If we only pay attention to the ancients, as White Buffalo taught us about the ancestors, and about his reverence to Great Spirit, we can learn from history about who we are and how to live in harmony with nature – with life itself."

"You certainly put a lot of thought into your theories."

"So much of it has come from my dreams of Laurinda and her time there. Plus, I've read a lot of others' thoughts on the subject."

"It's the ouroboros that's the difference. I think you ought to present your findings to academia at the university. I have many connections, now that I'll be heading up the dig," Michael said.

"That's a thought, but they'd probably think I'm crazy."

"Any theory comes across with much speculation, but that's what archeology is all about. So much of what we uncover comes with so many unanswered questions. Oftentimes, answers come from the guesswork of theorists. I think your thoughts on this are brilliant!"

"Well, you know that my spiritual symbol is a spiral, which caught my interest even more when I saw the triskelion, leading me to the theory of the ouroboros. The night that White Buffalo died, I spent time with him before the sun came up. His spirit spoke to me, leaving me with wisdom that I will never forget, which I think is what the triskelion symbolizes in its depths. 'We leave the world of the physical to join with the spiritual eternality that returns us back to the essence of our soul's journey, in the constant spiral of our greater becoming...'"

CHAPTER
Twenty-four

The full turning of several suns had passed. Laurinda and Balogue, now in their prime, were parents of two children - the eldest, a green-eyed, red-haired boy named Lakaar who was four suns old, and the youngest, Saurina, a tiny, dark-eyed, red-headed girl, now three.

It was the time when days were long and warmth returned to the island. Balogue, along with the most vital men of the village, had gone to sea hoping to provide a large catch that would feed the community through the upcoming seasons of shortened days of sunlight. However, after a few passings of the full moon, the men had not yet returned.

Never before had Laurinda made a personal request of the gods, for her prayers were always for her people's highest good and not for herself, but her heart was breaking at the thought of losing Balogue. With every bit of her power as the Druid Priestess, Laurinda decided to go to the circle of stones to commune with the gods. But first, she prepared to present herself well to the gods by wearing her golden crown and torque set with emeralds. She donned her finest white linen léine, having worn it only once before on the dawning of the Celebration of Light at the Tulach. She wore her bracelet of gold, and the ruby ring, both gifted to her by Balogue.

Standing in the circle of the stones, Laurinda held her head high, reaching for the heavens. "To all the gods, I beseech you. Please make known to me of Balogue's fate. My heart is hushed, for I am lost without him, and so I call on your great wisdom. If I am to be without him, let me know now, so I may be strong for our children and for the other families. If Balogue has gone on to the Otherworld, I ask that I know now, otherwise I will be patient and wait." Her voice cracked, and she was on the verge of breaking down into tears.

Laurinda took a deep breath and closed her eyes. She paused in expectant stillness, waiting for an answer, a sign - anything. She soon heard a rustling in the nearby forest, and she opened her eyes. Just outside the circle stood a mighty stag with a doe and their two fawns. Laurinda smiled, ever grateful to see such beauty in nature. Rarely did she see them together as a family. The stag suddenly ran away, deep into the forest. Laurinda could barely see the buck's magnificence in the shadows, leaving the doe alone with her two fawns.

Laurinda remained perfectly still and waited, but the stag did not return. The doe and her fawns approached her with caution, slowly stepping inside the stone circle. They stood motionless, looking deeply into each other's eyes. Laurinda leaned over and touched her forehead to that of the doe's, and she gently placed her hand on the neck of the beautiful animal. She then released the tears she had been holding back, finally admitting to herself that Balogue would not return. The doe remained still as her fawns stood near their mother.

Stepping back from the doe, she said, "Thank you, beautiful being. I will never forget you. Now go quickly from here. Take your fawns far away from all the people, so your babies may grow to be strong and mighty beings." At that, the doe and her fawns swiftly turned away from the circle of stones and ran into the forest. Laurinda sadly had her answer. Balogue was not to return. She finally conceded that the sea most likely claimed the life of her great love, leaving her to raise Lakaar and Saurina by herself.

She turned away from the stone circle and left the forest, running briskly like the wind to the top of the hill. At the edge of the cliff, she climbed the tower of the abandoned fort, and for a few minutes, she looked out over the sea, her vision blurred again by tears. Her long, golden-red hair blew wildly in the wind as she bid farewell to Balogue. She removed her gold ring, set with the ruby, a gift from Balogue when they married.

When she wore the ring, it enabled her connection with the gods, helping her to sense the best course of action to take. She kissed the ring and raised it toward the heavens. "To the gods of the sea and sky, I ask that you find my love and bring him safely home."

As the sun began to set, its golden rays turned the far cliffs to varied shades of red, as memories of her time with Balogue flooded her mind. "It appears that you are now gone, my love, but I remain hopeful that you will come back to me," Laurinda said aloud. "I know that the gods have not completed their work with you, nor have I. Never will I forget how we played together as children. The woods were not thick enough for me to hide from you when we ran until our feet became as green as the grass. When we splashed about in the sea, we did not even feel the cold, because we were caught in the warmth of each other's joy.

"In our youth, not so long ago, we saw each other in a different way. No longer were we children. I finally recognized your heart - your gifts - the wonder of you. We knew there was no other, and as our bodies joined, we transcended into worlds beyond our knowing.

"I feel empty without the warmth of your body next to mine. I miss your wisdom, your laughter, and I can no longer gaze into your eyes that change from blue to green when you are filled with passion. Our children need their father, for you taught them strength of character and hope for better days. Already, they are good people, and you would be proud to know how they have grown, but the emptiness in our hearts and our home will never be the same without you.

"I have known you before, my love, and I will know you again. If you are now gone from my life, I declare today that you and I will again meet to live out our days together in another time and another place. And so, I send you my most profound love that extends far beyond what Mother Earth leaves for us to know. I will never give up hope that you will return safely.

"At the base of the tallest standing stone of the stone circle, I will now bury this ring in the scallop shell we found together on the sea's edge. There, it will remain until you return to me, for my connection with the gods will not be complete until you do..."

Michael and Sophia began their day at dawn. As they walked to the area where Laurinda and the people of her village once lived, Sophia wanted to chat with Michael about something on her mind.

"I know that Hailey is a joke to many people of this area, but it's my sense there is deep pain beneath her colorful façade."

"I have to say, I know very few people with less self esteem than her," Michael said.

"Well, there is no one who doesn't suffer from self esteem issues at one time or another. I certainly struggle with it at times. You do. We all do. With some of us it is obvious, as it is with Hailey. Others keep it hidden with our sense of humor or with a carefully constructed façade of self-importance. I think we need to have more compassion for her, and some empathy as well."

"I can't disagree with you. I must admit, there's so much there to like about her," Michael said. "She's very smart, she runs a successful bed and breakfast, and when she's not running herself down, she can be genuinely sweet and charming."

"I offered to have her over for tea."

"Make sure it's hot enough, and the cup isn't cracked, and the napkins are folded right, and the spoons are polished…"

Sophia whacked him on the arm. "I *am* going to make sure Lou Ella isn't around."

"Good idea. Lou was kidding around the other night, but if Hailey had pushed a few more buttons, that could have gotten ugly."

"Well, I still feel bad about embarrassing her when she invited herself to go with us to India."

"I do, too. That spun out of control fast."

"There's a lot more to Hailey than we know, buried beneath all the makeup and obvious attention calling to herself. I'd like to give her a chance and hear her out. She's coming over tomorrow afternoon, when you and Pádraig take the group to Lily and Colin's pub for lunch."

"I didn't know I was doing that."

"Now you do," Sophia said with a grin.

"Yes, I knew that." Michael rolled his eyes. "But hey, havin' a few pints of the black stuff with Lily and Colin sounds like a craic. Hopefully, cousin Geoffrey will pop in for a spot."

"Your Irish brogue is getting better. So, getting back to why we're here today, I know the many treasures we found in the stone box belong to Ireland. Besides, what would I do with a torque and a couple of crowns anyway?"

"Some might put them on e-Bay, under priceless ancient Druid do-dads?"

"On the other hand, the gold bracelet, rings, gemstones, and pearls - well, a woman can always use more jewelry."

"I know what you're getting at," Michael said.

"Now, here's the thing - last night I went back into the life of Laurinda again. Her husband, Balogue, was lost at sea, so she buried a ruby ring that he gave her for their wedding at the circle of stones, never to be unearthed until he returned to her."

"Do you remember where?"

"Yes, at the base of the tallest standing stone."

"Since it's just the two of us today, let's begin our dig there. If we find the ring, I see no reason that you shouldn't keep it, since you were Laurinda at one time."

"You're definitely a smart man."

"Yes, I know. But what if Balogue shows up? Will you leave me and run off with him?"

"How do you know you *aren't* him, smart guy?"

Michael blinked five times. "I know I would never hear the end of it if you don't look for it. Besides, you're the reason we found this ancient community in the first place. So, let's get digging and see what we can find."

They went into the forest, where some of the stones still stood. At the base of the largest standing stone, they carefully began to dig in two thousand years of soil and sediment. Sophia knew just where to find what they were looking for. After several hours, they unearthed a small pot with a lid.

"Oh, my, look at this," Sophia said.

"Careful," Michael said as he gently lifted the pot and brushed the dirt away. "Honey, this is the real deal."

She cautiously lifted the lid, their hearts racing in wonderment. Enclosed was the scallop shell holding the ruby ring in perfect condition.

Sophia sat back for a brief moment, feeling a sense of sadness wash over her.

"What is wrong, my sweet? I thought you'd be overjoyed if we found the ring."

"The ring buried here means that Balogue may have never returned home from the sea. It's rather heartbreaking, really."

Sophia's amethyst began its familiar glow, as the area around them lit up in the brightest golden-white light, indicating that the ruby ring was yet another talisman.

"I love it when that happens!" Michael said.

"It never gets old, does it?" Sophia said, her mood lifted yet again.

Michael put his loupe up to his eye and examined the stone closely. "This is a large flawless oval cabochon ruby set horizontally in the ring. It's held with a bezel, etched in the same runes as all of the other talismans. With the rough lifestyle these people led, I would expect the gold to be pretty banged up. This gold must be the same metal as the golden bowl and chalice, because it is flawless - no scratches, and no wear on the piece. Here, take a look."

When she did, she instantly shifted to what she thought was Akrotiri, long before the time of Roxana, when there was no obvious volcanic activity.

Michael took the ring and placed it on Sophia's right middle finger. It fit perfectly, as if it was specifically made for her. Sophia immediately felt a palpable energy course through her body as she looked into the ruby. Everything around and within her became the same golden light as when she had her near-death experience. Again, she was aware that she knew everything there was to know, while feeling radiant and liberated of the world's concerns.

Michael knew that look in Sophia's eyes all too well. As her protector, he interrupted her vision, and he wrapped his arms around her and held her tight.

She pulled away from his arms. "Wow! That was powerful! Each talisman works even more potently than the one before it. I wonder what will happen when I wear this ring, using all the other talismans combined."

"I'm not sure if it's the talisman, or if it's you that is more powerful. I think it could be both, but I'm concerned. As you find more of these pieces, they take you to dimensions and times that I'm not sure I'll be able to retrieve you. I know I can't stop you from using them all together. So, if I might suggest that when you do, everyone should be with you to combine our protective energies for your sake."

"That's a good idea. Let's plan to do that before we go to England and Scotland."

"Or... before we go to Dharamsala?"

"That's an even better idea! As my dear German friend, Ingrid, used to say, 'You're so gute and schmart!' I have an idea. Shoshana and I found a great pub in Liscannor when we went to buy her wedding dress. Why don't we go back to the house and get cleaned up, then drive down there to celebrate the beginning of the dig?"

It was mid afternoon, and no one was in Joseph McHugh's Pub except a man who appeared to be the owner. He wore a windbreaker, as if he was about to close the place down.

"Are you still open?" Sophia asked, looking particularly fetching in her long layered summer dress and shawl draped over her shoulders. She looked around the pub at the wood finishes, beamed ceiling, and the welcoming blazing fireplace.

"Aw, sure, look it," the owner said. "As long as there's someone here other than me, we're open for business. Come on in and make yourself at home. Sit anywhere ya like." He shot a broad smile aimed at Sophia, and took little notice of Michael.

"Where is your uh…I forget what you call it," Michael said, pointing toward a hallway.

"The jacks?" the man said. "It's down the aisle and to the left."

"Jacks! Thanks so much. I really need to remember that…"

Sophia took her seat, watching the man walk around and rummage through shelves, evidently looking for something specific behind the bar. Eventually finding it, he came back to Sophia with a tall white taper candle in hand. He unscrewed the lid off a saltshaker, poured out most of the salt into the trash, and then placed the taper inside the saltshaker. From out of his coat pocket, he pulled a lighter, flipped open the lid, and lit the candle. He deliberately and firmly set it down on the wooden bar top in front of Sophia.

"There," he said, "call it atmosphere..."

Sophia burst out laughing as Michael returned and sat down. "What?"

"So, what do ya fancy on this fine day, lad? Fierce warm weather we're havin', don't ya think?"

"Yes, fierce it is! What kind of beer do you have?" Michael asked.

"Well, as ya might guess, I have Guinness, Guinness Extra Stout, Guinness Special Export, Guinness Smooth, Guinness Barrel Aged Stout... there are 20 varieties of Guinness – do ya want the whole list, or do ya prefer my sunny disposition?"

Michael laughed. "Well, I-"

"I also have Murphy's Irish Red, and O'Hara's Celtic Stout. I also have stronger spirits if you're a mind to be frisky – or maybe a Bailey's, or an Irish Coffee, if ya want something hot. I'm tiring out here, if ya don't mind..."

"Irish Coffee for me, please!" Sophia said, laughing.

"I'll have an O'Hara's," Michael said. "Let's see if my people stack up to the Guinness clan."

As the barkeep prepared Sophia's drink, he asked, "Would ya like me to brace it with a bit of Bailey's, Miss?"

"Sounds good to me, and you can call me Miss anytime!"

He topped it off with a tall spritz of whipped cream and added some chocolate shavings to the top.

"Thank you, kind sir," Sophia said. "It's almost too pretty to drink."

As she put her hands around the warm mug, the man noticed her ring. "That's a mighty fine ring ya have there,

Miss Anytime. Might the stone be a ruby?"

Sophia couldn't help but smile at his wit, "Yes, it's an extraordinary setting, isn't it?"

"Don't know jewelry much, but it's like hen's teeth - like some of the ancient Roman pieces we find around here."

"I'm not sure how old it is, but I love it," she said.

"If I didn't know better, I'd say it lights up the room, or perhaps it's just you. I hope ya don't mind my saying this, Miss, but you are a breath of fresh air, here at Joseph McHugh's. And yer beau is fetchin', too. Are ya two here on holiday from the States?"

"We just moved here. We built a home near Doolin. If I may introduce my husband, Michael O'Hara, and my name is Sophia." They all shook hands.

"Rory Fitzgibbons. Welcome to County Clare. Here at Joseph McHugh's, I'm the manager, bartender, chief cook, candle lighter, and bottle washer most of the time. Ya wouldn't happen to be the Americans who built the house into the hillside, would ya now?"

"Yes. How did you know?" Sophia asked.

"There aren't too many Americans building new homes around here, and yours has caused quite a stir. And you, Michael, do ya fancy your O'Hara's in a glass or a bottle?"

"A bottle is fine."

"That's good, 'cause all of our glasses are dirty." He removed the cap and placed the bottle on a napkin in front of Michael.

Michael shook his head, smiled, and took a sip from the bottle. "I have a cousin in the Gardi, and Sophia's aunt and uncle own the Pat Cohan Bar in County Mayo-"

"From the Quiet Man," Rory interrupted. "Colin and Lily's place."

"Oh, you know them?"

"Indeed. It's probably the most famous pub in all of Ireland, at least to those who have seen the movie. Can I get ya something to eat? This week is Guinness Week, with Guinness Braised Chuck Steak with Horseradish Mashed Potatoes, served with Hearty Guinness Wheat Bread, and Guinness Cheddar Cheese. For dessert, we have Guinness Gingerbread Bundt Cake."

"I almost feel like I'm being disloyal to Guinness, drinking my O'Hara's here. That sounds good for both of us, don't you think, Sophia?"

She nodded, licking off some of the whipping cream from her upper lip. "Rory, do you think you could find a clean glass so you can pour me a Guinness?"

"Ahh, I'm just pullin' your leg. I can find at least one clean glass around here. Ya know there's a science to pouring a Guinness."

"So I've heard. I'd like to see this," Michael asked.

"All right then, I'll be happy to pour you a pint of Gat, but it's truly a test of patience, don't ya know. First, we have a 20-ounce tulip glass with the gold harp on the side of the glass facing up. Ya tilt the glass at a 45-degree angle as ya pour the tap toward ya, filling the glass to the middle of the harp. Now, if you notice, I am setting the glass down. I'm going to go get your food, but you're not to touch the glass, because we have to wait until we see the distinction between the dark ruby red body and the creamy white head at the top."

In a couple of minutes, he returned with a tray of two plates of beef and mashed potatoes, bread, and cheese. "Now that it's settled, I place the glass level under the tap. This time, ya push the tap away from you, pouring the Guinness slower, right into the center of the foam until it rises a *wee bit* above the rim of the glass. Now, we have to wait again until it's settled. Never, do ya understand, I say *never* do ya take a glass of Guinness until the bartender hands it to ya. Do ya understand, Michael?"

"I understand-"

"It's *important* ya understand, boy-o!"

"I get it! I get it! Sheesh..."

"Ya don't have ta yell – I heard ya the first time." Rory winked at Sophia and finally placed the glass in front of Sophia. "Did you know that 10 million glasses of Guinness are consumed daily?"

"And not *one of 'em* drank before the bartender handed it to 'em," Michael said.

"Here's to 10 million and one!" Sophia said. "Sláinte!"

"Sláinte!" Michael said.

"So, I hear you're an archeologist, Michael."

"I guess there are no secrets to be had around here."

"Ya know what they say, the smaller the town, the bigger the gossip."

"You'll have to stop by and pay us a visit, so you can add some truth to the gossip," Sophia said.

"Aw, go way out of that!" Rory said.

"No, really, my wife invites everyone to our home, no matter where we live," Michael said.

"From where in America do ya hail?"

"Colorado."

"Pretty country, from what I've heard."

"Some of the prettiest in the States," Michael said.

"We have a log home in a mountain valley with a stream that runs through the middle of the property," Sophia said.

"So you have two homes, both here and there. You must be skiers," Rory said.

"We have the best of both worlds, I must say," Sophia said. "Here, we have green everywhere with the ocean nearby. There, the valley is lush and green, even though Colorado is a dry climate, but nearby are beautiful mountain views. And no, neither of us ski. We leave that mostly to out of state visitors and the younger folks, who seemingly have money to burn."

"Are you enjoying the food?"

"It's delicious! We're going to have to tell Mary and Lou about cooking with Guinness," Sophia said. "They are a couple of sisters who do the cooking for us when we entertain."

"You're not a cook, yourself?"

"Sophia specializes in brown food," Michael said.

"Yeah, if you ever want to stop by, I'd be happy to fix you a mean toasted cheese sandwich, potato chips, and hot chocolate."

"Don't forget the dill pickle," Michael said.

"Of course, that's the pièce de résistance! It's always about the garnish. Actually, Michael is the gourmet. He loves to cook, but when we have as big a group like we have now, we want to spend time with them, instead of him spending all his time in the kitchen. That's why we have help."

"Here's your bundt cake. If you think the beef is good, wait to be surprised! So, I understand you're going to begin, ah what do you call it, a pit?" Rory asked.

"I think you mean, a dig."

"A dig... isn't that quare interesting! What are you digging for?"

"We're not quite sure yet, but we think there are remains of a prehistoric site where people lived at least as far back as two thousand years ago, maybe more."

"Way back when about 80 percent of Ireland was covered with forests. Now it's only one percent forest land - bit of a shame, really," Rory said.

"Yes, when people settled here, specifically after the Bronze Age, people changed from hunter gatherers and became farmers. They cut down the forests to make room for their crops."

"So, is this dig of yours from that time?"

"We'll know more once we begin in a few weeks, but I think it may be from the Neolithic Period - the late Stone Age - because nearby are the dolmens and such," Michael said.

"I imagine you get really busy here in the evenings," Sophia said.

"Aw, sure look it, especially on weekends in the warmer months. We do cater to the locals as well, providing for weddings, wakes - parties of all kinds, really. We have a whale of a time. The pub has been here since 1899, and once was a boarding house for guests."

"It's charming. We'll have to bring our guests here for a Guinness experience," Sophia said as they got ready to leave.

Rory stepped out from behind the bar with a bar towel draped over his left arm, and he bowed at the waist to Sophia. "You're welcome any time!"

Sophia smiled, "I'm sure we will see you soon, and remember that you are welcome to come by and see us too."

"Thank you. Will do! Ya take care now," Rory said...

Chapter
Twenty-four

Three months had passed since Laurinda was certain that Balogue and the men from the village were lost at sea. Lon was aging, and he sensed the time was right to step down from his responsibilities as the Archdruid. For many suns, Lon held the same role, as did his father before him. He wanted Laurinda to take his place, but it was up to the community. They all gathered in the stone circle, and during their sacred ceremony, they unanimously chose Laurinda to take her father's place. To celebrate, a bonfire blazed in the middle of the stone circle - shining its light far into the surrounding forest, while everyone in the village took part in the celebration with food, drinking of mead, drumming, song, and dance. Thus, she followed in the family tradition, with the exception that she was the youngest Archdruid, and the only woman in that level of standing among all the Druids of Eire.

Western Eire had fallen into difficult times, with many men lost in the hostilities between differing villages. Fishing that year was not as successful as in previous years. The storms at sea were violent and deadly, accounting for the loss of so many more of the communities' men. The climate was colder with more rain than in years past, and so the starving people became desperate and angry. Laurinda's people lived along the coastline, not far from the cliff's edge, where the temperatures were cool and the winds were high. Far from their village, along the coastal sands, it took an entire day to dig enough shellfish to mix with corn for a hot stew to feed the village.

In order to provide enough for all, they made soup with a variety of fish, wild boar, deer meat, and dried meats, including goat, mixed with roots and mushrooms, adding rye, oats, and barley, of which they had plenty. Flatbread, baked on a hot rock in the fire pit, was made with ground grains. Occasionally, they mixed seaweed with milk and honey for something sweet to eat. They still had their storehouse of preserved foods saved for times of emergency.

The villages along the shoreline were constantly defending their communities from outsiders, who attempted to steal food, livestock, boats, and tools. The abduction of young maidens sadly became a common occurrence, who soon became the wives of their captors, eventually bearing the children of their enemies. Safe return to their own village was a rare occurrence. The peaceful serene life of Laurinda's youth had changed into one of rivalry, dissension, and tremendous strife.

Winter was especially cruel in Eire that year, with temperatures cold enough for snow to fall. Winds were so strong that no one dared go near the cliffs. Even the strongest man could not protect himself from the powerful gales, for if the wind blew him over the cliffs, the fall was 700 feet to the violent sea below.

Villagers spent most of the short winter days inside their subterranean homes built into the hillside, sheltered from storms and the cold. They ate sparingly from their storehouse of foods prepared during the prior summer and autumn. Although food was scarce, Laurinda was grateful to the gods that she and her people were safe. They had plenty of grain, fresh water, and wood for the fire to cook and keep them warm. Lon and Magda, who lived with Laurinda and her children, were in their forties and ailing from maladies that came from a rainy, cool climate and advanced age, but the ravages of time did not stop Lon from being an exceptional bard.

Many an evening, the community gathered to hear Lon tell legends of mythical beings and their ancestors, who performed great wonders. His deep voice resonated within the large subterranean room with walls shored up by stone and mortar. They gathered to hear colorful chronicles about the ancient history of their people, of nature, and their world. His narrative made the long dark nights tolerable until the springtime brought longer days. The tales were rich in wisdom, laced with fantasy, and the flight of imagination. Children went to sleep, dreaming colorful images of historic gallant heroes defending their homeland, or of mystical fairies bestowing their magic with a wish and a prayer.

Lon began to tell the saga with a deep voice that echoed off the walls of stacked stones. Wild firelight danced at his feet, as the shadows on the wall behind him passionately illustrated his dramatic tale with each movement of his hands. Not only were the children entranced, their eyes wide with wonderment, but the adults also basked in his ability to weave a story into a captivating tale.

"Long ago, in the days before this was an island, the terrain was once joined with other lands in all directions as far as the eye could see. As the center place and heart of Mother Earth, Eire stood tall. She stood high above the surrounding lands, with waterfalls that gushed from her highest mountain peaks, becoming flowing rivers leading to lands in the faraway distance. Animals lived here in plenty, but there were very few people, for humanity was in its inception in this part of the world.

"There was a season when the nights were long and the heavens opened up with rain that came ceaselessly. Every day, the rains poured as if the gray skies from above were emptying out onto this very part of Mother Earth so the heavens could again become blue. There was so much rain, that the lower lands surrounding Eire washed completely away by the powerful rivers that joined together, soon becoming the sea that now surrounds our island home. The silt and sand from the terrain around Eire finally settled to become the faraway lands that we now may only reach by boat. The only hint that we were once connected to Caledonia, across the sea, are the red stepping-stones, which remain on the northeastern edge of Eire. Many people and animals floated away. Their descendants now inhabit faraway lands, but Eire continues to call them home, for she remains embedded in the hearts of people all over the Mother Earth.

"The gods spared our home during that time of rain, because Eire was, and still is the center of Mother Earth. She is of utmost importance to the balance and well-being of all who reside on her. Without Eire, all other lands are nothing, and this they know. This is why so many are drawn to Eire, and always will be to the end of days, for they desire to return to what they know as their homeland.

"One of the few people who remained on Eire was Treoc, a young man, strong and wise for his years. He was tall and fine of features, with chestnut hair and eyes of amber. For countless times when day turned to night, Treoc saw only animals and wondered if he was the last human on Eire, for nowhere did he see another.

"The rain continued, and there was no respite in sight, for Treoc could see the skies to the west developing into a deep brooding gray, promising even more rain to come. Treoc was hungry, and although he was weary of the wet and cold, he went down to the far shoreline to dig for clams. There, he came across fresh footprints in the sand. Whoever it was could not have been there much earlier, or the prints would have washed away in the surf.

"So eager was he to know there was another person nearby, he quickly gathered his catch in a deerskin bag and followed the footsteps until they led to a narrow pathway up the hillside. The tall grass was so wet that a visible path remained, soon leading him to the crest of the cliff that hovered over the coastline from whence he came. His heart raced as he anxiously looked all around for the other person, who could not be far away.

"As he approached the pinnacle, he heard a woman's voice calling out to the gods. He soon noticed a petite young woman with long red hair, who stood at the cliff's summit. Her arms were wide open and her head raised high to the skies. She spoke with clarity and fortitude, and although she was small in stature, he could hear the resonant power in her words almost blending with the booming thunder.

"The skies cracked open as lightning danced in several places around the young woman. Treoc immediately fell flat on the ground, attempting to save himself from the fire in the skies, but the young woman did not move. Steadfast in her stance, she held out her arms, beseeching the gods of the sky to unite with her in their almighty power. In fact, it appeared to Treoc that she *absorbed* the lightning's power, being of even greater authority than just moments before. From what Treoc could tell, the woman did not flinch, but out of the corner of her eye, she noticed Treoc fall to the ground.

"The woman began to dance - her movements entrancing Treoc as he clung in fear to Mother Earth. The woman seemed to know where to step as the fire from the skies continued to strike the ground around her. From where she stepped away, the lightning struck that very place.

"Treoc was astounded. *Is she controlling the fire in the skies? How does she know where to step? She is indomitable!*

"The more passionately she danced, the harder the rains fell. Treoc could scarcely hear himself think as the cold raindrops violently splattered against him. Suddenly, she stopped dancing and bowed in reverence to the gods of the skies and then to Mother Earth. The rain ceased just as quickly, and the sun's rays peeked through a split in the dark roiling clouds over the sea.

"*Could it be that she controlled the storm? It certainly seemed that she directed the lightning.* So many thoughts were running through his mind.

"Treoc sat up in wonderment of what he just witnessed when the young woman confidently approached and offered him her hand. When their hands touched, he felt the power of the lightning transfer from her hand to his. He stood and pulled away to look at his palm as if he could see the energy as a physical entity.

"'It is how I gain my power,' the woman laughed. 'Lightning has become my friend. You poor man, you look as if you have seen the spirits.'

"'I have certainly seen power beyond my imagining, and now I feel it through your hands,' Treoc said, wiping the raindrops from his face. 'It also dances in your green eyes. How do you do it?'

"'I become the power that already exists within me and all around me. I let go of my thinking mind and open up my heart, willing to receive that which is mine to become.' She turned and began to walk down the hillside. 'Come with me. I have a pot of stew cooking,' she said as she took her long, waist-length hair, heavy with rain, and rung out the excess water from her tresses.

"'Thank you. I am called Treoc,' he said, as he followed the tiny woman down the hill to her home, very much like the ones we live in today. As they drew closer, he could smell a fire burning and saw a trace of smoke rise into the cool, wet air. Before they reached her home, he gathered some large wet leaves to wrap the clams to steam in her fire pit.

"When they got inside, where it was dry and warm, she found him fresh, dry clothes to wear. She changed and laid their wet clothing over a branch that hung not far from the burning fire pit. As they ate their meal together, he learned her name was Juna. All her people washed away to lands unknown, as did his. She too began to wonder if she was the only one left on Eire. After an evening of sharing stories, they both fell asleep next to the fire, in the comfort of knowing that they were no longer alone.

"As far as they knew, they were the only ones remaining in that part of western Eire. And although it was only the two of them, they soon felt deep love in their hearts, dedicated to the well-being of the other. Over time, they built a larger home in the hillside with several rooms, fortifying the walls with stone to make space for the several children of their family. Thus, Treoc and Juna became the first people of our lineage.

"Juna possessed powers of knowing. She joined with the wisdom of the animals, whose connection to the gods was as close as their breath. From them, she learned how to sense storms, how to adjust to the seasons, and how to love. She then discovered she could call forth storms, and then cause them to cease into the nothingness from which they came by calling forth the same power of the gods within her. That was why the gods chose her to remain on Eire, for Juna was gifted with this ability by the gods themselves after the rains washed away her people to the faraway lands.

"Treoc respected her control of the storms, for his abilities were just as powerful. Peace and tranquility reigned from his center. When their children were in conflict, he would enter their atmosphere and change would swiftly come about, the children finding themselves in concordance with each other, instead of quarrel.

"There were things he simply knew. In the same way that Juna moved just ahead of the lightning when it struck, Treoc knew when to go fishing for the greatest catch. He knew how to adjust to change and unexpected events, when never was he taught how. He knew what to plant and where, and how to care for their crops to create a storehouse of food. Treoc knew which plants to blend so that healing would quickly take hold. All he had to do was speak his word, while holding only love in his heart, and a broken leg would miraculously mend. He was a peacemaker and a healer - for he had a knowing.

"After a few turns of the sun, they began to connect with others. Treoc knew just how to respond to strangers as they began to join them on the western part of Eire. Most of the newcomers were peaceful people, living as best as they could to raise healthy families, but a few were thieves and marauders. Enough challenge was created by the few who only wanted to plunder and take, that the rest of them decided to pool their interests and live together in community, knowing there was greater power in numbers. Thus, our village began to grow.

"Once, during the time when the sun was high and the days were warm, thieves ransacked their village, attempting to steal not only their belongings and their food, but their children, too. Treoc took a stance with the other villagers, not in resistance, but with love's generosity. They were strong of body and mind, but their connection with the gods was so powerful that an invisible shield separated the thieves from the children of the village. The thieves' resistance rendered them powerless, and soon they surrendered, for their legs could no longer hold them upright. The children of the village, in laughter and song, brought them fruit and nuts to eat, and by love's presence the thieves transformed, which came to them through the children's innocence. Treoc then gave them a choice, 'You may return from where you came, or you may join us in peace, but you must make an unwavering choice in this moment. What is it to be?'

"Each of the thieves joined the community, becoming some of its strongest members. Over time, they brought their families, and soon this part of western Eire was known for its mighty people, who lived in peace and tranquility.

"After the rains, the people that remained here were very special people that the gods kept here so Eire could flourish. The best of the best continued on, and those people are your ancestors. Each of you stands on the shoulders of a mighty people. They stand strong so you can see far to the horizon. Their blood runs through your veins. You breathe the very air that they breathed while you walk in the footsteps they left behind. You now carry on with your own legacy to shine on as they did. As you reach for the stars, you take action upon that which your dreams beckon you to become.

"Over thousands of years, the people on Eire became a very strong people. Today, we live their legacy, as we create our own heritage for generations to come. Never will you be forgotten. Forevermore are your names etched on the stars that shine above. Never will you be insignificant, for each of you are as important and as powerful as Juna and Treoc. As did they, you possess the power of the gods, for you control your own destiny as easily as your dreams drift on the winds with love.

"So sleep well, my children. Dream of the grandness of Mother Earth, dream of her tall oak trees, the seas, rivers, and loughs, and all of Nature, for in your dreams is your greater becoming..."

Sophia awoke from her dream in wonderment of Lon's tale. There was no doubt in her mind the legend of Juna and Treoc was closer to truth than fiction. All those of Apeiros carried on the same connection with the Infinite Intelligence, possessing powers beyond human awareness. What they tapped into was ancient. It was the Truth of the Ages, and now that she had slipped into other dimensional fields, she was certain that Love held the power over everything.

Chapter Twenty-five

That morning, Sophia called Hailey to invite her for an early lunch instead of late afternoon tea, giving them more time to talk while everyone else was gone. Hailey came to the house all gussied up, expecting to see some of the others, but was apparently disappointed to discover that it would only be the two of them.

The Ello Sisters prepared a lovely fresh salad with local garden greens and freshly baked bread, served with Irish cheese. They sat out on the deck to enjoy their lunch, while Sophia broke open a bottle of her favorite chilled dry Riesling, hopefully to help their communications open up as well.

"So, Hailey, were you raised here in Doolin?"

"No, I grew up in Dublin. After university, I married a man from here. We divorced after two years, and he left me his family's cottage, because he wanted to live in the States. I turned it into a guest cottage, knowing I could make a good living, with all the tourism here. May I have some ice for my wine?"

"Oh, sure," Sophia said. Hailey followed her into the kitchen. "We really enjoyed staying there. I chose it because it's an authentic Irish cottage that looks like it could be a few hundred years old."

"Aye, around two hundred and twenty-five," Hailey said.

"Is that right? I love the native stone on the exterior, slate roof and floors, and all the wood interiors. The big stone fireplace in the kitchen is particularly charming."

"My ex's ancestors built the cottage in the late 1700s. They used to cook all their meals over that fire. I live in the carriage house out back, which was once a barn. It's small, but it's just me. I don't need a lot of space."

They came back out with a small bowl of ice and sat. "Being a proprietor of a business like that is a full-time job, with all the cleaning after each guest and the upkeep of the property," Sophia said.

Hailey chilled her wine with several chips. "I do stay busy. Tourism is heavier in the late spring into the early fall, but I do have guests during the winter months. I hire on help, if I want to get away for awhile. Sorry, might I have a wee bit more spinach? I love that with me cheese."

"Yes, I believe we still have some." Sophia dutifully got up, and Hailey followed her back into the kitchen.

"Sophia, I'm really grateful you invited me over. I felt the perfect eejit at the party when I barged in on you and your mates. I was right mortified. I hope all is forgiven."

"Oh, Hailey, please don't worry yourself – in fact *we* are the ones who owe *you* an apology. Michael felt so bad by making it sound as if you weren't welcome, or worthy of-"

"Well, let me say, I had the most marvelous chat with Ananta, later in the evening. She is such a gracious woman, and she explained everything. I feel so silly, thinking a visit to see the Dalai Lama was like a trip to Disneyland Paris." They laughed together and walked back out to the deck with the extra spinach.

"I'm so glad you understand," Sophia said. "And I want you to know you are welcome here any time."

"Oh, thank you so much, and you know that my door is always open to you and Michael. He is such a charming man. And funny! In fact, that Markos and Gaston also tickle my fancy. You have such lovely friends."

"Thank you. They're very special people. I love each one dearly."

They quietly ate their lunch as nearly a minute passed, uncomfortably.

"Sophia?" Hailey finally said. "Do ya mind a personal question?"

"Of course not."

"We just made acquaintance a wee bit ago, but I feel like – like I've known ya a donkey's years. How do ya do it? I feel so at ease here with ya."

"The feeling's mutual, Hailey."

"I don't have many friends. I work so much, and finding a gentleman caller around these villages that I feel comfortable with is like – well, truth is, no matter how hard I try, seems I get rejected from men and from friendships with women, too. I'm really quite lonely sometimes."

"I'm sorry. That must be difficult."

Hailey stopped eating and swallowed back a tear. "I know they call me 'Hailey, Who Can't Get a Date,' which is upsetting, but as the saying goes, the truth hurts."

"We can all be thoughtless sometimes, poking fun or talking behind someone's back without realizing what we're doing is hurtful."

"Oh, I bring it on meself sometimes, I ain't afraid to admit, with my picking, and nagging, and yammering on. I can't tell you the times a gentleman caller left skid marks outside my house after a short evening out. One of 'em run right out from under his toupee – left it right out there in the garden."

Sophia burst out laughing. "Oh my gosh, Hailey!"

"The songbirds had themselves a fine nest that spring, I tell ya."

Sophia needed a minute to compose herself. "Hailey, you're a treat," she finally said.

"Tell that to Pádraig and a host of others. Oh, Sophia, I just don't know precisely what it is about me that sends 'em scurryin'."

"Could it be that you are trying too hard?" Sophia asked, pouring Hailey a fresh glass of wine, and offering her the bowl of ice as well.

"What do you mean?"

"So much of the time, people are more comfortable with others that allow themselves to be vulnerable, causing everyone to let down their guard," Sophia said.

"Yeah, but I always want everything to be perfect, at least by appearances. I even work very hard to keep myself looking young."

"But is that natural for you?"

"No, but it's what I think is expected of me, being a single woman."

"You've met Anja, Ananta, Lestari, Shoshana, and Yesinia. What do you think of them?"

"Oh, I could never compare with any of you. You're all so beautiful and exotic, being from far away countries and such."

"Could it be they think that about you? To them, you're exotic too, being from a far away country, and with your fair skin and pretty hazel eyes."

"Oh, my skin has wrinkles here and there, if ya put your eyes to it. And I keep my hair dyed bright red because it's practically a calling card of the Irish to have red hair."

"Yes, for those who have naturally red hair. But why is it so important to try so hard to be something different than you really are?"

"I reckon it's because I don't think very well of meself," Hailey said.

"And why is that?"

"Me ma was a beautiful woman when she was young, but she believed that she lost her looks as she got older. Being an unhappy and jealous sort, she went out of her way to remind me how plain and unattractive I was. She didn't really want me, you know, often reminding me that I was a mistake. So many times she told others, while I was within earshot, that when she found out she was pregnant with me, she thought the world came to an end. She never forgave me for being born.

"Growing up, nothing I ever did was good enough, according to her. I wasn't pretty enough, or skinny enough, or smart enough. My hair was too dull, too frizzy, and I had too many freckles. When I was fifteen, she taught me to wear heavy makeup to hide my freckles and add color to my fair skin. I started dying my hair a couple years later." Hailey began to tear up again. "My da was a good man who truly loved me, but the drink got in his way. So growing up with little care from my folks, I reckon, caused me to seek attention from any man I could find." Hailey broke down and sobbed.

"I'm so sorry, Hailey." Sophia reached across the table and placed her hand on Hailey's arm. "You know, there are facts, which are the things that happened in the past, and then there is the truth - which is the beauty and grace of who you are right now, in this present moment, and most of the time they are quite different from each other. What your mom said to you came from ill feelings she had about herself. It wasn't about you. It feels that way, but it wasn't about you. Whatever opinion anyone has about anything or anyone is a reflection of themselves and not the person they are targeting with their criticism or judgment. What is truly right for you is *your* truth, and you sense that it is so, because it resides in your heart. You know it when you have those moments of wisdom when you get those intuitive nudges.

"And I want you to listen to me now, Hailey, I think you are a lovely woman, and everyone in Apeiros does, too. Clearly, you are smart, or you wouldn't be able to manage the business of your cottage like you do. You have a great sense of style, having decorated it beautifully, plus you helped us feel so welcome."

"Oh, some of the furnishings are dated, and I need to put some paint on the walls."

"We all have things we'd like to change and update, but here's something you might not be aware of. I just gave you a sincere compliment, and you found a reason to dismiss it as if you aren't worthy, but you are. I truly mean it when I say your bed and breakfast is charming and warm."

"I try so hard to please, but I guess I've become like my ma, nothing or no one is ever good enough. Like when I met Geoffrey the other night. I tried my best, but he shut me down."

"I suspect Pádraig had a hand in that."

"Aye, I suppose you got an earful about my one and only date with him. He's a kind man, but hard to please. All he wanted was to go on about his late wife."

"Well, you know, he lost her not that long ago."

"But that was more than two years now."

"It takes at least that much longer to grieve for a loved one. We grieve so deeply because we have loved so well, and when that is gone, we're left with the memories of what once was."

"Aye, I reckon. Could be I was yammering on so much that he couldn't get a word in edgewise."

"May I make a suggestion?"

"Of course."

"When you're talking to someone, just keep asking them questions. Be interested in them - what their interests are, their hobbies, what makes them tick. I don't know anyone who doesn't like to have someone pay attention to them, especially when it's sincere. You'll get to know them well, and if they reciprocate by asking *you* questions, then you have a friendship already in its beginning stages."

"That's what you've done for me today, isn't it?"

"Yes, but I genuinely wanted to get to know you better, and the way to do that is to ask questions and take interest."

"So, I ask again - how do ya do it?"

"What's that?"

"Be so confident."

"You know, there are so many times that I'm not confident, but when I'm in the company of others and get to know them, my confidence grows, because I take the emphasis off myself. Then, I don't feel like I'm the center of attention, and I become more relaxed. It's easy, really."

Hailey sat back and swirled her wine. "Not tryin' so hard. I must admit I fancy that, for sometimes it gets me completely knackered."

"It *can* be tiring, can't it?"

"And look at you. Your hair's so lovely, and you don't cake the makeup on. How do ya master such a natural look?"

"You know, Hailey, years ago I used to do professional makeovers for people. I have all these fun cosmetics. If you're willing, maybe we could try some fresh new colors on you. Are you game?"

"You would do that for me?"

"Sure! It's always fun to try out something new. How about it?"

"Ya know, it does sound like a craic."

"Follow me upstairs – and grab that other bottle of wine..."

It was a proper girls' afternoon out. In the master bath was a dressing table with a lighted mirror. Sophia prepared the table with moisturizers, a variety of cosmetics, cosmetic brushes, and nail polish. She also brought out a tray with teacakes.

"Sit here and start with this coconut oil to remove all your makeup," Sophia said. When Hailey removed her false eyelashes and wiped her face clean with a warm washcloth, her fair skin glowed.

"Look how beautiful you are!" Sophia said.

"Oh, that's just the wine talkin'. I look a fright."

"Ok, now another part of this makeover is you learning to accept a compliment. Let's try it again. Look how beautiful you are!"

Hailey giggled. "Right. Thank you, dear Sophia!"

"You're welcome – now, before we try some new colors on your face, what would you say if we color your hair a shade that complements your coloring?"

"I've never had anyone do this for me. I always do my own hair, but I'll give it a try."

"This is fun, pampering you today! I think this dark auburn shade is right for you. It's a touch of red, but a richer color that is more sophisticated. I can add soft highlights to give it some dimension. What do you think?"

"My natural color is an ash brown, but I think the auburn would be fetching."

Sophia colored her hair and wove some highlights to add light, then shampooed and conditioned it...

Downstairs, the Ello Sisters arrived with groceries from the market. Their husbands went to the pub with the others, and the sisters planned to prepare a simple meal for when everyone returned home. As they began unloading groceries, they heard wild laughter coming from upstairs. They exchanged a curious glance, and then returned to their business...

"What would you say to a sassy mid-length haircut?" Sophia said. "With all your natural waves, it would be easy to care for, and you'd be the talk of the town."

"Caution to the wind!" Hailey said. "Let's do it!"

Sophia cut her thick hair in a layered, shoulder length bob, so Hailey could leave it in its natural wave, or style it with a curling iron. While she waited, Hailey filled Sophia in on some town gossip, which led to more laughter and wine. After Sophia dried her hair, she turned sections into loose pin curls and clamped them with tiny claw clips. "This is a very fast and easy way to curl your hair for fifteen minutes while you're putting on your makeup."

Sophia applied an ivory foundation on Hailey's skin, then eye shadow in a couple shades of gray over a neutral light peach base on her lids. After applying soft peach blush to her cheeks and at the hairline along her temples, she penciled in her eyebrows, finishing the eyes with black/brown mascara to Hailey's long lashes. She concluded with a copper red lip color, and a dab of clear gloss on the middle of her lower lip. Sophia removed the clips from the pin curls and loosely ran her fingers through her hair, finishing with a light hair spray.

"Aren't you gorgeous! And look, even some of your freckles show through, giving you that youthful look that you've had all this time."

"I don't even look like myself! I'm pretty, even without the false eyelashes."

"You *are* pretty, and you don't *need* the eyelashes. Now for the clothes..."

"New clothes, too?"

"We're about the same size. Here, try on this long ruby summer dress. It will go well with the sandals you have on."

Hailey went into the walk-in closet to change, and emerged a different woman. "I fancy it! I never wear dresses like this."

"It's perfect for you. Here, try these delicate garnet dangle earrings and the matching Y necklace. They'll go well with your coloring and with the dress too, and let's add a pretty set of silver bangle bracelets. Voila!"

"Everything is so lovely, but now that I look at my blue nails, they don't go, do they?"

"No problem. Let's do a manicure. We're doing the works today."

"Right, you choose. You seem to know what looks good on me."

Sophia removed the metallic royal blue nail color, clipped down the length of her nails, filed them to a soft oval, and applied a light peach, almost the color of her skin.

"This is subtle and also elegant. Pretty, don't you think?"

"Aye, I like it! For years, I've worn long nails in bright colors. This is such a change, but they look so nice."

"When you wear a neutral nail color, it extends your fingers to make them look long and elegant. And when you want to glam it up, do that. Your nails are really strong. You don't have to wear polish all the time. You could just oil and buff, and they will look great."

"I'll have to try it. What do I owe you for all of this?"

"Nothing, it's yours."

"No no! I'll have none of that!"

"Hailey, I have more clothes and jewelry than I need. Why don't we call it the beginning of a good friendship."

"Oh, aren't you kind?"

They raised their nearly empty wine glasses. "What's a good Irish toast?" Sophia asked.

"May the good Lord take a liking to you, but not too soon!" They clinked their glasses together with a good laugh.

"Here," Sophia continued, "let's add this paisley shawl as a final touch." She draped the shawl over Hailey's shoulders and around her arms, letting it fall gracefully down her back. She then stood behind her, took her by the shoulders, and turned her to the mirror. "Look at you, Hailey. Look at the real you – the magnificent you."

Tears welled in Hailey's eyes. "Oh, Sophia, I don't know what to say."

"I think the fact that you are glowing from the inside out is a good enough thank you for me. Hey, I hear everyone downstairs. Why don't you join us for dinner? Are you ready to wow them?"

"I'm nervous. I've looked the same way for twenty years."

"I've heard it said, it's not the number of people that look at you, but the people that smile at you that tells you who you are in the world... and you welcome that smile because you're beaming from the inside out. They will notice you without you even trying, because it's your natural beauty coming through. Just try it. And while you're at it, ask lots of questions and take an honest interest in the people around you. Before you know it, you'll have lots of friends to spend time with."

"Aye, it's worth a go, isn't it?" Hailey looked in the mirror and adjusted herself.

"Let me go downstairs first," Sophia said. "Just take a few minutes by yourself, look in the mirror, and welcome in the new you. Give me five minutes, and then you can make your grand entrance..."

Everyone was around the dining table, enjoying cocktails and appetizers before dinner. Sophia joined them, noticing that Geoffrey O'Hara was there.

"Geoffrey!" Sophia said. "Good to see you."

"I hope ya don't mind. I wandered into Cohan's and was waylaid by this happy group who insisted I join ya for supper."

"The more the merrier. You're always welcome, cousin!" Sophia said.

"I hear you had tea today with Hailey, Who Can't Get a Date?" Pádraig said. "Did ya run out before ya found a blend she liked?"

"Uh, Pádraig-" Michael said.

"Pádraig? A word, please?" Sophia motioned for Pádraig to join her in the corner of the room, away from the others. "Pádraig, I love you dearly, but from now on, it's Hailey O'Donnell. If you call her Hailey, Who Can't Get a Date one more time, I will tie your tongue around your nose, is that clear?"

Stunned, Pádraig nodded. "As rain, lass."

"By the way, she knows that you and others call her that stupid name, and it hurts her deeply."

Pádraig turned a light shade of red. "I suppose I made a holy show of it. I didn't mean no harm."

"If you really got to know Hailey, you'd have some compassion for her, and you would like her. We have to remember who we are, and the work we do in the world, and today that begins with you."

"Aye, lass, it does. I promise, ya won't have to tell me again, or I'll tie me tongue around me nose, meself." He gave her a wink.

Sophia kissed him on the cheek, and they went back to join the group.

Hailey suddenly made her entrance, gracefully walking down the stairs. Everyone fell silent and simply stared at the stunningly beautiful woman who came into the room. She smiled and strolled in, looking around the silent room. "What, did someone die?"

"No!" Darius laughed with everyone. "Hailey, it's good to see you, my dear. Are you staying for dinner?"

"Aye, if you'll have me," she said, blushing a bit.

"Hailey," Pádraig said, "your hair's a stunner. I love the change."

Hailey paused, and with a smile looked at Sophia. "Thank you, Pádraig."

Geoffrey, who seemed shell-shocked, stood from his

seat and pulled back the chair next to his, offering it to Hailey. "Uh – Geoffrey O'Hara? We met the other night?"

"Of course we did," Hailey said. "You're the Garda." She gave him a playful nudge in the ribs. "Ya aren't gonna arrest me, now are ya?"

Geoffrey poured her a glass of wine. "Only if you steal me heart."

"Okay!" Michael said. "Let's eat!"

The room instantly filled with laughter, conversation, and good food. The Ello sisters put on their usual feast and floorshow as everyone dug in.

Sophia watched contentedly, counting her blessings as she looked about this room of magnificent, loving friends. Her heart soared when she felt a sudden, light tap on her shoulder. She didn't look, for she knew she wouldn't actually see White Buffalo standing behind her – but she knew he was there.

She leaned back in her chair and simply smiled...

CHAPTER
Twenty-four

As sundown began to reflect its deepest golds, rusts, and reds along the 700-foot Cliffs of Moher, the wedding party arrived by pony and trap at O'Brien's Tower, the highest point on the cliffs. The tower was restored in 1978, but was originally built by Cornelius O'Brien in 1835 as a viewing area for 19th century visitors. From there, they could see the Twelve Bens, a circular mountain range on the western part of Ireland, the highest elevation at 2,392 feet.

As the group gathered on the steps of the tower, Shoshana was the last to arrive. Markos assisted her off the trap as she stepped down in ivory slippers, carrying a mixed bouquet of summer garden flowers. She was stunning, dressed in a v-neck ivory appliquéd tulle gown, with a deep V to the waist down her back. Her long brunette hair, tied to the side, fell in loose curls down the front of her left shoulder. She wore her mother's pearl necklace, a gift from her father to celebrate Shoshana's birth. Sophia made her a delicate pearl and peridot bracelet. She wore Evangeline's gold and peridot earrings, made in Israel and left to her by White Buffalo.

Christofer, smartly dressed in a dark gray suit and ivory shirt and tie, stood at the top of the rounded stairs with tears in his eyes, awestruck by his stunningly beautiful bride. The golden colors of sunset highlighted his dark good looks, with his olive complexion, wavy dark hair, and rich amber eyes.

So moved was he by officiating the marriage of his two dearest friends, Markos could barely keep his voice from quivering.

"We welcome all of you this beautiful evening in this ancient part of the world, bathed in the colors of sunset overlooking the vast ocean. We all stand in support of our dear friends, Shoshana and Christofer, as they join in marriage.

"Although they have known each other over four years, today they begin anew. Marriage is not just a formality, but is a holy sanctuary where two people consciously join their ideals and dreams into that which serves them as they grow together as a couple. Here, they join their souls, two individuals merging as one.

"Christofer Aleksanderi Thanos, do you take this woman as your beloved, your wife... and Shoshana Gabriella Abraham, do you take this man as your beloved, your husband, as you both stand strong in truth, while creating a life of joy? Will you live in peace, restoring harmony and maintaining order and balance? With compassion and grace, will you live in gratitude for your abundance, living in health to the best of your ability? Will you bask in the world's beauty, recognizing oneness in each other, all in love and awareness?"

"I do!" Shoshana said.

"I do!" Christofer said.

"Do both of you continue to honor and support each other in your differences as you grow and change?"

"We do."

"Do you hold true to each other in body, mind, and spirit?"

"We do."

"Shoshana, the first time I saw you, my heart opened wide," Christofer said. "There was a magic in the atmosphere, indicating that my life had instantly changed. I could have married you in that moment. I stand here as a man, committed to a lifetime of wonder with you. I support you, and find you a stunning and intelligent woman, whose heart has room for millions of souls, of which I am fortunate to be one. May I always be supportive as life offers us change and growth. One thing, of which I am certain, my love for you will continue to expand as we nurture each other through the years."

"My beloved Christofer, you fill my heart and mind with a love so great, that the life we are beginning as husband and wife promises the wonderment of eternal grace. I am so grateful for your strength and artistic talents that lured me into a life of color and constant change. I stand by your side, and I lay with you in love's embrace, for together we flow downstream, enjoying life eternal. I promise to sit with you in collaborative understanding, always with a listening ear. Life will never cease its wonder as we look to the future with the eyes of our souls, in alignment with God as our anchor. In this, we are empowered beyond our vision of the life we see for our future. Christofer, I love you fully and completely to the end of my days."

"And so, each of us here today stand in the truth of this union," Markos said. "In that, we support them, we love them forward, and we bless them - wishing them prosperity in all that they do. May we all agree, by saying Aye."

"Aye!"

"It is my great honor to present to you, the world's most recent married couple, Christofer and Shoshana Thanos. You may both join —-"

Christofer and Shoshana were already in an embrace, as he held her, swinging her back in a deep dip while kissing her.

"in a... kiss!" Everyone cheered.

Sophia stepped up on the tower steps to straighten Shoshana's hair for pictures, when she suddenly slipped into the life of Laurinda, having been in that very location two millennia before. Everything of the current day disappeared as she envisioned her life as the Archdruid, searching far out to sea for her beloved Balogue. She looked down at the ruby ring on her hand as everything turned to white.

Michael, recognizing the look in Sophia's eyes, came up the stairs and put her in his arms, grounding her in his strength. "Come back to me, my love. You're safe. I've got you." They walked down the stairs and stepped away from the group that surrounded the newly married couple, unaware of Sophia's shift into another dimension. "Are you alright?"

"Yes, thank you for rescuing me, once again."

"It won't be the last time. Are you okay?"

"I'm fine, really. Let's go celebrate."

As photos were taken at sundown, the Ello Sisters returned to the house to ready the wine and hors d'oeuvres. Set up on the balcony overlooking the great room, the band played an Irish ballad as everyone returned. On the terrace were several round tables, draped in shimmering ivory satin, each with a centerpiece of garden flowers. White lights in a canopy hovered over the terrace, casting a warm glow in the evening twilight.

"Let us raise our glasses to the bride and groom!" Michael said. "Shoshana and Christofer. May life bring you only days of wonder, and nights filled with warm embraces!"

"To Shoshana and Christofer!" They all raised their glasses.

On each plate was the menu of a combination of Jewish and Greek cuisine:

Hors d'oeuvres

Dolmades
Stuffed grape leaves

Gravlax
Vodka dill cured salmon on rye bread

Kefledes
Savory meatballs on pita bread with tzatziki sauce

Dinner

Avgolemono
Greek soup

Braided Chullah Bread

Israeli Salad
with avocado

Beef Brisket

Gyros
with tzatziki sauce

Potato Latkes

Horiatiki Salad
with feta cheese and kalamata olives

Dessert

Irish Wedding Cake
Elaborate fruitcake with butter cream frosting,
with fresh strawberries, blueberries,
blackberries, and green grapes

Baklava
Multi layered, buttered phyllo dough
with nuts, honey, and cinnamon

Galaktoboureko
Custard pie in phyllo dough

Kourabiedes
Greek butter Cookies

Chocolatey Rugelach
Crescent cookies rolled with chocolate hazelnut spread

Neapolitan Hamantaschen
Jewish triangular cookies,
filled with strawberries and chocolate,
finished with a dabbling of vanilla icing

After dinner, many locals in the community were invited for dessert. When everyone arrived, the Ello Sisters brought out a silver tray with a traditional Irish wedding cake. Shoshana and Christofer cut the cake and fed each other the first bite. A champagne toast was made, after which trays of Jewish and Greek specialty cocktails were offered:

The Greek Mojito
Santorini Sunrise
Aegean Fizz
Cardamom Blush Cocktail
Mazel Tov Cocktail

Tables and chairs were moved to the sides of the terrace, and everyone danced to lively Irish music, highlighted by Geoffrey and Pádraig competing over a dance with Hailey, Gaston and Lou Ella dancing an Irish jig, and Hailey stunning everyone with some fancy River Dance-type steps. She urged Michael to join her, but after a few attempts, he admitted that his new hips weren't quite River Dance-ready.

In all, it was a party not to be forgotten.

After the festivities, Shoshana and Christofer spent the night in the separate studio apartment over the garage, away from the rest of the house. When they entered, the burning fireplace welcomed them, along with soft romantic music. On the coffee table in front of the sofa was an ice bucket with champagne, draped in a white linen towel, two Waterford crystal champagne glasses, and chocolate dipped strawberries.

The bathroom was lit by candles, with rose petals scattered around the edge of the jetted bathtub. Another ice bucket with champagne sat on a small table next to the tub. A variety of bubble bath, bath salts, and lotions sat on a tray for their enjoyment. Two long plush white terry cloth bathrobes hung on a hook, with their names embroidered on each. On the bed were red rose petals scattered over the turned down sheets, with lit candles adding to the romantic ambience...

Late the next morning, the Ello Sisters brought the lovebirds a tray of orange juice, coffee, and a brunch to last until dinnertime. In the afternoon, the newlyweds enjoyed champagne and strawberries during a bubble bath as Shoshana snuggled in Christofer's arms.

They joined the group at six for dinner, after which Christofer poured the finest Santorini wine from his own vineyard.

"We want to thank everyone for the most beautiful night of our lives," Shoshana said.

"Yes, thank you so much!" Christofer said.

"I so wanted to marry this wonderful man, but had no idea how to go about it. You all made it so memorable for us. We couldn't have planned anything better than the beautiful wedding on the cliffs. Thank you, Markos! You were spectacular. You might think of marrying people for a living. You know, some of the best ways to meet new people are at weddings. You'd never be without a woman in your life, my friend."

"He's rarely without a woman as it is," Christofer said, laughing. "Then, there was the dinner and party afterwards. Sophia, thank you for taking on all the planning for our wedding - the flowers, the band, the photographer, all the decorations, and invitations to the community. It was all so beautiful, but who would expect anything less?"

"We especially want to thank the Ello Sisters for the most magnificent dinner," Shoshana said. "Never would we have thought to bring a bit of both traditions home. We absolutely loved the traditional Irish wedding cake. If any of you are ever in Santorini, you are welcome to stay with us, and we will shower you with hospitality that you've shown us."

"With gratitude! L'Chaim! To Life!" Christofer said.

"L'Chaim!" They all raised their glasses.

No matter how tired she was, it didn't stop Sophia from dreaming of her past lives, and that night she returned to the life of Laurinda...

Chapter
Twenty-four

As the Archdruid, Laurinda spent many of her days as an advocate to her people. She worked as an intercessory, mediating disagreements of one party with another, using reason and logic. Occasionally, she acted as a judge to bring order and balance to the community. She diligently worked with her people, convincing them to remain loyal by honoring others in the same way they revered the gods - to live in peace amongst themselves.

When there was a greater challenge, she spent time in the circle of stones, communing with the gods for their wisdom, and seeking guidance for her community's future needs. So often, when she spent time wading in the sandy shoals, Laurinda found herself talking aloud to Balogue as she looked out on the far-reaching ocean. She sought her husband's warm heart and wise counsel, and time and again she received some form of acknowledgement that he was there for her.

Late in winter, the food stores became scarce. People grew restless and frustrated while fully dependent on the skill of a hunter's kill of a deer or boar. Winds on the cliff's edge could be treacherous. Thirty-foot waves powerfully crashed against the cliff walls, washing away multiple layers of rock. The upper edge of the cliffs often fell away, no longer supported by the stone foundation far below.

Eventually, the entire village would be in jeopardy at the behest of the sea. Laurinda and her wise elders came to the decision to build a new community farther downhill from the cliff's edge, beyond a large ridge of an outcropping of rocks. For a series of moons, Laurinda's people remained busy, digging deep into the hillside, strengthening walls with layers of stone and mud mixed with woody grasses and ash to create strong new homes.

With the village oftentimes in jeopardy by unwelcome raiders, Laurinda asked Lon to build a stone strongbox for items of value. On the outside, he etched spiral designs into the slate and carved the lid so it would snugly fit the box, sealing it well from the elements.

There, they placed precious items, such as Magda's pouch filled with many loose pearls brought to her by Lon from his travels when they were young, along with her gold wedding ring. Lon placed his gold crown and ring into the box, given to him by his father when he became the Archdruid, knowing he would not wear them again. Laurinda had many beautiful pieces that Balogue brought from neighboring lands - a pair of gold earrings and a carnelian ring from the Mediterranean, as well as a few other loose gemstones. When Saurina came of age, Laurinda would give these to her.

Reluctantly, she placed her gold cuff bracelet into the box that Balogue gave her the night they decided to marry. Until then, she had not removed it from her wrist. She also had several large clear crystal points that she valued, with the desire to pass them along to Lakaar. Lastly, she laid her gold crown and gold torque, inlaid with large emeralds, into the box, sadly thinking it was best to keep them safe. She wanted to save these pieces for her children when they were old enough to appreciate their value and beauty. In time, she would appoint a new priestess or priest when she passed along the torque and crown.

Lon buried the box just outside their new subterranean home, about a hand's width below the surface of the ground. He marked the location with a dome-shaped rock, its diameter the length of his foot, in which he etched a spiral on the top of the dome. Around it, he laid sod over the surrounding bare ground. Their precious items were now safe from marauders. Soon, the only indication of the hidden box's whereabouts was the rounded stone surface that barely peeked through the green grass.

That night, as the cold settled in, Laurinda told a story, as she often did, to her people who gathered around the fire where it was safe, warm, and dry.

"One of our ancestors taught our people how to live well. Her name was Rionach, a mighty woman, whose powers were of the gods. She was tall, lean, and strong, with shiny long hair the color of the deepest lough. Her eyes shined brightly, yet with the depth of the nighttime skies - a sapphire blue - one could get lost in her gaze. In her long flowing skirts, she moved about as if she floated above the ground, gliding along with an easy grace that attracted both people and animals into her company. But even though she was so powerful, Rionach possessed a quiet reserve, both steadfast and calm in her stillness.

"Whatever tasks her people had to do, she also did. She fished and hunted game, sheared sheep, and wove garments from their wool. Rionach often sowed fields and harvested crops. She cooked and told stories around the fire, in the same way I tell you stories most every night. Rionach did her best to be a part of the community, because in the same way she loved and cared for herself, she loved and cared for her people.

"The way she loved came with an understanding we can all easily remember. First, she knew that where she stood, right here in the present moment, was her access to all the gods. She, like the mightiest oak, was rooted to the core of Mother Earth, enabling her to stand strong, no matter the storm, while also having complete access to *Síoraí* - the eternal.

"Síoraí - where there is no past and no future, where all things exist. Síoraí is what has always been and forever shall be, right in this present moment, where time does not exist. In this present moment, there is no past, and no future - only the eternal now. Here, we ascend, rising above all concerns, where we join with the gods in worlds without end; far beyond this island home we call Eire. Here, we become the power of the gods, where we are one with everything.

"When we are true to ourselves in this way, we rise above and stand tall with our heads held high to receive the crown of starlight that rests gently upon our heads. In our sovereignty, this radiance becomes us as we extend that joy to all those around us - to all people, all animals, the trees, the sea, to all of Mother Earth. The light within us is like the lightning of the skies. It is immediate, powerful, and the brightest thing in our presence. This, my people, is who you are!

"Second, Rionach knew the power of community, the connection to all that reside on Mother Earth. As you extend your arms, you reach out with the power of the light within you to the one next to you, and they do the same. Our task is first to be that light for ourselves, and for others who are ready to receive that light, so they too can shine. As Rionach did, love yourselves and others as the gods love you. Be grateful for who you are, and for all that you have, because you will recognize your value and importance, while seeing the value in those around you.

"In our heavenly state, we are tall like the oak, while reaching out to those we love through our humanity. This is where the two forces meet, for this is the union of both heaven and earth, right at the heart. Only from the heart do we ascend above the earthly domain, while giving of ourselves in service, being that light to all that reside on Mother Earth. In living this way, we all can live and love well - right from the heart of here and now. When we live from the heart, it is not about doing anything, but about being, for the gods live in all that we are. In that, when we are busy in our day, the gods bless everything we do.

"Rionach left us one more simple wisdom to live by. You can do anything you want to do, as long as it brings no harm to anyone or anything. That seems simple enough, does it not? But this simple law causes us to think before we act. It causes us to make choices out of the purity of love, instead of shame, greed, revenge, or jealousy. In everything, we are at choice. So ask yourself, is your choice for the good of all? Is your choice life giving? Is your choice for love? I leave these wisdoms for you to sleep on tonight, because you come from the gods. You are meant to be happy, to be prosperous, and to live well in love..."

CHAPTER Twenty-eight

That evening, all of Apeiros gathered for dinner. Michael tapped his wine glass to get their attention. "This morning, Ananta received a phone call. As it turns out, His Holiness the Dalai Lama had a change in plans. He was expecting a visiting European dignitary, but the gentleman's plans were delayed indefinitely because of a health challenge. So, there's an opening next week for us to have an audience with His Holiness, if we would like to fly to Dharamsala."

The room erupted with excitement. "What do you mean, *if* we'd like to go?" Markos said. "Of course we would!"

"I talked to Pádraig," Sophia said, "and he put me in touch with a travel agent he works with, who is already searching for a group airfare and lodging arrangements."

"So that brings us to the next discussion," Michael said. "Sophia recently acquired another talisman."

"Indeed?" Gaston said, rubbing his hands together. "What? Where? When?"

"A stunning ring we discovered near Michael's project," Sophia said.

"Ah, another revelation coming your way?" Gaston said. Sophia nodded with a smile.

"With each one, her powers expand to such great lengths that I feel it best if she used them while all of you are present. She doesn't know what will happen - if she will go into another one of her past lives, or shift into another dimensional field, where she communicates with the Réalta. Are you all willing to support her tonight after we finish our meal?"

"Yes, of course," Shoshana said.

"I remember when she was the High Priestess of Akrotiri, and how powerful she was then," Markos said. "It's been a long time since we've been a part of her woo woo. Wasn't the last time when we summoned Algernon Gillette - to cleanse his spirit?"

"Yes, it's been a while. Chayton, you haven't seen Sophia in action yet, have you?" Irina said.

"No, but White Buffalo mentioned how powerful she is."

"Very well then," Michael said. "Once we're finished eating, let's clear the table while she gets out her talismans..."

Michael dimmed the lights as Anja and Ananta lit white candles around the great room. At Sophia's request, Michael played a recording of gentle ocean waves over the sound system. They sat on large floor cushions around a coffee table in front of the fireplace. Sophia sat at the table with her talismans before her, the fiery golden chalice reflecting on the golden bowl filled with fresh well water. Around her neck was the gold chain holding the amethyst amulet. She wore her aquamarine ring on her right forefinger, as did the other twelve people of the group. Next to the chalice, she placed the hourglass filled with marble sands from ancient Greece. On her left middle finger, she wore her newest acquired talisman, the golden ruby ring. Lastly, in her left hand was the golden ammonite, set with the labradorite at its center.

Sophia had no idea what she was going to do, or what would transpire, but she trusted Great Spirit, God, the Infinite Intelligence, that whatever emerged would be for the good of all.

"If you will all rest your right hand with your aquamarine ring on the table like the spokes of a wheel." Sophia closed her eyes. "We are gathered here, each of us one with the Source, the all-knowing Infinite Eternality of our souls' greater becoming. In this present moment, as we align with the Divine, we rest in that infinite power of Love and Awareness that resides in our every breath. In ease and grace, we humbly open to greater knowledge of the dimensions beyond what we now know as time and space. May we be astonished and brought to wonderment, and from what we experience, may we use it for the greater good of what we bring to the future of our world. In advance, we give thanks for this experience, knowing we are already blessed. And So It Is!"

She first turned over the hourglass as the delicate sands began to fall with the power of gravity. In her left hand, she held the ammonite, and in her right, she loosely held the chain from which the amethyst gently swung to the right, indicating they were all in the right place at the right time. She placed the ammonite into the water in the golden bowl, and turned her hand so the firelight of the chalice cast its light on the ruby ring.

A beam of light shined from the ruby, so bright that it would have blinded the average person, but those of the circle had already ascended beyond the earthly realm where nothing could bring them harm. They were within the realm of the gods, far beyond human ideals of spirituality. Every one of the talismans became white light, joining in union above the table in a brilliant ball of light that washed out the world of their awareness, taking all to the origins of the Order of Apeiros.

Beyond the veil, they observed a land of opulence, layered with mountainous emerald green forests. Waterfalls gushed to flowing rivers, which led to a multitude of lakes below. Abundant wildlife thrived both on land and sea in the warmth of sunshine, yet with a coolness in the air of early spring.

Not far away was the ocean's edge, with a massive shoreline of the finest white marble sands at the base of rising cliffs, upon which was a thriving community with buildings made of pristine white walls, constructed from wood, stone, and a mortar made from the sands of the shore. Built on a grid, the city contained multi-story houses and places of trade, clearly built and designed by a sophisticated society.

Instantly, Sophia recalled a previous time when she was briefly aware of this same advanced culture, but this time, from her ascended perspective, she witnessed in greater detail how they utilized the earth's elements in ways far more advanced than present day technology.

At the top of one building was an array of massive crystal panels, tipped to receive the sun's light at different times of the day from dawn to dusk. The energy was stored to supply the city's needs. On a nearby hillside, wind generators churned, collecting an additional source of energy for the community's use. One of the river tributaries flowed into a massive conical shaped crystal chamber, forming a forceful spiral of water inside its clear two-story walls. This additional energy source served a dual purpose. From it came healing tones that cured all forms of maladies. Around the chamber, people lay about in the white marble sands, or in the shallow waters of the river itself. The pitch of the crystal chamber changed throughout the day, so whatever the need, one could come at any time to receive healing sounds and vibrations, resulting in an equanimous society of health, peace, and harmony.

Sophia then discovered a part of the city where a magnificent new building was under construction. With laserlike precision, workers used sound and water to cut corners and edges of colossal stones to perfection with no need of mortar, for the blocks of stone fit perfectly together like a puzzle. Workers used powerful forces of water to move the stones into position.

Sophia then found herself standing on the top of a mountain, observing an approaching dark and foreboding storm. Not far were people involved in what appeared to be a sacred ceremony as lightning struck and heavy rains came. Surrounding the group was a circle of tall narrow metal columns. When lightning struck, the metal poles attracted the lightning bolts, creating a circular domed web of energy around the cluster of people. Suddenly, Sophia found herself as one of these people, energized in a way she had never experienced. She looked into the faces of the others who were equally vitalized by the lightning's power, recognizing each as the familiar members of Apeiros, who were also the council that governed the community.

Each was dressed in white as they all stood in a circle. The women wore long flowing silken gowns, and the men were dressed in casual white slacks and white linen button down shirts. Each raised their right hand with their aquamarine ring toward the center of the circle, as the familiar column of white light radiated from their combined energies. Each one spoke aloud the Divine Attributes of Peace, Joy, Harmony, Grace, Health, Oneness, Order, Balance, Abundance, Truth, Compassion, Beauty, all under the umbrella of Love and Awareness.

Sophia said, on behalf of the group, "We gather again in this blessed circle, joining our individual strengths so we may hold the highest blessings for Gaia, her inhabitants, and for the universe itself. As we stand in this circle, we are a representation of Gaia. In your minds, hold the image of Gaia cupped in your hands. Imagine your personal attribute blanketed around her as I speak a blessing for her:

"We bless all forms of water, here on Gaia, from the polar ice caps, the glacial fields, and snow-covered mountaintops, down into the deepest recesses of the surrounding oceans. We hold blessings for all water that flows - for all seas, aquifers, dams, rivers, tributaries, brooks, creeks, lakes, ponds, bogs, marshes, bayous, and waterfalls.

"We send blessings to all parts of Gaia that, by all appearances, seem to be desolate and dry, but all are affected by the power of water - that of the rocks, deserts, and arid lands.

"We bless all forms of moisture in the sky - the clouds, rain, snow, sleet, fog, and mist. For every being made of water, we send blessings to every two-legged, four-legged, winged one, finned one, creepy crawly, and all beings in existence not yet in our awareness. We bless all plant life, from the tallest of trees on the land, to the most miniscule foliage that lives in the sea.

"In this spiral of the blue waters that infuse and surround Gaia, we send this life-giving energy out to our galaxy - to our suns, moons, planets, and stars. Beyond that, we send this blessing of love to all galaxies, nebulae, and the space in between, to infinity.

"We then return that energy back to ourselves, as we feel the ever-expansive spiral of life churning within our DNA - within our body, and in our subtle bodies - within our mind, soul, and spirit. In this, we stand in our individual and collective power, and we are so grateful, knowing that we are blessed, we already know it is so!"

Sophia suddenly understood the workings of the community as she remembered who she once was. She had returned to a recall she had lived before, as it played out again in her memory. Sophia heard familiar voices that came to her through the ethers, and although the language spoken was alien, she could somehow comprehend the communication as if it was her native language. She connected with those around her on a soul-level, within the wider expanse of the all-powerful, ever-present, upward spiral of the Universal Intelligence.

There, at the table in Ireland, Sophia spoke aloud to the other twelve as a channel, not knowing if they could hear her, or if they were with her on the hillside in the ascended dimension. Nevertheless, she conveyed the message she received:

"Welcome to our domain. Do not concern yourself, for you will soon comprehend all the information you receive. Just allow it to fill your mind and heart, and soon, more details will become clear to you. Be sure to meditate and sit in stillness often. In this way, you will more easily prepare for the next time when you return to us. Know that there will be countless times when you come here, for you are an integral part of who we are and what we bring to the entirety of the universe. Remember to keep your heart open wide, for when you live from love, protection from anything you perceive as harm is yours. In this, your intuition will guide you, filling you with the depth of gnosis - the knowledge of the spiritual mysteries. All that you need to live well is easily sourced. Remember to invoke mindfulness - breathe and smile, staying in the present moment. In this mindset, you are always safe."

Sophia looked into the water at the runes etched in the bottom of the golden bowl, entranced by the wisdom coming through her, on behalf of them all.

"You are our daughters and sons. Each of you are one of us, and together, as a collective whole, we are the Réalta. Who you once were, you are now. Who you are now, you will forever be within the evolution of your soul, which is what links you to all aspects of life - to humans, animals, all beings, plants, and all the elements - to eternity itself. Your soul connects to all that is life giving, far beyond your comprehension, and that is why you are now here. Again, where you are in this realm is who you once were, and who you will ever be, for you are infinitely unstoppable.

"Humanity thinks in terms of horizontal time, which is past, present, and future. Whereas, in the truth of all things, the reality of everything that ever occurred, or will ever happen, is what some might call vertical time. All of life happens within this eternal moment of now. Some indigenous people see it as all the directions coming together. The four directions meet at the center, with the earth and sky at the one point of reality - eternal and endless. This is the point of power, the point of light, which is the center of the never-ending, expansive spiral that extends outward to all that has ever been and will ever be. You know it as sacred geometry - in the Flower of Life - you see it in the physical perfection of a sunflower's center. All power resides in this singular present moment where, to humanity, what seems to be time does not actually exist.

"Those you have recalled other lifetimes discovered this singular truth. All of you in the Order of Apeiros understand this truth as your reality. This is the way of being - the Sacred Way of the Heart, the center of all things. Being in the present moment of now is where you heal, create, and join the Universe in Love.

Here in the presence is where God resides. And when we join with it in solidarity, in oneness, we are in the presence of the Presence.

"Sophia, when your father, Patrick, conveyed to you to Know Thyself, he passed on what he finally understood to the depths of his being. To Know Thyself is to know the soul – to come from the heart's wisdom, the connection between all aspects of life eternal. This point of eternality is when what seems like miracles occur. This is when inspired ideas come through, where all things that have ever been merge into that singular moment of inspired absolute brilliance. At that point, life emerges from the paradigms of the known, from what just happened moments before, into the expansiveness of eternal creation.

"All of the individuals you tap into are you, because all beings are of one mind. This is what you call oneness - oneness with other people, with animals, with plants, with Gaia herself. You will discover more of your other lives as you progress in your work. These other lifetimes will continue to teach you about who you are. Learn from them and love them in return, for they too live on in vertical time to infinity, affecting worlds without end. Each of you is a creator of worlds, an architect of infinite universes. Life is endless and expansive, into infinity.

"As you begin to think in these terms, whatever is needed will come easily to you. The limited thoughts of someday or somehow will no longer exist, but instead you will understand how to think from the point of now, because you will be living fully in the present moment, where all power exists. From that frame of mind, you will pinpoint exactly what you desire and bring it easily into fruition. Your thoughts and actions will be inspired, for your intuition and sacred gifts will be a way of life for you, to dimensions beyond your imagining. If you temporarily forget, just remember what Patrick 'knew' when he left you the wisdom to 'Know Thyself.'"

Sophia emerged from the vision on the mountaintop and returned to the room. She removed the ammonite from the water and turned the hourglass over.

"Listen to the sounds of the flowing water. Slowly come back into the room, feeling your chair supporting you, and remove your ringed hand from the table."

Everyone moved around on their cushions.

"Would anyone like to tell me what you experienced?" Sophia asked.

"I don't know who Patrick was," Chayton said, "but when you mentioned him, I saw a tall, wise grey-haired man - an elder - who, I assume, was once a member of Apeiros. He was in conversation with you, Sophia, telling you to Know Thyself, as one of the last things he said to you. Am I right?"

"Yes, that's correct," Sophia said with tears in her eyes. "It's true that one's soul never leaves. Thank you, Chayton. Anything else?"

"He was there with us, on the mountaintop, when we were surrounded by what appeared to be a geodesic dome of electricity," Chayton said.

"Yes, I saw him too! Patrick was a sage. Do you remember your position there?" Sophia asked.

"Yes, I was the Educational Director, teaching both children and adults through the use of crystal-like panels, written in the language that is on all of your talismans. Once we read a crystal, another instantly appeared, with words, pictures, and some type of technology like a video. There also were holographic, three dimensional images to learn from. Anything to be known was inscribed on these crystals. It was like a train of thought, leading from one subject to the next. It was absolutely fascinating!"

"I can still feel the tingling energy from the lightning in my hands," Anja said. "The interesting thing was, it was a torrential rain, but we didn't get wet inside that electrical dome. That's a good thing, because the dome not only energized us, but protected us, as well."

"At the time, I didn't think about that," Christofer said, "because it was a normal existence for us there, but now that I'm away from the experience, I'm quite astounded by it all. I was the Director of Arts and Music. I painted murals on many of the building's pristine white walls. The people who worked with me also did physical sculpture and works that were like holographic images to decorate a home or business through light and sound. The topics were endless. We also had a dynamic theatre arts program as well, with both an outdoor amphitheatre that overlooked the ocean, and a magnificent indoor performing arts center."

"I want to go back and see that!" Ananta said. "I was the Head Chef for Gaia. My crew and I prepared food and sustenance for the grand sovereign and her guests, and for all the people at times. It was quite a challenge, because the guests were not average. They were foreign dignitaries, far from what we know them to be here, in this time period."

"What types of food did you prepare?" Shoshana asked.

"It was all vegetarian and vegan, from an abundance of plants and fruits harvested on the island. You should have seen my kitchen! What I could do with that kind of technology today!"

"It seemed like an island to me, too," Markos said, "but I wasn't certain. It must have been a large island, maybe like it is here in Ireland. My job was a Cultural Attaché - a diplomat, communicating through various languages for visiting guests. Evidently, where we were was a nucleus of sorts. It was a hub of trade, of commodities, and of wealth. Clear and present communication was very important."

"Markos and I worked together, both speaking numerous languages," Irina said. "I was like a Concierge Extraordinaire, providing hospitality for visiting dignitaries, and for local people, too. My job, as a concierge in Constanta, barely touched on the various duties that I had on the island."

"Isn't it interesting that the work we do now is what we did then, or, I guess in another dimension?" Lestari said. "I was a conservationist, working for the well-being and conservation of the surrounding ocean life, for sea animals and plants, as well as land animals and plant life. It was a well-run organization, with no political strife whatsoever. Everyone seemed to work for the well-being of the life of the seas and the land."

"I was thinking the same thing," Darius said. "It seems that our soul's journey has something to do with the work we do. Irina and I worked together in the hospitality field, and I was the administrator, working closely with the Grand Sovereign. Patrick was one of her sages - in fact, each of us was on her council. That was part of why we were standing inside the protective dome of lightning - to physically regenerate as leaders of the island."

"I was an ambassador," Yesinia said, "who traveled to different locations on behalf of the island. Some of the travel was physical, and some was astral, where I was transported energetically to communicate the good works we promoted. Evidently, it was as Markos said, the island was a nucleus - a center place - for the planet, as it was."

"As you might expect, I worked with the ancients," Shoshana said. "I was the Protector of Antiquities, both physically and spiritually, to save the traditions for future generations. There was no need for a grant, because the work was of utmost importance to preserve the society's history."

"Yes, I also worked with Shoshana," Michael said, "and I was also the protector for the Grand Sovereign. However, it was not as much a physical protection that I provided, but one that was spiritual - constantly holding her in what we call love and awareness. That was the work of our council - similar to what we do today as the Order of Apeiros."

"Well, I didn't have a physical job like I do now as an owner of an antique store," Gaston said, "but I was a medium and an intuitive - a sage. There, on the island, people worked closely with others to help guide them, communicating with the spirits of those who had gone on before them, and also through the higher realm on their behalf. I, like all of you, was on the council, in support of the Grand Sovereign. Also, I don't know if any of you were aware, but White Buffalo was there with us, as was Jocelyn, François, and Mika and Jelani. We were all there together, doing the work of the Order."

"It was like a reunion," Sophia said. "There were others, too, who were part of Apeiros long before we were a part of the group. It was as if time did not exist, and yet it contained all time, if you get my gist."

"My job was Trade Administrator," Anja said. "However, the items were not like what we make here - clothing, art pieces, and decorative items. They were pieces of eternal value, such as your golden bowl and chalice. We also made crystal hourglasses, filled with the marble sands of the shoreline. All of your talismans we made, now that I think of it, and there were others, too."

"That leaves you, Sophia. I have a feeling you were the

Grand Sovereign," Anja said.

"Certainly not in the traditional sense of someone sitting on a throne, but my task was being a conduit of the Réalta, an Oracle, taking their wisdom and passing it along. The crystal panels that Chayton worked with, I created - at least the writing, the runes, as we call them, was my work."

"You physically etched the panels and all the talismans with the runes?" Shoshana asked.

"No. It was through deep meditation that the runes would come to me through my thoughts from the Réalta, and then they naturally appeared on all the pieces. The technology of that realm was far more advanced than what we know today. I now understand what White Buffalo told me long ago, that my thoughts and words would be recorded for time immemorial. However, they weren't my thoughts, but were that of the Réalta, downloaded, if you will, through me. Like now, I was a channel.

"I then passed on the knowledge I received to my council - all of you - and we made decisions on behalf of the well-being of the island, its people, and all sentient beings that lived there. The way we thrived affected other lands and innumerable worlds around us. Our purpose was of utmost importance, because it also affected a variety of dimensional fields all at once, through the power that resides only in the present moment."

"So, that's why you're considered as the most powerful oracle of all time," Lestari said. "I mean, I know of your power, but it all makes sense, now that we've traveled back in time to that island."

"So, there are a number of things to discuss," Sophia said. "First, we all are the incarnations of the original Order of Apeiros. Our souls evolved to who we are now; doing the same good works in the world. Second, I was considered the Grand Sovereign because I channeled the Réalta, therefore preserving their knowledge and guidance, and then communicating it to the council, and to the people. I could only do that because each of you did your individual work to support the whole, along with others of Apeiros, which was a much larger body of people then. I was a conduit, a channel that received the information, the knowledge, and wisdom, to pass on to future generations for the betterment of what we now know as our world. But so were each of you. You were - *you are* - a channel, receiving intuitive guidance for the betterment of yourselves and for all."

"Who are the Réalta?" Ananta asked.

"They are who some refer to as Star People. Réalta, in Gaelic means star. The term 'Star People' has been used by so many for centuries, and what I understand about them is far greater than our understanding. They know all there is to know. They are God, or gods, entities, the Ancients. Some consider them to be extraterrestrial beings."

"Are they the Grandfathers?" Chayton asked.

"Yes, and the Grandmothers," Sophia said. "They possess all that we aspire to be, at our best and then some. It's like this, from what I understand: The more I know, the more I know what I don't know, and they are there to fill my mind and heart with intuitive guidance and inspired thought. Of course, you all know that the word 'inspire' comes from Greek, meaning *breath within*, giving life to thought and deed, motivating the actions we take."

"Where does God fit in?" Yesinia said.

"It's my understanding that the Réalta is God, in all forms," Sophia continued. "God, Spirit, Infinite Intelligence, whatever we refer to as the higher realm that is greater than the human mindset, is the all-knowing, ever-present, all-powerful force that has ever existed, and always will exist, far beyond the realm of humanity and that of the universe as we know it. The Réalta is an infinite number of entities that are always present for our higher good, always for our benefit. They embody the qualities and attributes that we hold most dear - that of joy, peace, harmony, order, balance, abundance, health, grace, truth, oneness, beauty, compassion - all under the umbrella of love and awareness. We are the manifest reality of the Réalta, of God, of the Infinite Intelligence. Every living being is. The difference is that some of us know precisely what our soul's task is, while some are yet to discover it, although that calling, if you will, is ever at work within each of us.

"Now that you've had a taste of the origins of the Order of Apeiros, perhaps you will have better insight to the importance of *your* calling, your mission, or that which I prefer to think of as your passion for life.

"The last and most important piece I want to share with you is that we didn't go *back* in time. We ascended into a dimensional field that encompassed the entirety of the universe, but it is far greater, far more advanced with a broader spectrum of what the Universe - God - Spirit, or the Réalta, if you will, has in store for us. What we all witnessed today was just an introduction to that dimensional field. As we re-visit, and even contemplate our experience, we become it yet again, because we are literally living our eternality. It becomes us, as a greater expanse within us as our evolutionary, greater becoming.

"The island where we were is known to some as Atlantis. It is a place where a relative few have gone and experienced. Plato only captured a tiny bit of it, based on stories he heard that were passed down for millennia.

Some think Akrotiri on Santorini was Atlantis, and I tend to believe that it was, but here's the catch - Atlantis is that Nirvana, that paradise, that Heaven, if you will, that place that is not physically available to us, but it still calls us. It's an ideal, a dream of the best we can imagine, right here on Grandmother Earth. Most ancient societies have such a place in their ancient tales. Another thought of where Atlantis once was is on Malta, or Lemuria. Another is Dwarka in the Arabian Sea, on India's Saurashtra Coast. But, I believe, we truly witnessed it in our own way, and we will again. That is the use of these talismans, and in that, I am the Grand Sovereign, because I'm the one through which these talismans are activated. But again, without all of you, I couldn't do this. We do it together."

"When can we go again?" Markos asked. Everyone was lit up with the possibilities of returning to the island.

"I don't know, but I do know this - now that we've done this, our visit to Dharamsala will be even more meaningful when we have an audience with His Holiness the Dalai Lama."

"Maybe we can do it there," Ananta said. "And that brings me to saying good night. I must fly back tomorrow to prepare for your visit. Good night, my precious Apeiros family!"

"Sweet dreams, Ananta. We look forward to sharing your world with you there," Darius said...

CHAPTER
Twenty-nine

That night, Sophia dreamed in an entirely different way than her past visions and past lives, aware of the change as she began to slip into another dimension. She thought the difference must have been for a couple of reasons. It may have been because the entire group returned to the origins of Apeiros, where a shift in consciousness occurred. Or perhaps, because she now had the ruby ring that tapped into a greater knowledge of the Infinite Intelligence, it opened her to even greater levels of awareness. Michael was right, and wouldn't he love to hear her admit that the acquisition of another talisman made her more aware, and more powerful. The idea was both humbling and alarming. With each new talisman, she had no choice but to adjust, not only to new information, but to a heightened perception of life and its offerings.

In this dream, she did not recall her own past life, but that of another, as if she watched a first-person tale in a movie about a man, whose name was Stephen McCarthy...

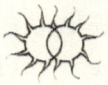

I was born in Trinidad, Colorado, founded in 1862, soon after coal was discovered in the region. It's located in Las Animas County on the central southern border of

Colorado, at an elevation of 6,010 feet. Trinidad is located 21 miles north of Raton, New Mexico, and 195 miles south of Denver. In 1878, the railroad reached the town, making it more accessible to both the east coast and the west. A few of its claims to fame was in 1882, when Bat Masterson served as town marshal, and around 1900, Damon Runyon, who grew up in Pueblo, started his career covering sports for the newspapers and managed a semi-pro baseball team in Trinidad.

It's a mighty fine town, shadowed by Fisher's Peak, just a stone's throw to the south. It has many beautiful three- and four-story red brick buildings on Main Street, where back in the late 1800s, Trinidad was in its heyday, welcoming travelers along the historic Santa Fe Trail. The primary economy, back when I grew up, was coal mining, which drew many European immigrants to work in the mines.

In fact, that was a bad time in Trinidad, because of the notorious Ludlow Massacre, also called the Colorado Coalfield War, that happened as the result of a labor dispute that lasted from September 1913 through December 1914. Conditions in the mines were dangerous, with the risks of explosions, collapse of mine walls, and the constant threat of suffocation. The coalmine death toll in Colorado was more than twice what it was in other coalmines across the United States, with over 1700 deaths from 1884 to 1912. In 1913 alone, 104 coalmining deaths occurred in the state, and over 200 were killed in 1910. The worst single disaster was the Hastings mine explosion in 1917, which killed 121.

The Ludlow war started when national unions tried to move in and organize miner strikes, which didn't sit well with the big mining companies, who evicted the striking miners and their families from their company owned homes in the coal camps. In retaliation, the unions built tent villages for the strikers in locations that blocked strike-breakers from the mine entrances, many who were beaten and a few shot and killed. The mining companies employed hired guns to protect strikebreakers and threaten the strikers.

The violence escalated, but the strikers were no match for the strikebreakers, who had more firepower financed by the mine owners. About October of 1913, Governor Elias Ammons called up the Colorado National Guard, supposedly to restore order, but most people think the governor was sympathetic to the mine owners. Things quieted down through the winter, but the state ran out of money to fund the National Guard, so the governor recalled them but left enough men and resources for the Colorado Fuel and Iron Company to form its own militia to guard and protect its non-union workers.

By the spring of 1914, the violence resumed when a strikebreaker was murdered. On April 20, 1914, the CF&I guardsmen confronted the strikers at Ludlow, and a gun battle broke out that lasted all day. The 1,200 strikers burrowed into pits dug to protect their families as the militia fired machine guns at the tent colony. In all, about 21 colliers, wives, and children were killed, and the entire tent colony was burned to the ground. All in all, up to 199 deaths occurred during the coalfield war, but Ludlow was the most notorious because the women and children who died were trapped and suffocated in a pit under a burning tent.

I don't know why I rambled on about that, because it was a bit before my time, but I guess it's because my grandparents on both sides of the family settled in Trinidad about the time of Ludlow. They were Irish railroad men and women, for the most part, and weren't involved in the coal strikes.

So, getting back to the start of all this, as far as I was concerned, was on October 4, 1918. That was the day I was born, as Stephen David McCarthy. The name Stephen came from a friend of my folks, named after his grandfather Stephanos, who came from the Greek island of Crete. So, my name is spelled with 'ph' and not a 'v'. My parents liked him, and they always liked the name. So that's what they called me and where I got my start.

I had one brother, Sam, who was six years older than me. Now, I'll tell you about how I got my face cut when I was two and a half years old. I have to laugh. My little granddaughter looked at my scar one day and asked me what happened to my face. I told her that I had fallen on a milk bottle and cut my face. She looked at me a minute and said, "You ought to put a bandage on that!" You know, it takes a kid to really put you in your place.

Sam and I had gone to the store. I was two and a half, and Sam was about eight and a half. He was not a very big kid. When we got to Dionisio's store, which was just catty corner across Kit Carson Park from where we lived on Rosita Street, we got the bottle of milk. I cried, of course, because I wanted to carry the bottle of milk home. Sam thought I could handle it. So, he handed me the bottle of milk and we started out.

Sam got a hold of the back of my shirt collar. He would keep hanging on to me to keep me going. Well, just a block from home, I fell on that doggone bottle and it cut my face from the corner of my right eye, clear down under my nose. That flap of skin opened up and just hung there. I guess it was bleeding something terrible.

Sam was trying to carry me, but our cousin, who was with us, was so scared that he held back and wouldn't help Sam out. We finally got to the house and Mother came running out. She called our aunt, who lived right across Kit Carson Park, who got there very shortly after I got home. Mother had me out on the back porch, trying to stop the bleeding. I can still remember seeing Dad. He was coming home from work, and I saw him jump over the fence. I can still remember seeing him running up to the house, wondering what was wrong.

In the meantime, my aunt called old Doctor Alfred Friedenthal, who we all thought was just one step under God. They got my face pinched up, using clamps. Today, they would have stitched me up and there wouldn't be a scar, but they used eight clamps to stop the bleeding. So, that was the way I got the scar on my face. There on Rosita Street, I still remember our telephone number - 714W. Isn't it funny, the little things you remember?

When I was about seven or eight years old, my grandmother, who was a practical nurse, also took care of the ladies around town when they were pregnant. She was also the caretaker and housekeeper for the Tavoularis family, who were Greek. Johnny Tavoularis, the husband, had two children, a boy and a girl, who were a little bit younger than me. Evidently, his wife ran off, or something. Johnny was a gambler - nice man - but a gambler. Grandma would tell stories about how he would come home late at night, and he usually would give Grandma a bag of money and ask her to put it away for him, to keep it safe. She had a hiding place, there in the basement. Then, he took that money and would sometimes be away from home for a week or two at a time. It was kind of a traveling thing. He gambled in Trinidad, in Raton, Pueblo, and Walsenburg, and maybe in Denver.

One night, after Johnny came home, there was a pounding at the door. Grandma answered, and when these two men stepped inside, Grandma said Johnny turned ghost white. He said for her not to worry – he had to go out, but he'd be back later. Grandma said Johnny looked scared, and he kissed his kids before he left and told them to always mind Grandma. And that was it. Johnny never came back, and nobody in town ever dared to even talk about Johnny again.

Grandma took care of those kids for a long time until she got sick, and that's when we took in the kids and kept them in our home. We had them for several years.

Believe it or not, the Mafia was big in Trinidad in those days, but was called the Black Hand back then. As a kid, I didn't know much from anything then, but looking back on it now – who knows? I don't know if she knew it or not, but Grandma was a bagman for old Johnny Tavoularis! It's a lucky thing Grandma was kind of naïve about it all, otherwise maybe she would have disappeared too!

We had a big family when I was a kid. I remember all the Thanksgivings and Christmases when we all got together, mostly at our house. Mom would have these big dinners, and we'd have twenty to twenty-five people, all family - aunts, uncles, and lots of cousins - great gatherings.

Two of my aunts and uncles and their kids all moved to Dawson, New Mexico, which was about 60 miles from Trinidad. Once in a while, we'd make the long trip to Dawson to see the folks, and believe me, that was a long trip. We had to go up over Raton Pass, winding up in the switchbacks in an old Model A Ford up to the top and then back down into Raton. The whole journey was like I said, 60 miles, but in those days when a car could only go maybe 25 miles an hour in the mountains, 60 miles was a real long trip.

One time, I was playing with my cousins, and we were up on a spoil tip at an abandoned mine. That's a large mound of rock and sledge that they excavate from a mine. We were playing cops and robbers. I was about fifteen feet above the ground. I was backing up to look at some of the kids that were above me, because I was going to shoot them. Anyway, I backed off this thing, fortunately, right into a pile of old cinders, but I broke my shoulder. So, my aunt got me bandaged up in a sling, and we left Dawson to get back to Trinidad, to see old Dr. Friedenthal.

Sam was driving, and we got about ten miles from Dawson, when a doggone car ran us right off road into a ditch and kept driving on. It was wet and rainy, and I was lying in the back seat with Mother and my aunt. Dad and Sam were in the front seat, and we were stuck in that ditch. Finally, a car came along and helped us get out of the ditch and back up onto the road. Eventually, we got to Trinidad about three or four in the morning by the time we got home.

Again, Doc Friedenthal took care of me and got me all patched up. I've had my bones broken several times - both my wrists were broken, my shoulder, and got my face cut up, the list goes on. I've always seemed to be accident prone. Some say it's because I move too fast.

Neither Sam nor I took part in organized games at school - baseball, football, and so on, other than intramurals. We didn't have the time to devote, to go out for the school teams, because when we got up that high, we had to start working.

When I was thirteen years old, the year before my freshman year, my first job was at a filling station not too far from our home. In fact, it was right down on the next corner away from Dionisio's store. I started at ten cents an hour as the air boy. This was during the Depression times, about 1928-1930 - the Big Depression. Dad was on two days a week at the Colorado and Southern Railroad. The other times, he also worked at the filling station. Both he and Sam were high paid employees - they got fifteen cents an hour. Of course, they did everything; grease cars, change tires, and that sort of thing, where all I did was be the air boy. When a car came in, I would wash the windshield. I'd check and fill the tires, and check the water in the radiator.

Times were tough then. I don't know how they did it, but Mother and Dad kept everything going with the income we had, 'cause it wasn't very much. I don't know that we missed anything, but it was rough. Everything that Dad, Sam, and I made - all of it went into the pot. That's how we paid the bills.

One of the guys, there at the filling station, had an old Model T truck. When people would call, needing help with a flat tire or something, one of us would go out to help them out. Well, the first time a call came when I was there, he asked me, "Can you drive?"

"Well, sure I can drive." I could do anything. Anyway, I got out there and got that truck to start up, and then I put that dern thing in reverse instead of going forward. I ran over the water pipe and I had water shooting up 20 feet into the air.

When he came running out, he said, "I thought you said that you could drive!"

"Well, I did! I hit that pipe." He didn't appreciate that very much. That was my first experience driving the truck. He wasn't mad about it for too long, figuring I had tried. From then on, I was able to drive.

So again, catty corner, across Kit Carson Park was Dionisio's store, owned by an Italian family. We all liked them. We all traded at that store. I can remember going in there, getting little old penny candy from Mr. Dionisio - real nice people. They were connected to the Black Hand, too. Trinidad was a kind of stopping place from Chicago, through to the West Coast. Gangsters from Chicago, Denver, and Pueblo, when they had to hang out and get away from the law, would come down there and, evidently, stay right there at Dionisio's store.

One Sunday morning, about 2:30 a.m., that doggone Dionisio's store was blown up. There wasn't anyone killed, as far as we know. There was no one there at that time, but it blew groceries all over Kit Carson Park. We tried to see what happened in the middle of the night, but the next morning, we all got out and went into the park with baskets, picking up canned goods that were thrown from the explosion.

We found out later that under Dionisio's store were living quarters, evidently huge living quarters, dug under the store. They had tunnels where the people that holed up could get out, in case the federal people came after them. They would go through these underground tunnels from under Dionisio's store that led to the arroyos, and that's where they could get away.

I worked all through school, and I always had it in my mind to get into the music business or to be an actor. Sam was a saxophone player, and naturally, I had to have a saxophone, too. Finally, I had an orchestra through my senior year in high school and into the year and a half that I went to Trinidad State College.

I worked many jobs. Of course, I mowed a lot of lawns, but I also worked as a salesperson for the J.C. Penney Company, a nice store right on Main Street. When I graduated from high school and went on to junior college, I had a job with Stromberg's Men's Clothing, also on Main Street. It was the nicest men's clothing store in town, which I enjoyed working there. My boss, the manager of Stromberg's, also the brother-in-law of the Stromberg brothers, was also an orchestra leader. He had the most popular orchestra in Trinidad for years and years. He understood. On Saturday nights, he would let me off early, so I could go with my band. We played 'purtnear every Friday and Saturday night during my school years. We always played somewhere, because dancing was the main entertainment in Trinidad. Either we went to a show or we danced. Of course, we met in our homes for dance parties. We did that often, because it was the only thing we had to do. There were a lot of good dancers in Trinidad.

I don't remember much from my early school years that was very outstanding, but I followed right along after everything that Sam did. When Sam was in high school, he was a cheerleader. So, naturally, when I got to high school, by gosh, I wanted to be a cheerleader too. And I did. I was first the assistant, the second cheerleader. Then from there on, for my sophomore, junior, and senior year, I was the lead cheerleader. As such, of course, I knew everybody in school. God, I think I knew everybody in town.

I had a great time in high school, yet I was almost to the point in my senior year where I was going to flunk out. There was one class, my chemistry class. It was vital that I passed that class so I could graduate. So I went to my chemistry teacher and told him I had to have that credit to graduate. I promised not to go to college, so he might as well get me through.

He said, "Well, Stephen, you promise you won't go on to college?"

"Yes, I promise." So he passed me and I got through. I

never was a very good student, but I sure had a good time in school. At our school, the total enrollment was about 750 students. When I graduated in 1936, we had 160 graduates that year. It was a lot of fun growing up there.

I went on to junior college in Trinidad. The first person I ran into, who I knew, was the teacher of my bookkeeping class; my high school chemistry teacher. I can still remember him sitting there and looking at me, saying, "Stephen, you promised you wouldn't go on to college!" He was kidding.

I went on for a year and a half, and didn't graduate, because Mother and Dad sent me back to Chicago, to Columbia College of Radio and Dramatics. That was about 1938 or '39. That's where I met Mazie Buchanan, which was probably the luckiest thing that ever happened to me. She was the prettiest little thing, about 5'1" tall, with sparkling brown eyes, and brunette shoulder length hair. She wore it half-up and half-down, as they said back in the day. I was about a foot taller than she was, being 6' tall and slender. At that time, I had a fine head of dark brown hair. Can't say that about myself today, because the few hairs that I have on the back of my head are now gray and wispy.

Mazie and I went to school together, and of course, I had to come back before long, because I knew I was going to be drafted. Mother and Dad moved to Denver while I was in school. I returned home in October. After Mazie finished school, she went to work for a Chicago radio station, doing the kind of work she really wanted to get into. It was a really great time for her. My Mazie just happened to be the first woman disc jockey in the entire city of Chicago.

It was not long before I came back home, when one of the most unhappy things that ever happened to me occurred. It was a terrible thing. Sam was married to

Lucille. They had a little girl named Samantha, Sammie for short. They lived in Albuquerque. Sam finally got a job he'd always wanted, driving a bus with the Greyhound Bus Company. He always loved to drive. He drove one of the smaller busses with about 25 passengers. He was driving to Roswell, and at one of the stops, he got a hold of some poison fish. He was very sick.

Mother, Dad, and I went to Albuquerque and got Sam, Lucille, and the baby, and brought them back up to Denver. The second day after we got home, on October 16, 1941, Sam died, which was a very traumatic thing, of course. I don't think Mother and Dad ever got over it. Mother was still at the hospital with my aunt when Dad and I got there around 3 a.m. You see, Sam had a bad heart, caused by rheumatic fever when he was a little boy. When he got that food poisoning, he got so sick that his heart couldn't take it.

The morning that Sam died, when I got home, I was in the bathroom, standing at the sink. I turned around and Sam was standing there, just as clear as can be. He just looked at me. I don't remember him actually saying anything, but then he just disappeared. I still think that I saw him there. I was, of course, very upset. It was a traumatic thing when Sam died. He'd always been a hero and a role model for me.

Then I was drafted. Sunday, December 7, 1941 was my first day in the Army. That morning, I had just gotten into Fort Bliss, Texas, in El Paso. It was about seven in the morning, and while we were waiting to be processed, we were playing football, when I broke my ankle. They were carrying me to the hospital when word started to come through about the Japanese bombing Pearl Harbor. That's when we actually went to war. We were all looking at each other wondering, 'where the Hell is Pearl Harbor?' We soon found out what a terrible thing it was. I always said the Japanese heard that I had been inducted into the Army, and they figured they'd better get this thing over with before I was trained, or they'd lose the war, which, of course, they did.

After my ankle healed, I took my basic training at Fort Warren, Wyoming. I was in the Quartermaster Corps there. When we finished basic training, I was shipped out to Fort Ord, California, where I joined the 3rd Division for about eight months. When I asked to be sent to OCS, Officers Candidate School, I was accepted. I remember the captain of my company called me in and said there was not an opening in Quartermaster OCS, but there was one in Infantry School. I could wait at least another month for an additional allotment for Quartermaster School, where I probably would have eventually been assigned to some kind of non-combat duty.

I remember rising up out of my chair, saying, "Sir, I've come into the Army to fight. I'll go to Infantry OCS."

He said, "Cripey! You must be crazy, but if that's what you want to do. Okay, we'll shoot you out."

At that time, I was a corporal, and they sent me to Fort Benning, Georgia, where I spent three months in OCS, when I graduated as a Second Lieutenant. Luckily, I was assigned the 89th Division, which was stationed in Colorado Springs, Colorado, where I spent 'purtnear a year.

Mazie and I were married in February 13, 1943. We wanted to have our wedding on Valentine's Day, but the chaplain, who we were fond of, was transferring out. So, we moved up our marriage one day so he could officiate at our wedding. Mother and Dad, my grandparents, and a few friends came from Denver for the wedding out at

Camp Carson. They all stayed at the Antlers Hotel in Colorado Springs.

Grandpop wanted to get his pants pressed. So we took his pants down to the cleaning shop. Pop was sitting in the bathroom with no pants for a long time, and finally Mazie called the cleaner, who had made some kind of error. They hadn't even started to clean or press his pants. Mazie got the thing straightened out and got the pants back, so we finally made it to the chapel at Camp Carson. We had a big group for the reception at the Antler's Hotel, and had a lot of fun.

Mazie and I rented a little house not far from Manitou Springs, a little bit west of Colorado Springs. Living there turned out to be kind of a fiasco. I had to get up so early in the morning to leave the house about five o'clock to get out to camp in time for reveille, which left Mazie there alone much of the time.

It snowed a lot in Manitou, and I remember one morning Mazie went out to pick up the newspaper. I was having a cup of coffee, and I walked in just as she was going outside. I told her there was a lot of snow, and I'd be happy to go get the paper, but she said, 'No, I can get it.' So she takes one step outside, and she slipped on the sidewalk and slid about thirty feet right down to the end of the drive, where the paper was. I couldn't help but laugh as I stepped out on the porch, but Mazie, who is the funniest person I ever knew, just looked around and then grabbed the newspaper, opened it up, and started reading right there in the snow! I laughed until I cried! Funny the things you remember, even when it was so long ago.

One night, there was a prowler that got up onto the back porch. Mazie was there alone. There were Coca Cola bottles in cartons, and she said those doggone bottles started exploding, scaring the prowler away. I later got to thinking about it, wondering if maybe it was a bear attracted to the sweet smell of the cola, and he knocked those bottles over and broke them. But that was enough to convince us that it was no place for Mazie to be by herself. So, we moved into town to a house on Cache la Poudre, where we spent most of our time when we were in Colorado Springs.

I remember one time, when we had Mother and Dad down for dinner. Mazie never did a lot of cooking. Her mother and aunt did those sort of things. Mazie had a real nice dinner, but the gravy didn't turn out as well as she would have liked it, because we had to slice it, rather than pour it. But Dad made a big fuss over it, saying it was the best thing he had ever tasted. Dad was like that. He'd eat anything, and he always liked it.

My claim to fame was while I was with the 89th Division, 355th Infantry. I was the platoon leader, and made quite a good showing in the exercises out in the field. The general came out and was very complimentary. I was the first member of my graduating class at OCS to receive a promotion to first lieutenant. Unfortunately, it seemed like everything that happened from there on, happened just at the wrong time to get my promotion to captaincy. I served as company commander when I went overseas, but I should have had my captaincy. At the time, there were no openings for captains. They brought in officers from other branches of the 89th Division - medical corps and so on. Being overstaffed with captains, they filled in the infantry companies and battalions with men of that rank.

I had a regimental commander, who was a fine man. He did everything in his power to get me into the right spot for promotion, but things changed and we missed. I heard later that he went overseas. Some kind of foul-up happened and he blamed himself for losing some of his men, later committing suicide. I hated that, because he was a real fine man.

Mazie and I were still in Colorado Springs when the 89th Division was transferred out. We first had maneuvers in California, at Hunter Liggett Army Base, when I got into some poison oak and was sent back to Fort Ord Army Hospital. At the time, Mazie and three of the other officers' wives were staying at a place in Carmel, which wasn't far from Monterrey. I called Mazie to let her know that I was in the hospital, and she came over right away. When she came into the hospital ward, she walked right past my bed, because she didn't know it was me. I was so swollen, that my eyes were almost shut and my face was 'purtnear twice its size.

I spent quite a while there - sort of a miserable time, but it was awful nice having Mazie there, so I could visit with her every day until I got well enough to go back to my outfit that was stationed at Camp Roberts, after coming out of maneuvers at Hunter Liggett. There, camped outside of Camp Roberts, we ate out in the field, but I got to eat at the mess inside a couple of times while visiting with my cousin, who was stationed there. Poor guy, he was never happy, and never seemed to adjust to the army life. He was finally transferred to Newfoundland, which wasn't a very good spot either. He never was in combat, but spent quite a bit of time up there before he was discharged.

After Camp Roberts, we went back east to Camp Butner, in North Carolina. We were stationed there for a very short time, six weeks, if that long. Mazie joined me there. We got an apartment in Durham, North Carolina, where we also bought a car. We enjoyed ourselves while we were there, but soon had to sell the car and let go of the apartment, because we were sent to Camp Shanks, in New York. From there I would go overseas. Before Mazie left for home, we went to Washington D.C. to meet up for dinner with an old school chum of mine, and his wife. Then I got my orders to go overseas.

Mazie returned to live with her folks in Aurora, Illinois, near Chicago, to work for Elgin Watch Company, the largest watch company in the world. Because of the war, Elgin switched its civilian manufacturing to the defense industry, making military watches, chronometers, fuses for artillery shells, aircraft altimeters and other instruments, along with sapphire bearings for army cannons.

In New York, we got on the ship in the evening. About half of our guys were seasick before we even left the dock. I always thought that, if you felt you were going to get seasick, you did get seasick. One of my buddies said that his banana tasted the same coming up as it did going down.

We left New York on a Liberty ship, built by the Kaiser Shipbuilding Company out of Rhode Island. They were turning out ships fast to use as troop ships. We went out on a convoy with several hundred ships in all. We zigzagged clear across the Atlantic Ocean to confuse the enemy. We got to Scotland, where we went up through the Firth of Clyde to Glasgow. We got off the ship, and were put on trucks to go clear down to the south of England, where we went across the English Channel to Le Havre. I was not in an invasion group. There was no combat at that time, thank goodness. This was after D-Day, June 6, 1944, in Normandy, the largest seaborne invasion in history. D-Day was a terrible thing - an awful lot of lives lost there.

When I finally got my assignment overseas, I served as an executive officer of a company of approximately 300 men. My company commander was a full-blooded Indian. He was a real fine man. Like me, he was a first lieutenant, but he was a senior first lieutenant over me, so he was in charge of the company.

From Le Havre, we got onto trucks for a time until we got to a train station. The officers were assigned to different train cars. My commander and I were distributing the officers onto each car. I was going to take a certain car, but found another officer already on it. So, by the time I went to get another assignment, they had all been taken care of. So, I hopped on the last train car.

It was night when we left. We traveled through Paris, but the only thing I saw of the city was from the door of the boxcar with about 40 men inside. We had a real trying experience on the train, because that night, there was an accident. One of the cars in the middle of the train jumped the tracks and rolled over. As it turned out, that was the car originally assigned to me. The officer was the last man to get on the car. He was standing in the doorway that popped open when the car rolled over, and he was killed.

On the train, we finally reached our destination. Then we unloaded onto trucks. Here again, I was assigned to a specific truck, but the truck had two officers on it already. So, I went back to get into another truck. Well, during this truck ride, that doggone truck that I was supposed to be on ran into another vehicle, and one of the officers was killed.

I guess somebody was just looking after me.

I didn't want to let close calls like that bother me, because there was danger all around us, and if I let it get to me, I wouldn't be much good to me or my men. Later that night, we bivouacked in the woods. We were getting close to the fighting now, because all night we could hear shelling not too far away. These dull thuds and faint flashes of light, like a distant thunderstorm, one after another, all night long – sometimes close enough to shake the ground. Everybody knew, by next light, we were going to march right into that storm.

It was hard to sleep out there, so I sat up and suddenly noticed this young fella was also sitting up – a ways off and away from the rest of us - just staring out in the darkness. I was 26, so I wasn't really that old myself, but this boy was probably not more than 18 or 19. I thought I should go tell him to get back with the rest of us – you know, safety in numbers.

Poor kid was scared. His hands were trembling - I can still see him struggling to get a cigarette in his mouth - and I could see he'd been crying, although when I crawled up to him, he rubbed his eyes and acted like he wasn't. I asked him where he was from – just to try to help him calm down. Said he was from Erie, Pennsylvania. I tried to make some more small talk. I said everybody here was scared, and it was nothing to be ashamed of. That if we all stick together, we'd get through this.

But, the strangest dern thing, I'll never forget his face when he looked at me. It was like he'd seen a ghost. His face was white as a sheet, and his eyes were dull and almost lifeless. He looked at me, and he said something that to this day I can still hear his voice in my head. He said, "Lieutenant, I ain't gonna get out of here alive..."

Sophia woke up in a sweat, knowing she had just begun to see into Stephen's life - that of being a soldier in World War II...

CHAPTER
Thirty

"I thought I'd stop by to see if I could lend a hand before you fly off to India," Pádraig said.

"You read my mind!" Sophia said. "I planned to call and see if you could take us to Shannon Airport tomorrow, but you'll have to get a couple more drivers and vehicles."

"Consider it done."

"And something else, Pádraig, the Ello Sisters and their husbands are going to London for a few days while we're gone. Would you consider house sitting to take care of Digit? We would certainly pay you, and you could use the pool, and the jetted tub, and the refrigerator is full of food."

"Sure look it. I have a few day tours on the slate, but I can look after the place and the magic little four-legged black kitty. I do believe she fancies me."

"I'll have you know, that is an enormous compliment by her. Digit doesn't take well to just anyone," Sophia said.

"Well then, I'm honored."

"Ahem... you might want to close all the doors to the rooms when you stay here," Gaston said.

"Close the doors?" Sophia asked.

"Well, we never told you," Darius interjected, "because you were in Hawaii, and there was no real reason to do so."

"And we thought," Gaston said, "if you found out, you'd think we're were slipping, and you'd put us in a home."

Sophia laughed. "What happened?"

"Well, Digit made herself scarce for a few days, and we feared we lost her," Darius said.

"There was nothing to worry you about," Gaston said. "I did some of my woo woo in the great room, and we discovered her lying in the middle of a beam overhead, staring right down at us with those big golden eyes. You know, cats like high places."

"Clear up on the beam?" Sophia said. "That little nut. Sometimes I can't find her, either, but I never thought of looking there. How did you get her down?"

"I got some of those irresistible cat treats out of the pantry, and persuaded her to come to us," Darius said.

"Yes, and then Darius took most of your blank canvases and placed them around the banister railings, so she wouldn't 'beam her way' out of our reach again. We shut all the doors to all the rooms, and she slept with one of us each night with the door closed. We were the ultimate cat sitters, I assure you!"

"*That's* why my canvases were in disarray," Sophia said.

"I prefer to think of them as 'being re-arranged' in that chaotic studio of yours," Gaston said with a satisfied grin.

"Yes, and we took an extension pole and duct taped it to the handle of a kitchen mop and cleaned off your beams," Darius said. "Those beams were covered with paw prints of this tiny little cat." Digit jumped up into his lap, head-butting Darius' hand, clearly knowing she was the topic of conversation.

"Duct tape - a man's best friend," Gaston said.

"Unfortunately, I wasn't able to use it to extract Gaston from the elevator," Darius said.

"How's that?"

"Nothing," Gaston said. "So, Pádraig, just keep in mind Digit is very independent, and she often likes her solitude."

"Right then, the doors will be shut, and I'll bring extra bags of cat treats to keep her in my spell. How does that sound?" Pádraig said.

"I'm sure she'll be in good hands," Sophia said...

A week later, everyone arrived safely at the Dharamsala-Kangra Airport at Gaggal, in the Indian state of Himachal Pradesh. Ananta had been there for a week, preparing for their visit. When they arrived at their hotel, she left each of them a personalized welcome basket, filled with snacks, bottles of water, and toiletries, which was certainly appreciated after their 24-hour-long journey. They had three days to adjust to jet lag, and to prepare themselves before their audience with the Dalai Lama. Ananta also left them information about the city.

About Dharamsala

Dharamsala means spiritual dwelling or sanctuary. It is a hillside city on the edge of the Himalayas, with an elevation from 4500 feet to 7112 feet, surrounded by deodar cedar forests and rhododendrons. Its population is over 31,000 people, and is mostly a farming community, growing rice, wheat, and tea.

Things to see and places to go:

- Dharamsala has beautiful tea gardens, known for its world-renowned Kangra green tea. My personal favorite is their Masala Chai.

- The area is a popular site for bird watching.

- If you want to go trekking, there are many paths to take, from one that is two kilometers long, to some that take several days.

- Rock climbing over the ridges of the Dhauladhar range is popular for the adventurous type.

- The markets in Lower Dharamsala are fun to go through, with many offerings of India.

- There are many restaurants, serving Indian, Tibetan, and Himalayan fare. A few serve western foods.

<u>Weather:</u>

- July is monsoon season in our subtropical climate. Temperatures can reach as high as 108 degrees Fahrenheit this time of year, but so far, we are fortunate that the temperature has been only 80 degrees with no rain. Let us keep our fingers crossed.

The afternoon before they were to attend a group meeting with the Dalai Lama, they met to review details about the life of His Holiness.

"Ananta, I would first like to learn a bit more about Buddhism," Darius said. "Buddha is not one to worship, as Christians worship Jesus, correct?"

"Yes," Ananta said. "Let me begin with what I was taught. It all began with Siddhartha Gautama, who was born as a prince of the Shakyá kingdom in modern day Nepal, around the year 563 BCE. 'Siddhartha' means, 'he who achieved his aim.' He was also named Sakyamuni - Sage of the Shakyás. His father was an elected chieftain, and his mother was a Maya born Koyiyan princess, who died soon after his birth. A mountain hermit seer named Asita announced that the child would be either a great king or a great Sadhu - a holy man. Eight Brahmin scholars predicted the same.

"His mother's youngest sister brought up Siddhartha, who was destined to live the life of a prince, with three palaces built for him for different seasons of the year. He was described as being pleasing to the eye - quite handsome with blue eyes, and a god-like form, with a most beautiful, clear, and radiant golden complexion.

"His father shielded him from religious teachings, and from knowledge of human suffering. At age sixteen, his father arranged for him to marry his cousin, who was also sixteen. She gave birth to a son, and they lived a life with everything provided for their needs. Siddhartha spent 29 years of his life as a prince, but he felt his life of material wealth was not the life for him.

"He left his palace, his wife, and son to meet his subjects, despite his father's intentions to shield him from the sick, aged, and suffering. First, he encountered an old man, then one who was diseased, a decaying corpse, and an ascetic. In his shock at the suffering of mankind, the roots of Buddhism began. Striving to overcome all of the suffering, he chose the life of an ascetic, or monk, living exclusively on charitable donations to survive. He practiced yoga, attaining high levels of meditative consciousness, and was asked to succeed his teacher, but again, he was not satisfied.

"He realized the life of extreme asceticism didn't work for him, and he discovered the Middle Way - a path of moderation, through the Noble Eightfold Path, which consists of eight practices: right view, right resolve, right speech, right conduct, right livelihood, right effort, right mindfulness, and right samadhi, which is meditative absorption or union.

"Some of you may know the story of him sitting under a pipal tree in Bodhi, India. The ficus tree is now known as the Bodhi Tree, where he vowed to remain until he found the truth. It is said that after 49 days of meditation, at the age of 35, he attained enlightenment and became known as the Buddha, or 'Awakened One.' In his awakening, he realized the complete insight of the Four Noble Truths. Part of the third truth is Nirvana, which is the goal of the Noble Eightfold Path, symbolized by a wheel that resembles a ship's wheel."

"Are you saying that being awakened and enlightened are the same thing? Is Nirvana also enlightenment?" Anja asked.

"That's a good question!" Ananta said. "Awakening or enlightenment is an event, whereas Nirvana, simply stated, is a transcendent state - a way of being in which there is no sense of self, having been released from the effects of karma and the cycle of death and rebirth. Nirvana is the final goal of Buddhism. Personally, I think of Nirvana as the ultimate state of grace.

"The moment of awakening, or enlightenment, is a single moment of profound spiritual insight, where we understand that all beings are awake, but most don't realize it. Enlightenment is realization, a building upon other moments of enlightenment, which can occur many times in a lifetime."

"So, if we awaken fully, we dwell in the state of Nirvana, free of suffering, while helping others to do the same?" Anja asked.

"Yes! This is the Way, the Turning of the Wheel of the Law. From the state of Nirvana, the Buddha began to teach the dharma of Buddhism, which is universal truth. A company of Buddhist monks soon formed, becoming more than 1000 monks in short order. In his teachings of the dharma, he taught the Middle Way, the five basic moral precepts, which are refraining from taking life, stealing, acting unchastely, speaking falsely, and drinking intoxicants. Along with meditation, these are the foundation of Buddhism.

"He taught the Four Noble Truths - The Truth of Suffering, The Truth of the Cause of Suffering, The Truth of the End of Suffering, and The Truth of the Path that Leads to the End of Suffering, which is Nirvana. The path that leads to the cessation, or the process of the ending of suffering, is the Noble Eightfold Path, the practices that I mentioned before.

"His father, Suddhodana, having heard of his son's awakening, sent ten different delegations to ask him to return to Kapilavastu. The first nine delegations did not deliver the message, but instead joined the sangha - an assembly or community of monks, nuns, novices, and laity. However, a childhood friend of the Buddha was the leader of the tenth delegation, who did deliver his father's message, and he also joined the sangha. Two years later, the Buddha agreed to return, making the two-month journey on foot, teaching the dharma along the way, which is the teaching of Buddhism - the truth and nature of reality or universal truth.

"The Buddha and the sangha were invited to the palace for a meal, followed by a dharma talk. His father then became a sotapanna, meaning one who entered the stream, the first of the four stages of enlightenment. Many members of the royal family also joined the sangha, including the Buddha's son, Rahula, who was seven years old. Later, he became one of his father's ten chief disciples.

"Before his death, Suddhodana became an arahant, meaning worthy or noble - one who has attained spiritual enlightenment. After his father's death, women wanted to join the sangha, thus creating the order of nuns, with the Buddha realizing that males and females had an equal capacity for awakening. So, for 45 years, the Buddha traveled, teaching all types of people, from nobles to servants, and even those who had committed heinous acts, such as murder and cannibalism. During the four months of the rainy season, they retreated to monasteries, parks, or forests, where people came to them.

"At the age of 80, the Buddha died after falling ill from eating his meal, entering parinirvana - the final deathless state. His teachings were passed down by oral tradition, and were first committed to writing 400 years later."

"So, theoretically, anyone can become a buddha?" Darius asked.

"Simply speaking, a buddha is an 'awakened one,' who has attained bodhi, meaning knowledge or wisdom - an ideal state of awakened intellectual and ethical perfection," Ananta said. "Buddha literally means 'enlightened one' - a knower. In Buddhism, we do not become *like* the Buddha. We work to attain buddhahood ourselves to become awakened. So yes, anyone can become a buddha. When one does, one can choose the altruistic path of a bodhisattva, which is an enlightened being, who rather than leaving samsara – the cycle of death and rebirth – he or she continues to help others to attain enlightenment. That was the work of the Buddha, himself. So, there it is – Buddhism, in a nutshell."

"Thank you so much, Ananta," Darius said.

"Now, I have questions about the Dalai Lama," Michael said.

"While I do work for him," Ananta said, "I will turn to Markos, who is much more knowledgeable about the life of His Holiness."

"I've had some food delivered," Sophia said, "so let's first take a break before we review his history."

CHAPTER
Thirty-one

"On to the Dalai Lama," Markos said. "Prior to the first Dalai Lama, there were at least 60 people preceding him in lineage, who were considered incarnations of Arya Avalokiteshvara – or, a Bodhisattva, as Ananta explained. Ten of these were Tibetan kings and emperors, and fourteen were Nepalese and Tibetan yogis and sages. His Holiness considers himself to be, in fact, 74th in line, traced back to the first incarnation of a Brahmin boy.

"The first Dalai Lama, Gendun Drup, was born in 1391, but was not named Dalai Lama until 104 years after his death. I invite you to research his remarkable life when you have time. He lived to the age of 84, longer than any of his 13 successors, with the exception of the 14th Dalai Lama, whom we shall soon meet.

"In 1682, a government minister kept the death of the fifth Dalai Lama a secret for fifteen years, ruling Tibet with a lookalike. Since the lineage of the Dalai Lama began, only half of them lived to their thirties. Some believe that the 9th through 12th Dalai Lamas were killed in palace conspiracies. Before His Holiness, the 14th and *our* Dalai Lama, went into exile, he was the paramount spiritual leader in Tibet and in 25 Himalayan and Central Asian Kingdoms. To over 50 million people, he was the source of philosophical and spiritual inspiration. Now, he is known throughout the world to billions."

"How did he come to be Dalai Lama?" Michael asked.

"In December 1933, the 13th Dalai Lama died early in life, making way for a leader of troubled times to come. In the process of his mummification, his head turned from facing south to northeast, considered a sign of the direction to look for the new Dalai Lama. The search then began for his reincarnation, which can take sometimes two or three years.

"In the meantime, Lhamo Thondup was born on July 6, 1935, on a straw mat in a cowshed in a small rural village in Taktser Amdo, in northeastern Tibet. He was one of 16 children, of whom seven survived, five boys and two girls. His father, a man with a short temper, was a horseman and a farmer of barley, buckwheat, and potatoes, and he also raised sheep. His mother was a kind and gentle soul, later known in her social role as Tibet's 'Mother of Compassion.'

"As a small boy, Lhamo would often pack a bag, saying he was going to Lhasa. In the chicken coop, he was often found sitting on the shelf in the hay. Perhaps he knew that someday he would be sitting on the golden throne. He always wanted to sit at the head of the table. It could be that he knew there were greater things in store for his life, other than being a farmer like his father.

"During this time, the Regent, Teting Rinpoche, went to Lhamo Lhatso, the sacred lake in central Tibet. It is believed that the female guardian of the lake, Palden Lhamo provides guidance, as an emanation of the Goddess Kali, the Shakti of the Hindu God Shiva."

"Who or what is Shakti? I have always wondered," Yesinia asked.

"She is the primordial cosmic energy - the divine feminine creative power - otherwise known as 'The Great Divine Mother,'" Ananta said.

"Thank you," Markos said. "I wasn't sure of that, myself. So, the Regent purposely went to sit in meditation by the lake, and there he envisioned three Tibetan letters, Ah, Ka, and Ma, along with an image of a three-story monastery with a turquoise and gold roof, and a small house with a strangely shaped gutter on the roof's edge. He thought the Ah referred to Amdo, the northeastern province, and Ka must indicate the monastery at Kumbum. Indeed, the monastery was a three-story building with a turquoise roof. The search went on through neighboring villages for a small house with an unusual gutter, until they found a house with gnarled branches of juniper wood on the roof.

"At the house, the group requested to stay the night, already knowing that the child's elder brother and great uncle were recognized as high-ranking lamas. The child recognized the Regent when he entered the house, calling out, 'Sera lama! Sera lama!' - Sera being the Regent's monastery. The Regent, disguised as a servant, spent the evening playing with the youngest child of the house, observing his ways.

"A few days later, they returned with a number of artifacts, such as prayer beads and drums, which were possessions of the 13th Dalai Lama, and several items that were not his. The items were placed before the child, leaving him with the option to choose from the collection. He pointed out each one belonging to the previous Dalai Lama, saying, 'It's mine. It's mine.'

"Soon after, Lhamo Thondup was recognized as the new Dalai Lama. He was taken from his family to a monastery in Kumbum, Tibet. Two years later, he was taken to the thousand-room Potala Palace in Lhasa, the capital of Tibet, along with his family, where he and his brothers fought with each other the entire way. He began his schooling with only one classmate, one of his brothers. If the Dalai Lama misbehaved, his brother took his punishment."

"Ah," Gaston said, "if only I had been selected." Everyone but Darius chuckled.

"On February 22, 1940, at the age of four, he was officially installed as the spiritual leader of Tibet, and forfeited his name Lhamo Thondup for Jetsun Jamphel Ngawang Lobsang Yeshe Tenzin Gyatso. So, Michael, you have nothing on His Holiness."

"I feel his pain," Michael laughed.

"He was more simply known as Tenzin Gyatso. Tenzin means the holder of Buddha Dharma, and Gyatso means ocean. Each of the 14 Dalai Lamas were named Gyatso. We know him as His Holiness the 14th Dalai Lama of Tibet, considered the living incarnation of the Buddha.

"At the age of six, the Dalai Lama became a Buddhist monk, with a shaved head, wearing maroon and yellow robes. He is the spiritual leader and head of the Tibetan government-in-exile, and refers to himself as a 'simple monk.' As opposed to the Buddha, he came from the most humble beginnings, to become one of the most recognized and beloved people of the world.

"The Dalai Lama is believed to be the reincarnation of his predecessors, who are manifestations of Arya Avalokiteshvara, or to Tibetans as, Chenrezi, the patron saint of Tibet, and Bodhisattva of Compassion, the holder of the White Lotus."

"Define bodhisattva again, please," Darius said.

"Bodhisattvas are realized beings," Ananta said, "inspired by a wish to attain Buddhahood - reaching Nirvana - but they delay doing so for the benefit and compassion of all sentient beings."

"In 1950," Markos continued, "three months following the Communist takeover in China, Mao Zedong announced plans to liberate Tibet from exclusive rule of the Dalai Lama, based upon his thought that Tibet was no longer an independent country, but a part of China. Soon, 80,000 troops of the Red Army raided remote areas of Tibet and approached Lhasa, its capital.

"Historically, by the 13th century, Mongol rulers gained authority in Tibet. Tibetans made the claim that their relationship was based on their common religion of Buddhism, and that the Mongols didn't stand with the Chinese. However, the Chinese considered differently. To them, the Mongol authority in Tibet was the establishment of 700 years of China's political dominion of Tibet.

"For two hundred years, relations between Tibetans and Mongols had gone awry. However, the 3rd Dalai Lama, known at the time as Sonam Gyatso, had gained a reputation for his great spirituality, thus receiving an invitation to meet with Altan Khan, chief of all Mongol Tribes. In 1577 - 1578, Sonam Gyatso traveled 1,500 miles to Mongolia, to meet with the Mongol chief, who, by that time, was given the title of King by the Ming dynasty. Altan Khan was the descendant of Kublai Khan, who lived from 1215 to 1294, also believed to be the reincarnation of his ancestor. When Sonam Gyatso died in 1588, his incarnation – the new Dalai Lama – was Altan Khan's great-grandson.

"Their meeting resulted in the re-establishment of strong Tibet-Mongolian relations, as Altan Khan and his followers soon adopted Buddhism as their state religion. Khan called Sonam Gyatso 'Dalai' - Mongolian for 'ocean.' The name Dalai Lama then became known far beyond the Tibetan world, and was thus applied in retrospect to the first two incarnations.

"In the 1950s, it was clear that Tibet had not grown with modernization, and was not prepared to defend itself against the Communist regime. Here they were, at the rooftop of the world, a country with no economic value, yet it was the size of modern Europe. Their army was ill prepared and poorly trained. There were no paved roads, few bridges, and a small number of people spoke no language other than their own. The Dalai Lama later wrote that, had the country modernized instead of turning away from reform, 'Tibet's situation today would be very different.'

"In 1950, The Dalai Lama was 15 years old, and it was his wish to negotiate with China, recognizing the need for Tibet to become part of the modern world. He said, 'I am just a simple human being. This is nothing special. I come from a small village with no modern education, and no awareness of the world.' His wisdom came from meditation - from the mountains, rivers, the wind, the trees, and the wide-open spaces, knowing he had a calling to lead his people away from danger. He felt that by meeting Chairman Mao, face to face, he could negotiate with the Chinese in a dignified manner. Little did he know, at the time, that he had an unimaginable burden to bear."

"Indeed," Christofer said. "Picture yourself at 15, confronting Chairman Mao over the fate of your people? Astounding."

"However, in 1951, the Chinese forced the Dalai Lama and his delegation to sign a 17-point agreement for a peaceful liberation of Tibet - officially incorporating Tibet into the People's Republic of China. As Red Army troops entered Lhasa, it created great financial difficulty for Tibetans, who had to feed them. At first, the Chinese were amiable, but soon the Tibetan Army was disarmed, and protesters were tortured, imprisoned, or killed.

"Mao invited the Dalai Lama to Peking in 1953. After much conversation, the Dalai Lama thought the Chinese would leave the Tibetan culture and its writings, but Mao leaned over to the Dalai Lama during their last meeting, saying that religion was poison, destabilizing, and slowing down the progress of any country. It was then that he realized Mao was an enemy of Tibet, and only deeper troubles were on the horizon for his people and his culture. By the end of the decade, he had to choose to stay in Tibet, or to escape into exile.

"Suspiciously, on March 10, 1959, the Dalai Lama was invited to attend a dance performance by the Chinese Army, unaccompanied. Over 30,000 people surrounded him in protection. In response, the Chinese began attacks on the Dalai Lama's palaces, and on the crowds themselves. That year, when the Dalai Lama was making the critical decision whether to stay in Tibet, or to go, due to the failed uprising against the Communist Party of China, he consulted Nechung, the state oracle. While in a trance, the oracle advised the Dalai Lama to escape Tibet, while drawing a map on a piece of paper of the route to take through the mountains to India.

"You see, since the age of 16, the Dalai Lama has based all his important decisions through the spiritual help of an oracle, by calling them 'supernatural counsels,' or 'consultations.' He works with a deity called Nechung Kuten, who speaks through a human medium, usually a monk. The oracle not only foretells the future, but he is also a protector and a healer, whose primary function is to protect the Buddha Dharma and its practitioners. So important is Nechung, he is given the rank of Deputy Minister, and is a principle protector of divinity of the exiled Tibetan government.

"While the medium is in a trance, the Dalai Lama poses questions to Nechung, who responds with inscrutable advice, which is often reserved and yet austere. It takes patience for the Dalai Lama to listen to and observe the oracle's prognostications. Dressed in a helmet weighing thirty pounds, while wearing heavy robes - all in all about seventy pounds of added weight, which an ordinary person would be overwhelmed - the oracle dances about and waves his sword wildly, finally bowing to the Dalai Lama. When he is complete with his insights, he collapses. Monks then take him away to recover.

"The current Nechung was once an ordinary monk, named Thupten Ngodup, who oversaw the sculpture and incense at a monastery in Dharamsala. In 1987, the deity chose Thupten as the medium, filling the monk with a physical sensation like an electric shock. The oracle is on call whenever the Dalai Lama needs a consultation. He is convinced that the oracles are correct in their advice, and seeks the counsel of the oracle in the same way he seeks the advice of his Cabinet, also using his own reasoning and wisdom in making important decisions. His Holiness knows that those of the western world cannot begin to understand his ancient method of intelligence gathering.

"So, getting back to his escape from the Chinese... at 10 p.m., on March 17, 1959, at the onset of the Tibetan uprising, His Holiness escaped through the unknowing masses of people in the middle of an assembly of guards supposedly on their rounds, with the help of the CIA Special Activities Division."

"The American CIA was involved?" Christofer said.

"Yes," Markos said. "Remember, this was during the Cold War, and the United States had a vested interest in helping Tibetans resist the spread of Communism. The

American government made numerous offers to help Tibet resist the Chinese invaders. While the CIA did train selected Tibetans in guerilla warfare, the Dalai Lama resisted because of his advocacy of peaceful resistance. He did, however, accept their offer to help him and his followers escape to India. He wore trousers and a long black coat, disguised as a common soldier with a rifle at his side, soon joining his entourage, including his mother and other family members, all of whom were leaving their beloved Tibet on horseback. For two weeks, they traveled through blizzards and mud, suffering from fever and dysentery. Finally, on March 31, they reached the Indian border, escorted by Indian guards, later reaching Tezpur in Assam on April 18.

"Prime Minister Nehru had already agreed to provide asylum to His Holiness and his followers. The Dalai Lama renounced all agreements with the Chinese, and announced the formation of the Tibetan government-in-exile, followed by the Chinese shelling the summer palace and machine-gunning the grounds outside. That year, 87,000 people were massacred. In the ensuing years, one million two-hundred thousand Tibetans were killed, 6000 monasteries destroyed, and temples were torn down. Through the years, the Chinese systematically destroyed everything of religious significance, all Tibetan art, books, and all things ancient."

"I have great empathy and compassion for the Dalai Lama and the people of Tibet," Chayton said as Irina rubbed his shoulder. "My people have much in common, having lost our homeland, our people, and way of life."

"I imagine you will have much to share with him," Markos said. "You might want to put together some questions to pose to him."

"I already have. I'm looking forward to meeting with him," Chayton said.

"Once in India, the Dalai Lama could speak freely," Markos continued. "He held news conferences, and soon the world knew of China's oppression of the Tibetan people. Later, in 1959, he met with Prime Minister Jawahalal Nehru, who agreed to set up schools for Tibetan children, with the Indian government bearing all expenses. In 1960, His Holiness and his followers moved to Dharamsala, India, shadowed in snowy peaks overhead. Before long, over 100,000 refugees fled Tibet, escaping Chinese persecution and trekking through the Himalayas to safety in Dharamsala.

"Let me give you a little background on Dharamsala. Dharamsala, McLeodganj, and Kangra were important centers of trade and commerce, but are located on the border of the Indian Plate and the Eurasian Plate. In 1905, the 7.8 magnitude Kangra Earthquake hit, killing over 20,000 people and 53,000 domestic animals in the area, and leveling over 100,000 buildings. There was not much left of the northern Dharamsala suburb of McLeodganj, at 6,831 feet in elevation. In March of 1960, Prime Minister Nehru was pleased to offer refuge to the Dalai Lama and thousands of his followers in McLeodganj, saying that, until then, it had been a 'forgotten ghost town wasting in the woods.'

"Mortimer House, in McLeodganj, was once owned by Lord Elgin, British Viceroy of India. After Lord Elgin died in Dharamsala in 1863, the home became part of the estate of Lala Basheshar Nath of Lahore. In 1960, the house was acquired by the Indian government as the official home of the Dalai Lama. He now lives in a modest monastery that overlooks the town. Now McLeodganj is known as Little Lhasa, because of its large population of Tibetans. Fifteen thousand Tibetans live in the Dharamsala area, most of them in McLeodganj, while over 94,000 live in India. McLeodganj is the headquarters for the Tibetan government-in-exile, along with schools, temples, and monasteries. The city is no ordinary Indian town. It's an important tourist and pilgrimage destination, made up of writers, poets, filmmakers, and hippies that share the town with young Tibetans, many of whom do not know of their homeland. Kiosks are set up with people selling their wares. The bestselling souvenirs are Tibetan merchandise and pictures of the Dalai Lama."

"To this day," Michael said, "Tibetans can't freely practice their religion in their country, and they risk their lives if they try to escape. The Chinese police will shoot them."

"Oh yes," Markos said, "refugees still perilously trek the 1,200 miles over the Himalayas, seeking asylum. In Dharamsala they have a place to stay and food to eat. Each one is also granted a personal audience with the Dalai Lama. In 1970, the Dalai Lama created the Library of Tibetan Works and Archives, housing 80,000 manuscripts and resources related to Tibetan history, politics, and culture.

"In 1987, His Holiness received the Albert Schweitzer Humanitarian Award for his work in human welfare and social reform throughout the world. He won the Nobel Peace Prize in 1989 for his consistent non-violent effort for the liberation of Tibet." Markos opened a small notebook and put on his glasses. "In his speech, he said, 'I am no one special, but I believe the prize is a recognition of the true value of altruism - love, compassion, and non-violence. I accept the prize with profound gratitude on behalf of the oppressed everywhere, and for all those who struggle for freedom and work for world peace.'"

"Beautiful," Irina said.

"At the time, he lived on about ten dollars per day in Dharamsala. Today, the monetary prize is over a million dollars, which he gave to charity, saying he wanted to do something for those people on this planet who are facing starvation. He also became the first Nobel Laureate, recognized for his global environmental concerns. In 2006, President Bush awarded him the U.S. Congressional Medal of Honor for his work for peace and human rights. He has traveled to 67 countries, on six continents, receiving over 150 awards, honorary doctorates, and prizes in recognition of his message of peace, non-violence, inter-religious understanding, universal responsibility for human rights, and compassion. He has written and co-authored over 110 books."

"I read somewhere that many Tibetan monks and nuns have said that, if it weren't for the Dalai Lama and his followers having exiled Tibet, the world may not know of Tibetan Buddhism as it is known today," Michael said.

"Yes," Irina said, "and as we know, it goes further than that. He shows the world by example the power of love in action, through compassion and forgiveness."

"An interesting fact about His Holiness is that he likes to repair mechanical watches, music boxes, clocks, and cars," Ananta said.

"Is that right?" Gaston said. "I just can't picture His Holiness under the hood of my Cadillac!"

Ananta laughed. "He can look at the workings of a clock, take it completely apart, and put it back together again. He spends much time gazing at the night sky through a telescope. He also has a remarkable memory. I've heard that he can meet someone, and after several years have passed, he will recognize them, recalling their conversation from long before.

"Each morning, he rises at 4 a.m. for four hours of meditation. Then, during the normal business hours of each day, he begins with a hearty breakfast and listens to BBC radio. He then meets with visitors, later taking time to counsel his people and comfort refugees. He reads and studies non-fiction books, and is fascinated with quantum physics, astronomy, and neurosurgery. He respects every major world religion, and contemplates religious doctrine, but when he finds a conflict between religion and science, he often chooses the scientific viewpoint. Not only does he stand for all sentient beings on Earth, he believes there are sentient beings outside the Solar System."

Michael said, "I've also read the Chinese government continues to crack down hard on its Muslims – in fact, they say there's a new wave of repression on all faiths, especially Buddhism."

"Sadly true," Markos said. "One of his most pressing issues is the preservation of the Tibetan culture - its art, dance, music, architecture, and literature. In 1995, you may remember, the Dalai Lama chose Gedhun Choekyi Nyima, a little six-year-old, as the reincarnation of the 11th Panchen Lama. The Panchen Lama is one of the key individuals who will recognize the next Dalai Lama. However, the Chinese government rejected the boy, and arrested the young Panchen Lama and his family. At the time, he was the youngest political prisoner in the world. Chinese officials chose their own young boy as the Panchen Lama, who will identify the next Dalai Lama according to their own terms. The Dalai Lama feels deep compassion for the young man."

"Whatever became of the first boy?" Lestari asked.

"The Chinese government has always maintained he is

alive, well, and thriving in China," Markos said. "The Dalai Lama has also confirmed word from reliable sources that the boy grew up and received a normal education."

"Isn't China primarily atheist?" Sophia asked.

"Yes," Ananta said.

Sophia shook her head. "I know they practice Taoism and folklore, and some are Buddhist, but they don't recognize the Dalai Lama as the spiritual leader of Chinese occupied Tibet, and yet they've chosen a child as the next Panchen Lama. Such a paradox!"

"I think we can all agree that so many choices of the Chinese government are contradictory," Darius said. "It's such a shame – as were the poor decisions made by the U.S. government and religious authorities toward the Native American people, African slaves, and indentured servants."

Markos agreed. "As with the Native people of the United States in the 19th Century, cultural genocide is still taking place in Tibet, as hundreds of thousands of Chinese immigrants are sent to Tibet to colonize it. Much of the city of Lhasa is now destroyed, with a lot of new Chinese businesses, Chinese restaurants - Chinese culture. The Dalai Lama's picture is banned from all temples in Tibet. Anyone found possessing a photo of the Dalai Lama, or speaking of him can result in a prison sentence. For years, the Chinese have brutalized, tortured, jailed, and killed anyone proclaiming independence for Tibet. Tibetans in China live in a constant state of fear in making any suggestion of freedom and independence."

"One of the Dalai Lama's greatest challenges is to encourage his people to forgive and move forward with an optimistic view of their future," Ananta said. "As a great promoter of peace, he educates Tibetans not to hold hatred for the Chinese, using the policy of the Middle Way - not one side for victory, and the other for defeat, meaning mutual benefit for both China and Tibet. He teaches that all people are the same, with the idea that everything is inter-dependent - everything is interconnected. Our interests are connected to their interests; therefore, destruction of your neighbor - of your so-called enemy - is actually destruction of yourself."

"Our survival and our future are linked to one another," Markos said. "He emphasizes that the power of truth comes through openness, through freedom of speech, and the freedom of information, which is open and honest. Peace, smiling, warmth, sharing, all are much more power-ful than violence. He teaches about the sacred friend. Anyone can love a friend, but a sacred friend is someone with whom you are in conflict. They remind you of your basal instincts, and because you are a conscious human being, you must choose the higher road. Your sacred friend causes you to grow, to become a better person, and to rise above the challenge of the conflict. He constantly tries to find common ground with his enemy, the Chinese - his sacred friend - who he has forgiven.

"The Dalai Lama refers to his death as a 'change of clothing.' He is certain that his successor will be found out-side Tibet, and perhaps from India. He suggests his rein-carnation could also be a woman. It could also be that he will select his own reincarnation, while he's alive, known as madhey tulku, in which he will train his successor."

"Now wait a minute. How could he choose one who is his reincarnation?" Christofer asked.

"I wondered the same thing," Anja said. "Could it be his reincarnation is one who is a part of his soul? We all know that the soul is what connects us all, which is oneness. Could it be that we are all reincarnated from each other? I know when I feel that soul connection with another, even with a stranger, it is a deep and abiding union."

"Makes sense to me," Michael said.

"As you might guess," Ananta said, "the Dalai Lama is happiest when doing spiritual things - spending most of his waking energy in pursuit of a perfect form of enlightenment."

Markos agreed. "He follows the method of his personal hero, Mahatma Gandhi, with passive, peaceful resistance. He favors active engagement with the Chinese people and government as a solution to Tibet's problems, believing it would be wrong to isolate China. The Dalai Lama will tolerate no violence or protest of China in his name.

"While he appreciates festivals, because they bring joy and happiness, he doesn't like ceremonies and rituals in his honor. He always laughs about himself. In conversation, he is quick to make judgments, but is also as quick to admit that he is wrong. He is unconcerned with status. His visitors sit in a chair of equal height, because he does not consider himself superior. He makes a deep impression on those he meets, not only because of his spiritual nature, but because he holds the gaze of the person with whom he is in conversation. He leans forward in his seat, truly interested in what they have to say. Some say, when in conversation with the Dalai Lama, it is like he's looking deep into their soul.

"When meeting with dignitaries that are overly impressed with themselves, he settles back into his chair, indicating he has lost interest. He is quick to dismiss them, cutting short the meeting. At times, he will leave the room. When traveling by plane, he does not travel first class, but coach, and does not stay in exclusive hotels. He has no passport, but travels with the use of the yellow document of a refugee.

"When in a room full of people, he carefully watches the crowd and makes sure to greet everyone before he sits on his golden throne, from where he will smile and joke, and can be slightly mischievous in his personality. He will look about the room with an intelligent and vigilant gaze. He makes people feel comfortable in his presence, and is not intimidating. When talking with you directly, he will most likely ask direct questions, putting you at ease right away. He is always present and accepting, saying that his greatest inspirations are in every human he meets. One thing I find to be very interesting is that he never charges money for his speaking engagements."

"How does he make money for his causes?" Gaston asked.

"It's all done through donations," Markos said. "When we first see him, we will be a part of a large group of people at his modest monastery. Do not rush up to meet him. Security is very strict. They will hold you back. By the way, no phones are allowed in his presence. However, if you bring your camera, you may take his photo. The next day, we will join him for a private audience, and then for dinner, prepared by our very own Ananta. You probably already know this, but each one of us has been screened and scrutinized before our private audience with him."

"It is important to understand the protocol when in company with His Holiness," Ananta said. "Be sure to wear professional business attire. If you desire, you may present him with a long white silk scarf, called a khatan, using both of your hands. His Holiness will bless the scarf and place it over your head and around your neck, as you slightly bow your head to receive the khatan.

"When addressing him directly, say, 'Your Holiness.' When speaking of him, say, 'His Holiness,' after which you may say 'you' or 'he.' While sitting, avoid pointing your feet at the Dalai Lama. The feet are the lowest part of the body. One never points their feet at a lama, which is considered disrespectful.

"When the Dalai Lama enters or leaves a room, you should stand. Allow him to sit first, and then take your seat. If you leave the room, back away while facing him for several steps before turning to leave. When eating with him, wait until he begins eating or drinking, unless he specifically requests you to do differently. Incidentally, Buddhist monks are vegetarian, because they honor all sentient beings. However, the Dalai Lama does eat meat, because he became quite sick while eating a vegetarian diet.

"When speaking with him, it is permissible to look him in the eye. However, when you shake hands with him, use both your hands, not just one, which indicates that you honor that which you hold in your hands. When we dine with His Holiness, pass a plate or receive a plate with two hands."

"How well does he speak and understand English?" Gaston asked.

"He understands English very well, but he speaks with a very strong accent that is a bit of a combination of Chinese and Indian," Ananta said. "I confess sometimes I must stop and think about some of your American words and phrases, so try to speak directly and slowly. He is very charming, and he has a wonderful sense of humor, so don't feel as if you have to be formal and reverent with him. In fact, he encourages us to be happy and lighthearted."

"Lastly," Markos said, "I will leave you with a few quotes from His Holiness the Dalai Lama:

'This is my simple religion. There is no need for temples; no need for complicated philosophy. Our own brain, our own heart is our temple; the philosophy is kindness.'

'All humans are the same. In that we all want to be happy and free from suffering. This is the reason why all humans, without exception, deserve our love and compassion.'

'Love is the remedy toward those who appear to be our enemy. We can counter negative actions, but still treat people with kindness.'

'Taking time out to find inner peace is important to remember why we are here...'"

CHAPTER
Thirty-two

After attending the group meeting with His Holiness the Dalai Lama, everyone from Apeiros anxiously awaited the following day, when they would hold a private audience with him and share a meal prepared by Ananta. Each had questions, but no one was sure if they would get a chance to speak with him directly. If not, they all agreed that simply being in his presence would be enough.

Ananta always prepared the most delectable dishes for the Dalai Lama, but since her dearest friends and colleagues were going to enjoy the meal as well, she worked overtime to make sure their dinner was one they would not forget. This would also be her first meal to share with His Holiness.

Before dinner, everyone introduced themselves to the Dalai Lama. They all stood around him in a circle as he went from one person to the next. Following proper etiquette, each shook his hand with both hands, knowing they were holding the hands of a blessed one, as it instantly became clear that he felt the same for each one of them.

"Your name?" the Dalai Lama asked.

"My name is Irina Vasilesui Blackwood, Your Holiness."

"From?"

"I am originally from Constanta, Romania, but now I live in Taos, New Mexico."

"From shores of Black Sea - beautiful country - Romania," the Dalai Lama said.

"Yes, it is. I lived there my entire life until two years ago, when I met this wonderful man."

The Dalai Lama smiled. "Taos is sacred land."

"It is very peaceful there," Irina said.

"You speak many languages - also powerful seer."

"My gifts enabled me in my job, as a concierge, to anticipate a guest's needs, sometimes before they knew what they needed."

"In your new task of foundation your group, your gift of seeing and knowing will be great service to world."

"We have already utilized our spiritual gifts in service to what this foundation will provide in its many divisions. If I may introduce my husband, Chayton Blackwood."

"Chayton, you are Native American?"

"Yes, Your Holiness. I am Lakota Sioux."

"Which Sioux nation from?"

"Sicangu Oyate, the Upper Brulé Sioux Nation, Your Holiness."

"Ah, Rosebud Reservation, Black Hills - very spiritual country."

"Yes. Grandmother Earth is very powerful there. We are blessed by Great Spirit."

"I feel great compassion for your people. To lose one's country, way of life, and so many people, difficult. Know this, no one ever lost, no noble task ever forgotten. Your people live to do great things in world and for humanity."

"Thank you for your empathy and compassion, Your Holiness," Chayton said with a tear in his eye.

"Your people blessed," the Dalai Lama said. "Important maintain heritage, language, culture. Your voices now heard in world. White Buffalo a great man."

"You knew him?" Chayton asked.

"Heard him speak in London. We laugh together after." He laughed and looked directly at Sophia, who was already wiping back tears. He nodded at her and smiled. "You know!"

Chayton laughed with him. "He brought all of us so much joy."

"His message was wisdom with clear heart and kindness. You, Chayton, bring greater wisdom, now as wisdom keeper, dream interpreter, and medicine man, to Native people, to all humanity. You blessed with noble purpose."

"Thank you, Your Holiness." Chayton bowed his head.

The Dalai Lama moved on. "Tell me name and where from?"

"I am Shoshana Gabriella Abraham - Thanos, Your Holiness."

"You are Israeli?"

"Yes, but I now live in Santorini, Greece."

"Ah, you are archeologist at Akrotiri."

"Yes, Your Holiness."

"Noble work, bringing truth to history."

"I love my work. The ancient people are family to me."

"You are intuitive and empath - very sensitive soul."

"Yes, sometimes too sensitive for my own good."

The Dalai Lama laughed. "Sensitive souls hold love for world. That is most important purpose of all. Remember, breathe, keep grounded, and all will be well."

"Thank you, Your Holiness. If I may, I would like to introduce my husband, Christofer Aleksanderi Thanos."

"It is my honor to meet you, Your Holiness," Christofer said.

"You are an artist. You paint iconography in Greek Orthodox churches?"

"Yes. It is one of the ways I express my art."

"Wonderful way to tell story of Jesus, who blessed humanity with teachings of the Way. You paint other things?"

"I do murals. I also restore the traditional houses of Santorini."

"Cave homes, yes?"

"You've been there?"

"Beautiful charming layers - white domes on white cliffs, trimmed in same blue as caldera."

"Yes. Santorini is an enchanting place. We love it there. You must come and visit! I will put you up in our finest traditional suite."

"Thank you. Santorini - good place sit in contemplation and watch blue waters. You are clairvoyant, clairsentient, and clairaudient - good combination."

"Yes, but sometimes in Greece, I have to see no evil, hear no evil, and speak no evil, Your Holiness."

"Wise man," he nodded with an enchanting laugh. "You are the couple, recently married?"

"Yes, we were just married in Ireland."

"This your honeymoon?"

"*This* is our bucket list, Your Holiness," Christofer said. They shared a good laugh. "We can't think of a better way to start out our marriage than to be here with you tonight."

The Dalai Lama took their hands in his. "May your marriage be blessed with years of kindness, compassion, and great love."

"Thank you, Your Holiness," Christofer said as he looked down at Shoshana, who fought back tears.

The Dalai Lama moved to Markos. "Tell me who you are."

"My name is Markos Xenakis, Your Holiness."

"What? You don't have several names?" the Dalai Lama said, jokingly.

"We would be here all night if I told you all of my names," Markos chuckled.

"Thank you for consideration of time, Markos. You lived in Egypt, speak eight languages, yes?"

"I do. I am not sure how you know that."

"Not mystical. Ananta tell about you all before you visit, yes?"

"Oh, yes, of course!" Markos said, laughing.

"Ah, but we know similar things, yes? You are prophet and sage."

"I think I know that power more from my past lives than I do from this life."

"Soon you see more how your spiritual gifts serve world. You and Sophia share past lives." He looked again at Sophia and smiled. She grabbed Michael's hand and dug her nails in. Michael just stood still and winced.

"Sophia was my adopted mother long ago," Markos said. "In fact, all of us have shared past lives, Your Holiness."

"We all know each other in many dimensions, what we call time - in great ways that surprise. Life blesses us all."

"I couldn't agree more, Your Holiness."

The Dalai Lama next turned to Anja. "Your name?"

"I am Anja Dembele, Your Holiness. I am from Senegal."

"Your name, Anja, means 'grace.' I like that. It fits you."

"Thank you, Your Holiness."

"Your people create handmade goods to sell."

"Yes, we are thankful to have a thriving business. My husband, Ibrahim and I, until recently, sold the goods of our community all over the United States and in London, but now with our thriving online business, we've changed the way we work in the world."

"You are shaman?"

"I am, like my mother and grandmother. My abilities have helped me envision the future that helps our community grow and prosper."

"These hand-crafted goods bring creativity and beauty to all people of the world. Your artistic and spiritual talents are gifts to more people than you will ever know. Keep shining through your humble heart."

"Thank you, Your Holiness."

"And you, what is name, and where from?"

"My name is Kadek Lestari Darma, and I am from Bali, for now."

"Are you leaving Bali?"

"I have had some recent changes, and may be moving elsewhere."

"Just know self-forgiveness is only form of forgiveness. Those we leave behind, we will meet again, maybe in another lifetime. Bless your past, be grateful for lessons, then let go."

Lestari's eyes filled with tears. "Thank you so very much, Your Holiness."

"Love always leads way. Future is bright, filled with promise of great service to love. Your gifts of healing will soon be well used."

"Oh, thank you, Your Holiness."

"And your name?"

"My name is Yesinia Maria Alessandra Maldonado, Your Holiness. Up until recently, my brother and I had a touring company throughout Peru and the Amazon."

"Not Amazon - online business," the Dalai Lama said, laughing.

"No," she laughed. "The Amazon Basin."

"You are humble, powerful shaman."

"The power lies in humility, Your Holiness."

"I see your body and emotions healed from recent car accident. Know this, you are broken open to new ventures that call you - you will soon use shamanic gifts more."

"Thank you, Your Holiness. You are a great gift to the world."

"As are you." He smiled, then turned to Gaston. "Ah, so many young here – nice to see one my age!"

"That will be my brother, Your Holiness," Gaston said, pointing to Darius. "I am as young as these other children – I just matured faster." The Dalai Lama lit up with a smile and laughter. "My name is Gaston Marcel Delacroix, Your Holiness. I own an antique store in the French Quarter of New Orleans."

"Ah – antiques - you appreciate history. Oh, but you are the one - the very powerful medium."

"Something I have not done much of lately, Your Holiness."

"Soon you will. Love will find you again, if you allow it."

Gaston was taken aback. "I am surprised, but I'm willing, if you say so."

"The heart says so. Sometime when sad from loss – hold on too much to sadness and not enough to strength and joy - of lessons gained from love."

Gaston put his hand to his mouth, perhaps to hold back his tears. For once, he was speechless. "Thank you, Your Holiness," he barely whispered as Darius put a loving hand on his back.

The Dalai Lama beamed at Ananta and held his hands out. "Ananta Dubashi, my chef."

"Yes, Your Holiness. Thank you for inviting us to have an audience with you."

He looked around at the others, gesturing at his belly. "Since Ananta cook for me – my middle grow bigger!" His full laugh charmed everyone. "You have special meal for us tonight?"

"I do."

"Your food - a gift to all my guests, Ananta. You are intuitive. You cook - easy to you. I miss food when you are gone, but I see you and companions serve humanity and world. So, I will have suffer when you away." He smiled in his playful, mischievous way.

"Maybe I'll put some of your favorites in the freezer to tide you over."

"Good idea. I like that!" He shifted to the next person in the circle, dramatically looking up and laughing as he stepped on his tip-toes. "And you, up high - your name?"

"Michael Aengus Conlan Bohannan Liam Seamus Riordan O'Hara, Your Holiness."

"You have one more name than me - not often accomplished. I like that big man has big names. Michael, you are from?"

"Originally from New York, Your Holiness, and have traveled the world in my work. Now we have homes in Colorado and Ireland."

"New York and Irish. You come from long line of protectors – all those names?"

"All policemen and firemen, Your Holiness – and I should add woman, for I have a female cousin who is an NYPD homicide detective."

"But you? Not policeman?"

"No, Your Holiness. My grandfather wanted something different for my father, and for me, so we took a different path."

"Your relatives – any in 9-11?"

"Oh, yes, Your Holiness. Thank God all survived, but several of my cousins and uncles were first responders that day, one who survived the south tower collapse. He was rescued from the rubble. He's had a very hard time with his health and his personal life since."

"You are protectors, Michael, but sometimes must protect self. I pray and give blessing for him."

Michael choked back an unexpected tear. "Thank you, Your Holiness. My parents would be proud to know that all those they named me for were remembered here, with His Holiness the Dalai Lama."

"Important honor those gone before us. Bohannan - you are man of big sandwich?"

"Guilty, Your Holiness."

"Thank you for new addition to menu here in Dharamsala. Ananta made sandwich for lunch twice, for guests. It is only sandwich I need fork."

"That way you get every bite. So glad you enjoyed it."

"Purpose of your soul is protector. Very important role."

"I must admit, sometimes I feel I'm not needed. Sophia has powers that extend far beyond where I can provide protection for her."

"Part of your importance is her knowing you are near. Her success is partly because of your protecting. You are also prophet and seer?"

"I'm not sure that I know that, Your Holiness."

"You spend time very grounded. Let go of control. You will then recognize many spiritual gifts."

"I appreciate your wisdom, Your Holiness."

The Dalai Lama moved to Darius. "Ah, the older brother!"

They laughed. "I am the mature brother," Darius said.

"I like that! 'Mature' better than 'older.'"

"Darius MacPhaidin, Your Holiness. I also live in New Orleans."

"Ah yes, CEO of Delaney Hotels. I have stayed in many."

"I hope all your needs were well met."

"Very nice places. I like – what they call? Continental breakfasts."

"Your Holiness, my brother and I are building a new boutique hotel in New Orleans. We would be honored if you would be our guest."

"If I travel to New Orleans, I would be happy to stay at your hotel. You have a plantation house?"

"Yes. It is an Antebellum plantation house, built by my ancestors in the 1830s, who came from Ireland during the great potato famine."

"Were there slaves?"

"No, never," Darius said. "My family came from many Irish people who, for centuries, were indentured servants, otherwise known as White Slavery. When they came to the United States, they vowed never to enslave people. They also operated a fine hotel in the city of New Orleans, and for everyone in their employ, they paid a fair wage and offered decent housing. They were not as profitable to begin with, but over the years their reputation grew into a thriving business that has lasted for generations. I credit much of my success in business because of their nobility toward their fellow man and woman."

"A great sage, you are - very old soul. Your wisdom

serves lifetimes of people. This group holds consciousness for the world?"

"Yes, Your Holiness. We are called the Order of Apeiros, which has been in operation for thousands of years, and dimensions of time," Darius said.

"You are leader?" the Dalai Lama asked.

"No, none of us is the leader. However, Sophia is a most powerful Oracle. She is more the hub of the wheel, rather than the leader," Darius said. "May I introduce to you, my granddaughter, Sophia MacPhaidin Delacroix Delaney Gallagher O'Hara."

"It is my great pleasure to meet you, Your Holiness," Sophia said.

The Dalai Lama nodded and smiled. "You also have almost as many names as me," he said, laughing. "And you are married to Michael, so combine all names and you have big room full of spirits!"

Now more at ease, Sophia replied, "I only had two names until I discovered my lineage a few years ago, Your Holiness. In fact, if not for White Buffalo, I would not be here, and I would never have found everyone here, in this room."

"It is important to know from where you come, to better know where you are going," the Dalai Lama said.

"That is certainly the case for me, Your Holiness," Sophia said. "I have a different direction, now that I know my lineage and some of my history."

"There is more to find. You are powerful oracle."

"So I am told. I am greatly blessed, Your Holiness."

"Know Thyself. Know Thyself."

She looked into his eyes as tears welled in hers. "My father told me the same thing."

"It is ageless wisdom, known to old souls. In this, we

treat all humanity, all beings with kindness and compassion, no longer cause suffering. You possess most every spiritual gift, Sophia. You are prophetic, which includes gift of intuition, mediumship, clairvoyance, clairaudience, clairsentience. You are healer, seer, shaman, and someday you will be a sage. You are a mystic."

"Yes, thank you, Your Holiness. These are the gifts of all of us in the Order of Apeiros. It is how we hold the truth for the world..."

CHAPTER
Thirty-three

They gathered in the dining room as dinner was served, family style. At each place was a printed menu:

<u>Momos</u>
Tibetan steamed dumplings
stuffed with potato, cabbage, spinach, radish,
and carrot, served with a spicy chili sauce

<u>Tibetan Yoghurt</u>
with fresh strawberries

<u>Chicken Thukpa</u>
Nepalese chicken rice noodle soup
with carrot, red pepper, cherry tomato,
fresh cilantro, cumin, turmeric,
red hot chili pepper, and Szechwan pepper

<u>Tibetan Tingmo</u>
Bread stuffed with chopped onion,
chilies, garlic, and coriander leaves

<u>Cucumber Salad</u>
with toasted sesame seeds and
salsa vinaigrette of tomato and cabbage

Bulgogi
A Korean recipe,
with lean pork, marinated in soy and
chili sauce, fried and served on a bed of rice,
with carrots, onion, capsicum, cabbage, ginger and garlic

Tudkiya Bhath
A local dish from Himachal Pradesh
lentils, potatoes, yogurt, onion, tomatoes,
garlic, cinnamon, and cardamom,
on rice with lime juice

Naizha Cake
Tibetan zanbha, naizha (cheese,)
butter and brown sugar

Himalayan Rice Pudding
rice, sugar, coconut, golden raisins,
cashews, spiced with cardamom

Belgian Waffle
by Yannick Ramaekers
A secret 15th century classic Belgian recipe,
made into his own specialty by Yannik's grandmother.
A rich buttery waffle, crunchy on the outside, with an
aroma of 15 spices. Served with homemade coffee, saffron, and
almond ice cream encased in a hard chocolate shell.

Kanga Tea

Masala Chai Tea

"Ananta, excellent meal!" the Dalai Lama said. "Thank you for honoring foods of Tibet, the Himalayas, and here, in Himachal Pradesh. The Belgian Waffle was best surprise."

"Yes, thank you, Ananta. I love the variety," Sophia said. "And thank you for the menu. Now I can volunteer Michael to make some of these dishes when we return to Ireland."

"Are you kidding?" Michael said. "A menu from dinner with His Holiness? That baby is going to be framed and put on a wall somewhere."

"I noticed that we didn't have yak butter," Sophia said.

"Now, there's something you don't hear every day," Michael said.

"I'm just interested," Sophia said. "I've always heard about it, and I thought, hey, when in India..."

"It's not the tastiest of Tibetan drinks," Ananta said. "Yak butter tastes like extremely salty sour buttermilk. It is said that there is only one thing worse than a cup of yak butter, and that's another cup of yak butter."

The Dalai lama laughed. "It is true! I no like!" He made a sour face.

"Okay then, thanks for your consideration - or should I say your compassion for our taste buds." Sophia blushed, glancing at the Dalai Lama, who simply smiled at her.

Everyone gave Ananta rave reviews. As the table was cleared and more tea was served, the Dalai Lama brought up the subject of why he called them to meet with him.

"I thank you all for coming to Dharamsala. I enjoyed reading your information and biographies. Each of you - mystics. What you do in service for world intrigues me. One of qualities you hold - compassion - caught my attention - when Ananta and I first talk about how you serve world.

"She said all of you blessed man who killed your parents, Sophia. That is mindset and action of forgiveness, kindness, and compassion we must take to bring healing to world. This mindset begins at home, where we stand. Tell me your name again, religion, and spiritual gifts." He gestured for Darius to begin.

"I am Darius, and I was raised in the Catholic Church. I am considered a sage."

"And Apeiros?"

"For millennia, Apeiros, meaning 'the cause of all unity and measure of all things' – also 'eternality' - has been a group of thirteen people from all over the world, representing the world's major religions, belief systems, and cultures. We all have connected in some way to be members, through our lineage."

"Ananta?"

"I am a student of both Buddhism and Hinduism, and I am an intuitive."

"I'm Markos. I was brought up in the Greek Orthodox Church, but I have studied Islam, having read the Koran eight times. I am a prophet and a sage."

"Markos is also a known scholar of the life of Your Holiness - His Holiness, the 14th Dalai Lama," Sophia said. The Dalai Lama nodded his approval.

"My name is Yesinia. I am Catholic, and a shaman."

"I am Lestari. I am Hindu and a healer."

"I'm Gaston, and I was raised in the Catholic Church. I am a medium."

"My name is Shoshana. I am Hebrew, an empath, and an intuitive."

"I am Christofer, also raised Greek Orthodox. I have all the clairs - clairvoyant, clairaudient, and clairsentient."

"The clairs!" the Dalai Lama laughed. "I *knew* you were

going to say that!"

Christofer pointed at him as everyone laughed. "Very good!"

"My name is Anja. I am Muslim, and a shaman."

"My name is Irina. I grew up in the Eastern Orthodox Church. I am prophetic and a seer."

"My name is Chayton. I was raised as a Christian, but I best resonate with my Native beliefs and practices. I am a medicine man, a dream interpreter, and a wisdom keeper."

"My name is Michael. I was raised in the Christian faith. I am a protector for my dear Sophia, and I am also a prophet and a seer."

"I am Sophia. I am from New Thought. I am an oracle, and a mystic, but then I believe we are all mystics."

"Yes, that is truth of each of you," the Dalai Lama said. "You have qualities that give noble purpose to your work. Tell me more about these qualities."

"They all are attributes of the Divine," Sophia said, "under the umbrella of Love and Awareness of the Absolute, as Peace, Joy, Harmony, Order, Balance, Health, Beauty, Compassion, Oneness, Abundance, Grace, and Truth. Twice a year, we gather for two weeks, each time in a different part of the world. We discuss current issues of concern, bringing healing to those concerns, knowing as we bring healing, other issues are healed as well. Most importantly, we share good fellowship, and we try to choose a new and interesting place to meet each time.

"As a group, we hold rituals that include these thirteen attributes or qualities of the Divine, because when we are completely immersed in peace, for instance, we automatically feel the power of all the other qualities, most especially Love and Awareness. When we feel complete compassion, as you know, we also feel joy, harmony, abundance, and all the other qualities, with no room for anything of negativity, because the fullness of Love is just that - there's no room for anything but Love itself. We then return to our parts of the world, holding these qualities in everything we do - in our work, our relationships, in our faith, and our personal spiritual practices – and we go about each day, holding these God qualities for the world."

"Tell me why you are thirteen in number."

"The number thirteen is very auspicious and favorable," Gaston said. "The number thirteen is one of transformation, as it cleanses and purifies. It also represents eternal love. Thirteen is a sign from the angels of being connected to the ascended masters. It's a far cry from some people's fear of the number. The work we do also cleanses and purifies - creating an energetic shift - because the energies we hold naturally cast out negativity. As individuals and together, we work with angels, ascended masters, deities, with Mother, Father, God - Spirit - whatever name we call the Infinite Intelligence - to bring Love to the world."

"You can do ritual here?" the Dalai Lama said.

"You mean now? Here? With you?"

"I would like that."

"Oh, my!" Gaston said, in astonishment. "Yes, of course! Let's all go to the center of the room, away from furniture."

Sophia offered her ring. "Here, Your Holiness, place my aquamarine ring on your right pinky finger. I am wearing my amethyst, which should serve the same purpose. Ananta, it is because of you that we are here. Will you lead us, please?"

Everyone looked at each other in awe, not quite believing that the Dalai Lama was standing among them.

"It's my honor," Ananta said. "As we all stand in a circle, place your right hand that holds your aquamarine ring toward the center, like the spokes of a wheel. Each of you speak one of the attributes, feeling that quality of the Divine to the depths of your every cell, from your soul's expression."

As each person spoke, the room filled with golden white light, and at the center, where their hands met, a column of the brightest light began to form. "Peace" "Harmony" "Joy" "Compassion" "Order" "Balance" "Beauty" "Oneness." The light's radiance increased as each person in the circle shared his or her attribute. "Truth" "Health" "Abundance" "Grace."

Sophia, standing behind the Dalai Lama, whispered in his ear, and he spoke, "Love and Awareness."

The column of light possessed a vibrational tone more beautiful than any music of the earth. Each person radiated within the light, becoming the light, smiling and feeling all of the qualities combined in every facet of their being.

Ananta continued, "We stand in the truth of our being as we bless our planet and all that reside on her, for she is a heavenly body within the fullness of the Universe itself.

"We hold the high watch for all people, all mammals, amphibians, and reptiles that roam the earth, all sea creatures, all birds of the air - all sentient beings - and those beings we cannot see, or do not know yet exist. We bless all plant life from the tallest trees on land, to the smallest flora in the sea. We pray for the deserts, rocks, and arid lands, knowing that everything is filled with the life force so valuable to the balance of Earth's ecosystems.

"We bless all water, in every form that surrounds and infuses this beautiful planet, knowing it sustains, refreshes, and cleanses all of Earth and her inhabitants, for it is the most powerful life force of Earth. In our mind's eye, we see our earth and all her inhabitants breathing clean air, while blanketed in peace, as love is the heartbeat that generates her expansion into her upward spiral of evolutionary grace. In this, we are grateful. And So It Is!

"Gently remove your hand from the circle, seeing the light fade, but know that this brilliance is within each of you as it continues to shine in all that you do."

The Dalai Lama walked to the sofa and sat down, and they all gathered around him.

"Beautiful. Thank you. This, you do together as Apeiros, and privately?"

"Yes, Your Holiness," Michael said. "It's really quite simple, because it is done with feeling within the present moment of now - with everything we've got."

"Simplest things are sometimes the most difficult," His Holiness said. "We humans complicate things, but not necessary. All humanity important. All sentient beings important. I see what you do includes all beings, all humanity, all of Earth. This is good.

"We have religious spirituality, but there is another kind of spirituality without religious faith. This is your spirituality. It is when we increase good part of human nature and share happiness with one another - it is when we care - when we live in peace. It is my fundamental belief the very purpose of our life is happiness, joyfulness. No need for church or temple. No need for complicated philosophy or convoluted theories. Each person has potential to celebrate these good human values. Simply, we want happiness. That is ultimate answer. We don't want pain and suffering. We want happiness. That is basis for our civilization. Everywhere is same. Not talking about Nirvana, God, or Creator. Simply warm hearted person. This is noble purpose. This is my long-term hope for peace.

"Some would think that what you do is idealistic. However, it is more worthwhile what you do. This I know - invisible is far greater than what is seen - ninety-nine percent, invisible, one percent, material. You do math! What you do is very powerful energy. You live all over world. You create web of power and energy around Earth, holding warmth, love, compassion, and happiness for all beings. This is good. Thank you for including me tonight."

"It was our pleasure, Your Holiness," Gaston said.

"Please know that we include you, the Tibetan people, and the continuance of its culture in our hearts," Lestari said.

"This is good, and also hold Chinese in your hearts," the Dalai Lama said. "Chinese want happiness and joy, like all people. Pray for peace for China, for compassion - all qualities you hold for the world. I now hold you in my meditations, and you hold me in yours. Together we hold happiness and joy for world."

"Thank you for the opportunity to meet with you, Your Holiness," Sophia said. "We will always cherish this time spent with you. Our lives and our purpose is now more enhanced. We have a gift for you. It is an ornament of green Kyanite, set in gold on a gold chain. Kyanite is a stone of compassion and of the heart, bringing all of the chakras - the subtle energies - into alignment, and it also brings one into alignment with nature and the world. It also assists one in feeling the truth of the heart, and know if those you are talking to are speaking truth."

"I appreciate. Very nice gift. Thank you."

"Before we leave," Sophia said, "would it be possible to have your assistant take a couple of photos of you with our group?"

"Yes. I like that."

After the photos, Sophia presented her khatan to His Holiness for his blessing. When he placed it around her neck, she felt an electrical surge as she looked into his eyes, as if their souls were forever linked. He removed her aquamarine ring from his finger and placed it in her hand, wrapping both of his hands around hers.

Each one in the group presented his or her khatan for his blessing, leaving with feelings of being blessed in their individual calling, and in the work they did in the Order of Apeiros...

The ride back to the hotel was electrifying with quickening energy, and everyone agreed that sleep would be hard to come by tonight. Back at their room, after enjoying a nightcap with everyone in the hotel lounge, Sophia and Michael talked about their astonishing several days in Dharamsala.

"Well, my life will never be the same," Sophia said. "It was like being in the presence of White Buffalo again. They have the same heart."

"I thought of White Buffalo, too, especially when we were talking with him after dinner," Michael said.

"Other than our meeting with him, what did you like best about Dharamsala?"

"While you went to have tea, Darius, Gaston, Markos, Chayton, Christofer and I went to one of the local monasteries and watched the monks creating a mandala out of colored sand, which can take them up to a month to create. It's part of their religious study, because as they create this wonder of beauty, it is filled with their prayers. Monks sit on the side, ringing their bells and chanting. They don't buy bags of colored sand, they actually dye the finest of sand in a variety of colors of the spectrum. I've seen pictures and artwork depicting mandalas, but until you see one being created, none of them compare. I never realized the meaning of the mandala. It is an elaborate 3-D meticulous design of an imaginary palace, representing the entirety of the Buddhist philosophy. It represents the journey from the outside to the center, as one goes through life.

"The interesting thing is they don't keep it around for long. Once it is finished, it's destroyed and the sand is poured into a river nearby, indicating that nothing is permanent while letting go of attachment, which is the cause of loss and sorrow."

"I bet Christofer was entranced."

"Yeah, I think he was wondering how to do a mural in a similar fashion. I could see the wheels turning. So, tell me, what was one of your favorite moments, my love?"

"I've met so many wonderful people from all over the world here. While having tea at one of the tea gardens, I met a lovely older couple from France. At the conclusion of our talk, they handed me a piece of paper with their name, address, and phone number. They said they are traveling the world, and when they meet someone they particularly like, they invite them to be their guest in the French countryside. They said that Paris is not the real France, for the French countryside is the heart of the country. I told them their invitation was the nicest compliment I'd ever received."

"Do you think I could come along, too?"

"No, just me." Sophia rolled her eyes at Michael. "Of course, they said that you are also welcome."

Michael smiled and gave her a wink.

"I also met an Italian woman who now lives in Cabo San Lucas. She has a small boutique there. She noticed my jewelry, and I told her I've made jewelry for a living for some time. So, she invited me to visit Cabo and stay in her home – and I should bring some of my jewelry and art to sell there."

"That's a beautiful area, with a lot of tourist trade. You could sell quite a bit of your work there, and I could scrape the rust off my surfboard and try out these new hips."

"She said we could come anytime."

"Any other invitations?"

"I also met an enchanting Indian couple, who live here in Dharamsala. They also extended an invitation to return, and to stay in their mountainside home."

"All those invitations in four days, and I didn't get even one," Michael said.

Sophia gave her best Bacall impersonation, "Yes, dahh-ling, so many invitations and so little time."

Michael shrugged. "I mean, I've been invited to go to hell a few times in my day, but-"

Sophia burst out laughing as she reached out and gave him a big kiss. "I have an invitation for you..."

That night, tucked in the memory of being in the presence of a mighty peacekeeper, His Holiness the Dalai Lama, Sophia easily returned in her dreams to the life of Laurinda, the steadfast Archdruid, esteemed leader of fortitude, bard, and loving mother...

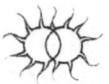

Chapter
Thirty-four

Whenever strangers passed through the village, they were welcomed with graceful hospitality, always with an offering of food and shelter. However, early spring brought a few travelers who were not receptive to their hearts and homes. These heartless few immediately sought out Laurinda, who had no idea of their origin, leaving her to feel no less than cautious and guarded.

The small band of ruffians contained only men about Laurinda's age, with the exception of their leader, who was a woman with grizzled hair, stooped shoulders, and knotted hands clearly crippled with pain. The old woman limped along, holding a long staff to support her twisted body.

"Destroy the village and take everything of value!" the old woman said, ordering her men about.

"Stop! Stop! This is not necessary," Laurinda said. "Please, tell me what it is that you want. We have little to share, but will be happy to give you what we can, if you will but lay down your weapons. Please, let us talk this over."

The old woman quickly swung her staff at Laurinda, but missed, for Laurinda was more nimble, easily shifting to the side. However, Laurinda was just close enough to gaze into the old woman's green eyes that quickly turned to black. Laurinda was stunned to recognize the woman as her sister, Gona. In ten suns, she had transformed into an ancient, crippled, gray hag.

"Gona?" asked Laurinda, not quite believing that this grizzled old woman was her sister, who was only three suns older than she.

"Oh, my daughter, please do not cause us harm," Magda said.

"Yes, let us talk!" Lon said.

"You once told me that I am no longer your daughter, did you not?" Gona said, glaring at Lon. "You exiled me from your home and hearts. Well, I am here to destroy everything in your lives. I have nothing more to say to you!" She turned to her men. "I said, destroy the village! Leave nothing standing! Take everything of value and burn the rest!"

"No wait! Certainly, we can come to an agreement. Please, Gona," Laurinda said.

"Hold her back," Gona said, pointing to her men with her staff. "Laurinda, if you say another word, I will strike you down."

The villagers were in shock as chaos ensued. There were very few men left to defend their community because of the losses at sea and recent conflicts between nearby villages. Those who remained were too old and feeble to fight back, or too young to defend their families. Women grabbed the children and ran from the scene. All the while, Gona stood back and cackled a laugh that sent chills through the people within earshot.

It took two men to hold the fighting Laurinda. All she could do was watch in horror as Gona's men ransacked the homes, piling any items with the least bit of value onto a shawl laid on the ground to take with them when they left. They smashed and destroyed what remained, and broke away the wooden door and window frames, causing the hillside homes to cave in. Lastly, they set the destroyed wooden roofs aflame.

What Gona and her men did not realize, was that their new village down the hillside beyond the rock outcropping was nearly complete, which contained many of their belongings already in place. Gona's men were destroying what was left of the original village.

The villagers knew to run to the woods, into the valley below, making it difficult for the intruders to find them. This left Laurinda, Magda, and Lon behind, attempting to reason with their deranged family member. Two of the men restrained Lon and Magda, leaving Laurinda alone to deal with Gona.

"Please, Gona, cease your plundering!" Laurinda cried.

"Stop! Let us talk!" Lon said, clearly shattered at the horror before him, all at the hand of his eldest daughter.

Gona raised her staff and glared at him, and he quickly ceased his attempts to communicate with her, knowing she could easily bring harm to Magda or himself. All three witnessed the resulting darkness of Gona's soul, which splintered into hardened brittle edges from her lifelong illness, the abandonment of her family, and living in a harsh environment. Gona had no ears for reasoning, no patience for mediation, and no heart.

With a nod of Gona's head, one of the men knew what to do next. He lunged at Laurinda, attempting to grab Lakaar, who held fast to her skirts.

"Leave them alone!" Laurinda said, screaming at him with the fury of a mother bear. She yanked away from the man's grip and grabbed a long burning stick. She swung with all her might, hitting his arm and setting his clothing aflame. He dropped his knife and ran away, endeavoring to run from the burning fire. Two other raiders tackled the man and rolled him on the ground, snuffing out the flames. Laurinda then grabbed the knife, and before another man reached Saurina, she sprung at him, imbedding the knife into his ribs.

Laurinda screamed to Lakaar, "Run to the woods!" Lakaar grabbed Saurina and scrambled away, leaving their mother alone with the band of vicious raiders, which was Gona's plan all along - to isolate her sister from anyone who would come to her rescue. All the while, Magda and Lon struggled to free themselves from the men who held them back.

The two remaining raiders grabbed Laurinda. She tried to wrench free, but as her sister limped toward her to meet face to face, Laurinda became still. Gona laughed, and all Laurinda could do was turn her head away, repulsed by her sister's putrid breath. Gona revealed what remained of her blackened, decaying teeth in a wicked smile.

"For years, I have waited for this day," Gona said in a raspy whisper. "On that small island of my exile, I imagined every detail of when we would again meet. How I have hated you - you, who was so loved, and for what - your red hair and blue eyes?" She leaned on her staff with one hand and reached up to take Laurinda's hair in her crippled fingers.

Laurinda tried to wrench herself free from the men, and from her sister's attention. "Leave me be! You destroyed our village! What more could you now do?"

"You should know. You destroyed my life, so I am here to make you and our parents suffer in the same way I have!"

By that time, three villagers crept back into the burning village to come to Laurinda's aid, but not before Gona saw them. She took her staff and struck Laurinda to the ground, and she pointed menacingly at the men. "Stay back, or I will destroy your precious Druid priestess! Come no closer!"

Gona had a fanatical look in her eyes, and all anyone could do was watch the gray-haired disfigured witch of a woman, wondering what would be their next recourse. Gona then began to seize up. She shrieked with frustration, for she had waited for this moment for ten suns, and now she was stricken, yet again. She fell to the ground, dropping her staff, her body jerking in its convulsions. When the spasms ceased, she laid still, exhausted and breathing heavily. The raiders held Laurinda, Magda, and Lon, waiting for Gona to recover. They were familiar with what actions to take when she succumbed to the seizures. All they could do was wait for her recovery.

But Laurinda took advantage of her sister's seizure and pulled away. She grabbed a flaming branch and charged the raiders who held her parents. The one holding her mother ran to the side. Laurinda raised the flaming stick high above her head, ready to bludgeon him, when someone from behind hit her on the back of her legs, and she collapsed in a heap.

Gona slowly pulled herself to her feet after using her staff to hit her sister. "Take them to the boat!" she yelled in her raspy voice.

The men grabbed Laurinda, Lon, and Magda, and forcibly took them down to the shoreline. The others followed with their plunder gathered in the shawl. The burned man and Gona trailed them, leaving behind the stabbed man to perish. Once they reached the shore, one of the men helped Gona get into the boat, without any sense of gratitude from her.

"On to the island," Gona said. The waves were brutal, taking every man on board to row against their force.

In the boat, Laurinda faced their island home and looked up at the cliffs that rose high into the skies overhead. In awe of the ocean's power, she watched the waves crashing and pounding against the towering stone cliffs that repeated as far as she could see to the south. She realized that the most powerful force upon earth surrounded her, and she surrendered to its domination, remembering what Balogue often said. *The last word always belongs to the ocean.*

Halfway to the small island, the men navigated the boat straight through the icy waves, causing the freezing ocean spray to shower over them. In an attempt to soothe her parents' discomfort, Laurinda leaned forward and reached out for her mother, but Gona violently shoved her sister away, accidently knocking Laurinda over the edge of the boat.

As Laurinda fell overboard, she grabbed Gona's woolen cape, trying to keep from falling. Instead, she pulled her sister into the cold waters with her. Gona, so handicapped, was unable to swim. In her panic, she reached out for the boat. One of her men, weary of her vulgar self-absorption, took advantage of the moment and shoved Gona farther out to sea with an oar.

Magda screamed as Lon lunged to the boat's edge, knowing there was nothing he could do to save them. Lon wrapped his arms around his terrified wife as she buried her head in his chest. Violent waves carried their daughters farther from the boat. The horrified Gona scrambled on top of Laurinda, attempting to save herself, and pushing her sister underwater. Lon and Magda screamed and reached out over the edge of the boat for one or both of their daughters, but the violent waves swept the two younger women away. In horror, they watched both of their daughters succumb to the ocean's power.

Now heavy with the weight of the water, their long woolen skirts and cloaks pulled them under the ocean's surface. Lon and Magda never saw Gona again, but Laurinda rose above once more, her eyes meeting theirs in a timeless gaze. Oddly, Laurinda took notice of the violent clashing of the waves and her parents' wailing, but as her heavy clothes pulled her under the surface, she became aware of a tranquil peace as the sea swallowed her up.

Laurinda no longer felt herself sinking in the icy waters. The storm ceased its fierce churning, and instead, she saw the clear aqua blue water, realizing there was no reason to breathe. She simply floated along, taking in the beauty of the water's serenity, which was now warm and soothing. Stormy clouds of darkened gray parted, revealing the brilliant sun overhead, with warm golden sunrays that penetrated deep into the water, bathing Laurinda in its light.

Thoughts and memories flashed through her mind, leaving Laurinda to feel only blissful love for everything in her midst. She thought of the story of Rionach, who lived from her heart center. Laurinda finally fully understood the meaning of the heart's power - that of unconditional love. It was about letting go, releasing all things that the mind created, and allowing the heart to shine its natural radiance, which was who she had always been.

She envisioned Lakaar and Saurina playing in the green grasses, knowing they would be well cared for among the community. The men would return Lon and Magda to their home on Eire, where they would raise their grandchildren to be strong and mighty leaders. Gona's men would join the village and become protectors of the people. The village would recover, for their new homes were safe. Their Druid life would eventually fill the island with generations of resilient, insightful, and spirited people.

Laurinda felt such love for her family, and yes, for Gona as well. There were no residual feelings of hurt or pain. Only love remained, for the ways of the physical domain were of the world, but not with her as she ascended to greater dimensions. Laurinda let go of life as she knew it, and felt herself sink deeper into the sea's depths. The sun's penetrating light became dimmer in the darkened recesses of the sea.

As she surrendered to the gods, she was surprised when she noticed a dark image above, plummeting straight toward her. She was deep enough in the dark waters that she could not see who it was, but she felt someone firmly grab her, wrapping one arm around her to hold her close as they immediately began to ascend to the surface together.

They emerged out of the dark and turbulent sea, both gasping for breath as she took notice of a large fishing vessel. A seaman from the boat tossed a rope in their direction. The man that saved her grabbed the rope as men in the boat towed them to where they could climb aboard a rope ladder. Onboard, shivering and wrapped in a blanket, it was not until she could breathe easily that she looked up at the man who saved her. She stood, completely stunned, taking notice of a lean and muscular, handsome man with wavy sun kissed auburn hair and beautiful green eyes.

It was Balogue...

On the horizon:

RÉALTA
Continuum Book Five

the journey continues...

Visit <u>ardyce.org</u> for updated information
on the Continuum Series.

Acknowledgements

When I was 14, I spent a portion of my summer with my aunt Hazel and Uncle Stan in Omaha, Nebraska, when my uncle noticed that it took me an extended length of time to read a short novel. Long story short, several months later I took a reading course through Evelyn Wood Reading Dynamics, a speed-reading comprehension course, which changed my life, resulting in my love for reading. Without the influence of my uncle's concern for my education, you may not be enjoying this book, because one must do a lot of reading and research in order to be a writer. I will always be grateful for his intervention.

Throughout the Continuum Series, it is my greatest intention to convey commonalities between the thirteen members of the Order of Apeiros through the foundational aspects of their varied cultures and religious differences where, at the core of their hearts and minds, they unite in oneness. Therefore, in this book, out of the deepest reverence and honor, I respectfully present the basic premise of the ancient religion traditions of Hinduism and Buddhism. Also included is the fascinating history and life of His Holiness the Dalai Lama, in which we journey into the beauty and strength of compassion and forgiveness.

Again, I am tremendously grateful for the talents, persistence, and fortitude of my husband, who is also my editor and publisher. He proficiently polishes my writing into a work of heart, making my dream of being an author more than a reality, but rather as an expanded vision of the passion for my life's work.

Through the lives of the characters in the Continuum Series, I express through storytelling what I learned from my two near-death experiences, in the straightforward and unswerving truth that God, or whatever name you may have for the Infinite Intelligence, is absolute Love and Awareness. It's simple, really! And so, if you feel the call to go deeper, after reading any of the books in this series, I invite you to join me in attending one of my workshops. Together, we will ascend into the magnificence of the eternal heavenly realm in the reflection of its grace, which is right where we are, here on earth, within the Eternal Now.

About the Author

Ardyce West is an optimum blend of spirituality and transformation. She is a Licensed Practitioner for United Centers for Spiritual Living in Colorado, as well as a certified Life Mastery Consultant and DreamBuilder Coach. Ardyce has expertly chaired large retreats and facilitated transformative healing workshops, assisting others in living a full spectrum wholehearted life through the brilliant guidance and intuition she provides for individuals and groups. Also an extremely accomplished artist, Ardyce has conducted many art and jewelry workshops.

Through captivating storytelling, Ardyce presents an empowering workshop featuring her two near-death experiences, which have resulted in her fascinating life, living through the grace of the Eternal Now.

She is the author of the metaphysical *Continuum* historical fiction series, including *Apeiros - Continuum Book One, Aeternalis - Continuum Book Two, Síoraí - Continuum Book Three, and Ouroboros - Continuum Book Four,* as well as the beautifully written poignant non-fiction book, *I Never Heard You Cry - A Compassionate Journey Through Abortion,* written to give a voice to the many who are affected by abortion, either through personal experience or through that of a loved one. With *Réalta - Continuum Book Five* in the works, Ardyce also wrote and illustrated her first children's book, *There Once Was a Kitty Name Digit.*

Visit ardyce.org for updated information.

Praise for
I Never Heard You Cry -
A Compassionate Journey Through Abortion

"*I Never Heard You Cry* . . . never approaches political edict or social commentary regarding abortion. Ardyce West focuses rather on the substantial number of people who do struggle with complex and deeply emotional post-abortion issues." - *Publisher*

"For me, a great book is one that leaves me moved and tingling when I complete its final passages. Ardyce West's book, *'I Never Heard You Cry'*, did precisely that for me. Not only will you be supported and inspired, you will find numerous springs of healing in this book. It is poignant as well as practical, offering compassion and insight in a controversial and troubled arena. Read this book and let your heart be touched." - *Dr. Roger W. Teel, Senior Minister and Spiritual Director, Mile Hi Church, Lakewood, Colorado*

"Ardyce West courageously shares her vulnerability in exposing her soul's journey of healing after her experience of abortion. Her insights give us all strength in moving forward after irreplaceable loss into greater awareness. *'I Never Heard You Cry'* is a significant and much needed work that will heal lives." - *Rev. Christian Sorensen, D.D., Seaside Center for Spiritual Living, Encinitas, CA*

"This is a book that will support healing and transform the way people look at abortion if they are willing to suspend fearful concepts. I highly encourage you to read this book and share it with your family, friends and even counseling clients. It will make a difference in how they view the experience of abortion and hopefully encourage them to open their hearts." - *Cynthia James, Author, What Will Set You Free, Revealing Your Extraordinary Essence*

"This extraordinary book isn't about pro-life, pro-choice, politics or religion. It's about people - the vast majority of us who understand that abortion is not a black-and-white issue that can only be addressed in absolutes. While it is an essential book for those who are struggling with unexpected and unattended post-abortion grief, it's also an excellent book for parents to share with their kids to help them learn about consequences and accountability." - *Kevin Cahill, Author, Sand Creek, Letters to a Rose, The Last Cafe, Knights of Harvest*

What reviewers are saying on Amazon.com:
"Few know how to heal the emotional wounds that accompany abortion. We don't talk about it much. This book is a good place to begin. It speaks with compassion, and offers signposts to acceptance, forgiveness, and healing." - *T. Nash*

"This book attempts to sort it out without all the screaming, finger-pointing and useless drama. I applaud this author for bringing some peace to all the pain on both sides of this serious and divisive issue." - *Jane*

"It has been written with such care and compassion while elevating us beyond the false oversimplification of this being a matter merely of either pro-life or pro-choice." - *Bruce*

"It was like finding Spring water in the desert of judgment that surrounds abortion and other such life decisions that many face in this complicated world." - *Suzanne*

"This book should be given to anyone considering or has been through an abortion." - *Susan*

"The book is about so much more than the journey through abortion, it speaks to me on many different levels about my own experiences in life." - *Frannie*

"I would highly recommend *"I Never Heard You Cry"* for anyone facing a healing process or anyone who works in an area of healing or spiritual counseling." - *Carol*

I Never Heard You Cry
a Compassionate Journey Through Abortion

is currently available on Kindle and other devices
Also available in paperback at Amazon.com and other
online stores.